"This roller-coaster thrill ride will keep reade[...] biting cliff-hanger, while the geopolitical pre[...] anyone thankful that a sovereign, loving God ultimately holds our safety in his hands, as Terry Brennan portrays so well. Please don't keep us waiting for the final resolution of this exciting thriller trilogy!"

—**JEANETTE WINDLE,** award-winning author of *CrossFire,*
Veiled Freedom, and *Freedom's Stand*

"Terry Brennan has done it again! This is an epic thriller. The stage is being set for the final parts of history. *Persian Betrayal* will grip you from page one."

—**GRANT BERRY,** author of *Romans 911*

"Amazing, awesome, powerful, anointed. *Persian Betrayal* will keep you turning pages and praying for the peace of Jerusalem."

—**MARLENE BAGNULL,** director of Write His Answer Ministries

"A fantastic combination of thriller, historical conspiracy, biblical prophecy, and Middle Eastern complexity—and you're never sure where the line is drawn between fact and fiction."

—**IAN ACHESON,** author of *Angelguard*

Praise for *Ishmael Covenant*
Empires of Armageddon Book #1

"A simply riveting action/adventure suspense thriller of a novel by an author with an impressive flair for originality and the kind of deftly scripted narrative storytelling style that holds the reader's attention from beginning to end. . . . Especially and unreservedly recommended."

—*MIDWEST BOOK REVIEW*

"Terry Brennan's new release is an engrossing ride into the dark world of political corruption that feels too close to home. In the epic unfolding of biblical prophecy, *Ishmael Covenant* catapults you across a landscape you've only imagined—on both a global and personal scale."

—**CHER GATTO,** award-winning author of *Something I Am Not*

PERSIAN BETRAYAL

PERSIAN BETRAYAL

Empires of Armageddon #2

TERRY BRENNAN

KREGEL
PUBLICATIONS

Published by Kregel Publications, a division of Kregel Inc., 2450 Oak Industrial Dr. NE, Grand Rapids, MI 49505.

Library of Congress Cataloging-in-Publication Data
Names: Brennan, Terry (Novelist), author.
Title: Persian betrayal / Terry Brennan.
Description: Grand Rapids, MI : Kregel Publications, [2020] | Series:
   Empires of armageddon; #2
Identifiers: LCCN 2020006298 (print) | LCCN 2020006299 (ebook)
Subjects: GSAFD: Suspense ficiton. | Christian fiction.
Classification: LCC PS3602.R4538 P47 2020 (print) | LCC PS3602.R4538
   (ebook) | DDC 813/.6--dc23
LC record available at https://lccn.loc.gov/2020006298
LC ebook record available at https://lccn.loc.gov/2020006299

ISBN 978-0-8254-4531-6, print
ISBN 978-0-8254-7498-9, epub

Printed in the United States of America
20 21 22 23 24 25 26 27 28 29 / 5 4 3 2 1

To my children:
Michael, Patrick, Meghan, and Matthew.
I am blessed.

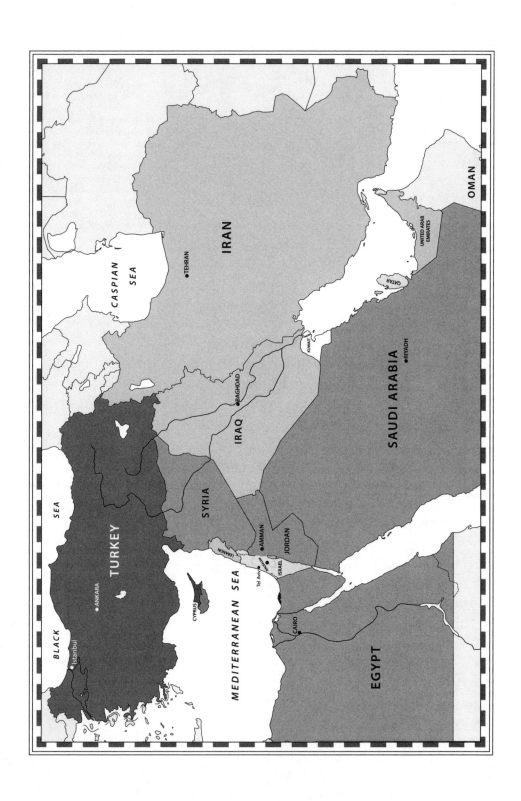

CAST OF CHARACTERS

United States

Brian Mullaney—Diplomatic Security Service (DSS) agent; regional security officer overseeing the Middle East; chief of security for Joseph Atticus Cleveland, the US ambassador to Israel

Abigail Mullaney—Brian's wife and daughter of Atlanta-based financial giant Richard Rutherford

Joseph Atticus Cleveland—US ambassador to Turkey transferred to Israel

Palmyra Athena Parker—Ambassador Cleveland's daughter

Tommy Hernandez—DSS chief for Ambassador Cleveland's security detail in Istanbul; transferred with Cleveland to Israel; Mullaney's best friend

Lamont Boylan—President of the United States

Evan Townsend—US secretary of state

Noah Webster—Deputy secretary of state for management and resources; oversees DSS

George Morningstar—Deputy assistant secretary for diplomatic security

Ruth Hughes—Political officer, US embassy, Tel Aviv

Jeffrey Archer—Cleveland's secretary at the ambassador's residence and the US embassy in Tel Aviv

Senator Seneca Markham—Former chair of the Senate Foreign Relations Committee, now retired

Richard Rutherford—Billionaire Georgian banker and DC power broker

Israel

David Meir—Prime minister of Israel

Moshe Litzman—Minister of the interior of Israel

Benjamin Erdad—Minister of internal security of Israel

Meyer Levinson—Director, Operations Division, Shin Bet, Israel's internal security agency

Turkey: Ottoman Empire
Emet Kashani—President of Turkey
Arslan Eroglu—Prime minister of Turkey
The Turk—Otherworldly pursuer of the box and the prophecy

Iraq and Iran: Persian Empire
Samir Al-Qahtani—Deputy prime minister of Iraq; leader of the Badr
    Brigades

Saudi Arabia, Egypt, Jordan, and Palestine: Islamic Empire
King Abdullah Al-Saud—King of Saudi Arabia
Prince Faisal ibn Farouk Al-Saud—Saudi defense minister; son of King
    Abdullah
Sultan Abbaddi—Commander of the Jordanian Royal Guard Brigade,
    personal bodyguards of the king and his family

PROLOGUE

The sharp aroma of charcoal—a thousand fires extinguished in the dawn's first light—mingled with the desert dew and hung in the early morning air. Standing at the forefront of the vast army of Israel, Joshua looked over his right shoulder, across the Valley of Rephidim. In the east, he could see the outlined bodies of Moses, Aaron, and Hur—the captain of Moses's personal guard—standing on top of a hill, the highest in the region. The sun was rising behind them, and the staff of God, raised high in Moses's hand, appeared to be shimmering, sparks leaping from it, crackling like bolts of lightning.

It was the sound of drums from across the plain that arrested Joshua's thoughts and brought his concentration back to the battle forming before him. Abner and Hiram stood at either shoulder. Behind him, aligned along an east-west axis on the southern rim of the Rephidim plain, stood half the army of Israel—thirty thousand fighting men from Joshua's tribe of Judah, each man carefully selected; another thirty thousand each from the tribes of Dan and Simeon; twenty thousand each from Reuben, Gad, Ephraim, and Asher. Behind that first phalanx stood a second wave of Jewish soldiers from the other five tribes—in total over two hundred thousand veteran fighting men.

Across the plain, Joshua estimated at least one hundred thousand sons of Amalek waited in the shadows of the dawn. Yesterday, a phalanx of these mounted desert raiders had fallen upon the last remnant of the Israelite column slowly working its way through the Alush Gorge. Joshua's soldiers rallied to form a wedge of protection around the weak and defenseless stragglers and repelled these descendants of Ishmael. But the Amalekites were back, even more determined to destroy the people of Israel and the army at its head. The enemy warriors, their black, green, and brown robes flapping behind them like battle flags, were mostly mounted on swift, powerful desert stallions. From a strictly military point of view, Joshua expected he would need to employ every one of his infantry to overcome the Amalekite horsemen. But then there was Moses—and the staff of God.

After glancing once more to the hill to the east where Moses stood firm, the staff held high, Joshua lifted his right arm, his old, nicked sword sharpened to a lethal edge. "For the glory of our God and in the name of Jehovah."

Behind Joshua, in a wave that reverberated through the ranks of soldiers, two hundred thousand voices joined in the declaration, "For the glory of our God and in the name of Jehovah."

And the host of Israel stepped out to cross the plain. In the distance, a great, swirling cloud of dust rose in the north, the mounted horde of Amalek racing toward them, committed to the annihilation of the Jews.

———※———

Twelve hours later, Moses still sat on a rock on the hill to the east, the staff of God held high above his head. His arms were pale, his fingers turning a shade of light blue. At times during the day, Moses actually dozed off in the heat of the sun. But the staff never faltered.

First Aaron and Hur, then in succession other teams of Moses's personal guard, took turns supporting his arms and the staff. And through the day, the army of Israel punished the bandits of Amalek, pushing them back across the field, slaughtering their horses as they fell, leaving alive no Amalekite warrior who came under their sword.

As the sun slipped behind the low hills to the west, what little was left of the Amalekite army withdrew in defeat, riding north to escape the inexorable fury of the Israelite fighters.

———※———

When the last stone was set in the altar, Moses approached and rested the staff of God on its edge. The army of Israel surrounded the altar, built at the base of the hill on which Aaron and Hur had held Moses's arms aloft during the battle. Moses lifted his left arm. "Come, Joshua."

Aware of the blood that covered his arms and his armor, conscious of the filth that crusted over his legs and his feet, Joshua held fast. He was covered with death. How could he approach an altar?

"Come, Joshua. Come . . . stand by me," said Moses.

The old man reached out his hand toward Joshua, who did not have the power or strength left to refuse. Joshua stepped to Moses's side.

Moses smiled at Joshua, then turned to the army and lifted the staff above his head.

"Today God fought for us," said Moses. "And he destroyed the army of Amalek. But know this." Moses took the staff and pointed it at the armed soldiers surrounding the altar. Deliberately, he moved the point of the staff in an arc that encompassed all of the army. "While we were on the hill, the Lord spoke to me. The Lord said, 'Moses, write this on a scroll as something to be remembered and make sure that Joshua hears it, because I will completely blot out the name of Amalek from under heaven.' We will call this altar Jehovah-Nissi, the Lord is our banner, for hands were lifted up to the throne of the Lord. And the Lord has sworn here, this day, that the Lord will be at war with the Amalekites from generation to generation."

The army of Israel raised a shout and sounded the shofar so that the hills of Rephidim rained praises on the bloody plain. But Moses stepped closer to Joshua and spoke so that only he could hear.

"My son, hear my words. The Lord has a message for you, your children, and your children's children. Remember what the Amalekites did here, when our people were weary and worn-out. They cut off those who were weak and lagging behind. They had no fear of God. Tell your children this . . . When the Lord your God gives you rest from your enemies and the land of the inheritance, you are still to go out and blot out the memory of Amalek from under heaven. The Lord says, 'Do not forget!'"

1

Hurva Square, Jerusalem, Israel
July 20, 2014, 1:14 p.m.

Rabbi Chaim Yavod raced into Jerusalem's Hurva Square, choking on the thick, swirling stone dust that encased the square in a malevolent fog. He leaped over huge shards of fractured stone and concrete—white, arched remnants of the Hurva Synagogue's once magnificent dome. A symphony of horror filled the square nearly as thick as the stone dust—moans of the wounded and maimed, wails of survivors as they stumbled over the bodies of those who were not, shrill and urgent sirens promising help but not prevention.

Only moments earlier he had been sent to fetch Rabbi Herzog's car. Then, in a mounding tide of rumbling destruction, the world that Chaim Yavod knew best was obliterated.

The convulsions of the first explosion ripped the door of the black Toyota out of Yavod's hand and knocked him back onto the uneven surface of the small parking lot. The ground shifting under his shoulder blades, Yavod felt three additional explosions shudder the stones of the street. He looked up, above the rooftops toward the north. What looked like a volcanic eruption of smoke, stone, and debris was roiling ever higher over the square that contained the Hurva Synagogue—outside of the Western Wall, the most revered symbol of Jewish worship in Jerusalem.

Now Yavod frantically scrambled through the destruction in the Hurva Square toward the smoking, shattered remains of the synagogue. The sickening fear tearing at his heart pushed aside any concern about delivering the envelope inside his jacket pocket—the decoded second prophecy from the Vilna Gaon. Israel Herzog, chief rabbi of the Israeli Rabbinate Council, his friend and superior, was probably somewhere under the collapsed dome and crumbled walls of what had once been Israel's most beautiful synagogue. Was Herzog alive . . . any other members of the council who were with him? Could he save them? Yavod pressed on through the escalating havoc.

The Old City, Jerusalem
July 20, 1:14 p.m.

The leader consciously forced himself to keep a leisurely pace in the midst of the mayhem. The bombers were three strides north on Habad Street, headed for the souks—the three, parallel covered markets of the Old City—and the Damascus Gate, beyond which they could disappear. All around them, people were racing: Israelis and Arabs alike ran toward the site of the explosions in the Hurva Square, while tourists, mothers, and children fled the dust and the terror.

The two bombers looked like worn and weary workmen headed to lunch when the leader thrust out his right arm and grabbed his partner by the sleeve of his dirty work shirt, causing a brief human pileup behind them. The leader pulled his partner close to a building facing the street.

"We need to go back."

"Risky," said his partner.

"Yes," the leader admitted, "but we need to see for ourselves. We know," he said, lowering his voice and looking side to side at the human tide moving past them, "that our work succeeded. But we need to give a report. It was a mistake not to make sure that the results were . . . effective. We don't want to make another mistake. You'll learn. Mistakes are not well tolerated. Come."

Ignoring his partner's unspoken reluctance, the leader turned to his left and began walking against the flow. He turned left on Hashalshelet, the Street of the Chain, away from the crowds, then quickly right into a narrow, curving walkway. Halfway along Tif'eret Yisrael Street the leader saw a stone walkway ascending between two buildings on his right.

"Wait."

He bounded up the stairs two at a time but stopped a head short of the top. In Israel, as was true throughout the Middle East, rooftops were often actively used as alternative living space, particularly in the cooler evening hours. It was possible this rooftop could be occupied. He peeked over the edge, left then right. No one. No chairs. No potted plants. To the right more steps led up to a second flat roof. He looked up to the higher roof, straight into the smoke and debris cloud gently settling over Hurva Square. He could hear the cacophony on the other side of the building, in Hurva Square, but no sounds closer. With a quick wave to his partner, he pushed himself over the edge and moved toward the second set of stairs.

He moved up these stairs more cautiously. He took one step and paused, then another and paused. The fifth step brought his head level with the upper roof. He peeked over the edge. This roof held signs of being used, but it was unoccupied at the moment. The vast, open Hurva Square lay beyond its edge. As if he were walking on an ice bridge in the spring, his body in a crouch, he edged to a small parapet wall at the end of the roof. A slight breeze carried the smoke, dust, and cries for help off to the west, giving the leader a fairly clear view of his handiwork—carnage, destruction, chaos.

Front to back, the Hurva sat on a north-south axis, the front of the building and the large, open Hurva Square on the southern side. He and his partner were now situated on a rooftop looking northwest, kitty-corner across the square, toward the ancient minaret of the Caliph Omar mosque on the far side. The Hurva, when it stood, was a massive square building of Jerusalem stone and masonry walls, almost its entire bulk covered by a huge dome. Now the Hurva looked like a squashed egg.

For maximum destruction of the synagogue, and everything and anyone inside it, the first twin explosions had cracked the spine of the building. Then another set of explosions obliterated the walls at the corners, causing the majority of the destruction to fall in upon itself, like a deflating accordion. But the blasts had also hurled huge chunks of stone wall and concrete arch in every direction around the building.

The trees in the square were shattered and stunted by the blasts, the umbrella-covered open-air restaurant tables that offered shade and respite for tourists were thrown against the walls of the adjacent buildings.

A retaining wall of Jerusalem stone, two stories high, was tied into and ran across the rear of the synagogue, accounting for the higher elevation of Ha-Yehudim Street. That retaining wall and a square chunk of the rear of the building attached to the wall were the only parts of the Hurva that had survived the blasts.

Below, butchery littered the vastness of the Hurva Square. Police and medical first responders were rushing around, looking for the living and covering the dead. Wails of grief battled with the still incoming sirens.

"Let's watch a moment."

US Embassy, Tel Aviv, Israel
July 20, 1:16 p.m.

In two hours, Rabbi Israel Herzog was scheduled to arrive with a secret that promised to make Brian Mullaney's life even more unpredictable and out of control.

The last two days—was it only two days?—had been relentless, seemingly endless, interrupted by only a few hours of sleep. He needed to shake off the weary exhaustion that was draining his muscles and dulling his brain. The daily security of hundreds of diplomatic staff rested squarely on his shoulders. Recently banished to Israel, his appointment as the US State Department's Middle East Regional Security Officer (RSO) was little solace for the fact that his career was on life support.

The phone rang.

"Mullaney."

"Sir, it's Floyd Bishop at the consul general's residence. There's been an explosion in the Old City. I think the Hurva's just been blown up."

Hurva Square, Jerusalem
July 20, 1:17 p.m.

Chaim skirted the eastern edge of the square. A slight breeze had begun to move some of the choking dust to the west. Scrambling his way around giant pieces of wreckage, tearing up the flesh of his hands on the knifelike edges, and avoiding the growing crowd of civilians pouring into the square to help, he fixed his eyes on his destination—an arched doorway on the north side of the synagogue, at the base of the retaining wall, that led to a lower-level hallway and the offices of the Rabbinate Council on the western flank of the Hurva.

Inside the arch, the door and its frame were no longer vertical. The door-frame canted to the right at a forty-five-degree angle, the door itself sprung open and hanging precariously from only one hinge. Chaim closed the distance, keeping a hopeful eye on the door for any sign of life and a wary eye on the still smoldering rubble mound to his left that continued to disgorge debris onto the square. He acknowledged to himself the fear that was adding lead weights to his limbs but, with a deep breath, cast the fear aside and pressed himself through the precarious opening into the underbelly of destruction.

The Old City, Jerusalem
July 20, 1:18 p.m.

The leader of the bombers had his eyes on the square below and his mobile phone to his ear.

"The synagogue is destroyed. The rabbis and their package are now buried under tons of wreckage collapsed in upon itself."

"Where are you?" asked the leader of the Disciples.

"On a rooftop overlooking the square."

"Remain. Make sure no one has escaped. Do not get caught."

The leader closed the phone and stuffed it in his pants pocket just as his accomplice poked him on the shoulder.

"You see . . . there is one. Looks like a rabbi," said the accomplice, as the thin, black-coated man gingerly approached a darkened archway in the retaining wall to their right.

They hunkered close to the parapet, their eyes on the slight figure who slipped into the darkness.

"He goes in," said his companion.

"Yes. And we wait until . . . if . . . he comes out."

US Embassy, Tel Aviv
July 20, 1:18 p.m.

Habit and training prompted Mullaney to swing his chair to the left toward the three-foot-square Jerusalem street map that was attached to a huge cloth board in his office at the US embassy in Tel Aviv, Israel.

Even though he had only been "boots on the ground" in Israel for two weeks, he knew where the consul general's residence was located—on Gershon Agron Street across from the sprawling Independence Park, in an Americanized compound less than a mile from the Old City.

Floyd Bishop was a seasoned and respected agent of the Diplomatic Security Service, someone who could be trusted. But Mullaney needed all the facts. "How do you know it was the Hurva?"

"I don't. I can't be certain," said Bishop. "But as soon as I heard the explosions and felt the ground move, I grabbed a pair of binoculars and ran up to the roof. We're on a rise, and the rear of the building looks out over the Old City. There was still a cloud of debris and smoke in the air to pinpoint the location. The explosion was pretty much due east of here, north of the Zion Gate . . . sort of split the distance between St. James Cathedral and David's Tower. I can't see it clearly through the smoke and ash, even with binoculars, but the Hurva is less than two thousand yards away from here in that very spot. And that's where the debris cloud is. If I had to make a bet—"

"Okay," said Mullaney, "take a—"

"Listen, Brian—excuse me, sir," said Bishop, acknowledging Mullaney's rank, "but that was a huge explosion—actually several explosions if I counted correctly. There's going to be a lot of dead people over there, sir. A lot of tourists. Could be some of ours."

Mullaney wiped a hand down his lined face and then scanned the map in front of him, calculating. In his nineteen years in the Diplomatic Security Service, he'd approached every assignment with constant vigilance, articulate intelligence, and an external calm that carried over to all those with whom he served.

Now the world kept blowing up around him. Mullaney was responsible for protecting the lives of every individual assigned to the US diplomatic mission to Israel and—by extension, he believed—responsible for every American soul in the land of Israel.

But he was failing miserably in fulfilling those responsibilities. First Palmyra Parker, the ambassador's daughter, was kidnapped and now—probably because of a decision he made—the historic Hurva Synagogue in the Old City of Jerusalem, Israel's most beautiful place of worship, was a smoldering pile of rubble. Only minutes earlier, Rabbi Israel Herzog called him from inside the Hurva, announcing that the Rabbinate Council had cracked the code of a two-hundred-year-old prophecy that Mullaney hoped would put an end to the death and mayhem that followed the scrap of parchment from Germany to Turkey to Israel. Was Herzog still in the synagogue when . . .

Mullaney held the phone to his ear, but there was little that was holding up his hope. "All right, Floyd, how many agents on duty over there?"

"Eight, at least—could be more if some of the agents stuck around after the shift change."

"How's your exterior security?" asked Mullaney. He visualized the long, high stone wall, topped by wrought iron fencing, that ran along the front of the compound on Gershon Agron Street.

"We're solid," said Bishop. "Mostly Israeli nationals—long-time service guys who are ex-IDF—with one of our agents in charge. We're solid here, Brian, and we're the closest."

Mullaney walked to the window and looked to the east where, forty-four miles distant in the Judean hill country, the contested city of Jerusalem was located. Still a formidable physical presence in his midforties, the spreading streaks of gray at his temples were a testimony to the daily stress he carried on his broad shoulders. Today he also fought the twin scourges of guilt and discouragement.

"All right, Floyd. Take a team of four and get to the Hurva as quickly as you can. I'll call Shin Bet and let them know you are going to be on-site shortly. Stay there until you get some information about any victims—and whether any of the victims are American citizens. And also check into the status of the rabbis at the synagogue. The chief rabbi there, Israel Herzog, was working with us on something very important. See what you can find out and call me back."

<hr />

Hurva Square, Jerusalem
July 20, 1:20 p.m.

Gray clouds of grit floated in the air, blocking out the sun as Chaim Yavod ducked under the skewed portal and entered the deeper darkness of the devastated Hurva. He left behind a swelling symphony of sirens and a frantic, growing assemblage—some with yarmulkes bobbing on their heads with every effort, others in shorts and T-shirts—frantically digging in the stony rubble that was once the most beautiful of synagogues.

Before him to the left ran a still discernable corridor, half of it collapsed, now an obstacle course of crushed stone and concrete shards, twisted reinforcing rods, and piles of rubble. Every few feet, a shaft of light sliced in through the shattered walls, now partially open to the sun, illuminating a frantic dance of dust and encasing the remnants of the corridor in a pallid fog. Yavod skittered around the fallen masonry, unaware of the blood trail left behind by his lacerated fingertips.

He had only been gone a moment to get the car requested by Rabbi Herzog.

He had only been gone a moment when the great dome was cloven down the middle, when the earth was rent from beneath his feet, when the unleashed roar of the explosions ripped past him like thunder down a valley's rift. Only a moment, but his world rested in ruins as devastating as the destruction under his feet.

He had to find the rabbi. He had to.

He reached the end of the corridor where three steps led left, to a lower level and the offices of the Rabbinate Council. What was once the ceiling had collapsed, reducing the corridor's height by half. Yavod lowered himself down the stairs, then bent over in a crouch, keeping his feet under him to navigate the ongoing debris field as he inched along the corridor toward the council's offices. The light faded. Yavod had to feel his way through the darkness. A gaping yaw of black stopped him. The front wall of the council's offices had been blown across the corridor, blocking most of it with a massive pile of ruin, leaving the interior of the offices wide open but shrouded in gloom.

Yavod scuffed his shoe through some of the rubble at his feet and found a broken piece of Shabbat candle in the dust. He lit the candle, held it in front of him at arm's length, and moved into the blackened office, pulling along an anchor of despair.

———◦◦◦———

US Embassy, Tel Aviv
July 20, 1:21 p.m.

Tommy Hernandez, Mullaney's right hand and head of personal security for US Ambassador Joseph Cleveland, stood in the open doorway. "What's up?"

Mullaney ended the call with Bishop and punched in a new number. "Bishop . . . from the consul's residence. Said it looks like the Hurva Synagogue has just been blown up," he said, the words as leaden as the despair in his heart. "Several explosions, he thinks."

"Herzog? The box?" asked Hernandez.

"Don't know . . . don't know anything yet," said Mullaney as he waited for his call to be answered, "but it looks like our enemies are getting more desperate. Why don't—"

The voice on the other end of the call didn't waste time with etiquette. "The Hurva is a pile of smoking rubble. This has something to do with the box, right?"

"Meyer—"

"You told me you would fill me in with all of the important details." The voice of Meyer Levinson, director of the operations division of Shin Bet, Israel's internal security apparatus, was firm but not stained with blame. "You can keep your promise on the helicopter. Get to Hanger C at Ben Gurion as quickly as you can."

"Twenty minutes, if I'm lucky," said Mullaney.

"Fifteen or we go without you."

"Okay, but you—"

The call disconnected.

Mullaney looked up at Hernandez, who was leaning against the door jamb. "Meyer a little testy?"

"Yeah," said Mullaney. He shook his head. "This day just keeps getting worse." He took a deep breath. *Too much happening . . . gotta stay in the game.* He pushed a button on the telephone console on his desk. "I need a car at the front gate, now."

He grabbed his suit jacket with one hand and Tommy Hernandez's left arm with the other and pulled him along toward the stairs. "I need you to stay with the ambassador," said Mullaney. "Don't let him out of your sight. I mean it, Tommy. Everywhere he goes, you go."

"We're in the embassy, Brian."

"Yeah, that's right," said Mullaney as he started down the stairs two at a time. "And I don't care. Have somebody with you at all times too. We're taking no chances. And call Pat McKeon at the residence. I want her and a second agent glued to Palmyra Parker. Double the watch here and at the residence. And double the watch at all the consular offices in Jerusalem. As of now we're running twelve-hour shifts and nobody gets a day off. Got it?"

2

Mullaney raised his arms so the Israeli soldier could fasten the harness around his body. He was seated on a bench that was bolted to the wall and ran down the length of the Sikorsky CH-53E Super Stallion helicopter which was now flexing its rotors in earnest. Meyer Levinson sat beside him on the bench, to his right, holding in his hands an identical twin to the headset and mic he had just slipped over his bald head. On the far bench were six uniformed Shin Bet officers, belted in but with no headsets. As the chopper lifted with a roar and banked hard to the east, Levinson handed the headset to Mullaney.

"Seven confirmed dead," Levinson said into the mic. "But there will be a lot more." He glanced left at Mullaney. "Tell me what I need to know, Brian."

Only yesterday, the story had seemed so far-fetched that Mullaney had been reluctant to share with Levinson what he knew about the metal box from Lithuania and the message it supposedly carried. Now, there was no hesitation. Mullaney had rehearsed his response on the drive from the US embassy. "Before leaving his assignment in Turkey, Ambassador Cleveland visited the synagogue of an old friend in Istanbul. He left that meeting in possession of a wooden box. Inside the wooden box was a metal box. There were kabbalah symbols hammered into the lid of the metal box." Mullaney shifted to his right as much as the restrictive harness would allow, to get a better look at Levinson. "Inside the metal box was supposedly a second prophecy from the Vilna Gaon, a prophecy that had been hidden and protected in the Istanbul synagogue for generations."

Levinson raised a cautionary hand. "Second prophecy? Vilna Gaon? Help me here."

Grimacing, Mullaney nodded his head. "Yeah, okay. I'm trying to keep this condensed. I'm told the Vilna Gaon was the wisest Talmudic scholar of his time—maybe any time. Literally, a genius with a prodigious photographic memory and a vast reservoir of both sacred and secular knowledge. Not only did he correct mistakes throughout the entire Talmud, he wrote a book about mathematics that was considered centuries before its time. Earlier this year the Gaon's great-great-grandson revealed the existence of a prophecy written over two hundred years ago that—"

"Messiah," said Levinson. "Yes, I remember. The prophecy said when the Russians take over Crimea it's a sign that the coming of Messiah is at hand. Put on your Shabbat clothes . . . Messiah is coming. Something like that."

"Right," said Mullaney. "The prophecy was written in 1794. The Russians invaded and occupied the Ukraine and Crimea just four months ago. Caused a bit of a stir, I understand."

"And this box supposedly had another, a second, prophecy from the Gaon?" asked Levinson. "But"—he twisted his head to look directly into Mullaney's eyes—"this prophecy was killing people?"

Again, Mullaney grimaced and nodded his head. "Well, something like that. We're not sure what was doing the killing, the prophecy itself or the metal box with the kabbalah symbols. But it appears that if anyone touches the box without the proper anointing . . . well, death is pretty swift."

"And gruesome?"

"Yeah, pretty bad," said Mullaney, staring at the floor of the chopper as he recalled the body of one of the housekeeping staff at the ambassador's residence, who inadvertently came in contact with the box. "Tongue turns black, hair falls out, start bleeding from the eyes."

"Sounds like a good reason to avoid the box," said Levinson. "But that's why the ambassador's daughter was kidnapped, right? To be held for ransom. Somebody wants the box or the prophecy. Or somebody wants its power."

"A whole lot of somebodies, it appears," said Mullaney.

"So why the Hurva?"

"That's my fault."

"Okay, we'll lock you up."

With a start, Mullaney looked up at Levinson, a man with whom he had forged a strong friendship years earlier during Levinson's assignment in Washington as head of security for the Israeli embassy. "What?"

Levinson's eyes softened, and he took a deep breath. "None of this is your fault, Brian. You've been through the ringer over and over the last two days. One crisis after another. And you must be exhausted. But"—Levinson put his hand on Mullaney's right arm—"you need to stay focused. None of this is your fault. There are some bad guys out there who are killing people for that box. And we're going to find them. Now, why the Hurva?"

Mullaney nodded his head, but this time with resolution, a determined set to his jaw. *Yeah, we are going to find them.*

"Two things the rabbi in Istanbul told Ambassador Cleveland," he said. "First, the expectation passed down for generations was that the prophecy would be in code—just as the first one was in code—that only a Talmudic scholar would be able to crack. Second, the rabbis who were guardians of the box believed the prophecy would reveal the name of the Man of Violence."

"Wait," Levinson raised his hand. "Who is—what is—the Man of Violence?"

"Honestly, I have no clue," said Mullaney. "Ambassador Cleveland was instructed to get the box to the Rabbinate Council at the Hurva, men who had the learning to open the box and understand the prophecy, and his task would be complete. One of the chief rabbis, Israel Herzog, came to the residence earlier today, and we placed the wooden box and its contents into his hands. He called me not long ago and told me that his council had deciphered the message. He said, *'Prepare yourself for another shock. What I'm bringing to you will radically alter the meaning of what was announced today.'"*

Less than two hours earlier, Israel had entered into a treaty and a mutual-defense pact with the majority of its neighbors: Egypt, Jordan, Saudi Arabia, and most of the Persian Gulf states, nations formed from the nomadic Arab people who, like the Amalekites before them, were all the descendants of Ishmael. From the day God chose between Abraham's sons—when Isaac was declared the heir of promise and Ishmael was banished into the desert—the two blood lines had been in conflict. That conflict became deadly when Israel was declared a sovereign nation in 1948. Since then the Arab states, the sons of Ishmael, had fought—and lost—three major wars against Israel, the sons of Isaac. Now, with the signing in Amman, Jordan, of what was being called the Ishmael Covenant, Israel was at peace with most of its former enemies for the first time in sixty-six years.

"The covenant?" asked Levinson. "The covenant and this two-hundred-year-old prophecy are linked?"

The helicopter banked left and started a long, looping swing back to the north.

"I don't know, Meyer," Mullaney admitted. "Honestly, I'm not sure if I understand what any of this has been about—at least not yet. All I know is that the metal box and the prophecy were at the Hurva when Rabbi Herzog called. I don't know if any of them—the rabbi, the box, or the message—survived the explosions. But my gut tells me we can't allow the box or what it contains to fall into the hands of whoever is behind all of this violence."

⸺◦◦◦⸺

Hurva Square, Jerusalem
July 20, 1:43 p.m.

The devastation to the council's offices was nearly complete. It looked as if the entire upper structure of the Hurva Synagogue had collapsed in upon itself and plummeted into the basement. Huge slabs of stone resting at wildly diverse angles were jammed into the area once occupied by the council. The flickering light of the candle guiding only one step at a time, Yavod pressed through narrow gaps, zigzagging his way deeper into the office toward the area where he last saw Rabbi Herzog and the council, his hope as wavering as the flame in front of him.

As if writhing in pain, the ruins of the Hurva bellowed forth a relentless, threatening groan, covering Yavod with a shower of small rubble, adding another cloud of dust to the nearly impenetrable air in the basement. He feared that his time was short if he hoped to escape the Hurva alive.

Yavod squeezed past the crushed and splintered remains of the resplendent Torah Ark that once dominated the northern wall of the Hurva's upper-floor sanctuary, carefully avoided a razor-sharp shard of concrete, and found himself staring at the table he had left just half an hour earlier. Two slabs of concrete had fallen into each other, creating an inverted V. Yavod could see nothing holding the implausibly balanced concrete in place, only a shimmering vibration in the dense dust above where the table was sheltered in the small opening. The table survived, but around it was death and destruction. Blood splatters covered the table and the surfaces of the concrete. One black-clad arm, its hand in a fist, protruded from behind the edge of the slab on the right. On the floor to the left, Rabbi Israel Herzog sat—tons of concrete in his lap. Herzog's unseeing eyes and silent mouth were open, his left arm outstretched toward the two boxes that still sat under the bloody lamb's fleece in the center of the table to his left.

Another death groan shook the Hurva. A large chunk of concrete fell, grazing Yavod's right shoulder. Instinctively, he put the candle on the desk. Lifting his eyes to heaven in a prayer for protection, Yavod put his hands on the lambskin, lifted the metal box and placed the skin-wrapped metal box inside the larger wooden box. He pulled off his black coat and once again remembered the envelope tucked into the inside pocket. He should get the deciphered prophecy to agent Mullaney. But then what about the box? He would have to give up the box also.

There was no time to think. Working swiftly, Yavod wrapped up the wooden box in his black coat, pressed it against his body with his left arm, picked up the sputtering candle—

And he stopped.

Rabbi Chaim Yavod looked down at the crushed body of his friend and benefactor, Israel Herzog, and began to recite the Jewish prayer for the dead, *El Malei Rachamim*. "God, full of mercy, who dwells in the heights . . . ," he finished, and then repeated the prayer over and over again as he left the dead behind and pushed himself through the tangled concrete canyons, back toward the light.

3

The Shin Bet helicopter landed in a cleared parking lot about one hundred yards southeast of the Zion Gate, the southernmost access through Jerusalem's Old City wall and the closest entrance to Hurva Square. Mullaney cast a quick glance at the pockmarked facade of the Zion Gate, bullet riddled during a series of ferocious battles during the 1967 war, in which all of Jerusalem and the entire Old City came under Israeli rule. But he had little time to reflect. Levinson and his squad were hustling through the twisting Zion Gate. Mullaney sprinted to catch up and jumped into the last of the waiting Jeeps as they headed north on Ararat Street.

Mullaney desperately clung to the side of the speeding Jeep as it careened through the twisting streets of the Old City. They came into Hurva Square at the southwest corner, near Bet El Street, and skidded to a halt at the very edge of the square. Before them was triage in public.

Red-and-blue flashing lights from ambulances and police cars parked along the perimeter of the destruction reflected off the broken pieces of white masonry blasted about the square. In spite of the heat, which was oppressive, hundreds of people were frantically scrambling over the debris, some tending to the wounded or the dying, some pulling away rubble with their bare hands.

His cell phone to his ear, Mullaney had to fight growing rage as he surveyed the destruction. "Bishop?" Mullaney said as his call was answered. "I'm in the square. Where are you?"

"On the east side, across the street from the square," said Bishop. "Jerusalem police set up an impromptu command post and threw up a medical tent on the sidewalk. Our guys are going through the square. They know to report to me here."

Mullaney looked around. *Good as any.* "I'm on my way."

He turned to Levinson, who was directing his squad members. "Jerusalem police have a CP over on the right. I'm heading there."

———◦◦◦———

Yavod threw the nearly spent candle on the floor as he approached the diagonal beam of light promising escape into Hurva Square. He felt naked. No hat. No jacket. Several of his fingertips were bleeding, and blood oozed around a ragged rip in the right knee of his trousers. He looked at the bundle tucked under his left arm. *Now what? What am I going to do with it? Where am I going to take it? How am I going to get there?*

Yavod stepped beside the now angular doorway and peeked outside. Shouts. Cries. People running. Sirens. And now a bleeding man with a box under his arm, trying to look inconspicuous. But he couldn't stay here. His right hand grabbed ahold of the tilted doorframe, and he stepped into the light.

———◦◦◦———

They say killers return to the scene of the crime. No one noticed.

The two bombers were tucked into a corner of the parapet. Other onlookers were on other rooftops surrounding the square, the drama of human suffering— other people's suffering—seducing them like a drug. Still, from this vantage point, they were virtually invisible to those on the other rooftops. They could see into Hurva Square but not be seen by the scores of people rushing to the rescue. And the police. Yes . . . the police.

"We can't stay here any longer . . . it's too dangerous."

The leader kept his eyes scanning across the mayhem he helped create, but his partner in crime was correct. They had stayed too close, too long. Each of them, the Disciples, had pledged their life—and their death—to hasten the arrival of the Mahdi. But . . . the leader of the Disciples would exact a stiff price if they were caught. "You're right, we need to—"

The words caught, stillborn, in his throat. He lifted a hand and placed it upon his partner's arm. Across the littered but open space of the square, a thin man emerged from the darkened archway to their right. Covered with stone dust, he clutched something under his left arm, close to his side.

"Is it the same man?"

"So it seems," said the leader. "He has taken off his coat and wrapped it around what he holds against his side." Even though it was covered, the leader could see distinct edges, a square shape.

The man emerged into the burning sun of the square, now cleared of dust, hunched over, stumbling, his right hand shading his eyes from the blinding light. He looked to his right, toward the ongoing rescue efforts in the rest of the square. Then, as if protecting a treasure, he wrapped his other arm around the box and headed in the opposite direction, to his left, toward a set of stone steps.

"He has the box," said his partner.

"So it seems," he said, looking left and right. No police watching. "We will not allow him out of our sight."

"But it has not killed him."

"So it seems."

The leader tapped his partner on the elbow. "Let's go." They pushed away from the parapet, launching them to their feet in pursuit of the rabbi, down the stairs, away from the roof, the street below, and the dead and maimed that never once crossed their conscience.

———

The man with the box limped away from the square and continued down Tif'eret Yisrael Street, deeper into the labyrinthian byways of the Jewish Quarter of the Old City. The leader moved into the light at the edge of the doorway and looked to his left, down the sloping Tif'eret Yisrael Street. Then he motioned for his partner and the two of them left their hiding place, turned left and followed the man with the box.

4

Hurva Square, Jerusalem
July 20, 2:12 p.m.

Brian Mullaney was on the far sidewalk, looking across the street into the destruction in Hurva Square. So far, his agents reported no Americans among the dead. But he feared that news would not hold up long. Hurva Square was a favorite haunt for American tourists. If nothing else a place to sit and rest their tired legs. He surveyed the ravaged landscape once more, but his attention was drawn to a thin man, limping and covered with dust, who had just emerged from a murky archway in the retaining wall at the far end of the square. For a heartbeat, Mullaney didn't understand why his eyes had stopped and fixed on the man.

Then he focused on both the man's behavior, and the bundle tucked under his left arm. From this distance, Mullaney could not be certain. But the bundle the man was clutching to his side was covered in black cloth. It appeared to be square. Boxlike.

Everything in Mullaney's instincts and his training clicked into gear. Disheveled and looking like he had just escaped a disaster, he must be one of the Hurva's rabbis. And now he was skulking away, protecting and hiding the bundle in his arms. This guy had the box!

The man looked to his right, at the mayhem in the square, then turned away, wrapping both arms around the box and pulling it against his chest. He limped toward a set of stone stairs in the northwest corner, against the massive retaining wall.

───⊰◦◦◦⊱───

Mullaney had his phone to his ear, Meyer Levinson on speed dial, when movement in his periphery vision pulled his attention from the dust-covered man. Up on the rooftops to his right, along the north side of the square, two men crouched against a low parapet wall. They were leaning over the parapet, chest high, staring intently at the dust-covered man with the covered bundle who started up the stairs to their right. Dressed as workmen, one carried a backpack on his back. As soon as the man was out of view, the two men on the roof turned and ran away from the parapet.

His call connected, shifting Mullaney's attention. "Yes, Brian?"

Mullaney took a moment to sift his thoughts, roll the tape of his memory. He felt certain.

"There's a guy—looks like a shell-shocked rabbi—with a wrapped bundle who just came out of an archway in the retaining wall at the back of the square."

"The box?"

Mullaney crossed the street and picked his way past the rubble and the life-and-death drama in the square. "Everything in my gut tells me he's one of the rabbis, and yes, he has the box."

"Where's he—"

"Meyer, I think the bombers are after him," said Mullaney, his eyes going back to the rooftop on his right. "There were two men on a rooftop to my right, watching the guy with the bundle. As soon as the guy started up the stairs in the northern corner of the square, the two guys on the roof took off fast."

"Which way are they headed?"

"North . . . two men . . . dressed in work clothes . . . one with a backpack . . . dark hair, midheight," Mullaney said as he skirted the ruins of the Hurva and weaved his way through a tangle of umbrella-covered tables that was once a tree-shaded restaurant. "I'm going after the guy with the box. I think that's where the other two are headed too."

"Deeper into the Jewish Quarter," said Levinson. "We'll be right behind you. But that's a labyrinth in there. Could be tough to find."

———

The further he got from the chaos of the Hurva, the more conspicuous Chaim Yavod felt. He kept to the narrowest, twisting alleys of the Jewish Quarter, but he knew he must look like an escapee from a mausoleum—covered in gray dust and dried blood, limping along in his ripped clothing. He rested for a moment along Tif'eret Yisrael Street, below a stone arch that offered release from the sun and the seclusion of darkness.

Where should he go? Home was too far away. He needed to get off the street. He needed to get cleaned up. And he needed to figure out what to do with this box.

———◆———

"He looks like death," said his partner.

They stood in front of a rug merchant's shop, examining a carpet while watching the rabbi's reflection in the shop window. "Then we should accommodate him," said the leader. "But first we need to herd him off these public streets into someplace more secluded so we can relieve him of his package. Stare at him."

———◆———

Mullaney was perspiring heavily under his suit jacket as he clumsily jogged the uneven, cobblestoned lane. But he couldn't remove the jacket without exposing the 9-millimeter fully automatic Glock holstered at the base of his back. The streets of the Old City of Jerusalem appeared to be one narrow, twisting, cobblestoned alley after another, all of them canyons of Jerusalem-stone houses rising sharply on either side that made it seem like you were walking below the street level of the city. Most of the streets of the Jewish Quarter angled downhill toward the east, some pouring out into the Western Wall Plaza.

The alley that Mullaney was carefully navigating was canted downhill, with three or four stairs every ten feet or so adding to the descent. Like many of the other streets in the quarter, ancient stone arches covered much of the alley, alcoves and hidden doorways materialized on each side, and stone stairways with iron railings headed both up and down at irregular intervals.

He came to an intersection and looked at the street names—elaborate white tile squares, about a foot on each side and about eight feet off the ground, painted with Jewish, Arabic, and English letters spelling out the exotic names. He was on Tif'eret Yisrael Street. Hamekabulim Street came in from the south on his right, and Bone Ha Homa Street branched off to the north on his left. No sign of the rabbi or the men who followed him away from the square. Mullaney pushed on, remaining on Tif'eret Yisrael Street and hoping he had made the right decision.

———◆———

Yavod lifted his right hand from the bundle and wiped it across his face, pulling the perspiration from his eyes. And he noticed two men staring at him.

His mind was spinning—Nissan Bek Synagogue? Yeshiva Ha Kotel? Close . . . but who did he really know there? But there was Herschel at the Matnas Cultural Center! He would help.

He cast a glance to his right. The intersection with the tight confines of Ha

Sho'arim Street was just a few meters away. A produce vendor had two carts of fruit against the northern corner of the intersection. *If I can get to Ha Sho'arim Street before they move . . .*

It was only thirty meters up Ha Sho'arim Street that a nearly hidden archway gave access to a narrow alley that angled toward the Cultural Center. *If I can get there . . .*

Yavod leaned into the wall under the arch, resting his forehead against the cool stone as he tightened his grip on the box under his coat. A woman and two children passed behind him, walking in the direction of the rug merchant's shop. Out of the periphery of his eyesight he could tell he was momentarily blocked from the men's view.

Without further thought, Yavod bolted to his right, running headlong for the intersection of Ha Sho'arim Street.

———◦◦◦———

The leader watched as the rabbi rested his head against the wall under the arch . . . clearly, he was fatigued. A Jewish woman and her children emerged from the arch and walked toward the shop, talking animatedly. He turned to his partner.

"After this woman passes, walk quickly toward the rabbi. We need to flush him out of that archway. When he's—" The leader glanced toward the archway.

The rabbi was gone.

———◦◦◦———

Mullaney came out into the sunshine. Two steps down was a small square, a rug merchant's shop on the left. Two men . . .

Like a match in the darkness, Mullaney saw a flash of movement under the archway on the far side of the small square. It was the rabbi. Running . . .

He quickly looked to the two men. One was wearing a backpack. Startled, the one without the pack slapped at the arm of the other man. They turned and would have run after the rabbi, but a woman and her children were just coming up to the shop and momentarily blocked their path.

Mullaney jumped off the steps as he pulled out his phone and hit the speed dial. "Tif'eret Yisrael Street, Meyer, heading east. A square on the far side of Bone-something Street. Running pursuit." He stumbled as he hit the uneven cobblestones and, reaching for his gun, he felt his phone slip from his hand and rattle on the stones behind him.

5

The fruit peddler was sitting on a stool, asleep under an umbrella, as Yavod raced past and turned left into Ha Sho'arim Street. Yavod pressed the box into his chest with his right arm and pushed out his left hand against the corner of the largest fruit-laden cart. The cart tumbled over, knocking the fruit peddler from his stool and crashing into the second cart, which careened into the narrow street he had just left.

With all his strength, he sprinted toward the alcove he knew awaited him on the right.

———⋙◈◈⋘———

Mullaney had seen enough stupid cop movies and was trained well enough to not even bother with the useless "Halt . . . it's the police!"

He concentrated on the two men disappearing under the arch on the far side of the square and, ignoring his clattering phone, took the Glock in both hands as he quickly ran across the square. The woman screamed and pulled her children close.

———⋙◈◈⋘———

The leader came out of the archway and slipped on a rolling melon. He pushed his right hand against the wall of the near building to keep from falling, then had to navigate not only an avalanche of produce, but also a startled, elderly Arab man who staggered up from the cobblestones, shook his fist, and yelled sharp-edged Arab words up the street to his left. He pushed one of his carts out of the way, directly into the path of the leader's stumbling advance.

A woman screamed behind him.

He gripped the edge of the wooden cart and was about to push it into the peddler's back when he glanced behind to the screaming . . . a formidable, focused man with a gun, running straight at them.

"Hamid! Behind you!"

———⊸⊰⊷⊶——

"Hamid! Behind you!"

Yavod was running headlong for the alley off Ha Sho'arim Street and tried not to be concerned with what was going on behind him . . . because his knee felt like it was about to collapse under the pounding. He came up quickly on a dark recess on the wall to his right, further shaded by the wide arch that spanned Ha Sho'arim Street at that very spot. Yavod virtually launched himself into the darkened recess . . . the access to the alley. If those two men hadn't cleared the intersection yet, perhaps he had a chance. Perhaps they would . . .

Two gunshots echoed along the canyons of Jerusalem stone walls, two more following in rapid succession. Startled, Yavod tripped over a step he did not see and pitched forward into the darkness.

———⊸⊰⊷⊶——

"Hamid! Behind you!"

Mullaney heard the shout and its echo under the narrow arch. The closest man, the one with the backpack, skidded to a halt just short of the intersection beyond the arch, whirled around as he dropped to a knee and pulled a gun from somewhere. Mullaney dove to the cobblestones, his Glock outstretched, and made himself a small target, flattened against the street, hard against the building to his right.

As he hit the rough surface of the street, two shots erupted from inside the arch and splattered stone shards into Mullaney's face. He flinched, protectively closing his eyes for a heartbeat. He felt darts of stone penetrate his skin, but his now open eyes were fixed on a backpack. Mullaney squeezed off two quick shots, the backpack flinched twice on the man's back, driving him headfirst into a sprawling pile of tomatoes.

Before "backpack" hit the street, Mullaney had shifted his aim to the left for the first man. In his sights was an elderly Arab, his caftan splattered and stained with assorted vegetables, his right fist raised in outrage. The first man was gone.

———⊸⊰⊷⊶——

The leader sprinted up the narrow street. The four shots told him two things. His partner had missed with the first two shots. He doubted the tall man in the suit had missed with the next two.

He pulled the gun from under his work shirt. His time was getting short. He needed to find the rabbi quickly, get the box, and figure out a way to escape. This street was uphill, cresting under a stone arch that spanned the street thirty meters in the distance. He did not see the rabbi.

He must already be over the hill.

———◦◦◦———

Yavod hit the ground hard, elbows and knees, shock waves rattling his body followed by pulses of pain through each of his extremities. The box in his right arm hit the stone pavement and ricocheted back, slamming into his chin, nearly knocking Yavod unconscious. Blood was pouring over his lips and down his throat and his head was swimming with stars and explosions of light.

His arms and hands flew up as he bounced off the stone alley, the box flying out in front of his battered body.

———◦◦◦———

At the intersection, Mullaney slowed to navigate both the cornucopia of fruit and the wild gyrations of the elderly Arab. He stopped at the corner and peeked around the edge of the building. The street ran uphill. The first man was nearing the crest of the street. But he stopped, as if someone had jammed a hand into his chest and turned to the right. It was then Mullaney saw the gun in his right hand.

———◦◦◦———

Despair was building in the leader's heart. This would not be a good report. The master of the Disciples would not reward this effort. No, he would . . .

As he neared the crest of the street, he heard a moan to his right, from inside a darkened alcove he had failed to see before. He turned to his right. Could it be?

———◦◦◦———

Pain coursed through Yavod's body as relentlessly as the blood flowed from his ripped lips. He groaned, his hands splayed on the slippery stones of the alley. The box? Where was it?

His eyes unseeing because of the fog in his brain and the darkness in the alley, Yavod stretched out his arms, his hands feeling in front of him along the stones for his coat and the prophecy Rabbi Herzog was so excited to decipher. He felt something cold. Metal.

***

His target only one hundred feet away, Mullaney leaned in against the corner of the building and leveled the 9-millimeter Glock at the man at the top of the street as he took one step toward a dark outline to the right.

***

A smile of evil intent spread across the leader's face. He lifted his gun as he stepped toward the darkened alcove.

***

His fingers on the metal, it felt as if someone had flipped a switch on a searchlight. Yavod's mind cleared. He was lucid again. The pain in his body was gone. He needed to get the prophecy to agent Mullaney. How . . . An exquisite agony erupted from Yavod's depths, radioactive torture racing through every cell, bursting with torment.

His scream was muffled as his tongue ballooned in size and turned black.

***

Mullaney drew in a long breath and held it. He centered his sights.

***

Boots were slapping, leather against stone, to his left. But the leader was focused on the alcove. He heard whimpering . . . a strangled scream . . .

"Stop!"

In a split second, the leader's mind processed three realities . . . his quarry lay helpless in the darkness before him; there were armed IDF soldiers racing uphill from his left; and, as he turned toward the threat, a fusillade of automatic gunfire chewed apart his chest.

They were the last thoughts to reach his brain.

———≈∞≈———

The echoes from the flurry of automatic fire were still reverberating down the canyon of Ha Sho'arim Street, but Mullaney was already on his feet and racing the one hundred feet uphill to the crest of the street when his training kicked in, he stopped, knelt in the street, put his gun down on the cobblestones and raised his hands over his head.

"Meyer?" he shouted. "Is that you?"

Two IDF soldiers crested the hill. One kept his Israeli-made Tavor automatic rifle aimed at the body in the middle of the street while the other centered his sights on Mullaney's chest. Meyer Levinson was right behind them.

Levinson looked past the body to where Mullaney was kneeling in the street. He put out his right hand toward the soldier with a bead on Mullaney then turned to his left, as if something had caught his attention.

"For God's sake, Meyer"—Mullaney was up on his feet, closing fast— "don't go near that alcove!"

———≈∞≈———

The squad of IDF soldiers—so young they looked barely out of high school, so well trained and well armed they were deadly, implacable foes—stood in a semicircle behind Levinson and Mullaney as the medics put the bomber's lifeless body on a stretcher and carried it down Ha Sho'arim Street to a waiting ambulance. But neither the soldiers nor the medics made a move toward the alcove at the crest of the hill.

Mullaney and Levinson stood a step back from the arched opening, Levinson's strong flashlight illuminating the space on the far side of the alcove.

Levinson played the light over a pair of legs in black trousers. The rest of Yavod's body was only visible by standing to the side of the alcove and looking up at the rising alley on the far side. The body was splayed out on the stone floor of the alley, as if Yavod were diving into a swimming pool. His shirt was soaked with perspiration, his pants ripped and covered with dirt and dust. His face was covered with blood, rips in the skin of his chin and lips. But it was the rest that rekindled a shiver of fear in Mullaney's heart.

He had seen this once before . . . the cleaning lady in the ambassador's residence. It was no easier to look at the second time.

Mullaney remembered meeting Yavod, Rabbi Israel Herzog's aide, when the rabbi came earlier that day to the US ambassador's residence in Tel Aviv at Mullaney's invitation. Now Yavod's body had undergone a gruesome transformation—and not from the effects of the explosions at the Hurva.

The hair of Yavod's head was skittered across the cobblestones in clumps, a few wilted strands still attached to his skull. His head was turned to the left, toward the alcove opening and visible to Mullaney, his eyes following the trajectory of his left arm as it reached out toward the two boxes that had fallen from his grasp and spilled out from under his suit coat. Yavod's eyes were wide in terror, blood pouring from his eyes and down his cheeks. His mouth was open in a silent scream, his tongue black and swollen and pushed between his lips. His fingers rested on the corner of the metal box that had sprung forth from the wooden box when Yavod crashed to the cobblestones.

"What do we do now?" asked Levinson.

"I'm not sure," said Mullaney. He pulled his eyes from the corpse and looked at the Shin Bet officer. "But nobody touches the box."

6

Riyadh, Saudi Arabia
July 20, 2:48 p.m.

Relentless, the sun's rays pounded off the baked blacktop of the runway at the far end of the King Salman Airport in Riyadh as King Abdullah returned from the press conference in Amman where the Ishmael Covenant was endorsed by the leaders of each nation. When the main cabin door of the Jumbo 747 opened, heat poured into the luxurious surroundings with a vengeance. The desert was no respecter of persons. It persecuted royal and commoner alike.

Crown Prince Faisal was up the stairs of the gangway and standing at the doorway before his father exited the royal lounge in the center of the plane. King Abdullah greeted his son warmly.

"You did well, Father," said Faisal, taking the king's left elbow and helping him down the stairs toward the waiting fleet of black limousines. "The event was great theater. Over one hundred million people worldwide watched the signing. But I didn't expect your return until tomorrow."

King Abdullah was seventy-six, stoop shouldered, nearsighted, and cursed with a weak heart—valves that didn't quite match in their rhythm. He descended the steps as if each one was an Olympic event and could feel the heat penetrate through to his skin, perspiration dousing his inner robes as he gingerly navigated the stairs. "Time is a luxury only the comfortable can afford," he said, reaching the tarmac. "Today, we cannot afford time." King Abdullah was grateful for his son's support. It was support that was becoming increasingly critical to the king and his plans.

The king of Saudi Arabia lived a pragmatically schizophrenic political existence. On the one hand, he was a disciple and protector of the Sunni Wahhabi clerics, who preached a sect of fundamental Islam that outraged some Muslims and emboldened others, like ISIS. On the other hand, the Saudi king often gave more than lip service to moderate Muslim positions in order to maintain his important but brittle alliance with the West, particularly the government of the United States. At the root of the monarch's delicate dance between these two widely disparate and often opposed worldviews were two foundational realities—a solemn alliance between the tribes of Arabia and the legalistic Wahhabi clerics in place for more than 250 years, and $120 billion a year in oil revenue.

After 9/11, the king and the Saudi government navigated a treacherously narrow path: publicly denouncing terrorism while trying privately to diminish Wahhabi influence over the affairs of the nation and the radical jihadism it spawned. It was a thin line that King Abdullah still walked—particularly now that Arabia's ancient enemy was once again exerting its power.

For fourteen hundred years, the Islamic faith had been riven by a conflict—often violent—over the rightful successor to the prophet Muhammad. King Abdullah's people, the Arab Muslims, overwhelmingly supported the Sunni faction. Persia, once conquered by Muslim armies for two centuries, fervently embraced the Shia sect.

Religious conflict was now added to the ethnic conflict between two proud people. That enmity took a dire turn in 1979 when the Arab Shah of Iran was overthrown by a religious dictatorship controlled by Persian Shia clerics. Their leader, Ayatollah Khomeini, preached that Sunni believers were not truly Muslims and called for the overthrow of the al-Saud family.

The Persian's hatred for his family and his people crystallized one overriding, all-encompassing truth in King Abdullah's thinking: he would do whatever was necessary to keep his family safe and in power—and in control of the $120 billion that flowed into his treasury every year. He was not about to relinquish his sovereignty, or his wealth, to the religious thugs of Iran who were racing toward operational nuclear weapons.

An iron-clad, ratified peace and defense pact between Israel and its Arab neighbors would present a formidable deterrent against the growing power and aggressiveness of the Persian Iranians. But Abdullah would not wager the future of his family on the possible, but unlikely, ratification of the Ishmael Covenant. He was focused on a power much greater than the power of oil. King Abdullah's desired endgame was a nuclear-armed Islamic caliphate—ruled by the Family Saud—from Pakistan to the gates of Europe.

Abdullah stopped at the bottom of the gangway and turned to his son. In spite of the heat, he would take this moment when there were no other ears to hear. "Faisal, the security of our family, the security of our nation, would increase immeasurably if this covenant with Israel were ratified into reality. If

Israel and all the Arab nations stood together in true unity, we could stomp the Iranians back into their holes. But after speaking personally with David Meir following the signing, I have even less hope of the covenant's viability in the Israeli Knesset. We cannot wager our future on the empty promises of others, especially the Jews. Contact the Pakistanis and accelerate the delivery of our weapons. Our only hope is the hope we hold in our own hands."

⎯⎯⎯◦◦◦⎯⎯⎯

The Old City, Jerusalem
July 20, 2:57 p.m.

Mullaney and Levinson stood in the shade of a building across the barricaded street from the alcove that became Chaim Yavod's tomb. Drenched with perspiration, emotionally crashing as the adrenaline rush of conflict drained from his system, doused with doubt, Mullaney struggled for control in heart, soul, mind, and body.

For nineteen years Mullaney had risen steadily through the ranks of DSS. Most recently he was adjutant to George Morningstar, the deputy assistant secretary for diplomatic security. Morningstar, a State Department lifer with a title that put him two blocks on the org chart from the secretary of state, was a man of integrity and good sense. Mullaney was fortunate to have Morningstar as an ally and a superior . . . until a breach of security at the Ankara embassy cost lives and required a scapegoat. Morningstar was shunted aside to an office in the basement of the Truman Building in DC, and Mullaney—collateral damage—was banished to Israel.

It was a bitter pill for Mullaney after two decades of exemplary service in the DSS. Before being exiled to Israel, he had expected his next promotion would lead to a permanent assignment in the upper echelons of DSS leadership in Washington—an expectation his wife and daughters had taken to the bank. But that hope now seemed as impossible as reconciliation with his recently deceased father. Not only was he facing a sudden path to obscurity, but he was also on that road alone. His wife, Abby, refused to make this move, remaining with his daughters in Virginia. A consummate professional, Mullaney was determined to do his duty. But he was also hoping to keep a low profile in Israel, exercise wisdom, get back into good graces—and back to Washington—as soon as possible.

Facing his sixth crisis in just twelve days, the chances of being reassigned to DC were rapidly becoming slim to none.

"Almost twenty dead already."

Meyer Levinson's eyes were fixed on the guys in the bomb suits across the street, but Mullaney could tell his mind was elsewhere.

"We've taken one hit after another from these guys," said Levinson. "We've been on our heels, on the defensive . . . from the beginning. We've lost too many good men already. That's got to stop."

"What are you thinking?" asked Mullaney.

"Offense," said Levinson. "I'm thinking offense. It's time for us to transform from defensemen into strikers—past time. I'm thinking we've got to take the fight to these clowns, wherever they are."

"How do you plan to find them?"

"I'm not sure," said Levinson. He motioned across the street with his head. "But there's the box. They want it. We've got it. I'm thinking they'll come to us. Instead I want to beat them to the punch."

Trained as a scientist in theoretical physics, on a tenure track at Hebrew University, Levinson had been lured from the academic world by Shin Bet, the highly competent and effective internal security apparatus for the nation of Israel. His intelligence, his daring, and his devotion to the Jewish state relentlessly propelled Levinson through the ranks of Israeli security.

Currently Levinson was director of Shin Bet's operations division, the antiterrorism branch of the service and home to the agency's frontline fighters, who relentlessly pursued—and usually crushed—any internal threat to the Jewish homeland.

Mullaney came to know Levinson professionally in Washington, when Levinson was the agent in charge of security for the Israeli embassy. They grew closer socially when they discovered the other's passion for the Chelsea Football Club, running into each other at DC's Airedale pub in Columbia Heights—a hotbed of Chelsea fervor—during the FA Cup tournament. Their friendship remained close, even after Levinson returned to Israel to help Shin Bet continue safeguarding the state and the people of Israel.

The IDF bomb squad leader, who looked like a teenager but who wore a captain's bars, carried his robot-looking helmet crooked in one arm as he walked across the street to where Mullaney and Levinson were waiting. The bomb squad had treated the box as if it were a massively destructive roadside explosive. Watching the drama of their dilemma was engrossing. But wisely, neither man offered to help.

"All secure, Major," the captain said to Levinson.

"I know it must seem like a whole lot of precaution for a small metal box," said Levinson.

"No, sir," responded the captain. "Small metal boxes have killed a lot of my friends. There's no such thing as too much caution. What would you like us to do with our little package?"

Levinson turned to Mullaney. "You have a vault at the embassy, correct?"

Mullaney grimaced and shook his head. "Bait?"

"You have any better ideas?" asked Levinson. He placed a hand on Mullaney's shoulder. "It's got to go somewhere, it's our best chance to draw these guys out, and it doesn't belong to me. Captain"—he turned to the bomb squad leader—"transport the package to the Shin Bet helicopter down by the Zion Gate and don't try to hide what you're doing. Then I want you and two of your men to get out of your blast suits and accompany the box and Agent Mullaney back to Tel Aviv. Get the box safely secured in the embassy's vault. Then the chopper will bring you home."

The young captain saluted, turned, crossed the street, and started giving instructions to his team.

"The ambassador is not going to be happy about having this box dropped back in his lap."

"Well," said Levinson, a satisfied smile creasing his face, "if I remember correctly, he's the one who brought this plague here in the first place.

Mullaney wanted to argue the point but knew he had no grounds.

"There is nothing in science that can tell us why that lethal little metal box kills people with such gruesome effectiveness," said Levinson, as he and Mullaney followed the bomb squad's armored cart down Ha Sho'arim Street. "So we know we're dealing with something outside the realm of science here. But I'm a little nervous about finding out just how far outside science we've wandered."

7

Washington, DC
July 20, 9:11 a.m.

"A bit much of the cloak-and-dagger, don't you think?"

Noah Webster, deputy secretary of state for management and resources at the US State Department, looked out the smoked-glass window of the Lincoln Town Car at the back entrance of Tully's Tap Room in the Woodley Park section of Washington, between the Smithsonian Zoo and the Washington Marriott. The Town Car was idling in a narrow alley populated primarily with trash dumpsters and back doors.

"Through the door and up the stairs to your right," said the driver.

"That's it?"

The driver simply looked in the rearview mirror. It was his only answer.

Richard Rutherford had sent his car, and his driver had delivered the invitation as Webster was leaving a breakfast of power brokers at the Hyatt downtown. The handwritten invitation said former senator Seneca Markham would appreciate Webster's immediate presence at a meeting with Rutherford, the billionaire Atlanta banker—the man Webster hoped would soon bankroll a successful campaign for the vacant Senate seat in Virginia.

It was Rutherford who held the strings to Seneca Markham and the campaign they quietly waged to block President Lamont Boylan's proposed deal with Iran. Rutherford was not so concerned with thwarting Iran's headlong rush to nuclear capability, but he was very concerned about the deal's plan to eliminate all economic sanctions against Iran—and return the two billion dollars in Iranian assets seized by American banks during the Iran Hostage Crisis. Assets that now, after thirty years of compounding interest, generated seven hundred million dollars in unfettered profit, growing every year, for those banks holding the funds. Most of which were controlled by Richard Rutherford.

Webster, at fifty-eight still lean and muscled like hardened steel, had served as Markham's chief of staff for nearly twenty-eight years, until Markham's poor health forced him to retire two years earlier. Senator Markham was the fount of incredible power and influence in Washington, and Webster used that power and influence with a religious ruthlessness, advancing both Markham's platform and his own personal agenda. Some, out of Webster's hearing, called it the reign of terror. But it accomplished Webster's intentions: the accumulation of power and the introduction to vast financial resources.

Handed a position in the State Department upon Markham's retirement, a position that included responsibility for the Diplomatic Security Service, Webster was enlisted by Markham into Rutherford's campaign against the Iran deal. Webster was to twist arms through the State Department and overseas, anything to block or delay an agreement that would return the seized assets to Iran. In return, Webster was promised an excessively funded run for the Senate seat.

So when Richard Rutherford called—or now retired Senator Seneca Markham beckoned—Webster knew it wise to change his plans and be available. But Tully's Tap Room? By the back door? Somebody was being very cautious.

At the top of the stairs stood two doors, one to the right and one straight ahead. The door on the right was open, and the room was filled with large cardboard boxes of supplies. Webster stepped to the closed door in front of him. Should he knock?

"Come in, Noah." It was not Markham's voice.

Webster turned the knob and opened the door. Richard Rutherford sat in an overstuffed wingback chair, the room's solitary window behind him. An empty desk occupied the left side of the room. Senator Markham was not in sight.

"Seneca was feeling poorly this morning," said Rutherford, his southern Georgia drawl making him sound like Colonel Sanders hawking fried chicken. "He asked me to pass along his regrets." Rutherford motioned Webster toward a second chair, this one facing the window, the sun in his eyes as he looked at the banker.

"You know, Seneca is very fond of you—like a son, he told me."

Webster's pride swelled as he settled into the chair. "I'm honored to know—"

"Me, I'm not so sure," interrupted Rutherford. "I think so far you've been pretty disappointing."

It was as if Rutherford had slapped him across the face. Immediately, the well in Webster's soul that harbored his sublimated anger burst forth like a plugged geyser. Insulted, he tasted all the prejudice he had suffered, the resentment that was fueled by the relentless discrimination against a black man in a white man's world,

Webster failed to identify his anger as pride. But he was quick to identify his adversary. A white man and a Southerner—an obscenely rich Southerner. He gritted his teeth as he tried to regain his composure. A Senate seat and then a run for president was the prize he pursued. Was it worth it?

"I am neither your lackey nor your servant." Webster spit the words out of his mouth. "Certainly not your slave. Treating me with disrespect will not get you what you wish to achieve."

"Stuff it, Webster. I don't need your attitude. What I need is results." The eclipse that was Rutherford eased closer. "I don't see any impediments to Boylan's folly rising up through the State Department. Secretary Townsend is President Boylan's gofer. Outside of Israel, a given, there is no international outcry against the Iran deal. And you and your Turkish pal Eroglu were supposed to have the Iraqis tied up in a knot by now."

Shortly before Markham retired, he had engineered Webster's unorthodox insertion into the higher echelons of the State Department's leadership bureaucracy. With the intent purpose of derailing President Boylan's Iran deal, Webster was introduced to Arslan Eroglu, the prime minister of Turkey. They were two men with a similar goal: gut the growing influence of Iran in the Middle East. Eroglu and Turkey's president, Emet Kashani, recognized the danger to Turkey that was posed by the growing power and influence of Iran and its expanding association with its embattled Shia brothers in Iraq. The emergent talk of a new Persia, a resurrection of the old empire that was once centered on Iraq and Iran, combined with the ongoing civil war in Syria not only continued political instability on Turkey's eastern border but also threatened Kashani's intention—less public but just as fervent—to expand Ottoman influence and power in the region.

So it was that Webster found himself in collusion with a foreign power, exchanging secrets with and funneling hundreds of thousands of Rutherford's dollars through Turkey's prime minister with the express, dual purpose of countering this flourishing Persian threat and killing the US president's nuclear deal with Iran. But so far, Eroglu's promises remained empty.

Webster uncoiled from his chair like a serpent on a hot rock—slow but deadly. He walked over to the empty desk and leaned against it so he was facing Rutherford from the side, getting the sun out of his eyes and forcing Rutherford to turn in his direction. Now Rutherford had to look up at him.

"It was you who insisted I should contact Arslan Eroglu in Iceland," Webster said. "Eroglu was your idea."

"Eroglu is an empty promise," snarled Rutherford. "I'm pouring a lot of money into a lot of bottomless pits. Tell me you've got good news . . . or maybe I should take my business and my money elsewhere."

"Yes, your money. I think you would be tempted to sell your soul to keep your hands on the Iranian funds harbored in your vaults."

Rutherford squared his shoulders and pierced Webster with a dismissive look of ridicule. "Don't be so naive, Noah. My soul? We live, and then we are nothing. Why should I be concerned with bartering something that doesn't exist? Money is good because it buys power. Unlimited money buys unlimited power. I don't pursue money. I pursue power. You would be amazed—perhaps rightly frightened—if you could fully grasp the realms of power my money, Iran's money, has purchased for me."

A ripple of dread invaded Webster's heart. He was navigating a very dangerous course with this man. One errant step could be fatal to his schemes and his future. But it was Rutherford who didn't fully grasp the risks Webster was willing to endure in order to see those schemes fulfilled.

"Senator Markham told me you had changed"—Webster's words were a whisper encased in brass knuckles—"ever since you met the man with the yellow eyes."

Rutherford physically recoiled in his chair. Webster watched as waves of surprise, alarm, and then resolve clouded Rutherford's countenance. Good. He had slapped Rutherford back.

"The senator told you about Ankara and the man with yellow eyes, eh? Well, what else did the senator tell you?"

Webster crossed his arms and looked down at Rutherford. He was feeling his confidence return. "That you asked the senator to help bring your son-in-law back home."

Even though his eyes still harbored ruthless reproach, Rutherford eased back in his chair and shrugged. "My granddaughters want their father home. How can I refuse them?"

"Tell your granddaughters not to get their hopes up," said Webster. "Mullaney is not coming home. Not on my watch. And I'm the one who controls his destiny."

Looking at the floor, Rutherford shook his head back and forth. "So foolish." Then he stood and took two steps, closing the distance to Webster to less than an arm's length. "I think you've lost track of something very significant, Noah. The reality of who is in control here.

"I want results." Rutherford leaned even closer. "I want Iran crippled, and I want the sanctions to stay in place. That's got to come from your end, Webster. And tell Eroglu I want to see some direct roadblocks thrown into Iran's path. Or . . . I withdraw my support—from both of you."

Webster's heart was burning with fury, and he could see the same fury staring back at him. But he wasn't about to be intimidated, or dictated to, by Rutherford. The time had come for him to play his trump card.

"You think your wealth buys you immunity, Richard," said Webster, his voice low but edged with a razor sharpness. "You think it buys you superiority. Perhaps . . . with some. But not with me." He held Rutherford's hard gaze and didn't flinch. "I believe it would distress you greatly to know that I have documented records of every contribution you've ever funneled into Senator Markham's campaigns and accounts—both the legitimate contributions and those larger contributions that flaunt every legal tenet of campaign finance. And I also have a matching calendar of every favor that Markham's done for you . . ."

"You are making a mis—"

"And," Webster continued, "more importantly, a record of every obscure amendment authored by Markham that would benefit only you and your empire. And I have those records safely resting in three very secure locations with instructions about when and how that information is to be made public. Enough information that would send both you and Markham to prison for a very long time."

Even though Rutherford's lips were pressed tightly together, he managed to squeeze out five words. "You *are* making a mistake."

Noah Webster's blood felt like an ice floe. Not from fear. But from resolve. He had come this far, risked this much. He was so close. Nothing was going to get in his way now. Not Arslan Eroglu. And if necessary, not Richard Rutherford.

"Mullaney stays in Israel and those records remain under my control," Webster whispered, "unless . . . of course . . . you desire to make a twenty-million-dollar investment into my campaign war chest." He ignored the fury that radiated from every pore in Rutherford's body. It was about time to teach this banker how the big boys played with power.

"Think about it, Richard." Webster turned and walked toward the door. "You know where to find me."

Ankara, Turkey
July 20, 4:16 p.m.

On a slope just downhill from the Ankara Castle, at the end of a cul-de-sac called Alitas Street, a small house was surrounded by high stone walls. Only the very top of the roofline was visible from the narrow street. Within those walls on a raised veranda facing east, under a pergola entwined with wisteria vines, Assan's master rested in the shadows, his body stretched out on a cushioned chaise longue.

The sun's rays and heat were just sliding behind the Turkish hills to the west, but it had been hours since that heat had insinuated its presence into the shadow under the pergola. A touch of the discomfort that is Ankara in July remained in the space. But moment by moment, the oppressive heat fled from the air.

His master, a man known only as the Turk, was small in stature, slight of frame. He was dressed in the traditional garb worn by the Turkish upper class during the height of the Ottoman Empire: baggy, blousy trousers—the salvar—over which was worn an ankle-length, robe-like garment with sleeves that flared wide from the elbows to the wrists—the jubba. His eyes were closed, his arms crossed and resting upon his ribs.

There was no sound under the pergola. The few birds that haunted the wisteria or lingered in the low pines of the courtyard erupted in a flurry of wings and fled the veranda and the courtyard as soon as the small man first approached.

His hands, long-fingered and pale, were habitually tucked within the wide sleeves of the jubba. He touched no man . . . and no man touched him.

———◦◦◦———

Human lifetimes had no hold on the Turk. He existed for centuries before being dispatched on this quest to destroy the written messages penned by a reclusive Lithuanian Jewish scholar, this Gaon of Vilnius. But for more than two hundred years, his avowed purpose was to ensure that the revealed prophecies contained in these messages would never be disclosed—prophecies that could devastate the calculated intentions of his master.

He pursued one ultimate goal. To change the end of the enemy's book.

———◦◦◦———

The world's three dominant religions—Islam, Judaism, and Christianity—had similar roots in the patriarch Abraham and a similar view of the future. The Islamic Koran, the Jewish Tanakh, and the Christian Bible each contained a meticulous rendering of a coming last days for the earth. In a two-stage vision of the future, each book foresaw a time of worldwide peace and prosperity. While each of the great religious books asserts that the era of peace would last only a short time, what was envisaged to come after the peace was wildly divergent.

Just as the Turk had adopted the traditional clothing of his host country, he had also adopted its religion, Islam, because it served his purpose. He was a diligent scholar of the Koran, and its doctrine provided a ready mechanism to accelerate the wishes of the One. But the Turk was also a scholar of the other religious writings. He needed to know and understand his enemy.

The Jews waited for their Messiah. His coming was projected in detail in the Hebrew scripture, the Tanakh—a compilation of the Law, the Prophets, and the Writings that were sacred to the Jews. It was the arrival of this Messiah, the Turk learned, that would usher in an end-times scenario in which Jerusalem would be the capital city of the Jewish Messiah-King who would rule all the world. Under the Messiah-King's divine authority, there would be no disease and no war throughout the earth, and the world would be united into one confederation with Israel enthroned in a place of prominence over all nations.

The Jewish Tanakh could also be found in the Christian Bible, which absorbed these same writings in its Old Testament, but also contained what is called the New Testament, the history of a Jewish Nazarene prophet named

Yeshua, who claimed himself to be the son of God, the Messiah. Outraged by his blasphemy, the Jewish religious leaders of his day had betrayed Yeshua into the hands of the Roman occupation, who crucified the prophet. But Christians further believed that after three days in a tomb, this Yeshua was resurrected to life, that he was lifted back up to heaven to sit at his Father's right hand, and that he would come again, return to earth in his human form, and lead the armies of God against the armies of the world in a climactic battle on the plains of Megiddo. Yeshua's victory in this battle would result in a thousand-year reign of peace, but that peace would end—once a new Jerusalem descended from heaven—in a climactic judgment where Christian believers in Yeshua would live on a perfected earth for all eternity. But this so-called Prince of Peace would summarily condemn anyone not professing he was the son of God. The condemned would be tormented through all eternity in an unquenchable fire.

The Koran, containing the words actually spoken by the prophet Muhammad, written down and organized after his death, was the sacred scripture of Islam, which the Turk revered as the only true path to bring forth the One he served. The Koran references many of the same characters and chronicles many of the same events as the Jewish and Christian scriptures. But as the last and greatest prophet, Muhammad was the precursor of the Mahdi, the final and greatest caliph, who would lead Islam's warriors in conquering the world. Under the influence of Islamic Sharia law, the Mahdi would reign for seven years over a golden age of universal peace and prosperity prior to the final judgment.

The Turk knew that all three religions held fast to the belief that the last days of humanity would be inaugurated by divine intervention.

But what was unique to the Islamic religion was the belief that Muslims today, by their actions and their intervention in this world, could accelerate the arrival of the Mahdi. In the same vein, the Turk believed, if he could hasten the Mahdi's coming, why could he not hinder or make impossible the emergence of the Jewish-Christian Messiah? If he could abort at least one of the Messianic prophecies of the Judeo-Christian scripture, would not all the others be rendered void? To that end, the Turk and his master had dedicated themselves to manufacture and manipulate the holy writings—to rewrite the end of the Bible.

When any possibility for the fulfillment of Messianic prophecy was destroyed, first would emerge a transcontinental Islamic caliphate with one ruler, the Mahdi. But out of that caliphate would arise the last and ultimate ruler for whom the Turk was only a messenger. This ruler—the One—would reign over a worldwide empire unhindered by the empty promises of any "holy" book, whether the Tanakh, the Bible, or even the Koran.

There were obstacles that needed to be overcome for the Turk and his master to achieve their intended goal. The anarchists of ISIS and its false caliphate must be wiped off the face of the earth, along with the Zionists, and the West lulled into false security while true Muslim believers infiltrated every level of society, government, and culture. But the most critical hindrance to his dream was the escalating nuclear arms race in the Middle East.

Neither the Persians nor the Arabs could be permitted to possess nuclear weapons and thus attain nuclear superiority and dominion over the Muslim world. For the Turk's plans to succeed, first a new Ottoman Empire must rise from Turkey, an empire ruled by the Mahdi that would stretch from India through the Balkans to the gates of the major capitals of Europe. An Ottoman Empire built on the back of a nuclear arsenal that would enslave its enemies.

And a nuclear arsenal was buried in hardened bunkers only four hundred kilometers from where the Turk now rested.

At the massive Incirlik Air Base in eastern Turkey, shared by NATO and Turkish air forces, were housed sixty American-made B61 thermonuclear bombs deployed to Turkey in 2009 as part of NATO's nuclear sharing policy. Belgium, Germany, Italy, and the Netherlands also received American B61 bombs to store on their soil as NATO expanded its program for nuclear deterrence against the Soviet Union. While the weapons were supplied entirely by the United States, each of the participating nations was responsible for storing and maintaining the weapons and the bombers needed to deliver those weapons. Necessarily, the Turkish Air Force and its officers were intimately knowledgeable about and involved with the maintenance of the weapons.

The Turk was keenly aware that the short-term history of the Middle East would be determined by the outcome of a nuclear arms race. Israel already possessed nuclear weapons. Now Iran—the nascent Persian Empire—was only two breakthroughs away from a viable nuclear weapon and a reliable delivery system. And the Saudis, terrified by a nuclear Persian Empire, had called in a debt—a shipload of Pakistani nuclear weapons as return for the billions of dollars Saudi Arabia invested in the development of Pakistan's nuclear weapons program.

Thus the Turk cast a covetous eye on those weapons at Incirlik, a craving that was at the root of a conspiracy—a shortcut to nuclear supremacy and ushering in the age of the Mahdi.

———— ◦◦◦◦ ————

Assan, his aide, stirred when his master withdrew his left hand from inside the right sleeve of the jubba and languidly raised it as if brushing aside a cobweb in his sleep.

Assan moved out of the darkness deep under the pergola. Not much more than skin and bones, dressed in a long, black robe, a black cowl over his head, Assan glided across the flagstones like a haunting wraith. He bowed his head. "Yes, Master. How may I be of assistance?"

The Turk opened his eyes and Assan could not hold his gaze. How many times had he been in the presence of the Turk? But still those eyes spoke of great power and greater violence. There was anarchy—no, madness—swimming in those eyes. They looked like a cat's eyes. The Turk's pupils were a pale yellow, and the irises surrounding the pupils were black. The space around the irises, the sclera, was swirling like a gray fog. But what made the Turk's eyes so difficult to engage was that the yellow pupils expanded and contracted as if they had a pulse, a life of their own.

Assan kept his eyes fixed on the flagstone floor.

"This day is an accursed messenger." The Turk's voice slithered through the air, the hiss of a whisper that contaminated Assan's thoughts. "We have failed miserably on several fronts."

A shiver rattled Assan's bones. The Turk did not suffer failure well.

"The woman was wrenched from our hands and the ambassador, who may know too much, still lives," he said, his whisper landing like a lash. "Now that demon box has returned into the hands of the American agent who continues to kill our Disciples. How is that possible? The box, and the message it carries, should be buried under the ruins of that Zionist sanctuary."

His master was not initiating conversation. Assan had learned that difficult lesson long before. So he waited, searching the cracks in the flagstones.

The Turk stood and moved farther into the dusk of the pergola. "Summon the leader of the Disciples," he said, his voice a shimmering menace. "Then we will pay the prime minister a visit. Eroglu's colonel should have the weapons in place by now. It is time for him to take action. But it appears the prime minister is reluctant to give the order. Perhaps the prime minister should no longer be our friend."

A cloud of dread projected from the Turk and swept over Assan, leaving behind an oily residue on his skin. But the cloud did not rest on him. It was directed toward another. Assan thanked the dark power—he had been spared.

⸺⧫⸺

Washington, DC
July 20, 9:44 a.m.

Richard Rutherford entered his black Lincoln Town Car limousine in the alley behind Tully's Tap Room. "Take me home." Then he pushed a button on the console by his right hand, and a smoked-glass partition rose from the back of the front seat and slipped into a padded dock in the roof. Rutherford could neither be seen nor heard by his driver.

He lifted an iPad from the briefcase on the floor, connected to the internet through an encrypted server, and entered a long URL destination he had committed to memory, even though he had used it only once before. His palms began to sweat as he waited.

"Yes?"

Memories flooded back when he heard the voice, memories that left Rutherford feeling both exhilarated and defiled.

"I have need of your Disciples," he said, the mic in his iPad picking up his voice.

The silent pause on the other end of the conversation lengthened. Rutherford's anxiety increased. Perhaps this was not a wise choice.

"For what purpose?"

Richard Rutherford allowed nothing to stand in his way as he built his financial empire. Not only were confidences betrayed, lives ruined, and competitors destroyed, but some individuals had also been sacrificed on his altar of greed. Perhaps not with his own hands, but there was blood on Rutherford's billions. He was single-purposed and resolute. Yet he now picked his words carefully.

"To ensure the continued invisibility of our endeavors, it has become necessary for Senator Markham's poor health to take a turn for the worse . . . a fatal turn."

"And your hands are too delicate for such a task?"

Rutherford knew he was being mocked, but he refused to rise to the bait. Markham had made a fatal mistake in telling his lackey, Webster, about the man with the yellow eyes. The senator was swinging out of control. Webster was still in a necessary position. But a message needed to be sent. "We can no longer be confident in Markham's discretion. He is a liability. There can be no trace. His death must appear to be from natural causes."

There was no video component to the communication. Which was just as well. Rutherford had tried to wipe his memory clean of their first and only face-to-face meeting. The man himself was creepy enough. But his yellow eyes—there was a seduction to madness in those eyes, the allure of wanton carnage. A shiver crossed Rutherford's shoulders as if a cloud had separated him from the sun.

"When?" the voice asked.

"As soon as your Disciples can be in place. To delay is to invite—"

"My Disciples are closer than you believe. It will be done. Soon."

"How—"

"Your debt to me has increased."

"Yes . . . I expected that," said Rutherford. "What—" The connection was severed.

For one of the few times in his life, terror flushed through Rutherford's veins. One of the most powerful men in the United States, he reached toward the console on his right. His hand convulsed. He felt as if his heart would explode. He did not know the cost. But he knew it would be high.

8

The telephone on Ambassador Cleveland's desk gave one short ring, the signal from his secretary in the outer office. "Yes, Jeffrey?"

"Ruth Hughes would like a minute, sir."

"Sure . . . send her in. And Agent Mullaney is securing something down in the vault. Please ask him to join us when he's finished."

DSS Special Agent Tommy Hernandez, chief of Cleveland's personal security detail, was in the corner of the office, going over duty rosters required for the higher threat level since the explosions at the Hurva. Hernandez was a native Texan whose expensive, finely cut suits and muscled, five-ten frame radiated power and confidence in any room. But his brown eyes twinkled with mischief, and the jester in Hernandez watched for any opportunity.

"Would you like me to leave, sir?"

Cleveland shook his head. "No, Tommy. Stay put."

Hughes stepped briskly through the door, all business as usual. The US mission to Israel's political officer, a former lawyer now in her midsixties, Hughes had been recruited by the State Department after a twenty-two-year career with Aramco—the former US-Saudi oil partnership. Hughes had proven so valuable to Aramco that she had been promoted from corporate counsel to a corporate officer and member of the board in 1976, when the Saudis first demanded twenty-five percent ownership of the company. She remained in a position of power for fifteen years, even after Saudi Arabia bought out Exxon, Mobile, and Texaco and took complete control of the world's largest oil and gas company in 1980.

"Good afternoon, sir," Hughes said, formally addressing the ambassador. "Please call on me if there is anything I can help with on the Hurva situation."

"Thank you, Ruth . . . and no need to be formal. Mullaney is at the Hurva with Meyer Levinson and his Shin Bet team. We should know something soon. But please, have a seat. Tommy," he said toward Hernandez, "you might as well come over here. I think you'll need to hear this as well. I take it you've discovered something about the Saudis?"

Her white hair pulled back in a matronly bun, defying her five-foot-four height,
Hughes radiated power in her pin-perfect black business suit, crisp white shirt,
and glowing pearls. For more than two decades as Aramco's chief contract
negotiator, she had played power politics with every government in the Middle
East. Which is why, only six hours earlier, Cleveland had given Hughes the
assignment to find corroboration of reports that Saudi Arabia was awaiting
delivery of a shipment of nuclear weapons from Pakistan. Hughes not only
personally knew the power players in the Middle East but also owned a contact
list that contained private phone numbers of the rich and the royal across the
region.

"I've never had so many calls end so abruptly as I have in the last hour,"
she said, frustration bubbling up as she settled into one of the chairs in front
of Cleveland's desk. "Something is happening, but not only are my sources not
talking, it's like their lips were forged shut on an anvil. We need to send somebody in there on the ground who can get close and listen."

"We certainly can't rely on secondhand or next-day reports," Cleveland
agreed. "There may not be enough time. We need to know more, and we need
to know now."

"Who do we have in the area?" asked Hernandez. "Most of our CIA assets
were driven out of the region under pressure from the Islamic clerics. Who does
the State Department have on the ground we can count on?"

"Not much," said Cleveland. "We've been incredibly crippled by Ambassador Alexander's sudden heart attack. When he died, we lost almost all of our
connections with the higher echelons of the Saudi royal family."

"There's Whitaker," offered Hughes. She knew involving this man was a
stretch, a Hail Mary. But who else did they have?

"Where is he?" Cleveland asked.

"Qatar. Assistant attaché for agriculture."

"Couldn't Webster bury him any deeper?"

Hughes lost the struggle to keep the smile from her face. Riley Whitaker was another State Department veteran who had been skewered by Noah

Webster's revenge. "Whitaker is not a bad guy," said Hughes. "He's a good diplomat, in fact. Except for going off the reservation about the proposed Iran deal, he's been a loyal soldier."

"So why the desert?"

"Because it was better than the Arctic. After Whitaker was identified as the source for that article in the *Atlantic* that excoriated Boylan and the Iran deal, some wanted to assign Whitaker to Reykjavík or Siberia. He needed to be given a penance tour, or others would have taken advantage. A slap on the wrist wasn't enough. He needed to sweat."

"Webster made that happen."

"Yes, sir. But now he's one of our most senior and experienced men in the region. And he's got something I didn't realize until twenty minutes ago."

"A bad sunburn?" asked Hernandez.

"Don't know about that," said Hughes. "But his father was Aramco. High in the food chain."

Cleveland pushed himself closer, pressing against the edge of the desk

"Really? How long? When?"

"His dad was VP Ops, spent a lot of time in the field. I met him once but never made the connection until now. Whitaker lived in Saudi Arabia from the time he was nine years old until his family returned to the States when the Saudis took full control in 1980. Student at the American school in Riyadh, played on a soccer team with King Abdullah's son, Faisal."

"Tough playing soccer in the sand," said Hernandez. "Now volleyball, that's another . . ."

Cleveland gave Hernandez a long stare down before turning his attention back on Hughes. "Are you kidding me? Whitaker knew Prince Faisal when they were kids?"

Hughes smiled. It was one of those rare moments of satisfaction—after days and nights of stumbling from one crisis into another, a moment to exhale, to enjoy some good news. "Not only Faisal. The Emir of Qatar's son Ibrahim went to the same school . . . played on the same team. Better yet? Riley took Ibrahim's cousin to the American school formal the year he graduated."

Cleveland's smile mirrored Hughes's.

"Well, let's get him. We need Whitaker, and we need him now."

Hughes looked down at her watch. This felt good. "The embassy in Doha tracked him down just as I was coming in. He should be giving us a call in five minutes."

—————◦◦◦◦————

"I won't get anything out of Faisal." Riley Whitaker's voice came out of the speakerphone on Cleveland's desk. "He's too much his father's son. But Prince Ibrahim could be helpful to us. There's only one problem."

"They're all in Jordan, and you're in Qatar?" asked Cleveland. Mullaney, Hughes, and Hernandez sat grouped around Cleveland's desk.

"Exactly," Whitaker replied. "And I don't expect them back here for days. Ibrahim is part of a group of us who get together each Monday night to play a little poker. He told us he wouldn't make tomorrow's game and wasn't sure when he would be back in Doha."

Cleveland looked up from the speaker, lips pursed in thought. "Mr. Whitaker, is the ambassador in his office?"

"I believe he is, sir. He's the one who asked me to give you a call. He told me to cooperate with you in whatever way you need. I am at your service."

"Good. Then pack a toothbrush and get to Amman as quickly as you can. See if you can get close to Prince Ibrahim and let us know what you hear."

"Yes, sir," said Whitaker. "But what am I listening for?"

Cleveland cast a quick glance at Mullaney, his chief of security, who nodded his head in affirmation.

"We have unconfirmed reports that King Abdullah has called in his debt with Pakistan," said Cleveland, "and a shipment of Pakistani nukes could soon be on their way to Riyadh. We need confirmation if that's true."

"Yes, sir . . . and that's not a question I'd want to ask over the phone."

"Wise choice," said Cleveland. "I've already contacted Embassy Air in Amman and they have a Sikorsky chopper on its way to Doha International. They will be wheels down in less than two hours."

"Old Camp Snoopy. I know it well. You must have been pretty confident I would take this assignment."

"Yes, I was," Cleveland admitted. "I know your story. I thought you might enjoy a diversion. And Mr. Whitaker?"

"Sir?"

"This assignment is dark ops, understand? A tight circle. I want you to report directly to my political officer, Ruth Hughes. No one else, understood? We keep a tight lid on this until we find out what we're up against. Agreed?"

"Yes, sir, absolutely," said Whitaker, his enthusiasm for the mission percolating through the phone line. "There's not a great deal of agricultural activity in the middle of this desert. You just saved my sanity. I'll stay in touch once I get to Amman. And don't worry, Mr. Ambassador. I'm confident the prince will help us."

"Thank you, Mr. Whitaker. But I always worry."

⸻⸻⸻⸻⸻

Gocuk, Turkey
July 20, 5:03 p.m.

Turkish National Police Colonel Fabir Matoush watched silently as the men under his command finished off-loading the wooden crates from the civilian truck convoy and into the Turkish National Police cargo haulers. He was frustrated. The trucks had been delayed. The transfer of cargo took longer than anticipated, and they were making the transfer in broad daylight. For this work, darkness would have been better.

"Those last crates," said his lieutenant, "they were so heavy you would have thought they were made of lead."

"Was the cargo divided correctly?" asked Matoush, ignoring the lieutenant's probe.

"Yes, sir," said the lieutenant. "Into three convoys, each with an equal number of green crates and white crates. The heavy ones—the red ones—were difficult to maneuver, but we divided those equally as well. The drivers are ready to leave at your order."

Made of lead? His lieutenant didn't know how close he had come to the truth.

The truth? The truth was that Matoush was more frightened than he had ever been in his life. He regretted listening to his cousin, the prime minister, with all of his heart. Certainly Eroglu promised lavish wealth and preached the salvation of Turkey, but Eroglu was not the one who would unleash a plague on the NATO base at Incirlik . . . Eroglu was not the one who was charged with securing and transporting nuclear weapons. Matoush would be living side by side with gruesome death until this mission was completed.

Matoush commanded seven thousand national police in the Adana District, only a short distance from the massive Incirlik Air Base. When the time came, those men he had handpicked would not be in uniform, nor would they be using police-issued weapons. They would need the most sophisticated, deadliest weapons available if they were to complete their mission. Chemical weapons—silent, but deadly sarin gas—which were contained in the red crates, sealed inside stainless steel vaults.

He had given much thought to his mission, how to complete it successfully. A full-on assault would not achieve the objective. Only stealth and silent death would allow his men to gain access to the hardened security bunkers that housed the B61 nuclear weapons.

When the time came, Matoush and his men—protected by laboratory grade biohazard suits—would release the toxins from locations hidden inside buildings throughout the Incirlik compound. There were sixty B61 nuclear bombs stored at Incirlik—seven-hundred-pound thermonuclear weapons. The most his men could hope to handle were thirty. If he could escape with only fifteen, that would be plenty.

The American atomic bomb that obliterated Nagasaki had a yield of twenty-one kilotons. The B61 nuclear bombs at Incirlik were adjustable and could deliver explosive yields over 330 kilotons. More than enough.

With thirty B61 nuclear weapons under his control—even if only fifteen—with the Russian bombers stolen during the collapse of the Soviet Union hidden in the Pontic Mountains to the north, and with the ex-Turkish Air Force flight crews in place, Eroglu would ensure Turkey beat Iran to the bomb and that the Persians could not hold his country as a nuclear hostage.

How would the Americans respond? It appeared Eroglu didn't care. The stolen Russian ICBMs hidden in the Pontic Mountains could reach America. Or Tehran. Or Jerusalem. Turkey would have the capacity to wipe out all of its enemies. And Prime Minister Arslan Eroglu, once he removed that fool of a president, Kashani, would be the caliph of a new, resurgent Ottoman Empire. No one could oppose him.

He would be like God.

Matoush feared he would not live to see God arrive.

Israeli Intelligence, Central Command Center, Jerusalem
July 20, 5:15 p.m.

It was a good place to hide a building that needed to remain hidden . . . in full view. A nondescript, Jerusalem stone building on Poliakov Street in the Kiryat Moshe neighborhood of Jerusalem, the Central Command Center of Israeli Intelligence was situated to the northeast of the government complex containing the Knesset building, Israel's Supreme Court, and the Ministry of Foreign Affairs. The nearby presence of the Prima Park and the Ramada Jerusalem Hotels and the Knesset Towers apartment complex, all only two blocks away, poured a relentless stream of traffic into Route 386, one of a confluence of other major roads that sliced through the bustling city.

Swept along and cloaked by the traffic, Israel's highest-ranking military officers and its most critical government leaders could quickly and unobtrusively converge on the command center without attracting much notice.

Today's hastily arranged emergency meeting was packed. Not only was the conference table crowded, but numerous aides leaned uncomfortably against the round walls.

David Meir, prime minister of Israel, sat in the middle of one arc of a large wooden oval table. The military helicopter returning Meir from Amman, Jordan, and the signing ceremony for the Ishmael Covenant had touched down only twenty minutes earlier on a rarely used helipad behind the Knesset. He was scrambling to catch up with the reports on the destruction of the Hurva Synagogue and the new dispatches from northern Israel and Gaza, where violence erupted almost immediately after he signed the peace plan and mutual defense covenant between Israel, Egypt, Jordan, and Saudi Arabia. Street protests were being planned for the next day by a wide spectrum of activists responding to one aspect of the covenant or another—Palestinians overjoyed at the creation of a new Palestinian state, Orthodox Jews and evangelical Christians to support the clause calling for construction of a Jewish temple adjacent to the Temple Mount platform, liberal Jews aghast at the thought of a temple, militant Jewish settlers enraged by the plan to evacuate and abandon Israeli settlements in what was to become Palestine, and a dizzying array of splinter groups already denouncing the covenant.

Then there was the report from Pakistan—still awaiting verification—that

Meir had folded and placed in his suit jacket pocket just before he exited the helicopter. That disturbing report was stuffed in among the many threats on Meir's life that Shin Bet had uncovered since the covenant was signed.

Flanking Meir were his two most trusted cabinet officers—Benjamin Erdad, minister of internal security, and Moshe Litzman, minister of the interior. Farther to his right and left sat the recently appointed minister of foreign affairs, a man Meir had yet to measure, and the chairman of the Knesset's powerful Foreign Affairs and Defense Committee, responsible for overseeing Israel's entire security apparatus.

Arrayed along the opposite arc of the oval table were the chiefs of the Israeli Intelligence Community (IIC).

Major General Uri Schatz, commander of the Military Intelligence Directorate, or Aman, the supreme military intelligence branch of the Israeli Defense Force (IDF), was the acknowledged leader of the IIC. But he shared that authority with the chiefs of Mossad, Israel's external security apparatus, and Shin Bet, Israel's internal security agency. It was a shared role that often created conflict.

Filling out the military side of the table were representatives from several of the tentacles Aman wove throughout Israel's intelligence apparatus: Unit 8200, the Israeli signals intelligence agency; the Information Security Department, the primary data mining and counterintelligence unit of Aman; and Sayeret Matkal, the IDF's premier special forces unit, directly subordinate to Aman.

Short, bald, and pugnacious, General Schatz was already on a rant. It was imperative that Meir not allow Schatz's arrogant bluntness to masquerade as reasoned assessment. Israel was in a more precarious position today than it had been on the day of its formation in 1948. Too much was happening too fast. A misstep now could prove devastating to his country.

"You have invited the enemy into the tent," declared General Schatz, pointing a finger at the prime minister. "And you have placed all Israel at risk. Hezbollah started dropping rockets on our northern settlements within minutes of the signing, a fusillade that has only grown in intensity. We are evacuating Kyrat Shimona as we speak. Hundreds are already dead. Gaza is a running patchwork of street battles. Hamas is more heavily armed than we expected. IDF forces are being chewed up and spit out into the dust. And the death count at the Hurva Square continues to rise. Just so you could sign a foolhardy peace."

To his right, Erdad shifted in his seat. and Meir knew the man was about to defend him. Meir gently placed a hand on Erdad's left arm while skewering General Schatz with an unwavering stare that had cowed many on the floor of the Knesset.

"General, we have just signed the most comprehensive and far-reaching peace treaty in Israel's sixty-six-year history, one that ties us together in peace with our brothers of the Abrahamic covenant and into unity against our greatest enemy—the madmen of Iran who are racing toward nuclear weapons and the delivery system that could soon annihilate the very state you and I are sworn to defend. What you seem to consider foolish I consider wisdom. We—"

Half an extinguished cigar was clenched in the corner of General Schatz's mouth. He took it out and pointed the chewed end at Meir. "So you will rely on the Arabs to protect—"

"General!" Meir's commanding voice brought the dust motes to attention. "You know as well as I, Israel will always rely on Israel, and no one else, for our future. Neither the Americans nor the Arabs have endured the Holocaust. As long as we have breath, Israel will never again allow an enemy to exercise the kind of power that can exterminate six million of our fathers and mothers, brothers and sisters. *Never again!*" Meir's fist pounded on the wooden table. The prime minister allowed the silence to build in volume, staring down each of the military men opposite him on the far side of the table. He stopped his eyes when they reached Schatz. "Allies, General? Yes, Israel will accept allies. The Americans have been vital allies until recently. But I do not delude myself, General. This peace is a peace of expedience. The enemy of my enemy is my friend, eh? In this moment, peace with our Arab neighbors makes sense—for us and for them."

"The Knesset will never ratify the treaty." General Schatz sounded like a truculent school bully who had been faced down by courage. His words lacked power.

"Whether the Knesset ever ratifies the treaty is unimportant." Meir leaned into the table, pressing his hands into the top surface. "King Hussein and King Abdullah have now recognized Israel's right to exist and joined Egypt in signing a peace accord. They cannot erase that line now that it has been crossed. That will never change. History was made today no matter what the Knesset does. We have formed a regional defense alliance with our closest neighbors who, not that long ago, were our closest enemies. Hamas? Hezbollah? Today, with an agreement for a Palestinian state, Hamas lost its relevance. At this moment, Egypt is destroying every tunnel from its soil into Gaza and arresting every gun runner who brought anything larger than a slingshot into Gaza. Tomorrow you, General, will coordinate with the commander of the Jordanian Air Force to immediately begin surgical air strikes on Hezbollah's rocket launching sites."

General Schatz looked at the cigar stub between his fingers. Then he took it and smashed it against the top of the table. He picked up the pieces of the squashed cigar and threw them into the center of the table. "If we entrust our future into the hands of the Arabs, that, sir, is your vision for the future of Israel."

David Meir stood from his chair. He was not about to relinquish his role or his responsibility to lead his nation. Without pointing a finger, Meir pressed his will against General Schatz's chest. "And you, General, will follow orders. Or you can go back to growing tobacco on a kibbutz rather than smashing it into a table. We're done."

9

US Embassy, Tel Aviv
July 20, 5:32 p.m.

Brian Mullaney looked at the clock on his office wall. Ten thirty in the morning at home. A good time to reach Abby, while the girls were at school. But he dreaded this call.

It had been four days since he'd called his wife . . . four days since he'd received Abby's letter that she and their daughters were now staying at her father's house in Washington. He should have called sooner, but part of him didn't want to have this conversation.

Sure . . . the last few days had been fraught with life-and-death crises. But was that only an excuse? Mullaney saved Ambassador Cleveland's life during a gun battle on Israel's Highway One. He had rescued the ambassador's daughter from a gang of murderous thugs. And the killers were still out there, pursuing an ancient prophecy and the lethal box that protected it—a box that now sat in the embassy vault, just a few floors beneath his feet. At the same time, Cleveland was trying to keep the Middle East from blowing up into a full-scale war and the ambassador needed his regional security officer by his side to keep him safe.

Would any of that make a difference to Abby? Probably not after four days of silence.

It was his fault. He had made the decision to accept the assignment to Israel, knowing full well he had promised Abby—after eleven moves in nineteen years—that he wouldn't make them move again, even if it meant resigning from the State Department's diplomatic security service. But then his name and his reputation had been unfairly tainted. He had been railroaded and scapegoated for simply doing his duty. Call it pride, but he was not about to jettison a hard-earned career with DSS while his name was falsely associated with negligence.

That's what Abby had called it . . . pride. Mullaney had promised and now he was trashing that promise to save his reputation. Well, Abby had promised her daughters they wouldn't move again, wouldn't have to change schools again. So she and the girls had remained in the States when Mullaney left for Israel. Now they were living with her father, Richard Rutherford, a billionaire banker who was one of DC's more relentless purveyors of power.

He looked at Abby's photo on his phone. Her smile warmed his heart. The memory of her curled up in his arms warmed his flesh. The smell of her hair—strawberry—filled his nostrils. And his spirit ached for those first days and early years, when they lavishly shared their passion for baseball, opera, and their faith. He was overcome by the spontaneous joy that erupted from her soft Southern spirit like a newly discovered sun. She was captured by his strength of character, his devotion to duty and honor, and his love of God.

They were bound to each other from the moment they met, even though their disparate careers—his in public service, first with the Virginia State Police and then the State Department; hers in preparing and polishing the public face of the biggest players in corporate commerce—often kept them in opposite orbits.

Their first ten years were bliss. The second ten a steady decline into stress and disappointment. The distance between them grew primarily, Mullaney believed, because he was too often absent in spirit, soul, mind, or body—or all of the above—from the lives of Abby and his daughters. And now the distance spanned half the globe.

Mullaney dreaded this conversation.

He opened Contacts on his iPhone and tapped the number for Abby's mobile.

———⟐———

If ice could travel through cell phones, Brian Mullaney's ear would have frostbite.

"I'm sure you've been *very* busy, Brian . . . too busy to at least call."

Mullaney's heart shriveled up in his chest. His wife was right. He was busy saving the world . . . too busy to save his crumbling marriage.

"I'm sorry," Mullaney said into his iPhone. "I should have called sooner."

"It's been four days since we last heard from you, Brian. Your daughters were frightened that something had happened to you. Four days since—"

"Since I got a letter that you had taken our daughters and left our home."

Silence filled the bandwidth between Washington and Tel Aviv, a vacuum that mirrored the ever-increasing void in his life where his wife and children had once resided. It wasn't only his job that was spreading the invasion of gray hair around his temples.

"Daddy invited us to stay at his house," said Abby without apology. "I thought it would be good for the girls to get away from home for a few days. When they're home, all they talk about is you. And when you don't call . . . well . . . they feel like you don't care about them." There was a short intake of breath. "I know what that feels like, Brian. I didn't want them to suffer those same disappointments."

"I didn't ask to come here, Abby," said Mullaney. "But I've got a job to do that is twenty-four seven, not nine-to-five. You know that."

"Only too well," Abby snapped. "Look, Brian"—her voice softened—"I understand the demands of your job. And I know how well you do it and the character you bring to that effort. And I know that today there are several hundred foreign service staffers whose lives depend on your vigilance to your duty.

"But you and I both know that your job is not the issue, Brian. I just want—for the first time in nineteen years—to see you put me, and your daughters, on the same level of importance that you put your duty. That's all. You have willingly upended our lives, and I've gone along with it for nearly two decades. Eleven moves, Brian. Without a complaint. Without a backward glance or a word of self-pity. You promised me that we were home for good."

The words stung, but Mullaney knew all too well that they were true. It had always been his career, his needs, that orchestrated his family's world. If he wanted to save his marriage, something needed to change. He needed to change.

What was most important in his life?

Mullaney was desperate to season his words with his heart. "Abby . . . I'm sorry I didn't call sooner. Regardless of what's going on over here, that was self-centered and inconsiderate of me. I apologize, Ab. I really do."

Across the miles, through the invisible lines of connection, Mullaney could hear Abigail's deep sigh.

"So what are you going to do?" she asked.

"Honestly, I don't know," said Mullaney. "Somehow I'm going to get home to you and the girls, and somehow I'm going to get home without abandoning my post and my responsibility here."

He knew that may not be enough . . . but it was all he could truthfully say at the moment.

"All right, Brian," said Abby, her words clipped. "I get it. But you've got to figure this out soon. Days . . . not months. I need you to make a decision for us, okay? Please . . . soon."

———◦◦◦◦———

US Embassy, Tel Aviv
July 20, 6:10 p.m.

"Is the ambassador free?"

Cleveland looked up at the sound of Mullaney's voice. Without waiting for an answer, Mullaney brushed past Jeffrey Archer's desk in the outer office and knocked on the ambassador's open door. "Excuse me, sir, but I need to speak—"

Before Mullaney could take a step across the threshold, Cleveland was on his feet. "What do we know from the Hurva, Brian?"

Cleveland crossed the unadorned Tennessee gray marble floor with thoughts of broken bodies filling his mind. For a moment, Mullaney appeared startled by his question. A quick shake of his head appeared to focus his mind.

"Thirty-two dead"—he handed the written report to the ambassador, but Cleveland's eyes never moved off Mullaney—"including Rabbi Herzog and most of the Rabbinate Council. Forty-seven injured, about a dozen of those in critical condition. But so far, none of the dead are American citizens . . . only two slightly wounded. They're at the hospital, and a DSS agent is with each one."

Cleveland's head dropped, his chin to his chest, and he slowly shook it back and forth. The weight of his responsibility always pressed most heavily upon the ambassador's heart when he was required to deliver terrible news to a loved one. "Thank you, Lord," he whispered, almost to himself. His chest heaved with a deep cleansing breath before he looked at Mullaney once more. "Small consolation for us . . . but no consolation for the families of the victims. I almost feel ashamed that we were fortunate when so many others . . ." He shook his head again and pointed Mullaney to one of the burgundy uphol-stered wingback chairs in front of his desk. "Here . . . have a seat."

The office, more pedestrian than plush, was devoid of the oak-paneled walls or massive vanity desks that filled important government offices across DC. Cleveland had inherited a Spartan but secure enclave, which matched his personality, and to which he added little in creature comforts. The walls were an ochre plaster, dotted here and there with haunting oil paintings of Israel's desert and mountains, which Cleveland already found soothing. One wall was the repository of the obligatory power photos of Cleveland with a Who's Who of world leaders.

In a corner, left of the main door, was a formal conversation grouping—stiff and uncomfortable Middle Eastern chairs surrounding a low, round, olive-wood table. To the right of the door, though, was Cleveland's one luxury—his only requirement as he traveled from one post to another—a well-weathered, tufted, brown leather sofa. It sat in the corner against the wall, opposite two equally weathered, brown leather armchairs. A couple of soft-looking throw pillows were tucked into one corner of the sofa. The generously proportioned leather sofa was a place where the nearly six-foot Cleveland often stretched out for an afternoon nap—once the doors were securely locked.

Throughout his three decades of diplomatic service to the United States, fifty-eight-year-old Joseph Atticus Cleveland had been revered by his colleagues, respected by politicians of all stripes, and honored by governments on three continents. The ambassador had formed an almost instant bond with Mullaney—his regional security officer upon whom so much depended—one of mutual respect and shared faith that was only two days old but already several layers deep.

"What do we know about the bombers?" asked the ambassador.

"We know they are dead," Mullaney said as he perched on the edge of the chair. "That's about it. And it may be some time before we find out any more. Israel's intelligence and military are more focused on the rioters in Gaza and the rockets in Lebanon. And Shin Bet is still trying to find survivors in the destruction of Hurva Square."

Cleveland leaned heavily on the desk, his face a skewered grimace, awash with anxiety over what . . . who . . . may yet be found in the wreckage. He dropped into his chair like a felled oak—slowly at first, with a stifled groan, then gathering speed as its mass obeyed gravity. Suddenly he felt old.

Cleveland's stellar reputation in the diplomatic corps was earned not only because of his ability to effectively maneuver through crises, but also because he was rigorously true to his Christian faith. Both friend and foe could depend on Cleveland's reliable integrity of character.

The great-grandson of a North Carolina slave, Cleveland was proud of his academic history, earning a dual-major bachelor's degree from Howard University, working his way through school, and then completing two programs at Harvard—for a master's in political science and a law degree.

Over the last century, Cleveland was only the sixth African American to serve as US ambassador in a country that was predominantly white. Closing quickly on career ambassador rank, one of the State Department's most rare and coveted titles, Cleveland had rebounded from heart surgery three years earlier and was now stronger and healthier than he had been in a decade. But his heart was captured and enthralled with his three children and fourteen grandchildren, so he was overjoyed when his only daughter, Palmyra—a recent widow herself—agreed to join him in Israel and take on the responsibility of running the ambassador's residence in Tel Aviv and managing his personal and social schedule.

"So we now have the box back, sitting in our basement vault, but still no idea who is behind all this and why they are so determined to destroy the box and what's in it." Cleveland looked up. "What *is* in it?"

"We're at a loss there too," said Mullaney, shrugging his shoulders and lifting his palms. "We know the box contained another message from the Vilna Gaon . . . probably a prophecy like the first one . . . we know it was in a code and Rabbi Herzog told me on the phone that the Rabbinate Council had broken the code and deciphered the message. He said to prepare ourselves for a shock, that what they discovered would radically alter the meaning of what was announced today with the Ishmael Covenant. But I'm afraid the message, and its meaning, are buried under the wreckage of the Hurva Synagogue. Unless . . ."

"Unless it's still in the box?" The question rose in Cleveland like the sun after a night of downpour, his words tinged with questioning hope.

"Possible," admitted Mullaney. "But who's going to open the box? Rabbi Herzog was the last guardian, the last one with the anointing, the protection from the deadly promise of those kabbalah symbols."

"Another problem we have to solve, Brian. But we need to call Secretary Townsend and bring him up to date. You know, sometimes I don't know how much to tell Evan. I know he and I are of the same mind about what America should be doing in the Middle East. But I also know he has an obligation to report what he knows to the president. And the way we see the world doesn't always match with the president's policy."

He looked at the clock on the wall. "Just after eleven in the morning in Washington. This should be a good time to catch the secretary in his office." Cleveland sat back in his chair and slapped his hands together in front of his chest. "But now, before that call, I believe you came in with something else on your mind. What is it?"

10

His housekeeper had gone home, but she had prepared a stew for dinner and left it simmering on the stove. Aromatic clouds of cumin and garlic and lamb greeted Arslan Eroglu, prime minister of the Republic of Turkey, as he entered the main floor of his home from the lower level garage. Lamb stew . . . one of his favorites. And another of his favorites, the lithe Myram, would soon be joining him. It would be a good night, one in which he could lay aside the growing anxiety he was dealing with both at home and abroad—both from Turkish President Emet Kashani and also from US Assistant Secretary of State Noah Webster. Let them dangle. Eroglu had his own plans, plans that included neither Kashani nor Webster—nor that madman with the yellow eyes. The Turk's ultimate concern was Israel, but Eroglu had his eyes set on western Syria—the ancient land of Assyria—whose annexation would be only the first step. One day he would usher in a new, powerful Turkey, the resurrection of the Ottoman Empire, once again sovereign over the entire half-moon of the Mediterranean basin, from Istanbul to Marrakesh. And he, Arslan Eroglu, would rule that empire, caliph of the Ottomans. That day was coming soon.

He walked through the kitchen to the far counter and poured some of the thick, sweet Turkish coffee into the small cup that was waiting alongside the electric coffee pot. The coffee was hot. He brought the cup to his lips carefully.

"Do not harm yourself."

Eroglu nearly spilled the coffee onto his five-thousand-dollar suit, barely holding the cup firmly enough to keep it from crashing to the quarry tile floor as he spun around to confront the voice. But he knew from the first word who it was. That voice always convulsed with menace.

The Turk emerged from the shadowed hallway that led to the rest of the house. Behind him remained an immobile, dark shape. His aide. Eroglu tried vainly to suppress the shiver that wavered his spine.

"How did you get in here?" Eroglu asked the Turk. He twisted at the waist and carefully placed the cup on the counter. Drawing in deep breaths for control and reminding himself not to get captured by the Turk's eyes, Eroglu returned his gaze to just below the chin of his surprise visitor. "And who sent for you?"

"Yes, thank you for the warm welcome to your home, Arslan." The Turk took a step closer and suddenly the succulent aroma of the lamb stew was obscured by a burnt tinge of sulfur, as if someone had struck an entire pack of matches. "I hope I have not disturbed your dinner, but I'm afraid there are some urgent matters we must discuss, and there is no time to waste."

"I'm afraid I have no time either," said Eroglu, leaning back against the counter and trying to regain that polished, aristocratic persona that he had worked for years to perfect. He also pushed aside a growing anxiety, wondering what was so important to bring the Turk out of his lair. "I have a guest arriving for dinner very soon."

"Yes . . . a guest." The words seemed to slide across the air, slick and oily . . . contaminated. "For dinner. Then I will be brief." The Turk removed his left hand from the right sleeve of his jubba, raised it slightly, and made an almost imperceptible motion with his cadaver-thin fingers. Assan emerged from the darkness of the hallway and carried one of the kitchen chairs to the Turk, who floated to the surface of the seat.

"It is time to put our plans into motion," said the Turk. "Send your emissaries to Iraq and to Israel and offer them the same thing—water. Lure the Iraqis into an agreement to support an independent Kurdistan to help thwart any expansion of Persia. And put into motion our action at Incirlik. We must remain at least one step ahead of the Persians and the Saudis—if we cannot thwart their attempts to secure nuclear weapons, then we must secure them first.

"Make no mistake, Arslan," said the Turk. "We are in a race for power and for survival, a race for nuclear weapons with the Persians and the Saudis that will determine who rules in the Middle East . . . which empire is resurrected. Seizing control of the nuclear weapons at Incirlik will be the catalyst for the birth of a new Ottoman Empire. Otherwise, we will be nuclear hostages."

Eroglu shook his head, keeping his eyes on the floor. "I've warned you. We need to be careful. We are taking a great risk. If the Americans figure out any part of our plan, they will wipe us from the face of the earth. And once the plot is set in motion, there will be no turning back."

The silence in the kitchen was so complete, Eroglu was forced to risk a glance. It was a mistake. The gray swirls of mayhem pulsed in the Turk's eyes, a riptide that threatened to pull Eroglu into its grip.

"Perhaps, Arslan, you have lost focus," said the Turk, his words a silken rebuke hiding a knife-edge of sarcasm. "Or perhaps you have lost faith in our ultimate goal and our ultimate victory. Yes, we long for a reawakened Ottoman Empire . . . Turkoman rule from India to Iberia. But the ascendance of the Ottomans is only a stepping stone.

"You and I, Arslan, have sworn ourselves to change the end of the book." The Turk's voice swelled with the threatening power of a thunderhead, his words echoing both in the kitchen and in Eroglu's spirit. "The Jews have sentenced themselves to failure. They have written promises in their book they claim predict the arrival of the Jewish Messiah—that the followers of the Nazarene adopted to legitimize their so-called redeemer. When we prevent the consummation of any of those promises, all the others crumble with it. Deny one prophecy, all are worthless. Do not forget that is why we must have that stipulation about the mountain north of Jerusalem in the water-for-gas treaty with Israel. In that way we defeat their Messiah before he can surface, and we hasten and ensure the coming of the Mahdi and his reign over all the world . . . a Muslim world.

"Yes," the Turk's words slithered across the quarry tile floor, "to fulfill our destiny, we cannot allow the ascendance of the Arabs or the Persians. But do not lose sight of the ultimate goal, Arslan. It's the book . . . and the Mahdi. All else is a gateway."

Suddenly, the silence was deafening. Eroglu could hear the clock on the wall as it clicked through the seconds.

"The Saudi's nuclear weapons," whispered the Turk, "are on a dock in Pakistan, waiting for a ship to arrive. The Iranian scientists in Fordo are weeks away from perfecting fission."

"I'm well aware of—"

"You will act now. You must."

Eroglu stiffened, resisting the urge to slam his coffee on the counter. *Who is this man to order me around?*

"I think you are forgetting yourself, forgetting who you are speaking to," he said. "What is your position in Turkey? Who are you to tell me I must? When Kashani is out of the way, I will rule in Turkey. It is for me to decide what this country *must* do. Remember . . . I don't need you . . . you need me," spurted Eroglu. "Without my support, your plots would be empty and worthless."

Eroglu felt the exhilaration of power and conquest.

"Yesssssss," The Turk's voice sounded like the hiss of a deadly viper, "in fact, I do have need of you. Look at me."

Eroglu set his neck like a steel rod, his eyes on the feet of the kitchen table, refusing to move.

"Look"—as if a strap of leather had been tied around his forehead and pulled tight, and despite all his efforts to keep it still, Eroglu's face began to rise, his eyes lift from the floor—"at me."

Tempests of fury gyrated in a wild dance in the yellow pupils, but it was the smile on the Turk's sepulchral face that nearly brought Eroglu's heart to a shuddering stop.

The Turk removed a corpse-like white hand from the left sleeve of his jubba. He turned it face up and extended it toward Eroglu. The prime minister felt the Turk's black eyes burn into his skull at the same time that he felt pressure in his chest.

"Come," said the Turk, curving his fingers.

The earth's gravitational pull shifted. The conscious dimensions of Eroglu's kitchen began to warp, morphing into a moving fluid where there were once walls and floors that appeared solid. In the grip of the Turk's hand, even from across the room, Eroglu could feel his mind pressing against bone. It felt like his brain was being drawn out from inside his skull, his lungs and heart and arteries being summoned to follow.

Not *by* the Turk. But *into* the Turk!

Panic overwhelmed Eroglu's remaining consciousness as he realized he was being consumed. What was left of his thoughts, his own thoughts, perceived teetering on the edge of a great, black abyss. The abyss was more than death. It was annihilation. And he was being drawn—

The Turk snapped his fingers shut and thrust his fist back into the sleeve of his jubba.

Eroglu collapsed onto the floor of the kitchen, exhausted, drained, gagging for breath but clinging to life.

"Yes, Arslan . . . I have need of you still," said the Turk. "But do not tempt me. You can be replaced."

—◦◦◦—

The heavy, metal knocker thudded against the front door. Consciousness was elusive. Eroglu could barely lift his head from the floor. The kitchen was empty. All that remained was the sickly stench of sulfur.

—◦◦◦—

US Embassy, Tel Aviv
July 20, 6:43 p.m.

The geopolitical landscape of the Middle East was changing as quickly as a traffic signal, and the US ambassador to Israel had just postponed a call to the US secretary of state, asking Mullaney what was on his mind.

Suddenly, Mullaney felt foolish. How could he bring his personal problems to Cleveland with all of the critical issues the ambassador was facing?

The Middle East appeared to be on the cusp of—perhaps already in the midst of—seismic shifts of power and influence. Old rules and old alliances were obliterated. And it was Cleveland's assignment, straight from the president's mouth, to find some solid ground upon which to restore America's influence in the region. For Cleveland, that was a heavy lift.

Partly because of his deeply rooted, family-nurtured faith and partly because of his years of frontline experience with the reality of the Middle East, Cleveland was all in with his support for Israel, its no-nonsense leaders, and its clear vision for what was truly necessary for peace in the region.

But US President Lamont Boylan had dispatched Cleveland to Israel with a clear directive to pressure the Jewish government into a two-state solution. While Cleveland acknowledged that a Palestinian state made geopolitical sense, the ambassador held grave reservations, based on biblical prophecy, about dividing the land of Israel.

A vocal and unabashed friend of Israel, a decade earlier Cleveland had walked a narrow but effective line during a three-year stint as United States ambassador to Jordan, making friends on both sides of the Jordan River, brokering backroom discussions between high-ranking officials from both Tel Aviv and Amman.

He would need all his skill, all his experience, and—particularly—all his friends to have some level of effectiveness during this crucial assignment to Israel.

So how could Mullaney be so thoughtless? His job was to help the ambassador, not add to his burdens.

"You are not adding to my burdens, Brian."

Mullaney laughed and shook his head. "I'm that transparent, eh?"

Cleveland leaned into his desk to draw closer to Mullaney. "Right now, the look on your face tells me your personal world has collapsed around you. What is it . . . and how can I help?"

Mullaney was always the strong one, the guy everybody turned to when they were in need. Asking for help felt foreign to him. But who else could . . .

"It's your family," Cleveland said matter-of-factly. "I'm sorry, Brian. Palmyra told me a little, that your wife and children were not going to join you on this assignment. I know this posting was sudden and unexpected for you. And for your wife, too, I'm sure. Is that it?"

So much ground to cover. Mullaney studied the creases in his knuckles as he tried to figure out what to say. Two things were certain—he would not lay the blame on Abby, and he would not leave his post until Cleveland and all the embassy staff were no longer in danger. It was his responsibility to accomplish those two objectives. Like the jet stream of a power wash machine, that decision turned his anxiety into clarity. He pushed himself back into the padding of the armchair and crossed his legs, feeling resurrected.

"I talked to Abby on the phone a little while ago. It's a long story . . . probably for another time. But the bottom line is that I made a promise to Abby and the girls, and now I have to live up to that promise. When we bought our house in Virginia, I told Abby that was going to be our home. Even if I had to resign from the service, I would not make her move again. Well, obviously, that hasn't worked out.

"After the embassy attack in Ankara, the world as we know it started falling apart, fast. All the blame fell on George Morningstar, and he took the biggest hit, exiled into the basement of the Truman Building, his career in the State Department on life support. And I was given a choice, get booted out of DC and into the desert . . . sorry, sir, no offense intended . . ."

"None taken," said Cleveland.

"Or resign under a cloud of suspicion . . . like I had done something wrong and was trying to run away or escape."

"I don't figure you for the running-away type, Brian."

"No, sir. Maybe I'm just too proud. Or maybe just a hard-headed Irishman who isn't left with much if someone steals his integrity. I don't know . . . but that wasn't the time to quit. That was the time to fight. And I couldn't fight back if I was no longer part of DSS, if I quit the service. So I took the boot and came here."

"Hoping to fight your way back to DC, vindicate yourself . . . perhaps rescue George Morningstar—a good man, by the way—and resurrect your marriage, correct?"

Mullaney nodded. "Pretty much, sir, yes."

Cleveland was nodding in agreement. "I understand, and I understand that feeling of betrayal and wanting to fight back. If I were a suspicious person, I might think that same betrayal boot hit my butt to get me out of Turkey. I try not to be paranoid, but . . ."

"Yes, sir. It's a pretty complicated mess. But to Abby, it's real simple. Our marriage is strained to the limits. She wants to live in Washington . . ."

"Yes," said Cleveland, "I know her father."

"Well, there's that too," admitted Mullaney. "But Abby feels betrayed—by me, by the State Department, by whomever. She's been a loyal trooper above and beyond the call of duty. And now she just wants her husband home at night and to finish raising our kids on US soil. After eleven moves and all I've put her through, that's really not asking a lot. If we're going to save our marriage, she wants me home."

"When?" asked Cleveland.

"In a month, if possible—before our oldest daughter's birthday," said Mullaney. "Mr. Ambassador, I've never quit on an assignment in my life. I won't quit on you . . . especially not now. But I can't quit on my marriage, and I can't quit on my daughters either. I'd like your help to get transferred back to Washington."

Cleveland leaned back in his chair and stretched. Mullaney's anxiety returned. Maybe this was a mista—

"Of course, Brian . . . I'll do whatever I can." Cleveland stood up and moved around the desk, taking the chair flanking the one Mullaney occupied. His face was as resolute as the grave. "After all you've done for me—rescuing Palmyra from those kidnappers, saving my life when we were attacked on the road to Jerusalem—I owe you more than you could ever ask of me. But I want you to understand something. The dust hasn't settled yet at the State Department. A lot of people are carrying around raw wounds about what happened in the aftermath of Ankara . . . some on your side, some not. I won't be able to take this request through normal channels, that would stir up a storm we would be best to avoid. And I don't want to make a public request to Secretary Townsend. But I'll tell you what I can do. I have a station situation report that I was to submit to the secretary as soon as I took up residence. It's a little overdue, but I think he understands. I'll put the request for transfer in the station situation report—very few eyes get to see that report. It will be a way for Evan to consider the request without being under any outside pressure. But I'll include it as an ambassadorial request—those are seldom denied."

Mullaney moved to the edge of the chair once more. "Thank you, sir. I—"

"But neither one of us has much leverage in Washington these days, so I can't promise you the request will be granted. And"—Cleveland held up a hand—"I have one condition. And I think it's one you've already decided in your heart."

For the first time in days, Mullaney smiled. He would follow this man into battle. "Yes, sir. I'm not going anywhere until we find the murderers out there and, one way or another, put an end to this violence. You have my word on that."

Cleveland nodded his head. "Good." He placed a hand on Mullaney's shoulder. "I'll get you home as soon as possible.

"But once we get on the phone with Secretary Townsend, let's not mention your transfer request just yet. There could be others listening. Let me get to Townsend privately. I don't want to put him on the spot today. I think that's our best chance."

11

Secretary of State Evan Townsend was an American patrician. Born, raised, nurtured, and educated in the lap of old money and presumed privilege, Townsend embodied the Hollywood stereotype of wealth and manners— distant and unflappable, regal in his comportment, unconsciously elegant in his custom-tailored clothes. But where Hollywood's caricature often portrayed the wealthy as people of little common sense, which trumped their Ivy League educations, Townsend was also brilliant, cunning, and fearless. His family had helped put Lamont Boylan in the Oval Office precisely because Evan Townsend had a passion and a vision for how he believed this world should work.

Even in those areas where the president had voiced a different view, Townsend was endeavoring mightily to bring his vision to reality through the formidable influence of one of the most powerful jobs on earth—the man who helped shape and implement the foreign policy of the United States.

But today, Townsend, the man on the other end of this FaceTime transmission, was clearly stunned. Cleveland and Mullaney had called Townsend's personal iPhone, hoping he would be alone in his office in the Old Executive Mansion across the street from the White House.

"Well, Atticus, I agree with you. It's only by God's grace that we don't have a list of American citizens in body bags at the Hurva. But you're telling me the destruction of the Hurva was not the work of terrorists bent on stopping the Ishmael Covenant?" Townsend was staring incredulously into his iPhone.

"No, sir," said Cleveland. "We don't believe it had anything to do with the announcement of the covenant. We believe it was another attempt to destroy the prophecy . . . and the box that protected it."

"And nobody knows what this expected prophecy contains?" asked Townsend.

Mullaney gave the ambassador a quick look.

"Go ahead, Brian."

The RSO turned his face to the screen. "Mr. Secretary, the rabbis knew," said Mullaney. "I had just received a phone call from the chief of the Rabbinate Council, Rabbi Israel Herzog, that they had deciphered the code of the prophecy and knew what the message said. Herzog told me that what they found would radically alter the meaning of what was announced as the Ishmael Covenant. He was coming here to deliver the prophecy to us. But moments later, the synagogue was destroyed in a series of explosions."

"But the box, the Gaon's box, was recovered."

"Yes, sir . . . but there is no one to open the box," said Mullaney. "From the time the box arrived in Istanbul eighty years ago, there has been one person—one guardian—who received an anointing passed down from father to son that protected the guardian from the lethal power of the box. Rabbi Herzog was the last of the guardians. He was the last one with the anointing. And Rabbi Herzog perished in the explosions."

Secretary Townsend was staring into his iPhone, clearly immersed in their story. When the silence stretched out after Mullaney stopped talking, he blinked his eyes and raised his shoulders in a hunch. "So that's it? The box can't be opened, so now the assassins will go home and leave you alone? I don't buy it," said Townsend. "How is all this stuff with the prophecy connected to the covenant? There's got to be a link. I can't imagine it's just coincidence. What do you think, Atticus?"

Cleveland pressed his lips together in thought and pushed himself deeper into his chair. "Mister Secretary, ancient enemies are now allies; ancient empires, like Persia, appear to be emerging once again. This new peace treaty and mutual defense pact between Israel and its Arab neighbors—this Ishmael Covenant—has completely altered any Middle East political strategy held by the United States and any other world power. We are in a new age. Nothing is what it was, and nothing is as it seems.

"In a world like that, Evan, there is only one constant we can hold onto, only one guiding light that might give us a clue as to what comes next and how we're supposed to deal with it. You and I know what that constant is, Holy Scripture, and I'm confident Agent Mullaney agrees with us. Current events in the Middle East appear to be on a collision course with biblical prophecy and warnings. With the world moving this fast, a lot of things will look like Armageddon. So it is at our own peril that we ignore biblical prophecy at a time like this or anything that might give us a clue to what comes next. Which is why I was so intent on being the first to know the content of the Gaon's second prophecy. But even without that knowledge, there is other prophecy we should not ignore."

Cleveland got up and stretched, then leaned in toward the iPad from the back of his chair. "Our conversation is secure and private, Evan?"

"Speak freely, Atticus," said Townsend, nodding his head. "There is no one else in the office, no listening devices, and this connection is secure and encrypted. Say what you need to say."

"Very well." Cleveland pulled the chair aside and perched on its edge, peering into the camera's lens. "This Ishmael Covenant makes all the geopolitical sense in the world. Logically, an independent Palestinian state is the only chance for sustained peace for Israel, and a political and military alliance of Israel, Egypt, Jordan, and Saudi Arabia creates a formidable, determined, and powerful deterrent to the deepening ties between Iran and Iraq and the emergence of a new Persia. It all makes sense. Except . . ."

As the pause lengthened and the silence grew, Mullaney cast a long glance at the ambassador. Clearly Cleveland was waiting on Secretary Townsend to fill in the blanks.

"Except for Exodus 17 and Joel 3, correct?" Townsend asked.

"Yes," Cleveland acknowledged, "it all makes sense, except this covenant is in opposition to Scripture." The ambassador turned to Mullaney.

"Do you know the story, Brian? In Exodus 17, the desert tribe of Amalek attacked the nation of Israel as it passed through the Valley of Rephidim on the way to Mount Sinai. After Joshua and the Israeli army routed the Amalekites, Moses pronounced a curse on Amalek and his descendants . . . a curse that was never to be forgotten. Through Moses, the Lord gave Joshua a timeless instruction, *'Write this on a scroll as something to be remembered and make sure that Joshua hears it, because I will completely blot out the memory of Amalek from under heaven.'* The people of Amalek were the forefathers of today's Arab nations. With this covenant, instead of destroying Amalek, Israel has just entered into a treaty that binds the Jews to defend the descendants of Amalek if they come under attack from any quarter."

"That sounds like a mistake," said Mullaney.

"Yes," said Cleveland, "and there is a prophecy in the book of Joel that is even more alarming. In Joel chapter 3, the prophet writes that God will put nations on trial and bring them to judgment for what they did to Israel, his inheritance, *'because they scattered my people among the nations and divided up my land.'* Establishing an independent Palestinian state from land that was biblically assigned to Israel is clearly dividing the land. It invites God's judgment."

Cleveland turned his gaze back to the camera lens. "Evan, you and I have our marching orders from President Boylan to get the covenant ratified and an independent Palestine established. Boylan's intention is to restore America's influence in the Middle East—and establish a legacy for himself. For a man who believes Scripture is true, I'm having a hard time reconciling this policy position."

Thirty minutes earlier, Brian Mullaney had come to Cleveland's office to seek help, to ask Cleveland to exercise his formidable influence to get Mullaney back home. But now Mullaney began to wonder how much influence Cleveland retained.

Sitting to Cleveland's right, Mullaney could see on the ambassador's iPad that Townsend was wrestling with this new information. The struggle to absorb, the calculation of its import, was written clearly in his narrowed eyes and the firm set of his mouth.

"You and I have a sworn duty, Atticus, to carry out the policy and directives of the United States government, whether we agree with that policy or those directives."

Secretary Townsend's voice sounded like a judge about to issue a bad verdict. A ripple of concern for Cleveland shimmied up Mullaney's spine.

Several thousand miles, the Atlantic and the Mediterranean separated the two offices. But Brian Mullaney could feel the presence of Evan Townsend's power in the room.

Townsend looked down at the top of his desk, ran his manicured fingers through his perfectly cut gray hair, and shook his head. "What a mess!"

His eyes came back to the screen. "Look, Atticus, I can understand what you walked into over there from the outset, with Israel and its Arab neighbors mobilizing their armed forces. And I can empathize with the pressure you were under as a father with Palmyra's abduction and rescue. And I can appreciate the dilemma this incredible story of the prophecy and the box created for you. I'll admit, I'd have to think twice before I decided to spin this yarn to the president or anyone else. So okay, I get it."

Townsend stopped. Took a breath. Mullaney knew what was coming next.

"Ambassador Cleveland"—Townsend's words were solemn, determined—"can you continue to fulfill your sworn duty?"

Cleveland threw back his shoulders and sat erect in his chair. "Yes, Mister Secretary, I have no doubt that I can, and will, fulfill all of my duty. And Evan . . . if there is ever a hint of that changing, I will let you know before a second heartbeat has time to begin."

On the iPad screen, Secretary Townsend was nodding his head. "Good . . . because I need you there . . . we need you there."

12

Three things were on Brian Mullaney's mind when he returned late on Sunday night to the ambassador's palatial residence in the Herzliya Pituach neighborhood of northern Tel Aviv, hard along the coast of the Mediterranean. First, he wanted to ensure himself that security was as tight as a rusty screw, and second he planned to check on Cleveland's daughter, Palmyra Parker, to make sure she was recovering from the effects of her harrowing kidnapping and the gun battle in the coastal plain north of Ashkelon that had led to her rescue. Then he wanted food and sleep. In that order.

It was a long time before he got to number three on his list.

On his arrival, DSS Agent Pat McKeon gave Mullaney a quick update on both Palmyra's condition and the status of heightened security measures around the compound. Both appeared to be improved since his last stop at the residence.

"Let's take a walk, Pat." It wasn't that he doubted McKeon's report, but Mullaney was in charge, and it was his responsibility to make sure the facility was secure. So they walked.

McKeon and two other agents walked with Mullaney as he conducted an extensive survey of the systems, personnel, and precautions in place at the residence, including updates and instructions with the agents and marines at each of the facility's entry points, those patrolling the walled perimeter along the Mediterranean Sea, and the lookouts and snipers housed in camouflaged positions around the campus. He reviewed the staffing patterns for that night and the next day, checked the functionality of all electronic surveillance, and planned strategy with the marine commander. It was getting close to midnight before Mullaney felt satisfied that he had covered all the bases. They were as ready as they would ever be. For what, he didn't know. But his adversaries had already proven themselves to be both bold and unpredictable, so he wasn't about to take any chances.

Only then did he turn his attention to the ambassador's daughter.

"She's in the garden," said McKeon. "She's been out there for hours, by herself . . . except for the two agents who have her in their sight at all times."

Mullaney stood in the corridor of the residence's north wing, which housed his office, and looked toward the gardens on the western flank of the sprawling complex. He turned back to his agent. "Thanks, Pat. You've done a great job today. Now I want you to stand down and get some rest. Tomorrow could be another long day. And I want you fresh. Okay?"

"Yes, sir," said McKeon. "And Brian . . . thanks for the second chance." McKeon had been duty officer yesterday when Parker had been allowed to leave the residence on her own and had been kidnapped from a nearby market by their unknown but relentless enemy. Yet it was also McKeon who had led the charge in the face of withering gunfire when DSS and Shin Bet agents had ambushed the kidnappers and rescued Palmer on the Nitzanim Reserve, north of Ashkelon, just before dawn that morning.

Still running through all the precautions in his head, Mullaney returned to the present and looked down at McKeon, who was a head shorter than Mullaney's six-two frame. "You're a top agent, Pat. I have the utmost confidence in you. Wouldn't want to have anyone else at my side in a fight. You've earned any number of second chances you need . . . but I don't think there will be need for any more. Go, get some rest, and I'll see you in the morning."

The smile on McKeon's face lit up the corridor. "Thanks, Brian. Thanks a lot."

The moon had yet to rise, and deep shadows lay under the trees and bushes spread throughout the extensive and well-maintained gardens of the residence . . . a space large enough to host over two thousand people for the ambassador's annual Fourth of July party. But Mullaney didn't need to search. His agents had given him Parker's location through the two-way mic-radio all DSS agents wore while on duty at the residence. Mullaney came around the corner of a hedge and found Parker reclining on a cushioned, metal lounge chair, a book in her lap but her eyes looking out over the black Mediterranean. She had picked a spot high on a rise, near the far right corner of the garden, that could see out beyond the compound's wall and had an unobscured view of the water.

Palmyra Parker turned her head as Mullaney walked up and seated himself in a padded chair, his back to the sea. He nodded his head toward the book in her lap. "Is it a good book?"

In spite of her ordeal, and in spite of the many wounds on her scalp where her abductors had recklessly chopped out chunks of her hair, Parker appeared peaceful, serene in the coolness of the garden, the light from a discreet lamp falling upon the lounge chair. She looked down at the book in her lap. "The best book," she said, her voice strong. When she returned her gaze to Mullaney her eyes were fixed, resolute, determined. "It's the greatest book ever written."

"Comforting?" asked Mullaney.

"Energizing," countered Palmer. "It's a call to battle."

Mullaney was stunned. "Haven't you had enough battle for one day?"

She shook her head and searched the reaches of the sea. "It's a battle that never ends, Brian. One that we didn't incite, but one we've been called to fight every day of our lives. Yesterday, we just happened to be on the front lines. Maybe we still are."

Palmyra Parker was thirty-eight and only four months a widow. Childless, looking for purpose and a change, she had agreed to join her father in Israel, maintain the residence and his calendar of events, serve as hostess for all occasions at the residence, and be the ambassador's companion at the embassy's official functions. Parker was tall, lithe, and stunning—her movements a testimony to the dancer she'd been. But now she had the look of a warrior, and her words fit her appearance.

Before Mullaney could ask any of his many questions, Parker had shifted position, turning on her hip to look at him more directly.

"Can I ask you a question?" Parker continued without pause. "After I was rescued, after the shooting stopped, do you remember me asking to know who the agent was who jumped in the SUV and protected me? When the explosions went off, the one who slammed the heads of the two thugs with me, slammed them into the side windows?"

Mullaney remembered the question. He also remembered he didn't have an answer. "Yes, I remember."

"There wasn't anybody there, was there, Brian?"

Now Mullaney could see where this was going.

"No . . . there wasn't anyone in the car with you except for the kidnappers, not until the IDF soldiers jumped in after the doors were blown off."

Parker was vigorously nodding her scarred head. "Right. See what I mean? There was nobody there, right?"

"Just you and the kidnappers."

Parker slapped the book in her lap. "But that's where you're wrong, Brian." Her words were more exclamatory than defiant. "There *was* somebody there, somebody who defended me and protected me before the soldiers jumped in the car. I know it, Brian. I know it for a fact. Just because you didn't see him doesn't mean he wasn't there."

Her green eyes were blazing in the diffused light with the fire of undeniable but unprovable conviction. She had an experience that was unexplainable. Except . . .

Mullaney remembered an experience of his own. Something that had also happened last night. "You're saying there was divine intervention?"

"I don't know what I'm saying," snapped Parker. She took a deep breath. "Sorry. All I know is what I saw. Something that I know happened that can't be explained. What does that make it?"

Mullaney felt like he was standing on the edge of a swimming pool, staring into the depths of the water. Was it too deep? Was it too cold? Would he jump?

He fixed his eyes on the flagstone under his feet. "After we raided the meat locker and you weren't there—and we saw the blood and the clumps of hair on the floor—I was a wreck," said Mullaney. "It looked so much like the death warrant of someone who had touched the box. I was terrified. I felt like I had failed you, failed your father. It touched a lot of the old lies I've tried to overcome all my life. I was useless and a failure . . . again. It all came crashing down on me in those few moments."

He had to stop. Gather himself together. How to say this?

"I was sitting on the edge of the loading dock, totally in despair. Then somebody put an arm around my shoulders, from my left. I thought it was Tommy. And I heard, 'You will find her. She will be safe.' I turned to my left, and no one was there." He waited, but there was no response from Parker. Stirred by the silence, he looked up into her eyes.

There was a knowing, twisted smile on her face. "Thank you, Brian. For your courage." She held his gaze for a moment longer. And the bond of warriors flowed between them, the bond of those who shared an experience few would ever understand. "Let me read you something."

Parker opened the book in her lap. It was a thick book, wrapped in a leather cover that was well-worn, nicked, and weathered. "I've had this Bible since I was in eighth grade. It was a graduation gift from my mom. She said it would help to guide me through my life. And she was right, oh so many times. I was just looking at the book of Ephesians. There is a long note connected to chapter 1, verse 3 about heavenly realms. The text note has some pretty heavy eschatological stuff, but it's basically saying there is this gigantic struggle going on in the heavenly realms between God and the powerful spiritual forces that oppose him and that the battles we face down here are connected to the battle in heaven. The note also says: 'the spiritual struggle of the saints here and now is not so much against "flesh and blood" as against the great spiritual forces that war against God in heaven.'"

"Wow," said Mullaney, trying to digest all he had just heard. "That's a mouthful. Eschatological? Don't think I learned about that in Catholic school."

"It means the part of theology that has to do with the end-times stuff," Parker said with a wave of her hand, "but don't focus on that. What do you think about this idea of a titanic battle going on between God and—what does it say?—'the powerful spiritual forces arrayed against him'? And that note where it says, 'As a result, the spiritual struggle of the saints here and now is not so much against "flesh and blood" as against the great spiritual forces that war against God in heaven.'" She bunched her fists on top of the Bible. "Did you ever think about that . . . that great spiritual forces were at war with God in heaven?"

"No," Mullaney shook his head, "not actually."

Parker started waving her hands in front of her. "Okay . . . but don't you get it? If there is a huge war going on in heaven between God and these other spiritual forces—which has to be evil, right—then why should we be surprised that the same war is occurring here and now on earth. And who's going to be fighting that battle? You and me, yes. But who else?"

Suddenly the torrent of words from Parker's mouth dried up. Mullaney sat there in silence, unsure whether he wanted to put voice to the things in his mind. Almost reflexively, it slipped from his lips. "You mean angels?"

"Yes!" Parker could barely contain herself. "Angels, Brian. Angels protecting me, encouraging you, probably protecting my dad when he didn't even know it. We're in a battle with an evil we don't know or understand. But it is a battle, Brian. A battle that is not over. And if we are in a battle between good and evil, why would we not expect good to come and help us out when we need it?"

"Or evil to keep pursuing us."

13

The swishing scrape of his leather slippers against the cold stone floor of the frosty subterranean room sounded like the slither of a snake on sand. The oil lamp he carried in his hand cast little light and no heat.

The Turk approached an ancient-looking wooden door. The door's lock moved easily, but the door itself gave a groan that could wake the dead as he pushed with his shoulder against its formidable bulk. Sound was no concern down here, far below street level, just downhill from Ankara's aged fort, the Citadel. But aside from the rasp of the heavy wooden door, there was no other sound. Only an escalating stench of putrid decay, overwhelming now that the door was open.

He moved with deliberate, measured steps. When a body had lived through centuries, haste was foolhardy. The Turk—as he was now called by those very few who knew of his existence—appeared in Istanbul in the waning days of 1938, following the trail of the Vilna Gaon's elusive prophecies. The Turk spent the previous 140 years in central Europe directing the activities of his Disciples, seeking to destroy the legacy of the Gaon, and serving the One. Then he was known by several names: the Prussian at one time, the Czar at another. Different names, but the same mission. Destroy the people of the book. Destroy any prophecy that foretold the coming of the Messiah. Destroy their legacy and their hope.

Over the last nearly eight decades, ever since the box had been carried to Istanbul for safekeeping, the Turk pursued his singular purpose with unrelenting determination. But he had gotten no closer to securing—or destroying—the box or procuring the key to dismantle the prophetic promises of the Christian book. He had been frustrated in Turkey just as he had been frustrated in Germany before the second war. In 1938 he had disappeared from Konigsberg like a fog on the wind and been reborn in Istanbul, where he was known only as the Turk.

Even though he remained determined and unflinching in his resolve, only a few months earlier, after being hidden and protected for 220 years, the Vilna Gaon's first prophecy had been revealed to the world, heralding the coming Messiah. Suddenly the urgent demands to find and destroy the second prophecy had become more strident, the threats more pointed.

None of which disturbed the Turk. He pursued a goal with eternal significance, a task that had not changed in more than a millennium. Thwart one prophecy in the accursed Book and all the rest would fall, worthless and unfulfilled. Block some of its prophecy and the end of the Book could be rewritten. But his foes were fierce and many. Hopefully the One would be merciful.

He had left the oil lamp by the door . . . it was always extinguished in this room. With the blackness wrapping itself around his body, his hands were inserted deep within the voluminous sleeves of his jubba. He had adopted these clothes on his arrival in Turkey. Protecting his hands suited his purpose and his caution. The Turk neither ate nor drank. He touched no man, and no man touched him.

He waited. The dark held no fear for him. It was home.

A shimmer in the black void, a dot of red light pulsing with life, and the iciness of the room was transformed in the span of a breath, as if a door to hell had been left open. The light grew and split into two, the red turning to yellow, the yellow dots swelling in size, gray thunder clouds flying across their surface. They blinked . . . mirror images of his own eyes: black pupils, yellow sclera with storms of gray making mayhem, eyes that projected hate and promised pain.

The Turk bowed before the eyes, first from the waist, then to his knees, then prostrate, his forehead pressed against the cold stone floor. "Exalted One."

"Rise." It was the sibilant slather of a voice, like the rupture of an underwater oil well polluting an ocean from the bottom up and bathing everything it touched in a slurry of decay.

The Turk rose.

"When will we ensnare the Jew?"

Satisfaction. Black as his heart was, the Turk smiled inwardly. The One needed him to see their plans fulfilled.

"Eroglu, so far, has been a willing pawn," said the Turk. "It is easy to manipulate those who are motivated by greed and power, since we can offer what they desire. And Eroglu dreams of great power. He is advancing on two fronts. Forces are in place to seize the nuclear weapons at the Incirlik Air Base. After tomorrow morning, emissaries will be secretly dispatched to Baghdad and Jerusalem. Iraq and Israel are both desperate for water. Ultimately, Iraq will agree to a Kurdish state and the partition of Syria because its rivers and lakes are turning to desert without Turkish water. And Israel will see no danger in signing a treaty to exchange its abundance of natural gas for the life-giving water from the mountains of Turkey.

"When we reveal the existence of both of these ongoing, secret negotiations, Israel will rush to consummate its treaty with Turkey. That is when Eroglu will introduce an innocent, last-minute request into the treaty, the proposal for the Mount of Olives. Once the Israelis accept the full treaty, one path to victory is assured. And when the nuclear weapons are under our control, the second path to victory will be in place. Either way, soon the Mount of Olives will no longer exist. Either we will level it and cover it with concrete and construction, or we will vaporize it and leave only a smoldering mound of irradiated contamination. Then any possibility of Zechariah's prophecy will be destroyed . . . that son of Joseph will have no place to return and rest his feet. The only savior to enter the new temple will be you, Exalted One. And we will hold the world at ransom."

It was all laid out, and the pieces were falling into place. The Turk was confident that this time . . .

"Where is the box?" The voice was a slippery hiss, but the words throbbed with power, pounding against his ears with accusation.

The Turk's confidence wavered, but pride tickled defiance in his demented heart. Still, he had not risen to this place through defiance. The two yellow eyes were piercing in clarity, trying to penetrate the thoughts of his mind, while all around them was a red, diaphanous vapor that, at times, could be construed as a face. A grotesque, tortured, malevolent face.

"It has been taken to the American embassy in Tel Aviv," said the Turk.

As if he had been struck by lightning, the Turk was driven, prostrate, to the floor. The skin along the back of his neck blistered and sizzled.

"You have failed me again! *Again!*"

The voice rent the air with the roar of an earthquake.

<hr />

US Ambassador's Residence, Tel Aviv
July 20, 11:40 p.m.

As soon as the words about evil pursuing them were out of his mouth, Mullaney felt the earth shimmy beneath him and the metal lounge chair move slightly sideways. In an instant, his training kicked in and all of his senses were on alert. In a second instant, the world settled back to normal.

Parker was looking at him wide-eyed.

"Did you feel that?" Her words were spoken with a hint of awe and a hint of concern. "That was spooky."

The entire compound seemed to hold its breath for a moment. You could almost hear everyone on the grounds exhale.

"Have you had many earth tremors while you've been here?" asked Mullaney.

"None."

"Then that shake gives me the creeps."

Ankara
July 20, 11:40 p.m.

The Turk's body was pressed into the cold stones of the floor by an onerous weight. He could not move, but he was not afraid. The One needed him. And the task was not yet complete.

As if a cadaverous hand grabbed him by the neck, the Turk was yanked to his feet. In front of him, the swirling red vapor surrounding the eyes erupted into a molten wrath, a lava flow of rage. The ground beneath him shook as the voice of the eyes rose in frenzied fury, each word the lash of a whip.

"The prophecy is back into the hands of the Nazarene's followers! Once again you come before me only to report failure. Why have you not slain that ambassador and this meddling agent? Extinguish them before they gain access to the message."

Barely standing his ground under the onslaught of venom, the Turk scrambled for a response. "There is no one to open the box," he gasped. "The last guardian perished in the destroyed synagogue. They may have the box but . . . but even if they could find a way to open it without perishing, they have no way to read the message. That understanding died with the rabbis in the Hurva. Our secret remains."

"But our enemies also remain. You must destroy them."

"The winged ones have intervened again," said the Turk. "One stood in the bowels of the Hurva, holding back the crushing tons of concrete to protect the box and the message. They are formidable."

"Have we not more power on this earth than those other immortals?" spat the voice, its volume and intensity building like an avalanche of bitterness. "We are eternally their equal, but this is our domain! The power of darkness rules this earth, not the power of light. We rule here. Defeat them!"

"As you wish, Exalted One." The Turk bowed his head before the presence of the One. But he had a plan to restore his place in that presence. "The winged ones are neither omniscient nor omnipresent," said the Turk. "Our advantage is in stealth and subterfuge. We will strike at the Americans and rip out their hearts before they can discover what rests in the box and use it to prevent us from ushering in the time of the Mahdi."

"Then strike quickly. Our time is limited. Already I can sense a narrowing in the future. The end is closer than you can imagine. That Jew's second message could interfere with all of our intentions. Change the story now . . . while we still have the opportunity. And do not fail again. If we fail, we both may spend eternity in the lake of fire."

14

Mullaney didn't know if he was more spooked by the earth tremor or by what Parker was implying.

Not only was it near impossible for Mullaney to accept the plausibility of the words that just emerged from Palmyra Parker's mouth, it was even crazier for him to harbor the thoughts in his own mind that were clamoring to be transformed into words. Why couldn't he just go to bed?

"You believe what you're saying, don't you." It was not a question. Parker nodded her damaged head. "Then you know what else you are saying, correct?"

One of the lamps that illuminated the garden was behind Parker, about six feet off the ground, partially obscured by palm fronds. Her eyes were in shadow. But he could see the firm set of her jaw, the tightness of her pressed lips. Her single nod was an announcement.

"If," said Mullaney, "we have angelic beings assisting and protecting us against the men who twice attacked your father, who kidnapped you—probably the same men who blew up the Hurva synagogue—then the logical conclusion is that these men . . . whoever they are, wherever they come from, whatever it is they want . . . these men also have, well, maybe not angelic beings, but other supernatural beings who are leading, guiding, and helping them. Do you believe that, too?"

A breeze came off the Mediterranean, carrying with it the smell of the sea and the taste of salt. Parker pushed herself up in the lounge chair, pulled up her legs, and wrapped her arms around her knees, tight against her chest. She was clearly seeking a safe haven. Her face was now in the light, and her green eyes were wide.

"Evil angels." Her voice was as soft as the sea breeze. "Yes. I believe we are in the midst of what the Bible calls this great titanic struggle. For whatever reason, Brian, God has enlisted us into the front lines of a battle against the powerful spiritual forces that are arrayed against him."

Mullaney felt the rebellion of good sense rise up in him. "But why us . . . why me? What have I ever done that enables me to be on the front lines of God's great battle against evil?"

"Why Gideon?" asked Parker. "Why David? Why Peter? None of them enlisted. All of them were drafted out of obscurity, called into service when it didn't make any sense and when they didn't feel capable or worthy. Besides, I think none of us can ever do enough or do the right things to be enlisted into God's personal service. We're called because he sees our hearts; he sees our potential. It's called grace, unmerited favor."

In his mind, Mullaney could understand Parker's logic and her faith. What he couldn't understand was the unreality of the real. "It didn't feel like unmerited favor when that Mercedes went airborne off Highway One and started doing flips with your dad inside, or when your kidnappers opened up with automatic weapons."

"That we survived was grace," said Parker.

Mullaney rose from his chair and turned toward the sea, away from Parker, looking for answers out over its black surface. He rested his right hand on the back of the chair. "What you're talking about is duty, not grace. We are drafted into battle or enlist into battle because of duty. I have a sworn duty to my country, to your father." Across the surface of the dark water, Mullaney imagined three faces, and he was reminded of another duty. He turned back to Parker but didn't sit.

"I had a telephone call with Abby this afternoon . . . at least I think it was this afternoon. I hadn't called her for days. She was scared, upset. She . . ." He wasn't sure how to tell—

"She wants you home," said Parker. "I don't blame her."

"It's more than that," said Mullaney. "My duty is here. But my duty is there too. I haven't always been very diligent in fulfilling my duty to Abby and the girls. She's hoping I'll put them first . . . for once."

The palms and the pines whispered on the back of the breeze. The faces Mullaney had imagined disappeared from the distant dark of his subconscious.

"I asked your father this morning to get me reassigned to Washington. He's putting it in his situation report."

"How much time have you given us?"

"I haven't gotten that far. Let's wait and see if the request is granted. But I hope I'll be around until we find and destroy this evil . . . until you and your father are safe once more."

"You could be faced with conflicting promises."

"Well . . . I know," said Mullaney. "Right now, I can only think about my duty, all of my duty. Do the best I can with each day and leave the rest in God's hands. If you're right—if we're right—and the fight we're in is supernatural, then God's hands are where the fight belongs. The battle is his. I'm just along for the ride."

"I think you're along for strength," said Parker. "For muscle—physical, emotional, and spiritual muscle. We may be in God's hands, but we are also under your protection. And for that, I am blessed."

15

It was good news. So this time, he figured he would FaceTime. He wanted to see Abby's face light up when he told her.

"Brian? Are you all right?"

Mullaney could not only hear the alarm in Abigail's voice, but he could also see the fear in her eyes. It had been less than seven hours since they last spoke. He should have known she would be worried.

"I'm sorry to startle you, Abby. Everything is okay," he said. "But I wanted to talk to you before I went to bed. It would be too late to call you in the morning."

"Okay?" The word was a question . . . she turned her head slightly to the side, uncertainty in her azure eyes.

"I've spoken to Ambassador Cleveland and asked for his help to get home," said Mullaney. "He's submitting his first situation report to the secretary of state tonight. In it he's promised to include an ambassadorial request, asking for my reassignment to Washington."

The silence was protracted and pregnant with possibilities. It looked like Abby was standing in a kitchen. Mullaney realized he was holding his breath, waiting for a response.

Abby sat down in a chair and closed her eyes. "Thank you." Her words sounded like a prayer. Maybe they were. But then she looked fully into the screen on her phone.

"But what does that mean?" Abby asked. "When will you be coming home? Will that request be granted? You've only been there a few weeks."

Mullaney exhaled. "Ambassadorial requests are seldom denied. I'm sure Cleveland will do his best to make a case. But"—he had to be honest with her—"Cleveland reminded me that neither he nor I have much clout in the department these days. A lot will probably depend on how the secretary responds to the request."

Abby looked as if she was about to speak, then stopped, her eyes downcast, a sigh lifting her chest and escaping loudly through her nose. She slowly shook her head, auburn curls brushing her face. "Please tell the ambassador that I appreciate his efforts on our behalf." She looked up. "I hope this request is approved, Brian. I really do. But . . . what will you do if it's not?"

Mullaney could sense the old wounds opening up, the litany of marital disappointments—and the eleven moves—that followed in the wake of his decision to join the State Department's Diplomatic Security Service. A nineteen-year veteran of the DSS, Mullaney's once prospering career was now on as much life support as his marriage to Abby. And he was desperately trying to find a tourniquet that could stanch the bleeding on both fronts.

"Abby"—Mullaney poured the earnestness of his heart into his words as he stared hard at her image on the screen—"you and the girls are the most important people in my life, our marriage and our family the most important thing in my life. If Cleveland's request is denied, I'll have to figure something out. Maybe—"

"You promised me, Brian," Abby cut him short. The edges of her face became rigid. It sounded like her fist hit the table. "You promised me that we were done moving, that our return to Virginia was the last move, that we would stay put, even if you had to leave the service."

Again, she was right. It was his promise. Still . . . "It all happened so fast, I felt like I didn't have a choice."

"Oh, Brian . . . there is always a choice. You could have asked Daddy. You know he could have fixed it."

The death stroke.

Yes, Mullaney knew both the counsel, and the requests, of billionaire banker Richard Rutherford reached to the highest levels of government in Washington. Abby was right. Daddy probably could have fixed it . . . prevented Mullaney from getting banished to Israel.

But Mullaney hadn't once eaten the crumbs from Rutherford's table since the first day he met Abigail Rutherford at a small Georgetown party. And he wasn't about to start now. Mullaney had seen firsthand what it was like being in debt to Richard Rutherford. Don Vito Corleone was a lightweight compared to Rutherford's debt collection. No . . . not in a million lifetimes.

"I'm sorry, Abby. I know you love and respect your father. But when I made a vow to you, to keep you, for richer or poorer, I made a vow to myself that I would provide for and care for you, for our family, out of my own resources, not out of your father's. You know I can't go there."

"Can't or won't?" Her sky-blue eyes flashed the fire of sunrise.

"Either way, it doesn't matter. I will not be in Richard's debt."

So . . . there it was. The immovable object. The granite cliffs upon which his life and his family were being pounded to shreds. Was it pride? Or was it wisdom? Did it matter?

"Well then," said Abby, her words an exclamation point. "You've made your decision. You've drawn a line in the sand, so I'll draw one too. I want you home, Brian. If you want to save our marriage, if you want to rescue our family, if you want to put us first once—just once!—I want you home. You can do it. And you know there are two surefire ways to get it done—ask for Daddy's help or resign your post."

Two impossibilities. How could he . . . "Abby, you know there—"

"I know, Brian. I've heard you say it enough times. There are two things you will never do: *'I will never shirk my duty, and I will never betray a confidence.'* Well, Brian, I need you to do your duty toward me, toward your daughters. I need you to do whatever is necessary, whatever you need to do, to get transferred back to Washington."

There was an "Or what?" hanging in the air between Washington and Tel Aviv, an "Or what?" that neither of them appeared ready to ask.

A sternness came over Abby's countenance. She looked like a judge about to deliver a sentence. The look on her face sent a shiver deep into Mullaney's spirit.

"It's your decision, Brian. Be stubborn. Be right. But that will come with a cost."

"Please, Abby—"

"Goodbye, Brian."

Baghdad, Iraq
July 21, 5:46 a.m.

The building housing the offices of the Dawa Party was nearly empty at this early hour. Only the janitors and a few sleep-deprived guards stood between Samir Al-Qahtani, deputy prime minister of Iraq, and his objective—the private sanctuary of the Iraqi prime minister, Khalid Al-Bayati, when the Iraqi parliament was not in session.

Both Al-Qahtani and Al-Bayati were Shia members of the Iraqi Parliament, frustrated veterans of the endless struggle of Iraq's Shia majority to wrest power from the Sunni minority that had controlled Iraq's government, and its treasury, for decades on end.

Al-Bayati, pushed into his role by the Americans, had relied on politics to save them. Politics that had merely embroiled them in a fight against Sunni bureaucracy while ISIS swallowed up thousands of acres of Iraqi desert, cities, and oil refineries.

But Samir Al-Qahtani had taken action to cut through the Sunni choke hold on the Iraqi government. Moving in force in the fading darkness before dawn, Al-Qahtani's Badr Brigades—an Iranian-backed Shia militia of well-equipped, fierce fighters—had launched dozens of armored vehicles and transport trucks with several thousand fighters into the streets of Baghdad, taking control of the city.

The vast majority of Iraq's population were Muslims of the Shia sect, fervent sympathizers and supporters of Al-Qahtani and his Badr Brigade Shia militia. So not only was there little opposition when police and government facilities throughout the city were surrounded by the Badr military, there were also celebrations and shouts of unity. Thousands of Iraqi citizens—Shia, all—poured into the streets, waving Iraqi flags and singing songs of praise to their Badr saviors.

Earlier, Al-Qahtani himself was in the lead armored personnel carrier, holding a white flag high above his head, as hundreds of the Badr militia advanced cautiously on the Assassin's Gate, one of the main points of entry to the heavily fortified American military base in the Green Zone. Warned to remain inside their compound, the American military waited impatiently while their commanders frantically sought direction from Washington. But the Sunnis would receive no help from the West to prevent Al-Qahtani from taking Iraq for the Shia majority.

Now, with the access points to the Green Zone surrounded and Baghdad effectively in his hands, Al-Qahtani strode down the wide hallway of the office building, his combat boots resonating off the marble floor, two dozen heavily armed fighters in his wake. The single guard at the door to the Dawa Party's office not only laid down his gun, but lay down on the floor beside it.

Al-Qahtani didn't bother to knock. He passed through the empty reception room and into the prime minister's office.

Kahlid Al-Bayati, his eyeglasses perched on the end of a bulbous nose, looked up from the stack of paper on his desk.

"Good morning, Samir," said Al-Bayati. He stood up, moved away from his chair, and came around to the front of the desk.

"Come . . . sit," he said, pointing at the chair of power behind the desk. "I've been expecting this day would come. Tell me how I can help my Shia brothers."

Truman Building, Washington, DC
July 20, 11:50 p.m.

"Watch commander!"

DSS Senior Agent Declan Thomas looked up from the latest "flash traffic" report on his desk in the State Department's state-of-the-art operations center on the seventh floor of the Harry S. Truman building in Washington. "Yeah, Jonesy . . . whatcha got?"

One of the forty-five watch officers on duty in ops, Jones was standing inside his cubicle, his head above the partition, two aisles away from Thomas's desk, closer to the wall of television monitors that kept ops connected to American embassies and foreign service staff around the world. "I've got a military attaché on the line from our base in the Green Zone in Baghdad. He's says they're surrounded . . . militia . . . armored vehicles. The gates are blocked."

The team currently manning ops was responsible for the safety of thirteen thousand men and women who served with the US Foreign Service on assignment in other countries. Since the end of the Cold War, that protection often meant saving their lives. The list of Foreign Service personnel killed overseas was an all-too-grim reminder of how difficult that responsibility was to fulfill.

Around the clock every day, the sixty-five-person rotating crews in ops not only monitored the security systems and surveillance videos at every US Foreign Service installation around the world but also maintained constant feeds from every major broadcast news network on earth. In short, from the seventh floor of the Truman building, the staff of ops tried to keep a finger on the pulse of everything happening in the world.

"Transfer him to me," said Thomas. He turned his head to the right. "Clancy, pull up video of Baghdad." His phone rang.

"This is Senior Agent Thomas, watch commander in ops. To whom am I speaking?"

"Agent Thomas, this is Quinton Ballentine, a military attaché at the embassy in Baghdad."

The man's voice was low, hushed, barely audible.

"I've been assigned as liaison to the US troops that were deployed to Iraq last month for security in the Green Zone. About 05:20 Baghdad time, not long after dawn, a troop of Iraqi militia, led by a number of armored vehicles, approached the camp's main gate. Their commander was holding a white flag. I wasn't there, so I'm getting this secondhand, but I'm told the militia was Badr Brigades."

"Not good," spit Thomas. He raised his left hand to get his adjutant's attention. "Get Webster on the phone. Be ready for a call to the secretary. Go ahead, Ballentine. And speak up, will you?"

"Yes, sir . . . I'll try. The militia commander . . . some people think it was Al-Qahtani . . . told the duty officer that all American military were confined to the base and that his men would resist any attempt by our military to leave. I think all of our units have been told to stand down. At least nothing is moving at the moment."

Agent Thomas waited, but the line was silent.

"Ballentine? You there?"

"Yes, sir."

"It's been over an hour, Ballentine." Agent Thomas tried to keep his frustration in check and any reproof from his voice. But it was tough. "Why has it taken so long for you or somebody else to contact us?"

"Yes, sir . . . I understand," said the whispering voice from Baghdad. "I can't speak with certainty to the decisions of the base commander. But sir, the scuttlebutt is that base HQ is in an uproar. It appears the commander is embarrassed that he got caught with his pants down, so to speak, and he's trying to figure out what's going on before he contacts anyone in DC. I was told he's locked down communication until he gets some answers. The mood in HQ is pretty ugly."

"So why . . . how . . . am I speaking to you now?"

"Well, sir, I'm hiding in a closet with the door closed. I, uh . . . liberated . . . a military satellite phone. I think I'd be in for a world of hurt if the commander found out I was talking to you."

"Is that it? Is that all you have for us?" asked Thomas.

"Well . . . I have no corroboration for this. But I called a contact at the main police station," said Ballentine. "They were surrounded too. Militia and armored vehicles. But most of the police are Shia. They were out dancing in the streets." Agent Thomas waited for Ballentine to break the silence. "Agent Thomas . . . I think the Iraqi government just got overthrown. I think there's a coup going on and Al-Qahtani and his Badr militia have taken over."

"Hold on, Ballentine." Thomas turned to the desk on his left. "Call the secretary. I want him on the phone now."

16

Tommy Hernandez was already in Ambassador Cleveland's office at the residence when Brian Mullaney arrived, looking like he had wrestled with the night and lost. It was Mullaney who had requested this early morning meeting between the ambassador and his security team to try and get in front of the head-spinning events unfolding not only in Israel but throughout the Middle East. And a couple of sensitive items were for their ears only. But Mullaney looked haggard, preoccupied, his eyes distracted.

"Good morning, Brian," said Cleveland, standing behind his desk and flipping quickly through a stack of papers. "Are you okay?"

Startled back to the present, Mullaney shook his head. "Yes, sir . . . just tired."

"Coffee is in the corner, and I've called the kitchen and asked them to bring us up some breakfast."

"Thank you, sir," said Mullaney, closing the door behind him and joining Hernandez by the coffee carafe. "Meyer Levinson is on his way. He was grateful that he could get some time with the three of us this morning to review the events of yesterday and to share some new information."

"Good," said Cleveland. "We need to hear what Shin Bet has uncovered." The ambassador ran his finger down a sheet on the left side of his desk. "We'll need to—"

A rapid knocking sounded on the office door.

"That is real fast food," said Hernandez. "Which is great, because I could eat a mountain goat . . . if I had a mountain." He crossed the office and opened the door. Jeffrey Archer, Cleveland's secretary, stood in the doorway, wringing his hands.

"Excuse me, Mr. Ambassador," said Archer. "Deputy Chief Goldberg is on line one. He says you should turn on your TV. There's been a coup in Iraq."

Cleveland closed his eyes and pulled in a deep breath. *God, what's next?* He looked at Archer. "Who's taken over?"

Hernandez opened the doors on a credenza in the corner and turned on the television.

"Samir Al-Qahtani," said Archer. "The militia from the Badr Brigades moved into the streets of Baghdad before dawn. They blockaded our forces inside the Green Zone and deposed al-Bayati without firing a shot."

"That means—"

The sound from the television pulled all of their attention toward the credenza. A news anchor was doing a voice-over as choppy video of Baghdad's streets played on the screen. "—When Iraqi forces under the command of Deputy Prime Minister Samir Al-Qahtani, apparently allied with and supported by Iranian military personnel already in Iraq, swept through the city and overthrew the government of Prime Minister Kahlid Al-Bayati. Al-Qahtani has been publicly vocal in his calls for much closer ties with the Shia-led government of Iran. If this military coup succeeds—as it appears to be doing—this will be the first time all of Iraq and Iran have been unified since the Sassanid Persian Empire of the seventh century."

Cleveland turned away from the television and glanced at Mullaney. "Well, looks like something else has been added to our discussion list. This is going to be quite a day. Jeffrey, please show Colonel Levinson in when he gets here."

———✦———

Colonel Meyer Levinson, director of Shin Bet's operations division, the assault force of Israel's internal security apparatus, sat in Cleveland's office, tapping his foot and obviously barely constraining his pent-up energy. Mullaney had put aside his growing to-do list, including trying to catch up on the latest from Baghdad and the coup in Iraq, to concentrate on what he saw as task number one—tracking down the killers who still pursued the box. What Levinson was sharing was not making Mullaney's day any better.

"There's just no trace of these guys," said Levinson, "who they are, where they are, or what they're planning next. Our forensic team did a full workup on the bodies of the kidnappers killed at the Nitzanim Reserve. They are doing the same on the two bombers from yesterday. So far, no IDs, no hits in the fingerprint files, no records on any of these men—which is pretty interesting in itself—no hits through facial recognition. There were no other traceable mobile devices on any of them."

Past experience told Mullaney that the Israeli colonel was pursuing every lead with a passion that would match his own. Meyer Levinson was not only a dead ringer for Israel's rakish former general, Moshe Dayan, but as near a real-life superhero as Mullaney had ever known.

"So . . . what does that tell you?" Levinson asked.

"Professionals," said Hernandez.

"Yes, but professionals who have never even gotten a speeding ticket. Who until this week had never been connected with an illegal act. And not just hired professionals. This is an exclusive group, cohesive, covert, and committed to something they all believe in. These guys are not doing this for money. There is ideology or theology or some other *ology* behind their actions. These guys have the same tenacity of purpose we see in jihadists, but I don't peg them as Al Qaeda or ISIS. Since Mrs. Parker identified the language of her kidnappers as Turkish, there's a likelihood these men were Turkish nationals. But we get no hits through Interpol or NATO. We've shared their mug shots with Turkish national police and came up empty. And they have virtually disappeared."

"Killer ghosts," said Hernandez. "Sounds like a bad movie."

"Unfortunately this is no movie. And our reality keeps getting worse."

Mullaney had known Levinson for a decade, had faced more than one life-and-death situation with him. So Mullaney heard and understood the signals.

"What else is there, Meyer? What else have you discovered?"

Levinson reached inside a manila folder he'd carried with him and pulled out a sheaf of printed paper. He looked directly at the ambassador. "You're not going to like this, Mr. Ambassador." He turned his gaze on Mullaney. "Remember when we met at our headquarters to plan the raid on the Holon warehouse and I told you about some communication intercepts Mossad had uncovered?"

Levinson picked up the printed pages before him. He looked at the three seated around him. "Simply put, Mossad monitors every communication that comes into or goes out from Israel. Every one. And yes, this includes diplomatic communications, like yours with Washington. We maintain a record of those communications, and our computers can break down these communications into keywords almost instantaneously, whether the communications are encrypted or not. These"—he shook the sheets—"are some of the call logs made during the time we were searching for Mrs. Parker. Our team scanned for any communication containing the name *Parker* or *Palmyra Parker*. Initially we had a lot of innocent hits. But when we discovered her kidnappers were speaking Turkish, Mossad factored that into their algorithm and came up with something I shared with Brian before the raid.

"We recovered three wireless telephone conversations during the time just prior to Mrs. Parker's abduction—one between Turkey and the United States and two between Turkey and Israel—that mentioned Mrs. Parker by name. The last two also referenced a package.

"We reached far to discover these communications," said Levinson, "and the results are often incomplete. But what I wanted to show you was the origination signal on the call between the US and Turkey." Levinson handed the top sheet to the ambassador. One of the entries was highlighted. "If you will look at the code under *originating signal . . .*" He looked in Mullaney's direction.

"It's State Department, sir," said Mullaney.

Cleveland's head lifted, his eyes moving from the sheet in front of him to Mullaney, then to Levinson, back to Mullaney. "You're sure?"

"I had one just like it," said Mullaney.

The code on the call log was a signature address, like the signatures computers receive when they are linked into a network. Each device has a unique signature. But similar devices, devices used by the same company or on the same network, have similar signatures. It was one way of identifying and locating the device.

"*That* signature address," said Mullaney, "is for an encrypted satellite phone used at the State Department. I had one with an almost identical code when I was in DC."

In the wake of Mullaney's words, the environment in Cleveland's office was holding its breath, waiting . . .

Cleveland's voice was a fraction above a whisper. "We suspected we had a leak somewhere in the system." His words were flat, emotionless. "But this . . . this . . ."

"This is one big bad buckaroo," said Hernandez. "Somebody's playing footsie with the enemy."

"Yes," said Cleveland, nodding his head, "but this somebody is very high in the food chain." He looked across at Mullaney. "Last night I submitted the situation report, with your request. But I don't know if . . ." Cleveland stopped abruptly and turned his attention on Levinson. "Colonel Levinson, we are once again very much in your debt. Thank you. But I don't want to delay you from what must be a considerably difficult day. Is there anything we can do for you, or anything else you have for us today?"

17

US Ambassador's Residence, Tel Aviv
July 21, 9:04 a.m.

Tommy Hernandez was escorting Meyer Levinson to his car at the front of the residence, giving Cleveland a few moments alone with Mullaney. "It's 2:00 a.m. in Washington. I'm sure the State Department is up and jumping and Secretary Townsend has his hands full. So let's take a few minutes before we try to find him." The ambassador reached down to the telephone console on his desk. "Jeffrey . . . I'm going dark for a while . . . no interruptions unless it's the secretary, okay? Thanks."

His shoulders lifted, and a deep sigh escaped from Cleveland's chest. His eyes were still on his desk. "I'm beginning to think I should have retired last year." He shook his head and stepped from behind his desk. "I need a cup of coffee. Join me?"

Without waiting for Mullaney's response, Cleveland filled two US embassy mugs from the side table, took one, and headed for the battered, brown leather sofa in the corner. Mullaney, his hands wrapped around the other mug, settled into the wingback chair opposite the ambassador.

Cleveland stared at the coffee in his mug as if he were looking into a crystal ball, searching for the future. "There seems to be a lot of fear running rampant in the world today," he said. He moved his hands around the outside of the mug, absorbing the warmth like bright sunshine on a spring day. "And a lot of decisions are being made because of that fear. You know"—Cleveland broke the spell and looked up at Mullaney—"fear is not generally a trustworthy advisor. We need to be very careful not to allow fear to determine our course right now."

But what will determine our course? We're running headlong into . . .

A weight was resting on Cleveland's shoulders that he didn't want to recognize. So he punted.

"Brian . . . what is your greatest fear?"

Mullaney sat up in his chair and placed his mug on a side table, focusing on Cleveland. "One of those kind of discussions, eh?"

Feeling weary, Cleveland simply nodded.

"Up until yesterday, my greatest fear was being useless," said Mullaney. "That's what my dad used to hammer into my brother and me . . . don't be useless. My dad's identity was wrapped up in being effective and productive, being the rock that everybody else relied on and leaned against, being a man of character who could be trusted. That's what he taught us. *Don't be useless.*

"After talking with Abby twice in the last few hours, my greatest fear now is losing my marriage and my family. But you've taken care of that. At least now I'll have a chance to get home and try to patch my family back together. But I understand what you're asking. So what do I fear most? Being of no value. I fear being severely wounded. What if I didn't have use of my arms or my legs? I know some courageous people do wonderful things despite not having the use of their limbs or having lost a limb. Maybe I could do that too. But it scares me. What if I needed someone else to feed me? Or help me get dressed? Or if I couldn't get around?

"In order to do what I do, I need to be in full control of all my faculties—body, mind, soul, and spirit. If my mind started to go—if I lost my memory—what would I do? I'd be useless."

Cleveland was leaning in from the waist, focused intently on Mullaney and his words. "Why do you fear that?"

"Because I watched my Dad become useless. He was a state police officer in Virginia. He worked himself up through the ranks from a grunt rookie to commander of a field division of troopers. But then he got Alzheimer's. First he forgot people—names, relationships. It wasn't long before he forgot himself. My mom had to lock him in the house because he wanted to leave to go home. When he became violent . . . well, we needed to put him in a safe facility. He spent his last years curled up in a fetal position, trapped in his own mind."

Cleveland tried to imagine the terror that Mullaney must have felt, watching his father's life melt away and now carrying the unanswered question of whether it could happen to him too. And as a widower, he understood how the threat of losing something as close and personal as his wife and family could displace all of his fears from the past.

Cleveland found himself struggling with the same conflict—a new and present fear overwhelming the familiar fear that had been a foundation of his life.

"I have to agree with you," said Cleveland. "Up until yesterday, if you had asked, I would have told you that my greatest fear is disappointing my children. It's taken our family a long time and a lot of sacrifice to rise out of the dehumanization of slavery and the tobacco fields of North Carolina to a place where all of my children have university degrees and all of their children want for nothing. I've been given the blessed opportunity to represent my country in conversations with rulers and kings. My greatest fear was to disappoint my children and dishonor those lives upon which I stand."

Cleveland realized he'd been holding his coffee all this time and had yet to drink even a sip. He found himself lost in the rapidly cooling brown liquid, his mind visiting the memories of ancestors long gone.

"But today there's something else?" asked Mullaney.

Pulled back to the present, the ambassador finally put down his mug and settled into the comforting embrace of the worn, brown leather. "Today, Brian, there is everything else."

"Sir?"

"You were here yesterday when the secretary and I were discussing the implications of Exodus 17, God's curse against Amalek and his descendants, and Joel 3, the warning of judgment on anyone who divides the land, as they relate to the Ishmael Covenant," said Cleveland. "I'm sworn to uphold the Constitution of the United States and to support and advance the foreign policy of our nation. But what do I do, Brian, when that foreign policy is directly opposed to the things I read in my Bible? I believe the Bible is the word of God. The whole thing. I believe the Bible lays out the story of the history of man, from beginning to end. It's not a fable or a practical code of conduct. The Bible is the words of God written by men inspired by the Holy Spirit.

"The Bible has many parts—creation, the history of the Jewish nation as God's chosen people, the giving of the Law, the words of the prophets, the songs, and the Gospels and letters of the New Testament. I believe all of that is true . . . the inspired Word of God.

"So"—Cleveland pushed himself forward on the sofa—"how do I reconcile the story in Exodus 17, when Moses tells Joshua that he is to wipe out the name of Amalek from the face of the earth, with the covenant announced yesterday in which Israel is making a blood contract to defend the sons of Amalek? How do I reconcile the prophesy in Joel 3 that predicts judgment on any who try to divide the land of promise? There's more . . . how do I reconcile the words of Ezekiel 40? In a vision, a 'man whose appearance was like bronze' met Ezekiel on top of a 'very high mountain,' which is Mount Zion, and measured out for him the dimensions of the temple of God."

Cleveland leaned over the arm of the sofa and reached into a basket that sat on the floor, removing a well-worn book. "My great-grandfather's Bible," he said, showing it to Mullaney, "remember? I showed it to you, what, two days ago? Well, in the 43rd chapter of the prophet Ezekiel's book, he writes about a vision. Ezekiel and the rest of the Jewish people were in bondage in Babylon at the time, but in the vision, Ezekiel was taken back to Jerusalem. He was taken to the east gate of Temple Mount, where the glory of the Lord entered the temple of the Jews. Ezekiel wrote that the Lord spoke to him and told him that their temple was the place of his throne and where he would live with the people of Israel forever. In verse 12 the Lord says—it's the King James Version, so a bit old-fashioned: 'This is the law of the house; Upon the top of the mountain the whole limit thereof round about shall be most holy. Behold, this is the law of the house.'"

He closed the book. "Brian, the Ishmael Covenant proposes to allow Israel to build what would be the third temple of God. But on the side of Mount Zion . . . on the side of the Temple Mount . . . not on the top of the mountain.

"Now today the Persian Empire may have just been resurrected; we think the Saudis are trying to get their hands on nuclear weapons from Pakistan, and an ultraconservative army of religious fanatics has swept across large sections of Syria and Iraq under a flag of terror and violence. In a time like this, Brian, I look to the Bible for guidance, for wisdom, for understanding. If we as a people dispose of the Bible as a source of wisdom . . . well . . . we do it at our own peril.

"If"—Cleveland held up the book—"this is the inspired Word of God, what will happen if we ignore it? What will happen if all of our actions contradict what the Bible says? There is a long, verifiable history of what happens to a people when they defy God. Personally, I don't want to be around when that happens.

"And right now I'm trying to figure out how I'm going to fulfill both of my duties—to my country and to the Word of God—when they are moving as polar opposites."

Cleveland turned and looked at the clock. "And we better call the secretary."

18

"Don't be absurd, Arslan. No one is getting any sleep over here."

Deputy Secretary of State Noah Webster sat in his black Mercedes SL 550 in the parking garage under the Truman Building in Washington, the headquarters of the US State Department. As a result of the coup in Iraq, State staffers were arriving like a thunderstorm on a summer's evening, but the corner where Webster was parked was dark, secluded. And the satellite phone had perfect reception, even in the bowels of the Truman building.

"I've already received calls from Senator Markham and Richard Rutherford, both of them in a minor panic about what this coup may mean to our plans. Just yesterday Rutherford tried to strong-arm me with his arrogance, threatened to withdraw all of his support—from both of us—if we didn't start to show some results. And now this coup happens without us having a clue that it's coming? Arslan, we look like fools. Fools!"

Webster was pushing it. The prime minister of Turkey was well-educated and cosmopolitan, publicly committed to strengthening Turkey's military and economic ties to the West, but also a savvy political operative with grand visions for his own glory. His ego bruised easily.

There was a pregnant pause from the other end of the call.

"Tell your senator and your banker that it may be wise for all of you to withhold final judgment." Eroglu's words were defiant and sharp. "There will come a time to determine who has been a fool and who has been wise. I would wait until the game is over to determine who wins."

Yes, his ego bruised easily. "Don't take it personally, Arslan. There's a lot riding on the next few days. Do you have any insight into how things are playing out in Baghdad?"

"The Iranians are being very cool," said Eroglu. "They are claiming this coup is an internal Iraqi issue over which they have no control. And they are downplaying all of this speculation that the coup is a first step toward creating a new Persian Empire. The official word out of Tehran is that Iraq is a sovereign nation, but if there is any way the Iranians can assist their Shia brothers in Iraq, they would be happy to oblige."

"Smoke screen," said Webster. "And a poor one at that."

"What will the American president do now?" asked Eroglu. "Will he reconsider his nuclear deal with Iran?"

"Too early to tell," said Webster, "but that's what got Rutherford so animated. Rutherford's banks rake in hundreds of millions of dollars of interest every year that Iran's confiscated funds remain in his vaults. He's got hundreds of millions of reasons to want that Iran deal scuttled . . . and you and I are in line for a slice of those hundreds of millions. If we can kill the deal."

Rutherford might be facing financial losses, but Webster knew any resurrection of a new Persia was even more frightening to Eroglu and Turkish president Emet Kashani. A nuclear Persia on its doorstep would be a threat not only to Turkey but also to NATO.

"These are very uncertain waters," said Webster. "President Boylan could threaten to withdraw the nuclear deal if Iran doesn't completely get its hands off Iraq. Or he could push for the deal as a way to strong-arm Iran into concessions. But we can't wait to find out what he decides. What can you do, Arslan, to put a spike in the heart of this new Persia?" asked Webster.

"Kashani is spineless, but he's pliable," said Eroglu. "I've convinced him to accelerate our strategy against Persia and Israel. Tomorrow one of our emissaries will meet with Al-Qahtani in Baghdad, and another will meet with Meir in Jerusalem. The same trade bait will be offered to both—endless supplies of fresh water from the Pontic Mountains. Iraq's rivers and lakes are dry and desolate. Al-Qahtani will be compelled to accept our private offer of unlimited water in return for announcing Iraq's public support of an independent Kurdish state. In front of NATO and the UN, we will announce a gas-for-water treaty with Israel, betraying our promise to Iraq while upholding our concession of land for an independent Kurdistan. The Kurds are relentless . . . they will hound the international community to pressure the Iraqis to uphold their public promise of land. They will never allow Iraq to get off the hook. But we will not open our dams for Iraq or Syria."

Webster was intrigued. This was a double deal like he would concoct. "Betray the Persians . . . once the buffer of an inevitable Kurdistan is rooted in and accepted by the international community," he said. "Al-Qahtani will not be happy."

"Even less happy when Turkish troops swarm into western Syria and annex the province of Assyria back into the Ottoman sphere. But what can he do?" asked Eroglu. "Al-Qahtani still has ISIS swallowing up huge chunks of western Iraq. That's his first priority. But Turkey will have erected a formidable barrier to deter any future Persian aggression. Meanwhile the millions we're getting from Rutherford are being funneled into Iran to support the underground rebellion that is building against Khomeini's dictatorial government. Just enough to throw the country into chaos."

"I've got to get back inside," said Webster, "but I hope your schemes work. We need to show Rutherford some positive results. And we need to do it soon. Don't foul this up, Arslan. We've lost all our margin for error."

Webster could almost feel Eroglu recoil from the rebuke. It brought a smile to his face. Make the bugger squirm.

"Don't worry, Noah. My plans will be implemented. And you will see their results."

There was an edge to Eroglu's voice that suddenly made Webster wary. Was he . . .

"We will both receive our just rewards. Goodbye, Noah."

Webster looked at the satellite phone in his hand, now disconnected. And wondered what he had just been told.

<hr />

US Ambassador's Residence, Tel Aviv
July 21, 9:32 a.m.

It was two thirty Monday morning in Washington, still hours to go before sunrise, and it became very clear the secretary of state was not in a good mood. His personal cell phone rang only once. "I'm up to my eyeballs in alligators here, Atticus," he snapped into the phone. "But you would know that . . . so this must be important. My sleep has already been ruined. Now my gut tells me you've got something that is going to ruin the rest of my day. What's up?"

"We need to speak privately, sir."

There was a pause on the other end. "Is this more about the box that kills and the prophecy of doom?"

"No, sir," said Cleveland. "Mullaney is with me. And this is crucial . . . it hits us right where we live."

Mullaney could hear a long sigh from the other end of the phone call. "All right. I'll call you back in five."

Mullaney was about to ask the ambassador a question about Iran's involvement in Iraq, but in less than a minute Cleveland's personal iPhone rang. It was a FaceTime call.

"I've cleared the room," said Townsend. "You've got my attention."

"I'll make it brief," said Cleveland. "Our enemy has been in front of us every step along the way . . . long before we even knew we had an enemy. Whether it was the embassy attack in Ankara, or the car chase through the streets of Istanbul when I first received the box, or the attack on our convoy on Highway One, or the phone call that tipped off Palmyra's abductors that a rescue attempt was imminent, or the destruction of the Hurva Synagogue less than two hours after the box and the prophecy had been handed over to Jerusalem's Rabbinate Council for deciphering—whomever we are up against knows what we're doing.

"Mr. Secretary, I've been presented with credible evidence that someone in the highest echelons of the State Department has been in contact with the people who are after the box . . . the people who have put all our lives at risk."

Townsend's calm, detached facade cracked. "What a bloody mess." He sat back in his chair and folded his arms across his chest. "And you've got solid proof, don't you Atticus. Or you never would have brought it up."

There was no evidence of triumph in Cleveland's voice or on his face. "I'm afraid I do, Mr. Secretary."

Cleveland ran through the information supplied that morning by Meyer Levinson.

"There's no doubt about the signature address?" asked Townsend.

"Go ahead, Brian," said Cleveland.

"Sir, I was using the very same type of phone when I was in DC that had an almost identical signature address," Mullaney explained. "It's like looking at a car, Sir. I can tell you it's a Ford, but I can't tell you who owns it . . . not until we do some digging. I'm absolutely positive this signature is State Department, used by somebody in the Truman building who was not that far removed from me. Just one thing, Mr. Secretary. We can tell you when the phone was used and where it called. But we can't tell you who made the call. But I'll bet my socks the caller is someone all of us probably know."

For a moment, Townsend appeared to be lost, trying to absorb as real something that could have been his greatest fear: betrayal . . . by someone close. "What do you think, Atticus?"

Cleveland picked up a pencil from the top of his desk and danced the eraser across its surface. Mullaney wondered if he had heard the secretary's question.

He stopped the pencil in midflight and looked up at the screen of his iPhone. "I'm thinking a lot of things these days, Mr. Secretary. I'm not sure you would want to know most of it."

Cleveland took a breath. Mullaney could see he was about to take a leap of faith. "I'm convinced that the same group of murderers—at least those who remain alive—are responsible for my daughter's kidnapping, the Hurva bombing, and the murders following the Gaon's box. And whoever is directing their attacks is being fed information that only a few people know—very few inside the State Department itself. So what do I think? I think I don't know who to trust, Evan. And I believe you should think that way, too."

United States Secretary of State Evan Townsend sat in the early morning quiet of his private office in Washington, DC, his lips pressed together, his head nodding slowly as if he was agreeing with an interior monologue. Mullaney watched the iPhone screen and his heart ached in tandem with the grief the secretary must be wrestling with. One of his own . . . one of his closest . . . was a traitor, an accomplice to attempted murder. Who could he trust?

The words came before Townsend lifted his head. "Gang of Four, Atticus."

"Sir?"

Mullaney felt a shiver in his spine when the secretary looked once again into the lens of the iPhone. There was a deadly resolve on the countenance of Evan Townsend, the look of a gladiator about to enter the ring in the Colosseum . . . the look of a gunfighter stepping out into a dusty street . . . the look of a warrior who was determined to survive and destroy his enemy in the process. Evan Townsend was ready for a fight. Someone was going to be bloodied at the end of this.

"We keep a close circle, Atticus. A gang of four. You and me, Mullaney, and Ruth Hughes. I want Hughes in on this as well. I trust her and she's got the best contacts of any of us. We keep this to ourselves, and we find out who's responsible. That's it . . . Gang of Four. Not even your daughter, Atticus. Nor your wife, Mullaney. Ask Shin Bet to keep the circle tight as well. We keep this close until we can squash this traitor like a bug."

As if infused with a renewed life force, Townsend's body became more erect, his voice firmer, his tone more determined. "Mullaney, I want you to work with Shin Bet and track down everything you can discover about these calls. We need to know whatever we can about who was on this end. Atticus, I need you to do what you don't want to do . . . you need to pursue the policies of this administration, the directives of our president. And right now, that is to get the Ishmael Covenant ratified, including an independent Palestinian state. That needs to be your public posture and purpose. Anything else puts you and your staff in danger. Agreed?"

"Yes, sir, I understand," said Cleveland. "And I'll do my best to be successful."

"Thank you, Atticus. It's your character that infuses your loyalty . . . I knew I could count on you. In the meantime, I want you to unleash Ruth Hughes to scour every back channel and shadowed source at her disposal. Find out if there is any ripple of double-dealing coming from any quarter of the State Department. Often those looking in from the outside have a better view of a room than those sitting in its comfort."

Townsend looked at his watch, then back at the screen. "Gentlemen, there are seventy thousand people working for the US State Department," said Townsend. "And at least one of them is a traitor. Find him."

19

Cleveland got up, crossed the office, and walked behind his desk. Leaning over, he pressed a button on the phone console. "Jeffrey, could you please find Ruth Hughes and see if she is available to join us here at the residence. Or the embassy later, if necessary. Yes . . . we'll be leaving soon. Perhaps thirty minutes. Thank you."

He stood behind the desk, his hand on the phone, his eyes out the west-facing window behind his desk. Beyond the park-like expanse of lawn, the vast, blue, liquid carpet of the Mediterranean stretched unblemished to the horizon. It appeared to Mullaney that Cleveland was searching for something beyond the horizon. He lifted his right hand from the phone and rubbed it across the top of his bald head. When he spoke, his voice was as far off as the distant sea. "Who's on first?"

"Sir?"

Cleveland turned back to the room and almost seemed surprised that Mullaney was still seated over in the corner. "'Who's on first? What's on second? I don't know's on third.' It's an old Abbott and Costello routine . . . they were vaudeville comics who made a bunch of movies in the fifties. It was a baseball routine . . . pretty funny when they did it right. And I was just standing here thinking, Who's on first? What in the world is going on around us, and what do we deal with first?" He came from around his desk and walked toward the battered brown leather sofa in the far corner of his office. "It seems we have a lot to talk about."

<hr/>

They were back in the same place—Mullaney was sitting in an armchair, waiting for the coffee mug in his hands to cool, across the low table from the ambassador, who was nestled into a corner of the leather sofa—now wrestling with an additional set of concerns.

"I can appreciate the secretary's shock," said Cleveland, "but I'm troubled that we don't miss the important because we're paying attention to the urgent. The Ishmael Covenant is only a day old and already Meir's coalition government is beginning to crack, some Palestinians are rioting in Gaza, and others are dancing in Nablus. Now there is a military coup in Iraq, probably supported and guided by Iran, that has all the earmarks of a resurrected Persian Empire. Which will only spook the Saudis even more.

"For any normal day, that would be enough. But we also have a determined and vicious gang of murderers who will stop at nothing to get their hands on that bloody box in the embassy's basement vault, which leaves all of us—including Palmyra—constantly at risk. And the box, or its message, may have some bearing or impact on all that is playing out on the Middle East's geopolitical map. And now Evan wants us to track down a traitor in the State Department."

Cleveland turned his body in the corner of the sofa to look directly at Mullaney.

"I know we just received clear direction from the secretary of state . . . and we will follow that direction and obey his orders." He balanced his elbows on his knees, clasped his hands beneath his chin, and glared at Mullaney. "But is that the right thing for us to be doing now? Is trying to track down a traitor where we should be investing our time and energy?"

Mullaney waited, but Cleveland allowed his question to hang in the air between them. "Mr. Ambassador, I think the answer to that question is way beyond my pay grade."

———— ⋙⋘ ————

Mullaney and the ambassador were reviewing dispatches with details about the Iraqi coup when Cleveland's personal iPhone signaled a text message.

"That's unusual."

"Sir?"

"Webster wants me to call him 'without delay.'" There was an annoyed emphasis on the last two words. "This is not like Webster. He is a man who likes to remind people of his power and position. He usually has one of his assistants call or email me to set up a time for us to get on the phone. And he's not a man who easily breaks from his routine. Something is up—something with Webster personally or he wouldn't be contacting me this way himself."

Cleveland sat up straight, pulling away from the low table upon which were spread satellite photos of the armed militia positions blockading the entry gates to Baghdad's Green Zone. "I don't like the smell test on this one," said Cleveland. "Brian," he nodded toward the extension receiver beside the leather sofa, "please pick up the extension before I make this call. I'd be very interested for you to tell me what you hear in Webster's voice, his tone . . . what you think is behind the words he uses."

Mullaney moved to the sofa and lifted the receiver while Cleveland went behind his desk, settled himself in his chair, picked up his office phone from the console, and punched in the speed dial for Webster's office in the State Department.

"That took a while," snapped Webster as he answered the call. There was an unmistakably nasty edge to Webster's voice that put Mullaney immediately on edge and on alert. "When I tell you to call—"

"Good morning, Noah," Cleveland's interruption was silken, attempting to apply a healing balm to Webster's cutting arrogance. "I know it's very early, and I'm sure you are very busy sorting out the coup in Iraq. But it's thoughtful of you to reach out to us at such a critical moment." Cleveland glanced up and shared with Mullaney a wink and a shrug of the shoulders. "I appreciate your concern."

Mullaney held the receiver to his ear, the mouthpiece lifted above his forehead so even his breathing wouldn't be heard. There was a momentary, frosty silence on the other end.

"Just as I should be concerned," Webster countered. "I've heard nothing from you for more than twenty-four hours—nothing on the bombing at the Hurva, nothing on the status of the covenant, nothing on the search for the terrorists who have pursued you since Istanbul . . . or even *why* you are being pursued. It's your job to keep me informed, and you're not doing a very good job of it, regardless of the circumstances."

Mullaney watched Cleveland for a reaction to Webster's tone, but the ambassador simply leaned back in his chair and closed his eyes.

"Forgive me, Noah, I apologize for not keeping you informed. We appear to be moving so swiftly from one crisis to another that there is barely time to breathe."

"Crisis—yes—that's all you've seemed to accomplish since you arrived in

Israel," Webster snarled. The sarcasm in his voice was as thick as false flattery at an embassy soiree. "And you don't appear to be paying any attention to your mission. What is the status on moving Meir's government to ratify the covenant?"

Cleveland shook his head. "Prime Minister Meir has not scheduled a vote on the covenant in the Knesset. I think he knows he would lose. He's been very busy trying to drum up support. And he's got armed conflict on two of his borders, so—"

"I don't care about Meir's problems," Webster snapped. "I care about getting the covenant ratified and getting a Palestinian state established. That is our president's direction and our nation's policy. And our job—your job, Atticus—is to see that direction and policy fulfilled. And you apparently haven't made any progress on any of those fronts. Just what *are* you spending your time on, Atticus?"

Whoa, what a land mine, thought Mullaney. It was an "are you still beating your wife?" question . . . guilty no matter how you answered. Mullaney held his breath and hoped.

"There are no American fatalities as a result of the Hurva explosion," Cleveland said with a grace that Mullaney would have been hard-pressed to match, "and only two minor injuries. We have embassy staff constantly with each of the victims and their families. RSO Mullaney and his agents have been superb, working closely and actively with Shin Bet. And I'm scheduled to have a phone conversation with the prime minister in"—he looked at his watch—"in two hours. After that I'm having dinner with an old friend, Menachem Herzl, leader of the ultra-orthodox party, Shas. Shas is the glue that is holding Meir's coalition government together and Meir's biggest hurdle to getting the covenant ratified. We'll see what Herzl would like to receive in return for his party's support of the covenant. And then tomorrow morning I'm hosting a breakfast here at the residence for a half dozen members of the Knesset who are the most crucial members . . . if and when the covenant comes up for a vote. I will definitely call you as soon as that dinner with Herzl concludes, if that is your wish."

Mullaney was impressed, but not surprised. No wonder Joseph Cleveland was so highly regarded in the department. He was smooth and cool.

Cleveland was writing something on a paper on his desk. He held it out to

Mullaney, who rested the receiver on the sofa and quick-stepped to the desk. Grabbing the paper from Cleveland, Mullaney was back in position on the sofa, the receiver in one hand and the note in the other, as both he and the ambassador waited for Webster's response. Mullaney was surprised by what was written on the note. *Please have Jeffrey invite Menacham Herzl to join me for dinner tonight, and I'll call Meir myself and get on his calendar.*

"Is there anything else, Noah?"

Cleveland may have been trying to keep a note of triumph out of his voice, but it was pretty unmistakable to Mullaney.

"Yes, Cleveland . . . one minor issue," said Webster. The malice that traveled through the phone was palpable. "No one is untouchable. Do you understand me? Regardless of your tenure and in spite of your friends, if you don't follow my orders and immediately provide some positive results, I'll call in every favor in my black book if necessary, and I will cut you off at the knees and pull you back to the States in disgrace. You know I can do it. I don't have to find or create an excuse. And, if I do it, no one is going to be able to cry discrimination or racism. So I've trumped your last ace. Understand? Get in line, Cleveland . . . or get out of the way."

He was waiting for Cleveland to rip out Webster's black heart. But Mullaney saw no movement from Cleveland . . . only a grimace on his face . . . when he heard the crack of a slammed phone in his ear. He sat motionless, watching. Mullaney realized his mouth was open, primed for protest, but his mind was in shock—both at Webster's brutal rebuke and blatant threat, but also with the ambassador's placid submission.

Silence as fragile as cracked ribs settled on Cleveland's office. Mullaney was afraid to touch what he had just heard, concerned that any contact would just make the pain more intense.

Cleveland opened his eyes and slowly replaced the phone receiver. "Well," he said, "that could have gone better."

Mullaney was on his feet, took two steps toward Cleveland's desk before the cord snapped taught and the phone console pounded to the floor. He dropped the receiver at his feet. "That was more than disrespectful and uncalled for," he said, anger and embarrassment fueling his response. "It was downright illegal.

Webster can get fired for threatening your career like that. And pulling out the race card like that? You've got every—"

"Just Noah being Noah," said Cleveland. His voice tried to take on a mellow tone, but Mullaney saw the torture cutting deep crevices across the ambassador's normally placid features.

"What does Webster know?" asked Mullaney. The change was subtle—a slight upward movement of his head, stalled in midflight—and Mullaney knew his guess was accurate. But he still didn't know why.

"What do you mean?"

Mullaney took a seat in one of the two, straight-backed chairs facing Cleveland.

"I haven't been with you long, sir, but I think I have a pretty good line on who you are—a man of character and integrity," said Mullaney, the softness of his voice communicating the empathy in his heart. "And I have a very personal knowledge and understanding of how it feels to be railroaded—particularly by someone you don't respect—for something you haven't done."

He leaned in closer, resting his right hand on the front edge of the desk. "I don't care if he is the deputy secretary of state—and our boss—Webster just asked you to do something you know is a mistake, and you gave in to him without an argument. I don't know what he's holding over you, sir, but you looked like somebody was delivering a death threat on your daughter."

Cleveland broke eye contact with Mullaney and absently pushed a pen across the top of his desk. "I don't know what you're talking about," he said, not lifting his eyes. "The deputy secretary has given me a task to accomplish. Not the first time . . . not the last."

Pushing himself back into the chair, Mullaney took stock of Cleveland and his reactions. Something was terribly wrong, that was clear.

"This is not like you, Mr. Ambassador. Nobody pulls your strings. Sure, you're a good soldier and you are a man under orders—just like me. But this is different. I'm concerned, Mr. Ambassador. How can I help?"

In a gesture of futility, Cleveland raised his empty hand from the desktop, but not his eyes. "There's nothing you can do, Agent Mullaney. I do appreciate your concern. But there is nothing to be done—except follow orders and do what I've been asked to do." He looked up. "This goes back a long way, son. There's nothing either one of us can do about changing the past.

And sometimes your past dictates your future. At least where Mr. Webster is concerned."

Mullaney hesitated a moment, unsure just how far to push. But who else did Ambassador Cleveland have to talk to? So he jumped.

"Atticus . . . I can see you're grieving about something. You can tell me to shut up and mind my own business. But I want to help, if I can."

<hr>

Truman Building, Washington, DC
July 21, 3:48 a.m.

Noah Webster replaced the handset of his telephone, satisfied that his threats would keep Cleveland under his control. As he did, his eyes fell upon the printout of the report that was sitting on the top of his desk. The report was only six pages long. He opened it to the last page and looked once again at the paragraph that had given him pause.

How to best use this advantage for maximum leverage? There were so many possibilities. Drive a wedge between Cleveland and Mullaney, who appeared to have bonded as brothers in just a few days? Score points with Richard Rutherford?

"This is not a good idea, Noah. You're going to leave a trail."

Webster glanced up from the report. Nora Carson sat across from his slightly elevated desk—the vanity of a short man with dreams of grandeur—a grimace of anxiety etched in the creases around the outside of her eyes. He had ordered Carson to bring him Cleveland's situation report. At first she had refused—something he would have to deal with later—enumerating the risks he was asking her to take.

Undersecretary for management of the US State Department and Webster's chief of staff, Carson had proven in the past to be a valuable and reliable asset, an equally ambitious member of the department with her eyes fixed on further advancement. But recently Webster had sensed a disturbing level of doubt . . . hesitance . . . in Carson. Disloyalty? He needed to watch Carson closely. So much was at stake.

"How else am I to know what is on Cleveland's mind if I don't read his situation report?" he asked, a satisfied smirk animating his face. "He does report to me, after all."

Carson shook her head. She pushed away a loose thread of red hair as it fell across her brow and held steady under Webster's gaze. "Read it, yes," said Carson. "You could read it on your computer. But you're thinking about more than reading the report, aren't you?"

The last page of the report held only one paragraph, an ambassadorial request—a seldom denied format—from Cleveland, appealing for Brian Mullaney's immediate transfer back to Washington because of pressing family concerns. If he allowed the request to reach the secretary's desk, Webster would lose any leverage he was holding against Richard Rutherford, who—under pressure from his daughter—was also lobbying for his son-in-law's rapid return to the States.

"You're afraid he knows about the HR intern, aren't you?"

The grimace hit his face before he could stop its arrival. Now Carson probably knew she'd hit home. The HR intern. That big idea was proving to be a mistake. He thought he had slapped a lid on it. But now he wasn't so sure. And Carson had warned him.

"I warned you it was a bad idea . . . just like this one."

About a year after he took his position in the State Department, Webster saw an opportunity to gain advantage. He read an internal notice that State was looking for interns to serve in various capacities and departments. Human Resources was one. There was a young woman he met in Markham's office who had doggedly pursued him for months, looking for both political favor and physical intimacy. Favor he would dispense. He got her assigned to the intern's position in Human Resources while secretly paying her an exorbitant salary from his own pocket. Her assignment from Webster was clear: troll the personnel files of State Department employees and look for dirt that Webster could use to his advantage.

For six months it worked like a charm. Webster's heavily encrypted secret records were brimming with convicting tidbits of information that could threaten an otherwise stable career of State Department employees from attaché to ambassador. He even had his intern peruse Mullaney's personnel file on the off chance he might find something to use against Richard Rutherford. No one would ever get the drop on him without paying for their attack.

Many of the senior staff at State had dual titles and responsibilities. Something Webster had overlooked. George Morningstar, who was deputy assistant secretary for diplomatic security, also held the title of assistant director for threat investigations and analysis, responsible to investigate threats directed against US diplomatic personnel overseas and domestically. The department's IT security picked up on unusual patterns of activity, hints but nothing solid of possible system breaches to personnel records.

Morningstar assigned his adjutant, Brian Mullaney, a former Virginia State Police investigator, to look into the concerns.

Webster was furious but quick on his feet. He arranged a meeting with the woman he had inserted in the HR department. She suggested meeting near her home at the Airedale Pub, a Columbia Heights place she said was just a neighborhood sports bar. In an empty back room, Webster threatened to have the woman sentenced to federal prison for the rest of her life if she ever spoke a word. He left her with an envelope stuffed with cash—large bills—and a round-trip airline ticket to Cape Town, South Africa. He told her to stay there for a month—he would cover the expense—and he would be in touch.

As the woman rose to leave, Webster noticed two men walk past the alcove. One was Brian Mullaney. Mullaney was talking to another man who looked like former Israeli general Moshe Dayan. They didn't seem to notice Webster. But who could be sure?

"Whatever happened to that woman?"

"I don't know," Webster lied. He knew she never made it to Cape Town. And he also knew it would be impossible for any investigation to ever find her.

"Convenient, that attack on the Ankara embassy," said Carson. "Gave you the opportunity to get Mullaney out of the country, send Morningstar into the basement, and put an end to that records investigation." Carson was enjoying this too much. Time to make her sweat a little.

He held up Cleveland's situation report. "We're not here to discuss the past. We're here to protect the present."

Carson shook her head dismissively. "If you change anything, there will be a record in the system."

"I'm not going to change anything, Nora," said Webster.

He reached into a side drawer of his desk and pulled out a sharp-tipped felt marker. Sometimes, he thought, a little theater helped drive home a point. With a flourish, Webster swiped the marker across the words printed on the last page. He put the cap on the marker and tossed it back into the drawer. Then he picked up the report and held it out toward Carson.

"You are."

Carson glared at Webster, her cheeks almost as red as her hair. "You're asking me to commit professional suicide, Noah. Why would you do that? Why would I do something as foolhardy as altering an ambassador's situation report?"

Fair questions, both of them. And an accurate assessment. He was asking Carson not only to stick her neck out, but to lay it across the path of the guillotine. He needed to convince her the risk was safe . . . because that's where he wanted her neck, at the edge of a blade.

"Two reasons," said Webster, who still held the report in his right hand. "First, your mole in Ciphers can manipulate the electronic date stamps on the report as easily as he ran off this copy. Second, you have me watching your back to make sure no one even goes looking at the history of Cleveland's report. Bottom line? I don't want Mullaney back here in Washington. He's too much of a risk . . . more of a risk than you altering Cleveland's report to omit that request."

He shook the report in her direction. "So get to it, Nora. Remember—we're in this together," said Webster, the words more of a warning than an assurance, "and we're in this too far to stop now."

20

David Meir entered the quiet of his personal office a shaken man. In his wake came his closest allies—Benjamin Erdad, Israel's minister of internal security, and Moshe Litzman, minister of the interior. From the looks on their faces, they could have been returning from a funeral. Meir thought perhaps they had.

His coalition government was in a shambles . . . no, a crisis. Right now, it was a long shot whether his fragile coalition government would survive the month. Or a week.

Israeli politics and the governing structure of the country were perilous from the outset. More than thirty active political parties vied for seats in the 120-member Knesset in any given election, which made it nearly impossible for any one party to gain a clear majority of seats. Thus Israeli governance usually required the party that had gained the most seats to cobble together a coalition of other parties—often an ill-tasting stew of mismatched ingredients—in order to establish a functioning majority.

Coalition building and coalition killing were both actively pursued by Knesset members.

The elections were not determined by a prescribed amount of time, as every four years in the United States. Elections in Israel were held when the government in power, represented by the prime minister, called for a new election (usually when the prime minister's party was in a powerful or popular position), or when a "no confidence" vote was taken, proving that the government in power no longer had the support of a majority.

There were currently twelve active political parties represented in the Knesset, many of them small in number and insignificant as far as power. Meir's Likud party, a popular center-right party, held the largest number of seats, thirty-two. Next in line was the left-wing Labor Party, Likud's most fervent adversary . . . and no candidate for coalition building. So Meir was forced to reach into the splinter, issue-based parties to find enough seats for his coalition. The two that he was most reliant on, and most indebted to, were the ultra-right-wing Jewish Home party, who were relentless evangelists for expanded Israeli settlements in the West Bank, and the ultra-orthodox religious Jews of the Shas party—power brokers through the rise and fall of many Israeli governments.

And Meir found himself in a strangely ironic dilemma.

Meir, Erdad, and Litzman sat in the prime minister's small office off the Knesset floor, following a meeting of the Israeli cabinet to discuss the potential ratification of the Ishmael Covenant. The meeting was a street brawl.

Both Jewish Home and Shas had launched vicious opposition to the Ishmael Covenant, the peace treaty and mutual defense pact between Israel and its Arab neighbors—Jordan, Egypt, Saudi Arabia, and the smaller Arab states along the Persian Gulf. Jewish Home was up in arms that the covenant would establish an independent Palestinian state that would require the resettlement of thousands of Israeli families who now occupied contested settlements in the West Bank. And Shas was just as incensed that the covenant provided for the construction of a temple—the third temple of God—but not on Temple Mount, where the first and second temples were built. Instead it would be built on a platform that was to be constructed over the Kidron Valley and connected to Temple Mount at the East Gate.

In a plot twist unique to Israeli government, the Labor Party supported the covenant wholeheartedly. But could Meir get into bed with those beasts?

Adding to Meir's woes was a street uprising in Gaza that was gaining steam and collecting victims, and a flurry of rocket attacks from the Hezbollah launchers in Lebanon that targeted northern Israel. Meir was taking a beating.

"I don't see how we can align ourselves with Labor," said Erdad. The fifty-four-year-old former career military officer was sitting ramrod straight in a leather armchair facing Meir's desk. "They will suck every conceivable concession out of us to improve their position, and then they'll drop us into another no-confidence vote once they get everything they're after."

Litzman was sunk as low in his armchair as his spirits. "Shas and Jewish Home will never support the covenant," he mumbled, "and there are not enough seats remaining—even if we could convince every other party—to give us a majority. The choices are simple. We repudiate the covenant, which makes no sense since we just signed it yesterday; we join forces with Labor;

or we call for a new election—or the Knesset calls one for us. I see no wiggle room. And if we want the covenant ratified, only one of those options achieves that goal."

David Meir heard the arguments of his lieutenants. He still heard the echoes of the raised voices and unveiled threats that reverberated off the walls of the cabinet room. And he thought of the covenant, which provided Israel with concessions it had fought for in vain since its inception: unconditional recognition of the State of Israel without a demand to return to the pre-1967 boundaries, the guaranteed safety of Israel's borders, and Jerusalem—intact and under Israel's dominion—in return for a Palestinian state and the abandonment of dozens of contentious Israeli settlements.

After all this time and enmity, Saudi Arabia's fear of the growing militancy, power, and nuclear threat emanating from Iran—and perhaps the need for a united stand against ISIS—had forced a pragmatic friendship between the Arab states and Israel.

Israel had what it had longed for since 1949. Not only a homeland, but a secure homeland for all Jews.

And now Meir felt like it was all slipping through his fingers.

Meir picked up the brass bullet casing that sat on the front of his desk, right in the middle where he could see it every day. It was a bullet like this one that had killed Meir's father during the Six-Day War. He kept it in front of him as a reminder of the price that had been paid in the past—many times over—to keep Israel safe and free. He turned the casing around and looked at the firing pin mark on its base. Not this bullet, certainly . . . but one like it . . .

"It's not about us," he said softly, the casing twirling in his fingers. "It's not about Likud. It's about Israel. About what is best for Israel. The Hashemites of Jordan and the Family Saud have created a new reality by signing this covenant, a reality that will be nearly impossible to undo. A reality that heralds a brighter, better future for Israel."

"Don't forget about the nuclear weapons that King Abdullah has ordered from Pakistan," said Litzman. "We have to think of that new reality also."

Erdad shifted in his chair, facing Litzman. "That issue will be resolved tonight," he said. "The weapons will never reach the Saudis."

David Meir, prime minister of Israel, rested the bullet casing on the top of his desk.

"Benjamin," Meir said, looking up at his two Likud comrades, "please go visit with Naaman, discreetly. Ask him if Labor is truly ready to join Likud in forming a government. Allow him to tell you what it will cost."

21

Still in his battle fatigues, Al-Qahtani stepped out of the armored personnel carrier. A swift tour of the city had confirmed his confidence that his militia was in control of Baghdad and that the citizens of Baghdad were, for the most part, celebrating his takeover of the government. Reports from around the country recorded the same outpouring of joy and relief . . . except for the few remaining enclaves of Sunni Iraqis, now once again displaced from power. He found his aide waiting on the steps of the Badr Brigade's command center.

"You have visitors."

"Not surprising."

"Well . . . yes and no. The American general is waiting in your office. He is not very pleasant."

"Fool," spat Al-Qahtani as he took the steps two at a time. "He'll lose his command for this. An occupation force can never relax."

"He seems to be fully aware of his predicament. But you have a more interesting visitor."

Al-Qahtani stopped, one foot on the top step, and turned to his side. "Yes?"

"The Turkish ambassador to the Republic of Iraq arrived about twenty minutes ago requesting an audience."

Unexpected. "The Turks? What could they want?" asked Al-Qahtani.

"What do the Turks ever want?" The aide handed Al-Qahtani a blue file. It was marked "Turkey" and bore the seal of the previous prime minister. "Power, as always. He asked that his visit remain a secret. So I put him in the deputy's lounge and waited for your return rather than using the radio or the phone. The Americans are probably monitoring every electronic transmission."

Al-Qahtani opened the file as he stood on the steps and started flipping through the pages.

"Who would you like to see first?"

He closed the file and tucked it under his arm. "Let the American stew in his own self-pity," said Al-Qahtani. "Their days in our country are at an end.

I want to see what the Turks have on their minds. This should be much more interesting."

⸻◦◦◦⸻

Knesset Building, Jerusalem
July 21, 1:43 p.m.

Still smarting from the personal virulence of the arguments and accusations launched in the midst of his cabinet meeting—and the humbling decision to pursue a coalition government with the Labor Party—David Meir, prime minister of Israel, tried to cloak himself with the patina of dignity as he walked from his office toward the secure, underground garage of the Knesset. His aide was standing out of the way, to the side of the corridor, on the near side of the security checkpoints. Normally unflappable, his aide was bouncing on the balls of his feet, unable to contain his excitement.

Meir stepped away from his security detail to the side of the corridor. "Yes?"

"You have visitors," said Meir's aide.

"Not surprising. Who is it this time who has come to tell us we have betrayed the trust of all Israel?"

"Well, yes . . . you have that," said his aide. "Three members of the Jewish Home party chased me down, bellowing that you sold out every settler in the West Bank and demanding a meeting. They are cooling off in the small meeting room. But sir, there is another . . ."

"Yes?"

"The deputy prime minister of Turkey, Alexander Hursit. His head of security called from the street while they sat in their limo. He wants a private audience . . . secret, he said. I didn't know what to do with him." Meir's aide shrugged his shoulders and had a sheepish smile on his face. "He's in the janitor's break room. He didn't seem the least bit insulted."

Meir looked over at the elevator doors leading to his office level, then cast a glance at the corridor to his right, leading to the maintenance area. "The Turks must be awfully worried about this covenant. Probably desperate for a few friends in this rapidly changing world."

The aide handed Meir a thick manila file folder. "Notes on all of our recent conversations and negotiations with the Turks . . . Mavi Marmara; the pipeline . . . a little bit of everything. Just in case."

Meir took the outstretched file and smiled at his good fortune to be served so well. "Thank you. We know what we will hear from Jewish Home. Let us go discover what we will hear from Minister Hursit. This should be interesting."

— ⊰∘◦∘⊱ —

Parliament Building, Baghdad
July 21, 1:51 p.m.

Immediate revulsion squirmed up Al-Qahtani's back and over his shoulders as the ambassador of Turkey wrestled to move his immense bulk out of the armchair.

"Commander, may I present Ozlem Gokay, ambassador from the Republic of Turkey," said Al-Qahtani's aide. "I'll leave you now."

The revulsion became palpable as the soft, sweaty, fleshy folds of the ambassador's hand fumbled with and violated Al-Qahtani's military handshake.

"Mr. Prime Minister, it is indeed an honor," said the ambassador, bowing his bald head as bullets of sweat ricocheted off the floor tiles.

"Commander," snapped Al-Qahtani. "I have no need of political titles."

A smile that would pollute a garbage dump spread across Gokay's massive jowls. "Commander, then." He bowed. "I bring you the recognition and congratulations of the Republic of Turkey, the personal best wishes of President Kashani, and an offer of assistance in whatever way Turkey can help this popular, new government of Iraq."

Rubbing his now damp palm along the seam of his fatigue pants, Al-Qahtani forced himself to regain control. Everything about this smarmy man generated disgust. But growing inside of Al-Qahtani was an even greater sense of distrust. He needed to be alert and on guard around this man and listen carefully to what he said and how he said it. He was a diplomat, and diplomats the world over spoke a fuzzy language of inference and obfuscation.

"Thank you, Mr. Ambassador." He led Gokay to a pair of facing armchairs. "And please convey the thanks of the Iraqi people to President Kashani and his government." Al-Qahtani considered his next words carefully as he sat and waited for the ambassador to navigate his corpulence into the armchair. "I'm surprised, but grateful, for the swiftness of Turkey's recognition of our new government. How can I be of assistance to your government?"

"Oh, esteemed commander," gushed Gokay, an insincere smirk defiling his face, "it is the wish of the Turkish people to be of assistance to their brothers in Iraq. I come under direct orders of Prime Minister Eroglu. 'Ozlem,' he said to me, 'I have for you the most critical of assignments.' I have a message for your ears only."

Al-Qahtani waited, but Gokay sat folded into his chair, his bald head nodding as rivulets of sweat flowed into and around his ears. Al-Qahtani was being invited to take the bait. He knew a barbed hook awaited. So he refused to bite. Gokay's smile slowly faded. His eyes grew harder.

"Commander," he said with an exasperated sigh, "I come today to offer you all of the resources of the Republic of Turkey to help you rebuild and restore your nation. *All* of our resources, Commander."

Al-Qahtani looked into the polluted eyes of Gokay and knew he was bargaining with evil intent. *And what will this cost?*

Knesset Building, Jerusalem
July 21, 1:51 p.m.

Alexander Hursit was on his feet at the first crack in the door to the janitor's break room. Tall, regal, impeccable, the deputy prime minister of Turkey, a former investment banker, commanded respect not only by his presence, but also by his hard-earned reputation as a tough but fair negotiator. Meir and Hursit had squared off many times over issues critical to both their governments.

"Good afternoon, Alex," said Meir, stretching out a welcoming hand, "what a pleasant surprise. I'm sorry the surroundings"—Meir's eyes swept the cramped, musty room decorated with mops and brooms—"are a bit humble. But, why such secrecy?"

"An unfortunate necessity," said Hursit. "May we talk in private?"

"Of course," said Meir. He looked up at his aide who was already slipping out the door, then turned back to his guest. "Please, sit. What brings you here today?"

"Pragmatic politics, David. The best kind," said Hursit. They sat on mismatched metal chairs with cracked leather seats, between them a scuffed and dented metal table stacked on one corner with rolls of cleaning rags. "Your Ishmael Covenant has stirred up considerable anxiety in Ankara. The controlling axis of the Middle East just shifted overnight. So President Kashani and

Prime Minister Eroglu are suddenly feeling a bit isolated. And with the Russian bear flexing its muscles again . . . well . . . they dispatched me personally with a message for your ears only."

The man's eyes were clear, his words firm and unequivocal, his intentions honorable. Still, David Meir was a veteran of many backroom discussions. One thought took root in his mind. *And what will this cost?*

———✦———

Parliament Building, Baghdad
July 21, 2:03 p.m.

The warrior was more deeply engraved in Al-Qahtani's character than the diplomat. The warrior wanted to wrap his hands around Gokay's throat, rid the world of this vile creature, and throw his body onto an ash heap. He held that instinct in check.

"Thank you for your offer to my country." Al-Qahtani forced his words to be civil. "What are these resources you offer?"

Waggling his bulk, Gokay pushed himself to the edge of his chair.

"Western Iraq is starving for water. We—"

"We have you to thank for that," Al-Qahtani snapped. "It's your government that shut down the flow of water into the Euphrates River."

His eyes only half visible under the fleshy folds of his heavy lids, Gokay reacted to Al-Qahtani's words as if they were a slap to the face. "An unfortunate response to the enmity of Iraq's former government toward the people of Turkey, I can assure you," he said, his voice dripping with feigned offense. "But with the brave soldiers of the Badr Brigades restoring order to your nation . . . well . . . we wish to help our brothers."

Gokay appeared to be waiting for an apology. But Al-Qahtani remained silent.

"Very well," said Gokay, putting words to his pout. "Turkey will open the gates of its dams, restoring the flow of life-giving water to both the Euphrates and the Tigris. The farmers and shepherds of Syria and Iraq will be indebted to the leadership of Al-Qahtani for rescuing their lives and their livelihoods. From Kobane to Qa'im to Ramadi, from Mosul to Baghdad to Basra, lakes will be restored and life will return to the great rivers that water the land of Syria and Iraq."

Nothing, not even his audacious overthrow of the Iraqi government, Al-Qahtani admitted to himself, would have as powerful an effect on the lives of his countrymen than the restoration of fresh water to his nation. But . . .

"In addition, Commander," Gokay continued, "President Kashani has empowered me to offer Iraq the full support of the Turkish military, including our ground troops and armored divisions, in a coordinated offensive that will drive ISIS from both Syria and Iraq and destroy this cancer once and for all time."

An interesting opening gambit. The Turks were offering much. They must desire much. "In return for . . . ?" asked Al-Qahtani.

"Ah, Commander, and here I am most proud," said Gokay, trying valiantly to sit up straight. "The Kurdish people are the most populous ethnic group in the world without their own sovereign nation. President Kashani invites you to join with Turkey in ceding territory for an independent Kurdish state. Let us put right a terrible wrong."

Knesset Building, Jerusalem
July 21, 2:03 p.m.

"And what is this message you bring me today?" Meir asked.

"Don't believe everything you hear." Hursit leaned into the table and rested on its edge. "David, Turkey and Israel have been negotiating this pipeline treaty for more than ten years. You know my country has been Israel's friend since the early days of its independence, and we are still your friends today."

"Your country, yes," said Meir. "Kashani, I'm not too sure. He's been courting the jihadists for some time now."

"Posturing," said Hursit, shaking his head. "And you will see more of it in the next few days. Ignore what comes out of Baghdad. The future of Turkey lies in the West, in NATO, and in the European Union. With the covenant, this part of the world is now picking sides. Our side is with you, with the West. And we are going to make that clear when you and I sign that pipeline treaty."

Hursit sat up straight. "At this moment, David, a Turkish emissary is meeting with Samir Al-Qahtani. He is offering this new government of Iraq an alliance . . . unlimited fresh water to resurrect the Euphrates River and restore life to western Iraq along with Turkish troops and military support to crush ISIS.

In return, both Iraq and Turkey will provide land for a Kurdish Free State. Be assured, sir, that this agreement—like your Ishmael Covenant—will never be ratified. The Persians are as much our enemies as yours. We want their promise for a Kurdish state on the record, so the Kurds have a basis for pressuring the international community, the UN, for a state. And a Kurdish state to the east of Turkey would be a bulwark against the Persians. We plan to make that Kurdish state a reality, without giving up our water."

Leaning in, toward Meir, to signal his earnestness, Hursit opened his hands in front of him. "There are more than seventy major lakes and reservoirs—vast reserves of fresh water—in the Pontic and Taurus Mountains of Turkey. Israel needs fresh water. Turkey needs your natural gas. All the engineering and preparation for the pipeline are in place. It's time. The water is yours. We simply need to sign the treaty.

"Privately, Kashani and Eroglu are committed to sabotaging any rapprochement between Iraq and Iran. We must keep Iraq, Iran, and Syria as unstable as possible while we forge a new alliance of the West against this nascent Persian Empire."

Hursit stretched, then stood to his feet. "Your Ishmael Covenant is a remarkable piece of paper, David. But you and I both know that is all it will ever be . . . a piece of paper. You can't even get agreement in your cabinet, let alone the Knesset. So no, Israel will not sign a military alliance with the Arabs, which will leave you isolated once more, facing even more powerful enemies. You need an ally. So do we. Stand with us, David. Together, as the first line of defense for the West, we might even survive."

<hr />

Parliament Building, Baghdad
July 21, 2:17 p.m.

"It could take a lifetime for a promise to the Kurds to actually turn into a viable nation. That's a long time to wait for water."

"If Turkey, Iraq, and the Kurdistan Regional Government sign an agreement in principal to pursue a true, independent Kurdish nation, our government will see that as a good faith gesture on the part of Iraq, and the water will begin to flow."

Al-Qahtani's mind was spinning with calculations. "The Kurds claim a significant amount of territory as their own," he said. "Giving up land . . . you ask a great deal."

Since the fall of Saddam Hussein in 1993, a coalition of Kurdish politicians and militia leaders had claimed the creation of a Kurdish region in Iraq and, in the midst of chaos emerging from the US invasion of Iraq, began overseeing large swaths of territory claimed by Kurdish nationals. When Iraq's constitution was rewritten in 2005, that self-declared Kurdish enclave became an officially established region of Iraq, and the Kurdistan Regional Government was recognized by Iraq.

But the thirty million people of Kurdish descent were not only sprawled over the northern mountains of Iraq and Syria, but also into eastern Turkey, where those mountains extended. What the Turks were proposing was the annexation of land from all three countries—Iraq, Syria, and Turkey—to form an independent nation.

"Some inhabitable mountains in the north," Gokay dismissed, waving a portly hand. "In return, we put an end to the incessant Kurdish insurgencies against both our nations. And my good Commander, if it's territory that concerns you . . ." Gokay's shoulders leaned forward and his voice dropped in a stage whisper, "perhaps a time has come to put an end to the carnage of the Syrian civil war. President Kashani wonders, once Turkey and Iraq annihilate ISIS, perhaps the Syrian people would be happier . . . safer . . . living in a protectorate, a partitioned country, the eastern portion administered by Iraq and the western portion administered by Turkey."

Ah . . . at last. There it is.

The endgame became clear to Al-Qahtani. Turkey would rid itself of the rebellious and dangerous Kurdish Peshmerga guerillas who had been fighting against Turkish rule for over one hundred years and gain control of western Syria. Not a bad trade for them. And not a bad trade for Iraq, either. The new Persian Empire would expand more rapidly with the eastern part of Syria under its control. The Kurds? The Kurds hated the Turks more than anyone else, so Kurdistan would never become an ally of Turkey. In fact, for as long as it served his purpose, a strong Kurdistan would be an effective weapon against ISIS, a buffer to western Iraq, and a thorn in the side of the Turks.

Perhaps this is not so bad a deal.

Al-Qahtani stood to his feet. "Mr. Ambassador, please convey my thanks to President Kashani and Prime Minister Eroglu. Tell them my government is grateful for their recognition." He shoved his hands into the pockets of his fatigue pants. "As for this agreement you propose . . . let me sleep on it. We'll have an answer for you by tomorrow."

Knesset Building, Jerusalem
July 21, 2:17 p.m.

Calculating the angles, searching for pitfalls and hidden agendas in Hursit's speech, Meir's head was spinning with possibilities. He was grateful for the minister's straightforward candor. And he, too, had doubts about the viability of the covenant. But with so many suitors, what was best for Israel?

Meir stood and held out his hand. "Tell Kashani I am willing to talk. An agreement on the pipeline would be a good thing for both of us. We need your water and you need our natural gas. But . . . if we're going to do this, Alex, if we are to forge a true alliance between Israel and Turkey, we need to include much more than simply an agreement on a pipeline. So much more."

"Excellent," said Hursit, taking the prime minister's hand. "My president will be delighted. And Turkey will place all of its resources at Israel's disposal."

Pragmatic politics, Hursit had called it. And he was correct. But Meir, looking at his hand in Hursit's grasp, remembered it was the same hand that just twenty-four hours ago had signed the Ishmael Covenant, binding Israel into a peace treaty and mutual defense pact with Egypt, Jordan, Saudi Arabia, and the Gulf states. What would the Arab countries think now? Pragmatic politics? Then why did it feel so much like treachery?

22

"Where are you?"

Levinson's voice sounded breathless, as if he had dropped out of a marathon along the Tel Aviv beach just before making his call.

"At the embassy," replied Mullaney.

"Okay . . . grab whoever you need and meet me at the northwest corner of the Carmel Market parking lot. We're already rolling."

Mullaney's heart started beating faster. "What's up, Meyer?"

"We've found them," he said without explanation.

"But that's only a dozen blocks away," said Mullaney, running his fingers over the Tel Aviv map on the wall of his office.

"Clever fellows," Levinson admitted. "If it's your Turks, they've been operating out of the rear portion of a fire-engine-red building that has a taxi and limousine service in the front. Lots of activity twenty-four seven, lots of cars and SUVs in and out at all hours of the day and night. Now get moving. We're wasting time."

Mullaney punched a button on his phone console and nearly knocked the entire unit on the floor.

"Hey, Brian, I got . . ."

"Saddle up, Tommy. Two squads of four. Body armor and fully armed. I want to be in the cars and moving in less than three minutes." Mullaney took a breath. "It's the same guys who kidnapped Palmyra."

―――⊂∘∘∘⊃―――

"Try to keep it under a hundred, okay?" said Mullaney. He was hanging onto the handle above the passenger door of the black SUV as it raced down Herbert Samuel Street, the long stretch of Tel Aviv beach flashing past on the right. Tommy Hernandez had his foot on the accelerator, one hand on the steering wheel and the other on the horn.

"You said *fast*."

"Yeah . . . but also alive. Watch it!"

Hernandez whipped the SUV around a slow bus and then tested the laws of physics and the limits of the vehicle's suspension system through the sweeping left curve into Khananya Street. Defying most Israeli traffic laws, with the second SUV close to his tail, Hernandez cut through the Carmelit bus depot and pulled into the packed market parking lot. In a corner to the left, Meyer Levinson was leaning up against a post supporting a low, corrugated tin roof. Levinson gestured to the space under the roof and Hernandez pulled up alongside a sad-looking collection of dusty and dented vehicles.

The city of Tel Aviv was only eleven years old when the Carmel Market first opened in 1920. Smaller than the sprawling, open air Mahane Yehuda Market in Jerusalem, the Carmel Market was still the largest *shuk*—authentic, Middle Eastern open-air market—in Tel Aviv and stretched from Magen David Square to the north to the bus depot on Carmelit Street to the south. Making sales six days a week, its open stalls overflowed with products from produce and spices to electronics and clothing. It was one of the defining elements of the ethnic neighborhood Kerem Hateimanim, formerly a Yemenite enclave of narrow, twisting streets and decaying buildings, now—like most of Israel's cities—grudgingly enduring the first throes of gentrification.

In the shadows and privacy provided by the corrugated tin roof, Levinson had spread out a map on the hood of a dirty, gray clunker. "These streets? They are narrow to begin with but are regularly clogged with parked cars and cafés spilling out onto the cobblestones. It's a difficult area to get into. And your monster trucks will get IDed as cops in a heartbeat. So we'll use this fleet of Israeli specials," he said, patting the hood of the aged Volkswagen Jetta.

He pointed to a spot several blocks north of the market parking area. "The livery service terminal is here, just off this corner. This street, Malan Street, dead ends—to cars, at least. Pedestrians and motorcycles can get through. So there are only three very narrow ways in or out for vehicles. The livery building opens onto Nakhali'el Street."

"How did you find them?" asked Mullaney.

Levinson looked up. "Follow the money," he said. "We alerted banks and currency exchanges, asked them to call us if they had any large or ongoing currency transfers from Turkish lira to Israeli shekels. In seven hours we had three hits. Two of them gave this address."

Mullaney shook his head. He wasn't surprised. Shin Bet was good. "Okay . . . what's the plan?"

This time it was Levinson shaking his head. "I wish I had a plan, Brian. I'm afraid this one we'll need to wing it. We've had no time for surveillance, so we don't know what we're walking into. We don't know how many hostiles are in the terminal. It's a very busy place, but I would think some of the drivers are likely just that, innocent livery drivers. Here's what I'm thinking . . .

"There is a synagogue here, on Nakhali'el Street, at the foot of Elyashiv Street," Levinson pointed at the map. "And there is a Yemenite restaurant on Nakhali'el Street here, just south of Malan Street. And Malan Street is fully clogged with tables and umbrellas from restaurants on either side of the street.

"What I suggest," said Levinson, "is that we divide into four units—two DSS agents and two Shin Bet officers in each unit. One at a time, on foot, at irregular intervals, one unit will travel south from Rabbi Meir Street, and enter the synagogue. Once inside, two agents will access the roof overlooking the dead end and two will go through the back of the synagogue and try to work their way to the rear of the livery.

"A second unit will occupy the Yemenite restaurant. There are plenty of tables outside, on Nakhali'el Street. Two agents will walk in from the south and two will drive up on motorbikes. The other two teams will each squeeze into one of these clunkers . . . one will drive east on Malan Street to the intersection of Nakhali'el and the other will drive north on Yehya Kapah Street and park crosswise, at the east end of Malan Street, blocking any exit that way."

"Not bad for not having a plan," said Mullaney.

Levinson looked up from the map and focused on Mullaney. "Here's the deal, Brian. You and your agents will stand in place. You will block the escape routes, but you will not engage the enemy. Only Shin Bet agents will advance on the livery building. These are very tight streets, with restaurants in almost every block. A lot of pedestrians. And we don't know what we're running into. If this thing goes badly for us . . . well . . . I can take responsibility for my men. I can't take responsibility for yours."

Collateral damage, thought Mullaney. If there were any civilian casualties,

Meyer Levinson wanted to take the heat. "Understood," he said. "We'll block the exits and play backup if needed. It's your show."

"Excellent," said Levinson, nodding his head. "Now let's get the whole team together and go over this another dozen times."

———⋙∘⋘———

Every agent was wearing an Israeli wire, so all the units and all the agents could communicate. The agents in the restaurant were limited to their standard-issue automatics, concealed under their jackets. But the remaining attackers were each carrying the relatively new Tavor X95 assault rifles, converted to 9-millimeter submachine guns. Two had been fitted with grenade launchers. Mullaney was riding in the front passenger seat in the trashed Jetta, coughing its way east on Malan Street.

The unit at the Yemenite restaurant was in place—two men each at one of the outdoor tables, facing the intersection of Malan Street—and the last of the four men had just entered the synagogue. Hernandez was one of the men assigned to the roof. On a *Go!* signal from Levinson, all four Israeli units would advance toward the livery service building. All they needed was word that the automobile blocking the east side of Malan Street was in place.

Mullaney leaned toward Levinson, who was driving. "How close are you . . ."

Four things happened at once. The steady, telegraph staccato of automatic weapons fire erupted from the far side of Malan Street on the other side of the intersection; women started screaming; all of the people eating at the outdoor restaurants scattered in every direction possible, knocking over tables and clogging the narrow streets even more; and the chatter on the communications line was urgent, immediate, and nonstop—both the synagogue and the car at the end of Malan Street were under fire.

An old military axiom holds that battle plans last until the first shot is fired. With withering gunfire spewing from the location of the livery service before all of the teams could get in place, Levinson's plan was shredded.

The Jetta jerked to a stop short of Nakhali'el Street, and all four agents poured out. Mullaney, hunched behind the open car door, did a quick analysis of what he could see. He spotted numerous firing positions in the red building halfway down Malan Street, the majority of them ripping into the battered

Toyota blocking the east end of the street. He could also hear gunfire off to his left, from the location of the synagogue.

"Hernandez, what can you see from the roof?" Levinson said into his mic.

"Hand grenade in a mouse hole," came through the mic. "Bad guys scrambling out of windows and doors while other bad guys are laying down fire. The runners are not shooting—they're just running. All in civilian clothes, nondescript. Only the guys inside the building are shooting at us. The runners should be getting to you about now."

Mullaney looked around the door and peeked up the street as Levinson was calling Shin Bet headquarters for backup. Two men ran out of an alley in the middle of the block, between the car and the synagogue. Black hair. Gray jackets. Kalashnikovs pointed down the street.

"Two more following them," called Hernandez.

Levinson's voice cut through. "All hands . . . advance in twos . . . stage by stage . . . Shin Bet on point. Clear the streets . . . then drive them back into the livery building." He looked through the open doors of the car to the other side. "Brian, you're with me."

Sixteen agents opened fire almost at the same time. Like a lethal ballet troupe honed by training and acting on instinct, the pairs inched along Nakhali'el and Malan Streets, rapid, short bursts from 9-millimeter Tavors covering their advance. Corner to door, cover . . . door to door, cover . . . door to corner, cover.

Mullaney and Levinson hugged the west side of Nakhali'el Street. Two agents from the Yemeni restaurant on their flank and behind them crept up the eastern side of the street. All four agents were alternating shooting, each of them tearing shards of stone splinters from the corner of the building behind which the men with the Kalashnikovs were hiding.

But Mullaney kept his eyes on the alley that opened on the far side of the street.

He saw the barrel of a Kalashnikov poke from the end of the alley first. He took a breath for a heartbeat, then planted two, two-round bursts on the end of the alley just as the man behind the Kalashnikov put his head and shoulder out for a look. His head exploded.

But the man behind had learned a lesson. Only the gun cleared the end of the alley, pointed down the street, his finger hard against the trigger, spraying death in random patterns. The first two runners who were across the street got the message and did the same thing, spraying gunfire onto the far side of the street.

For a moment, the Shin Bet and American agents were hunkering for cover, trapped in a crossfire. The noise was deafening, multiple echoes of gunshots reverberating between the stone buildings that lined both sides of the narrow streets.

"The shooters from the building are now running"—it was Hernandez's voice—"and the runners are now shooting. Looks like they're planning a tag-team advance."

Another voice came through their earpieces . . . "North of you." . . . giving the agents on Nakhali'el Street a heads-up.

Mullaney could hear gunfire erupt from beyond the alleyway . . . agents from the synagogue, working their way south, down Nakhali'el Street.

The shooters were diverted by the new burst of gunfire coming from the agents working their way south. That was all the edge Mullaney and the agents needed. They popped out from cover and started emptying one clip after another onto the shooters' positions on each side of the street. Stone shards were flying as fast, and as lethal, as bullets. Mullaney had his finger pressed hard against the trigger, his sights on the shooter hiding in the alley, across and up the street from him. The Kalashnikov came out and both the gun and the hands holding it were flayed by Mullaney's weapon. The shooter fell to his knees in the alley, opening his back to the street. It was riddled by 9-millimeter slugs.

As if it was halftime, most of the nearby shooting stopped. The team on Nakhali'el Street had eliminated all four of the shooters. But the fight wasn't over.

"I want three men down the alley," Levinson barked. "Push them back to the livery. The rest with me. Clear Malan Street."

Levinson, Mullaney, and three other agents dodged across Nakhali'el Street and converged on the western end of Malan. One was cut down by heavy fire from multiple machine guns that were tearing up a delivery truck behind which two of the agents from the restaurant were trying to get off a shot.

"Some of the runners are breaking out." Hernandez again. "Headed west."

Withering fire was shredding the truck and tearing up the street.

"Can't stay here," Levinson said over the comm link.

Mullaney chanced a flash peek around the edge of the truck. What he saw tripped a memory from the movie *Heat*, with Robert De Niro and Val Kilmer, where a gang of bank robbers—heavily armed and oblivious to the police confronting them—slowly walked down a wide, three-lane street jammed with abandoned cars, laying down a murderous fusillade of automatic weapons fire that was shredding every vehicle in the street and wiping out every cop who made himself visible.

In his quick look, while there were still active shooters in the livery building, Mullaney saw at least six to eight men, heavily armed with rapid-fire assault weapons, weaving their way through the growing carnage on Malan Street—to the east, away from Mullaney and Levinson on Nakhali'el Street toward the car blocking the exit on Yehya Kapah Street. Like municipal workers spraying for mosquitoes, these men were sweeping the street, spewing bullets as they advanced toward the intersection.

"They're trying to break out to the east too," Mullaney transmitted, "where we're weakest."

Levinson had six men, including himself. Mullaney watched as Levinson looked to his left.

"Three . . . the building," he said, nodding his head in the direction of the livery. He turned back to the right. "The rest with me. Hernandez . . . we need you on the east end of Malan. Go!"

With that, six agents tucked their submachine guns against their shoulders and came out of the shelter of the truck, their fingers glued against the triggers.

Mullaney ran down the right side of Malan Street, ducking behind restaurant tables and delivery vans, stopping, firing, waiting for the next agent to work his way past, then up, firing, looking for his next safe haven. An explosion rocked the livery building to the left, blasting smoke and debris out of the building's windows and onto the street below. The shooters went silent.

"Grenade," said Levinson. "Let's go!" And he was up and running down the middle of the narrow street, firing at the backs of the men who were rapidly closing on the Shin Bet blockade at the east end of Malan Street. Mullaney was on his feet, weaving down the right side of the street, two other agents now running down the left side.

Two or three of the enemy had reversed course and were returning fire toward Levinson's group. A flurry of bullets slammed into the Israeli agent just in front of Mullaney, picking him up off his feet and blowing him backward into a wall.

For a heartbeat, Mullaney stopped, thinking about going to the agent's aid. But as if a giant hand had grabbed a fistful of the back of his shirt, Mullaney felt himself being flung behind a dumpster, the bullets clanging off the heavy metal like so many BB guns at a carnival shooting gallery. Before he took his dive, he could see the escaping killers were already scrambling over the car blockade and running in several directions on the curving, narrow streets.

Colliding with the ground behind the dumpster, Mullaney came to an abrupt and painful stop, scraping along the rough brick of the street's surface. But he was quickly to his knees, crouching behind the dumpster, his sights trained down the street. In the periphery of his vision, he thought he saw Levinson take out one of the shooters. But Mullaney's eyes were fixed on a man in a blue windbreaker and tan pants who had just turned toward the sound of Levinson's firing. He had an Uzi pressed against his side, the barrel swinging in Levinson's direction. Mullaney put two shots in the man's left ear, one for good measure into the back of his head as he spun to the ground.

The livery building burning to their left, all of the ambulatory agents on Malan Street raced toward the blockade vehicle at the end of the street—more to check on and assist the agents who were in the blockade vehicle than to chase the escaping Turks.

Running full tilt, Levinson ignored the mangled steel carcass of the car, jumping, planting one boot on the left front fender, leaping over the car, and landing on the street on the far side. Mullaney took a more reasonable route, circling around the back of the car. But both came upon the same scene. All four agents were down, pools of brown-red blood spreading across the stone street. Two were clearly dead, one an American DSS agent, and the other two were severely wounded, only one conscious.

"Agents down, need immediate medical help," said Levinson, even as he was tearing the left sleeve off his shirt and wrapping it tightly around one agent's mangled shoulder, the blood pumping out rhythmically from a severed artery, "Yehya Kapah Street, at the east end of Malan Street."

It was only then, when all the shooting had stopped, that Mullaney realized his ears were ringing from the thunderous battle. And he also realized that the scrapes on his knees were not his only wounds. He had a new part in his hair . . . a suddenly scathing tear along the left side of his scalp as if someone had laid the thin edge of a white-hot iron against the length of his skull.

Mullaney leaned against a wooden pole holding up an awning. A heavy cloud of burnt gunpowder hovered about six feet off the street's surface. It smelled like Fourth of July fireworks. But it looked like a war zone.

"Report!" called Levinson.

Bandy-legged, Mullaney picked his way around Levinson. On the ground, on the far side of Malan Street, was sprawled the DSS agent, his back to Mullaney so he could see the "DSS" stenciled on the back of his black jacket. The agent was broader in the shoulders, heavier than Mullaney. He pulled in a breath as he came up to the body, tugged on the shoulder. No . . . it was not Tommy! But this man was one of his. And he was not alive.

A medic was applying something to Mullaney's scalp that sizzled and stung, like a burger on a steel griddle. Levinson was squatting in the street, ten feet away, holding the head and shoulders of one of his agents in his lap, rocking on his haunches. The swarm of EMTs that had invaded Malan Street were not stopping to help this agent. For him, it was too late.

Tommy Hernandez, covered with dirt and ash, the clothes under his DSS-labeled jacket soaked through with perspiration, came up and sat next to Mullaney on a low, stone wall. In his right hand he held the smoking Tavor X95.

"Casualties?"

"Eight bad guys DOA," said Hernandez, his voice a weak, hoarse whisper. "Ed Mitchell?"

"Yeah . . . I saw him," said Mullaney.

"And two of Meyer's team. That guy," said Hernandez, nodding his head toward the street where Levinson still rocked. "That guy was Meyer's second-in-command. They've been together since '98. It's a—"

"How many got away?" Mullaney interrupted.

⇒◦◦◦⇐

Ankara
July 21, 4:12 p.m.

"Eight dead, Exalted One," said the leader of the Disciples. "It was a formidable force—Shin Bet and American DSS. Caught the Disciples by surprise. Still, eleven escaped . . . two wounded. I take responsibility."

The Turk sat in the garden on Alitas Street, twisting the phone in his gnarly, white hands. "Yes . . . I knew you would," he whispered—but the whispers failed to slake his rage. "Death is the price of war. The enemy also inflicts casualties. Where are you?"

"Baghdad . . . Persia is growing."

"Go to Israel immediately," said the Turk. "Take command. I have work that must be done here. But you will exact our revenge. You will rip the life from this agent Mullaney, and you will rip the life from the Jew, Levinson. Make them pay . . . blood for blood. Don't kill the American ambassador. Kill his daughter. Mutilate her. That will end his life in agony. Then recover the prophecy and the box or destroy them."

23

The underground room was dark and cool. Still and quiet. A small lamp illuminated a far corner of the room but failed to pierce the heart of the gloom.

Rabbi Mordechai Herzog—white-haired and two years past his eightieth birthday, wiry strong but thin as matzos—sat on a small wooden chair adjacent to the wooden casket that contained the now lifeless body of his son, Israel. The elder rabbi was offering *Aninut*, the first and most deeply personal stage of mourning in the Jewish religion. His son's body was washed and wrapped, prepared for the burial that would take place in an hour, well before sunset. The burial would be followed by the seven days of Shiva, the traditional Jewish mourning ritual. But today, Mordechai Herzog did not desire or require the *minyan*, the prayer circle of ten adult Jewish men who were mandated during mourning by Jewish tradition. No, today he wanted his son—who had succeeded him as chief rabbi for the Jewish Rabbinate Council—for himself, for his final leave-taking.

Rabbi Herzog grabbed the left sleeve of his black suit jacket and pulled. But the stitches wouldn't give. So he grabbed his white shirt in both hands and pulled with all his strength, buttons popping free and falling to the floor to observe *k'riah*, the customary rending of garments. The tinkling buttons were the only sound to break the traditional silence, Rabbi Herzog reciting his prayers in the solace of his own mind.

He was uncomfortable with the other coffin being in the same room, even if it was only temporary. Rabbi Chaim Yavod had no family in Israel, no one to care for his remains, no one to mourn for his soul. Rabbi Herzog was empathetic . . . but he had no mourning left over for a stranger. His grief for his dead son was overwhelming and consumed all his energy. He had nothing left.

"*Ha'makom yenahem*, Mordechai."

For a heartbeat, when he first heard the voice recite the opening words of the traditional and formulaic Jewish response to mourning, Rabbi Mordechai Herzog wondered if he too had left this world. But his heart beat a second time

. . . and a third. He opened his eyes and looked into the gloom of the room in the direction of the voice.

"*Ha'makom yenahem, etkhem betokh she'ar avelei Tziyonvi'Yerushalayim,*" the voice said again. "May God console you among the other mourners of Zion and Jerusalem."

Rabbi Herzog quenched a chill that started at the base of his spine. "Who are you, and why do you disturb the silence of Aninut?"

The darkened corner farthest from the light began to oscillate . . . vibrate and shimmer as if the very atoms of the air were dancing a waltz. Like the parting of the Red Sea, a shard of brilliance rent the dark in two, and a massive form, the light at its back, approached Herzog's stool. A gasp of dread stillborn in his throat, Herzog's aged heart began to fail him.

"Be strong and courageous," said the voice, shimmering at the same wavelength as the vision approaching his chair.

Rabbi Herzog felt a river of life explode from his chest and race through his veins, flooding his muscles with strength and filling his faint heart with confidence and boldness. It took all his self-control not to shout in exclamation. "Who . . . what are you? Why are you here?"

Before his eyes, the dancing atoms began to coalesce, and the hint of form gathered substance. Rabbi Herzog's mouth opened, but no sound emerged as a man . . . a sort of man . . . materialized before him, tall, regal, massive in strength, dressed in the armor of an ancient warrior, his muscled arms crossed over a chest covered by a breastplate of silver, a gleaming scabbard hanging by his side from a wide belt of spun gold.

"I am Bayard."

Now Rabbi Herzog's eyes were as wide as his silent mouth, sucking in breath but powerless to utter a word in the face of such an apparition. Then, this sort-of-a-man unfolded his arms and held his hands, palms up, away from his body. From behind his shoulder blades unfurled vast, feathered wings, their breadth constrained only by the walls of the room.

"Speak."

Words stumbled from Herzog's addled brain, but none managed to complete the journey to his lips. "Aahhhh . . ."

The sort-of-a-man smiled. And all of Herzog's fear fled in a headlong rush before the power of that smile. "I am Bayard, sent to protect the guardian. Your

son was the last in the line of guardians. Forgive me . . ." the smile fled from
Bayard's face and he knelt on one knee, bowing his head, "I failed."

Herzog threw aside all of the rational disclaimers pumping out of his earth-
bound experience and responded to this man with the empathy of a grieving
father who now had forgiveness to dispense . . . forgiveness for an angel?

All he could muster was a whisper. "I forgive you."

Bayard lifted his head, his eyes well-watered, a solitary tear coursing down
his right cheek. "Thank you, Rabbi," said the angel, his words a reverent caress.
"You have restored my grieving spirit. Perhaps now, I can restore yours."

The angel stood, his feet braced apart, his shoulders back. "I am Bayard!"
he bellowed, the percussion of his impassioned words threatening to shatter the
foundation of the building. He pulled the sword from its scabbard and plunged
it point first into the limestone floor. "I am protector of the guardians, captain
of the host, slayer of evil."

"I . . . I . . . believe you," said Rabbi Herzog, his eyelids and his voice flut-
tering against the onrushing power of Bayard's declaration. "But . . . but . . .
who are these guardians? And forgive me, but who are *you*?"

Bayard looked down at the quaking old man, his blue eyes twin pools of
kindness and compassion. "I am from God . . . for you." He took a knee once
more, folded his expansive wings back behind his shoulder blades, and leaned
upon his sword so he could speak to Herzog face-to-face.

"The Vilna Gaon was taken into heaven in the spirit 220 years ago. There
he received two prophetic messages from the throne of God."

Rabbi Herzog could hear Bayard's voice and see his body, and he knew of
the Vilna Gaon, the Lithuanian rabbi who was the greatest Talmudic scholar of
all time, but still he found the reality before him almost unbelievable.

"Steadfastly opposed by the agents of evil, in spite of our protection, the
Gaon's pilgrimage to Jerusalem to deliver the prophecies to the rabbinate was
thwarted. Wisely, and at our direction, he left the second of these prophetic
messages with the Rabbi of Konigsberg, while the first prophetic message
returned to Vilnius with him. For 220 years, one rabbi after another, first in
Konigsberg and then in Istanbul, has entered into the role of guardian of the
second prophecy. Walking in the safety and power of an anointing, this same
rabbi was guardian of the bronze box—lethal to some—that housed and protected the prophecy until its appointed time. The first prophecy was revealed

by the Gaon's great-great-grandson just months ago. The appointed time of the second prophecy is within reach. But we are being opposed by a great, gathering force of evil.

"Yesterday morning, your son, Rabbi Israel Herzog, received the anointing as guardian from an unorthodox, but still valid source—Palmyra Parker, daughter of the US ambassador to Israel. Your son took the box to the Hurva Synagogue and the Rabbinate Council of Israel, where the box was safely opened and the second prophecy deciphered, as was intended."

A curtain of sadness clouded Bayard's countenance. Rabbi Herzog could see the anguish of the angel. "You didn't . . . couldn't . . . save him?" It was a question for clarity, not for malice.

"We of the brethren," said Bayard, his words as heavy as fog at night, "are endowed with gifts beyond the natural realm. We are created ones who were created like Adam: free from pain, free from death, and infused with knowledge.

"But we are neither omniscient nor omnipresent. We are limited," Bayard continued. "Evil exists. There are those of the brethren who fell from their place in heaven, who succumbed to pride. But they still possess the gifts with which they were created. They are evil, but they are also immortal, feel no pain, and are infused with knowledge. Evil exists, and evil is determined to prevail. Thus the cosmic battle between good and evil continues, a battle that has raged in the heavens since the fall of the angels and the fall of Adam and which will only end when the Son of God returns to claim his rightful throne."

Bayard lifted his hand from the hilt of his sword and extended it toward Rabbi Herzog. "There are prophecies that must be fulfilled, Rabbi, to herald the coming kingdom of God. We cannot, will not, interfere with life on this earth if that interference would prevent prophecy from being fulfilled."

The rabbi searched Bayard's eyes. "I don't understand."

"Understanding is not always available, not even to us," said Bayard. "But action we all understand. I have a task for you, Rabbi Herzog, a task your son would have fulfilled, were he still alive. Are you willing to stand in his place?"

The pulsing river of life quickened its pace and rushed through Herzog—flesh, bone, and spirit. He felt invigorated, empowered, equipped. And angry. They killed his son. He would not let them win.

"What do you want me to do?"

He felt no weariness, even though he had no idea how long he had been sitting on this hard, wooden chair. Eighty-two years old and Rabbi Mordechai Herzog was about to go to war.

"We need you to do two things," said Bayard, as he stood erect and placed his huge sword back in its scabbard. "First, speak to your brethren in the rabbinate. This so-called Ishmael Covenant is an offense against the Word of God. In addition to allying themselves with those the Lord said to destroy, what does it say in your Torah about dividing the land of Israel—the promised land appointed and anointed by God?"

Rabbi Herzog knew the verse. It was clear. "'In those days and at that time, when I restore the fortunes of Judah and Jerusalem, I will gather all nations and bring them down to the Valley of Jehoshaphat. There I will put them on trial for what they did to my inheritance, my people Israel, because they scattered my people among the nations and divided up my land.'"

"If the people of Israel agree to and support this covenant, they will join the nations in the valley of judgment," said Bayard. "Divide the land, tear asunder the nation, and the plunder of Israel will have only just begun. Speak . . . save your people, God's people."

"This I can do," said Herzog, nodding his white-haired head. "This I already planned to do. What is your second task?"

"Make yourself unclean."

If he had been a younger man, the fury that rose in Rabbi Herzog may have led to a wrestling match with an enormous angel. As it was, his spine stiffened, his chin dropped to his chest and he pierced the angel with a warning gaze over the top of his bifocals. "I am Ashkenazi . . . a rabbi of the cloth . . . a man who lives and breathes the word of God. Why would I ever willingly make myself unclean?"

Bayard nodded, long brown curls falling over his shoulder. "I do not ask lightly. Evil took the life of your son. Would you make yourself unclean to destroy that evil?"

Rabbi Herzog stood to his feet. "A thousand times over."

"Then come with me."

Before Herzog could process the thought of following an angel, Bayard's long strides took him to the far side of the room beside the second covered casket. He raised his left arm above the casket and passed his hand down its length. The lid of the casket opened backward on its hinges.

Bayard pointed to the body and Rabbi Herzog leaned over slightly to get a better look. The body was clothed in a soiled and rumpled black suit, the shoulders of the suit jacket covered in gray dust. A white cloth, stained in the middle, covered the face of the corpse.

The angel raised his arm once more and held his hand above the white cloth. "This will not be pleasant." Bayard moved his hand and the cloth slid from the face of the corpse.

Sensory overload threatened Herzog's consciousness. His eyes flew open, as if dynamited apart, while revulsion twisted his stomach and a retching gag was caught in his throat. The body of Chaim Yavod was a grotesque tableau of a gruesome death. Yavod's tongue, long, black and swollen, was thrust from his mouth as if he were begging for water. His eyes were as wide as an open window, rivers of dried blood running from their corners and down the open maw of his jawline. His scalp was a minefield of bloody patches as if his hair had been yanked from his head one fistful at a time.

Rabbi Herzog's breathing was short and rapid, his shoulders were rocking back and forth, and his legs felt like soft butter. One hand covered his mouth, the other covered his heart.

"This," Bayard said solemnly, "is the death bequeathed to all who touch the box without the anointing," The angel turned to face Herzog. "Your son and the other rabbis of the council had broken the code and deciphered the Vilna Gaon's second prophecy. Minutes before the synagogue was destroyed, he had dispatched Chaim Yavod to fetch his automobile. They were to drive to Tel Aviv to fulfill a promise—to first share the message of the prophecy with those who carried the box into Israel, Ambassador Cleveland from the United States and his head of security, Brian Mullaney. After the explosions, Yavod instead raced back to the Hurva. He found the dead bodies of your son and the other rabbis, but he also found the box that protected the prophecy. He must have touched the box."

"But . . . what . . ."

"In the pocket, inside Chaim Yavod's suit jacket, is an envelope. Inside the envelope is the translation of the Vilna Gaon's second prophecy. If you wish to fulfill the task of the final guardian—your son—you must reach inside the man's jacket and retrieve the envelope and then deliver the envelope to the American embassy in Tel Aviv. Or the evil that stole your son's life may prevail."

"But I must touch a dead man . . . and become unclean."

"Yes, for a moment."

Mordechai Herzog looked at the ravaged body of Chaim Yavod, at the blackness of his tongue and the dried blood that had seeped from his eyes.

"Fear not," said Bayard. "It is safe for you to touch him."

The rabbi drew in a deep breath, mumbled a prayer, placed his left hand on the edge of the coffin and reached under the filthy suit coat. His fingers found the inside pocket and immediately felt the sharp corner of an envelope. He pressed the envelope between thumb and forefinger and slid it out of the pocket, away from the body. Herzog released his breath. At no point, he believed, had his hand touched the body itself. Still . . . he was unclean. The envelope pressed between his two fingers, Herzog turned toward Bayard, unsure of what to do next. What he didn't expect was for Bayard to reach out and place his left hand upon Herzog's head.

"'The Lord bless you and keep you; the Lord make his face shine on you and be gracious to you; the Lord turn his face toward you and give you peace.'"

The words of Aaron's blessing flowed over Herzog like a cleansing stream of righteousness. He didn't realize his eyes were closed until Bayard spoke once again.

"Now you are once again ceremonially clean." His bright gray eyes bored into Herzog's consciousness. "And now you are also the guardian . . . guardian of the box and guardian of the prophecy. I wish you to bestow each assignment upon the esteemed warrior who guards the lives of those at the American embassy in Tel Aviv. Reveal the message to him. Explain its meaning. And then pass the anointing into his hands."

"But . . . but I . . . I don't even know what the prophecy says, let alone what it means," stammered Herzog. "How can I pass on what I don't understand myself?"

Bayard reached out with his right hand and held Herzog's head between both of his hands. The angel lowered his gaze and closed his eyes. His lips moved, but no words escaped from his mouth. Then he exhaled slowly, the breath a gentle breeze upon Herzog's face. And light infused the rabbi's mind— his thoughts and his understanding now existing in an expanding space of wisdom, a mental library with sunshine flooding in from floor-to-ceiling windows, a spiritual ecstasy of heart and soul. And a truth pressed upon Rabbi Herzog that was difficult for him to absorb.

"Now you know the truth," said Bayard. "Now you know the way. Now the truth has set you free. And you can have life."

Bayard removed his hands as Herzog searched for words to express what he now knew was true . . . the truth of all prophecies. But no words came.

"There was an earlier prophecy given to the Vilna Gaon," Bayard whispered, "that when the Hurva Synagogue is rebuilt for the third time, construction of the temple of God will begin. Now, with this latest explosion, the Hurva must be rebuilt for the third time. Then when the temple is completed, it will be prepared for Messiah. No consolation in your grief, I am sure, but . . ."

Nodding his head, Rabbi Mordechai Herzog understood Bayard was speaking of a second coming of Messiah. No longer heresy. "But my son . . ."

"Yes, your son perished in the explosions and, for that, I grieve with you," said Bayard. "But I have good news. Good news of your son and good news for you. Hear my voice and the words of heaven. The long-awaited Messiah of the Jewish people has already arrived—Yeshua Hamasheach, who shed his blood in atonement for all sin and who was raised from death back to eternal life on the third day. He is risen, Mordechai. Seek him! Your son did. I could not save your son's mortal body. But his immortal soul was redeemed by the blood of Yeshua, the Christos. Receive Yeshua, and your son, Israel, will be waiting for you when you enter eternity."

Rabbi Mordechai Herzog, formerly chief rabbi of the Rabbinate Council of Israel, faced a challenge even greater than believing in angels. *Jesus? My son accepted Jesus? And you want me to* . . . but now Rabbi Herzog knew the truth. He knew the One who is the Way and the Truth and the Life.

Herzog felt the hands lift from his head. "If you confess with your mouth that Jesus is Lord . . ." as Bayard's voice grew fainter . . . "and believe in your mind that He was raised from the dead . . ."

And there was silence. Dusk reentered the room. Herzog opened his eyes. Other than two corpses, he was alone in the room. And he had a decision to make.

24

The mammoth wharf was tucked into the armpit of the eastern spit of the T-shaped peninsula that was the port city of Gwadar in Balochistan, the far western corner of Pakistan's Persian Gulf coast. A flat, paved square of concrete, Gwadar Port was in the initial stages of an ambitious construction project financed by the Chinese government. Along its seawall were a half dozen soaring shipping cranes that looked like Imperial Walkers from the *Star Wars* movies.

Along the length of the wharf, six-foot-tall wooden crates stacked five high stretched into the distance in a dozen lines. The sun long set and moonrise still hours away, the canyons between the crates were as dark as the far side of Venus.

Suntil Rahaman leaned against one stack of wooden crates at the mouth of the canyon, directly adjacent to the rusting hulk of a coastal freighter that was moored to the wharf, a foul-smelling cigarette in one hand and a Colt M4A1 semiautomatic carbine in the other. Abdul Zadari, near invisible, haunted the shadows at the far end of the same long, narrow corridor. Both Rahaman and Zadari wore the uniform of Pakistan's Strategic Plan's Division (SPD)—the army group charged with the safekeeping of Pakistan's nuclear arsenal—but only one was truly SPD.

Sergeant Rahaman looked across the wharf to the gangway leading to the rotting freighter, taking in the other SPD soldiers stationed at the eastern and western sides of the vast wharf. His commander, Colonel Dawar, of the Inter-Services Intelligence (ISI) directorate, Pakistan's military spy agency, stood under a light on the platform at the top of the gangway, speaking to the freighter's captain.

Hurry, thought Rahaman. In spite of the fact that he had been assured that each crate was lead-lined, Rahaman remained anxious in the vicinity of the five crates directly across the corridor from where he now stood. He knew many of the technicians who worked for SPD in maintaining the nuclear arsenal, and he trusted few of them. The crates he faced could be benign, or they could be spewing out his death warrant. *Hurry!*

───※───

Riyadh, Saudi Arabia
July 21, 7:50 p.m.

Prince Faisal sat in one of the two chairs that faced his father's desk.

"And what of the shipment?" asked the king.

"On the dock, waiting to be loaded onto the freighter."

"Are we prepared for its arrival?"

"The quay where the ship will dock in Ras Laffan, Qatar, is secured and guarded by our men. The warehouse is empty and locked and the entire wharf will be evacuated and locked down when the ship is nearing the port. We have two teams of scientists, one as backup just in case. They will be on the wharf as the ship docks and will take immediate possession of the cargo."

"Good. Then we are ready."

Faisal crossed his legs and sat back in his chair. "A deterrent is of no effect if it is kept secret. When will we unveil our newest toy?"

───※───

Gwadar, Pakistan
July 21, 9:53 p.m.

Down by the rocky coastline east of the wharf, hidden by the coastal cliff, two black Zodiac inflatables nosed onto the shore in a shallow cove a few thousand meters east of the port, their electric motors silenced. Six black-clad figures slipped out of each boat and padded across the stone beach to the darker shadows under the cliff face.

───※───

Colonel Dawar moved out of the light and into the darkness of the canyon.

"The secure hold is prepared."

"Well hidden?" asked Sergeant Rahaman.

"Not even a sea mist could find it. They are preparing the rigging. Loading will start when the dockworkers get here in thirty minutes."

"Not soon enough for me. I'll be glad to be rid of these crates."

———◦∞◦———

There was little cover to conceal the leader and his men. He raised his head above the rim of the low, seaside dunes. Between him and the massive, flat slab that was Gwadar Port was an undulating, treeless plain of ochre sand and rock.

The leader had basically two choices for approaching the loading docks of the port. The most direct route to the sea edge of the wharf was to continue to the right, east along the coast, skirt the dormant volcano cone that stuck out into the sea, climb a series of low bluffs, and follow a straight, beachside dirt lane that led directly to the port platform.

The second route was longer, perhaps more perilous than the run along the sea. After passing the volcano cone, that option meant following the base of the cliffs that ran southwest from the beach to just short of the Akram Road, then turning north along a shallow ravine, crossing the Port Road undetected, and hugging a fence along the far western rim of the port complex.

To the west of the beachside lane was a broad, flat expanse of sand, several hundred meters, that was completely exposed. Suicide to move in that direction, even for his extraordinary team.

But the leader had made his decision even before his squad hit the beach. He turned to his second-in-command, pointed to his watch, and flashed five fingers three times. Once they reached the volcano cone, the leader would take his team on the longer run to the Port Road. Fifteen minutes later, his second-in-command would head out with his team of six along the beachside lane.

Their mission was clear. Converge on the port complex from two directions, destroy the nuclear weapons bound for Saudi Arabia, and escape undetected. Whatever it took, those crates were not leaving Pakistan tonight.

———◦∞◦———

As soon as he had reached his objective, lying prone on the ground along the fence line on the western edge of the port complex, his team stretched out behind him, the leader surveyed the concrete platform through his night vision binoculars. From his vantage point, he could clearly see the side of a freighter nestled against the dock. Several workers were making preparations for loading—a forklift was approaching a line of stacked wooden crates and a crane was lowering a cargo net onto the wharf.

"Report."

"Two special forces guards visible on this side. One at the edge of the platform; one near the shipping crates. Other military dispersed throughout the port."

"Yes . . . the same on this side. An officer of some kind with the guard near the crates. There may be others," he said. "Control?"

"Yes," came the response in the leader's earpiece.

"Start the diversion."

———◦◦◦———

Colonel Dawar turned toward the ship. "I'll be on the bridge during loading. You can—"

The explosion rocked the freighter over on its port side, scraping its hull against the tire bumpers protecting the wharf. The rattle of automatic weapons echoed from the far side of the ship.

Dawar spun on his heel and pointed to Sergeant Rahaman. "You stay here. Guard the crates." Then he spoke into the mic attached to his left shoulder. "Defend the ship." And he was running across the dock toward the freighter.

———◦◦◦———

The leader and his second-in-command each moved their squads in unison toward the dock while the diversionary attack erupted on the far side of the ship. Sound suppressors on their automatic weapons, the lead soldiers picked off the Pakistani military guards on both sides of the platform as other Pakistani military ran toward the ship. Silent, merging with the shadows, disappearing into the darkness of the canyons between the stacked shipping crates, the two squads converged on the line of crates that were still guarded.

———◦◦◦———

Rahaman heard the running feet coming up behind him through the corridor and spun around, his finger on the trigger of his Colt automatic carbine. Only a split second of hesitation saved Sergeant Abdul Zadari from being cut down by Rahaman's weapon.

"What's happen. . .

"Get back to your post," snarled Rahaman. "Dawar's got that under control."

"But look." Zadari pointed past Rahaman toward the freighter. "It looks like it's on fire."

Rahaman turned his attention back to the ship. "I don't . . ."

Zadari smoothly lifted the SIG Sauer pistol in his right hand and sent two 9-millimeter bullets through Rahaman's skull. The sergeant was dead before he hit the concrete. Zadari stepped over the fallen body, peeked to his left around the corner of the shipping crates, and waved an arm in the leader's direction.

The leader saw the waving arm first then the profile of Abdul Zadari giving them the all clear.

"Move," he said, but his team—blocked from the freighter's view by the stacked crates—was already advancing on the nearest rank of wooden shipping crates. "All the boxes marked *Water Project—Las Raffan*," he said.

As the black-clad attackers fanned out around the five marked crates, an agitated Zadari came alongside the leader, who was mostly hidden in the dark canyon between the crates, one eye on the work of his men and the other eye on the ongoing fight around the freighter.

"I hope this job was worth blowing my cover," snapped Zadari. "It'll take me years to rebuild what you just threw away." He looked up as their men were ripping open the sides of four crates marked *water project*. "So, what's in the crates?"

The leader shifted his attention from the swift, focused steps his men were taking.

"These four crates contain the components of four nuclear warheads con-structed by Pakistan but paid for by Saudi Arabia. These are the latest war-heads, deliverable by missile or bombers. And the Saudis just called in their order. And that fifth crate . . . the one we haven't touched . . . contains the fissile parts. That's the deadly stuff."

His team were pulling sets of wires from each of the crates.

"Time. Let's go. You're coming with us."

"This is my home."

"Not anymore," said the leader, who stepped in close to Zadari. "Look, you've done your part. More than your part. You can't stay here. You'd be dead in less than a week. Let's go."

<hr>

Back along the fence line to the west of the wide concrete expanse of Gwadar Port, the leader clicked the mic at his left shoulder.

"Yes?"

"Maintain your position and keep us covered until we make it back to the volcano. We're about to light it up."

"As you wish."

Zadari was lying in the pumice-like sand next to the leader, watching as the other members of the team connected ten pairs of wires to small black boxes the size of compact computers. "What are you going to do?" asked Zadari, looking back and forth between the shipping crates and their hiding place. "We're awfully close, don't you think?"

The leader turned on his side to watch his men complete the connections. "The engineering tolerances on nuclear weapons are incredibly precise. So it's not that difficult to render them useless. You can hit them with a hammer and throw off the engineering so they don't work. But, break them and they can be fixed. So we're going to melt them—all of the parts. We're going to melt them together. One big ball of useless metal."

"What about the deadly stuff?"

"Yeah, the deadly stuff," said the leader. One of his soldiers gave a thumbs-up. He returned the thumbs-up then snapped his wrist to the right. "That crate is lined with lead. Otherwise, we would all be cooked right now. Lead melts at 328 degrees Celsius. Here," he handed Zadari what looked like thick sunglasses. "Watch."

There was a low hum from behind the leader. Not much happened at first. Then the visible components inside the shipping crates began to glow, faintly at first and then increasing more intensely with each passing heartbeat. Suddenly, it was as if a new world was being birthed on the Pakistani wharf—five mini-suns flashed for the thinnest of seconds then disappeared in a roiling cloud of gray smoke.

As the smoke cleared, the contents of the open crates became visible—

gleaming, randomly shaped globs of molten metal now quickly cooling. The lead-lined crate was still sealed closed, but it was now contorted out of shape, gray stains of melting lead erupting on the surface of the crate.

"Control . . . break engagement." The leader turned to his squad. "Cut the wires, grab the boxes, and let's vanish."

25

The housekeeping crews cleaning the offices in the north wing of the residence had come and gone hours earlier. Brian Mullaney had been trying to read the same regional threat assessment for the past half hour. His head was throbbing from the pain of the wound in his scalp, his heart was heavy for the men who had been killed in the raid on the livery service, his spirit was furious that so many of the killers had escaped, and his mind was still wrestling with the venom of Webster's phone call. His eyes read the same paragraph for the fourth time and still had yet to absorb its content.

"If you stare any harder at that paper, it'll catch fire."

Mullaney looked up. Tommy Hernandez, dressed in sweat-stained gym clothes that gave him the look of an NFL linebacker, was anchored to the frame of the open door to his office. "Do they pay you time and a half?" he asked. "Because if they do, I'm getting gypped. And if they don't . . . then what are you doing here? They did give you a bed, right?"

Mullaney nodded to one of the chairs in front of his desk. "Shut the door, will you?"

Closing the door behind him, Hernandez crossed the room. "Now you really have me worried," he said. "Am I getting fired? Or a raise?"

After surviving DSS training together under the relentless battering of the marines at Quantico, Hernandez and Mullaney had forged a friendship that was now in its nineteenth year. Broad shouldered and barrel chested, his body thick with muscle, a flat-top crew cut bristling like porcupine quills, Hernandez knew Mullaney better than Mullaney's brother, Doak, ever could.

Hernandez sat in the chair facing the desk. "That was rough duty today," he said. "I don't know about you, but I was scared senseless coming off that roof. There were bullets flying everywhere. How's your head?"

His left hand started toward his head, but Mullaney stopped quickly. Nothing should touch that wound tonight. "Still hurts."

"Kinda goes with the divots on your face from the stone shards that ripped you up earlier. You're having a bad day, kemo sahbee. Oh—" Hernandez looked up. "Sorry, Brian. Did you have to call the families?"

Mullaney carefully shook his head. "They took care of that Stateside. But I've written the letters. Ed Mitchell had three kids." The words caught in his throat. "God help us, Tommy—how did that go so wrong?"

"Could have been bad luck," he said. "Or they could have gotten tipped off again. Or somebody spotted the car blocking the end of the street. Whatever happened, the day got deadly real fast. I'm sorry . . . sorry for you, Brian. You've got enough on your plate right now. Is this what you wanted to talk about?"

"No. And don't feel too sorry for me. Who knows, you might be getting my job," said Mullaney. When Hernandez's eyes flashed open and he started coming out of his chair, Mullaney put up his hand to signal *stop*. "Hold on . . . we've got a lot to talk about, and I'm certainly not the most important topic."

Hernandez took the towel that was in his hands, wrapped it behind his neck, and settled into the chair. "Well, you've got my attention," he said. "But I'll tell you right now, I don't want to hear about anything else on the list until you tell me about what's going on with you."

From the first day they started DSS agent training in Quantico nearly twenty years ago, Mullaney and Hernandez—unlikely pals—had bonded like brothers. And their friendship lasted and grew stronger even when they were posted to the opposite sides of the world. Like Mullaney's brother, Hernandez was one of the few people to whom Mullaney revealed his heart. And tonight, he needed counsel.

"We'll get to that shortly," said Mullaney, closing the report and tossing it to the side of his desk. "But first we need to talk about Atticus." He turned his shoulders to the credenza behind his desk and turned on a radio that was help-ing to stabilize a row of books. Classical music filled the room, soft but clear. Mullaney turned back to his friend. "And I don't want anyone else to hear it."

"What's going on?" asked Hernandez, genuine concern tempering his words.

Toying with a pen on the top of his desk, Mullaney kept his attention on his fingers. "You said to me once—was that only yesterday?—that the ambas-sador seemed to be carrying some great weight, something that was burdening his soul." He looked up at Hernandez. "Any idea what it is . . . what's weighing so heavily on him?"

"I wish I did," said Hernandez, shaking his head. "Just sometimes his eyes glaze over and he's a hundred miles away, and I can see in that moment that he's carrying a great burden of sadness. For a while, I thought he missed his late wife. And he does. But that's not the weight. I can hear it in his voice when he talks about her . . . there's nothing but joy in his memories. My sense is it's something in his past, some great regret. I don't know. I just wish I could fix it."

Mullaney weighed the pen in his hand while he weighed the wisdom— or folly—of bringing Hernandez up to speed on the recent conversation with Webster, and Webster's threats to Cleveland. But Hernandez, who had been in charge of Cleveland's personal security detail during his previous three-year posting in Turkey, had been at the ambassador's side a lot longer than Mullaney. He deserved to know—no, he needed to know—what was happening to Cleveland. And Mullaney was certain that Hernandez would never betray a confidence.

He dropped the pen on his desk and turned his full attention on Hernandez.

"After Meyer Levinson came by this morning with the details of Mossad's communications intercept of those conversations about Palmyra Parker, Cleveland and I called Evan Townsend and told him that whoever is feeding information to our enemy has access to equipment that is used by people in the upper echelon of State . . . that it looks like somebody high up is a traitor."

"Those guys were always one step ahead of us," said Hernandez, "and, in our business, we have to deny the possibility of coincidence. Did the secretary have any ideas? What does he want us to do next?"

Now Mullaney had a confidence he couldn't betray . . . even Hernandez was not to know of the Gang of Four. "Townsend's still trying to figure it out. He said he'd get back to us."

"Well, I hope it's Danny Foyle," said Hernandez. "He beat me in the darts tournament at Smiley's Tavern, and I want my trophy back. I won it three . . ."

"Not now, Tommy!"

It was as if Mullaney had punched Hernandez in the chest. The big man pushed back in his seat, his eyes wide and his hands out, palms up. "Hey, I'm sorry . . ."

"Wait . . . no," interrupted Mullaney, shaking his hands in front of his face, ashamed at his lack of patience and short temper, "I'm the one who's sorry. Tommy, I apologize for snapping at you. It's just"—he shook his head and realized the toll exhaustion was taking on his body and his temper—"about ten minutes after we got off the call with Secretary Townsend, Atticus received a call from Noah Webster."

"Now after what Webster did to you both, there's a guy who should get skewered."

"Yeah, well, you're not going to like this, either. Webster was on Cleveland like a bad suit. He didn't know Atticus had asked me to listen in on the extension. He was rude and abusive and read Cleveland the riot act . . . told him he should pay attention to his duties and follow orders. Webster told Cleveland it was his job to pressure the Israelis to ratify the Ishmael Covenant and berated him for wasting his time on worthless ancient messages."

"Webster has all the tact of a pit bull on a bone."

Mullaney leaned into the desk. "Tommy, Webster treated Atticus like . . . like . . ." He couldn't think of the right word. "Like an immature child. It was demeaning. Not only was he disrespectful, but at the end of the call, he threatened Cleveland—told him that it doesn't matter how long he's been an ambassador or how many commendations he's received, if he doesn't follow orders and get some results soon, Webster would make sure Secretary Townsend recalled Cleveland and they would find someone else who could get the job done." He took a breath.

"I was furious. And Atticus just looked at the top of his desk and drew circles with his finger. He had that look that you talked about . . . like he had the weight of the world on his shoulders. I said he should report Webster to the secretary, that nobody has a right to speak to him in that fashion. And Cleveland said, 'Well, that's just Webster. Evan knows what he's like.' He said to just leave it alone. Then he asked if I had anything else. I got the hint and left, but that conversation has been dogging me all day. I just don't get it."

Desperation gnawed at Mullaney's heart and soured his stomach. "What do you think is going on?"

The atmosphere in Mullaney's office had the feel of a funeral home an hour before the wake was supposed to start. Only family members seated in the chairs. The dead body still dead. No matter how much they loved, none of them was going to bring that dead body back to life. They needed a miracle.

"I wish I knew. What I do know is that Webster's the wrong guy to have as an enemy," said Hernandez, his words leaden. "Even worse to have as a friend.

But since he doesn't have any friends . . ." Even the wisecrack died on Hernandez's lips. "What are we going to do, Brian?"

For a long moment, the only sound disturbing the silent corridors of the ambassador's residence was the soft classical music from Mullaney's radio. "I don't know," he mumbled, as if talking to himself. "But nobody's going to threaten Cleveland and get away with it—neither the fanatics here who are after the box nor the fanatic back in Washington who is after Cleveland's scalp. I've got to protect him, Tommy. That's my job. At least for the moment."

Hernandez sat up straight and whipped the towel from behind his neck. "There you go again . . . what do you mean, at least for the moment? What's going on with you?"

Mullaney sat back and ran his hands over his face.

"Abby wants me home."

"Or what?"

"Or . . . I don't want to find out. Cleveland included a request for transfer in his situation report."

"Webster won't allow it."

"Webster won't know. The report is going straight to Townsend."

"Good luck with that. Webster is *The Beast with a Million Eyes*. You ever see that movie? Fifties monster flick. This big . . ."

Mullaney looked at his friend. "She's scared, Tommy. She's feeling abandoned. And she's reaching out like a drowning person, grabbing anything that will float. I've got to be there for her. I've got to get home."

Hernandez took the towel in his hands and threw it on the floor. He inched up in his seat and reached his arms across the desk, palms open, and facing up. "Let's pray."

―――――⟡―――――

Gwadar, Pakistan
July 22, 1:37 a.m.

The Israeli submarine came up to periscope depth off the southern coast of Pakistan, the captain's eyes peering through the scope before all the water had dripped clear. The commander of the Shayetet 13 raiding party was standing by his left shoulder, anxious to get his elite naval commandos into the boats and onto the beach just south of the Gwadar Port complex.

Equivalent to the US Navy Seals, Shayetet 13 was part of the Israeli Navy, its members rigorously trained in the use of advanced weapons, hostage rescue, and operations behind enemy lines. Tonight, the commander's men would call upon all of their training.

Israel's military intelligence apparatus received information that Pakistan was in the process of completing a shipment of nuclear weapons to Saudi Arabia. The Saudis had long funded Pakistan's covert nuclear weapons program, with the standing promise of providing some of those weapons to the Family Saud if they were ever called for.

Israeli intelligence knew the order had been placed and the weapons' components would be loaded onto a ship at the Gwadar Port. What they didn't know was when, if there was still time, or if they could even effectively destroy the shipment once they found it.

But the commander knew that if the weapons remained on the dock, one way or another, those crates were not leaving Pakistan tonight.

If they failed, a flight of F-15I Thunder dual-purpose fighters, highly advanced versions of the Boeing F-15E Strike Eagle, was already airborne, circling high above the Indian Ocean. Should the commandos be unable to destroy the weapons themselves, the bombs and missiles of the F-15I fighters would not only destroy the weapons, but also annihilate the entire Gwadar Port facility. Israeli High Command preferred the cleaner, more surgical commando raid. But . . .

Twice the captain had adjusted the viewfinder on the periscope. Now he shuffled his shoulders in a rolling stretch and massaged the back of his neck. He turned his head to the commander and then stepped away from the periscope.

"You're going to want to take a look at this."

The commander stepped up to the viewer. It took a few moments to dial in the range but then he, too, stepped back, shook his head and then went back for a second look.

"The cargo ship is half under water," said the submarine captain.

"And the crates on the dock . . . what . . ." The Shayetet 13 leader knew what he was seeing, but he didn't believe it. "It looks like that bunch of crates on the end of the line . . . looks like whatever was inside of them has been melted."

"Look at the last one on the left," said the sub captain.

"It's . . . more. What is that?"

The submarine captain moved toward the periscope and the commando leader stepped aside. The captain gently tweaked some of the controls on the view finder.

"There's a lot more metal coming out of that last crate," he said. "But it looks like whatever is inside has been encased in a molten metal coffin. Strange, though." He fiddled with the controls. "Looks like blood on the docks . . . along by the crates. But no bodies." He scanned the area with the scope. "No bodies anywhere."

The captain turned to the commando. "Somebody beat you to it. Those nukes are toast—literally."

"But who?"

The submarine captain shook his head. Shrugged his shoulders. "Mission accomplished. Down scope!"

26

Donovan's Corner, Virginia
July 21, 4:42 p.m.

"I was hoping you would contact me. The rumor mill has been running nonstop. If the stories are true—and I don't usually put a lot of credence into what I hear down in the bowels of the Truman building—it sounds like you and Cleveland have been fortunate to walk away with your lives. And that looks like quite a wound on your head."

It was late afternoon in Virginia, just over the river from Washington, DC, and George Morningstar sat in his car, which was parked along the side of a gas station on Ox Road, near Burke Lake. Woods behind him, Morningstar was in a quiet corner, his car pointed toward the highway so he could see whatever was going on in front of him. Old tradecraft, hard to unlearn.

Morningstar exited the State Department offices only minutes after receiving the text message from Brian Mullaney. He suspected this was a conversation he didn't want overheard . . . or recorded . . . by anyone in the department, so he took the extraordinary precaution of driving halfway to his home in Virginia, turning into a service station he had never used before, and finding this quiet and secure corner where he could speak freely.

Until a few months ago, Mullaney had worked as adjutant to Morningstar who, at the time, was deputy assistant secretary for diplomatic security at the State Department. Mullaney was on a steady path to the upper echelons of both the State Department and State's Diplomatic Security Service, the armed force of special agents that was entrusted with the security of every embassy and all State Department personnel across the entire globe. For reasons he had not yet fully grasped, both Morningstar and Mullaney were unfairly targeted as scapegoats in the aftermath of an attack on the American embassy in Ankara, Turkey. Based on some trumped-up rumors of security failures leading up to the attack, and after Morningstar was publicly identified in the media as the official in charge of security, he was exiled to a make-work position in the basement of the Truman building and his close aide, Mullaney, was rushed out of the country and unwillingly assigned regional security officer for the Middle

180

East. Billeted at the US embassy in Tel Aviv, Mullaney also found himself ultimately responsible for the health and welfare of Joseph Atticus Cleveland, the newly appointed ambassador to Israel.

Both Morningstar and Mullaney were fully aware that their chastening and punishment were the result of machinations of one Noah Webster—deputy secretary of state for management and resources and the official overseer of DSS and its agents—their reputations soiled and their careers endangered so that none of the dirt from Ankara would soil Webster's handmade suits. So when Mullaney's text said he wanted to talk about "our mutual friend," Morningstar had a pretty good idea of who they were going to discuss. And this was one discussion he was not about to have in a building where Webster appeared to have ears in every corner.

"Whatever you've heard doesn't begin to scratch the surface of what's been going on over here," said Mullaney. Even though the FaceTime screen on his iPhone was small, Morningstar could clearly see that Mullaney looked exhausted, and not only because it was nearly midnight in Tel Aviv. "One of these days I will share the entire story with you. But right now I have something more pressing, something I need your help with because, George, you are the only person I can trust with this."

Mullaney had not only been incredibly effective and productive as Morningstar's right hand, but during their two years of working together, the elder and more experienced Morningstar had come to look upon Mullaney with the same affection as a son. "Anything," he said. "What do you need? Oh—wait— don't forget to tell me about this crazy box that kills people."

The smile that crossed Mullaney's face was not one of mirth, but the smile of weary resignation. "Okay, but first let me tell you why I contacted you."

With a growing apprehension and a rising fury, Morningstar listened to Mullaney's replay of Webster's threatening phone call to Cleveland. "What a slimeball," he said when Mullaney finished. "What do you need?"

"I need to know more about Webster, and I need to know more about Cleveland's relationship with Webster," said Mullaney. "Nobody pushes around Joseph Cleveland. The man's too respected, too experienced, and too smart to let a guy like Webster walk all over him. But that's just what happened earlier today. And not only did Webster get away with it, not only did he seem to relish every moment of denigrating a good man, but Cleveland made up excuses for Webster after it was over. There's something wonky going on, some strange reason why Webster can treat Cleveland the way he did and know that he can get away with it. And I want to find out what that thing may be so I can crush it."

"And you want me to dig into Webster's past with Cleveland?"

"Yeah," said Mullaney. "I want to know . . ."

"Brian . . . you are entering into very dangerous territory here," Morningstar interrupted. "Webster is powerful, ruthless, and vengeful. If he finds out that you are digging into his past, his background, your next posting may be on Pluto—if you are still with the department. Are you sure you want to take this kind of a risk?"

A black panel van with smoke-tinted windows pulled into the gas station, and Morningstar's pulse quickened. Then he shook himself free of anxiety and returned his concentration to Mullaney, whose face was twisted in a painful-looking grimace.

"And for you to poke around in Webster's past would put you at risk too," Mullaney admitted. "I know. I've thought about it. Webster is a thug in a silk suit. A bully with no heart. But there's something else going on with Cleveland. It's not just Webster throwing around his weight or his position. I can hear it in his voice . . . it's a stiletto and not a bludgeon. Webster is not hammering Cleveland like a brute, he's slicing his carotid like an assassin."

Even though the words were incendiary, there was nothing Mullaney was saying that came as a surprise to Morningstar. Webster was a dangerous foe.

"I've got to do something. I've got to figure this out, George. I will not sit back and watch Webster vilify this good man, even if it wrecks any chance of me being reassigned to DC."

Morningstar was confused. "You just got there. And why would Webster allow you to come back?"

"I forgot to tell you." Mullaney stopped and took a breath. "Cleveland submitted his situational report to the secretary yesterday. He went out of his way to include in the report an ambassadorial request for me to be reassigned to Washington."

The ulcer that Morningstar had been battling for weeks thrust a stabbing jolt of pain into his stomach. *Oh, no . . .*

"Abby has made it clear that she needs me to be home," the words came tumbling out of Mullaney, full of hope and dread at the same time, "and that Virginia is our home, not Israel. Cleveland understands that I need to get back to DC as soon as possible. An ambassadorial request is always honored, if possible. That should make a difference with the secretary."

What do I do? How can I . . .

"Cleveland would do that?" asked Morningstar. "You've only been assigned to Israel for a few weeks. Are you sure Cleveland would stick his neck out that far, so soon?"

Mullaney was nodding his head vigorously. "Oh, yeah. He promised me . . . said it was the least he could do after I saved his daughter's life. I only hope the secretary has . . ."

"Brian . . ." Morningstar interrupted, but how to say it? How do you put betrayal into words? "I've read Cleveland's situation report. I wanted to make sure I watched your back, so I've cashed in a few favors so that everything that comes in from Israel gets blind copied to me."

Morningstar could read the question on Mullaney's face and the apprehension that followed.

"Brian, there was no request in Cleveland's report for you to be transferred back to DC." Morningstar felt like he had just ripped the heart out of his friend. "I read it all. No ambassadorial request, which would have been obvious, but no other hint of a request either. Brian . . . he just didn't mention it."

In his screen, Mullaney blinked a few times, like a man walking out of a coal mine and into the sunshine, but then he closed his eyes, squeezed down his eyebrows, and shook his head. "No, George, it's in there. It has to be in there. He promised me."

US Ambassador's Residence, Tel Aviv
July 21, 11:58 p.m.

Sleep-deprived, saddled with layers of anxiety, barely keeping fear at bay as if he was walking downhill with a brimming-over water bucket in each hand, Brian Mullaney held onto the edge of the desk in his office at the ambassador's residence in Tel Aviv. Surely he must have been mistaken. He misunderstood what Morningstar was saying.

"No, George, it's in there. It has to be in there. He promised me."

Through the lens of his iPhone, he searched the face of his friend . . . his trusted friend. And he saw nothing but sadness and loss.

"I'm sorry, Brian. I read the report thoroughly." Morningstar's hand came up and covered the lower half of his face, rubbing back and forth across his chin. He shook his head the way a doctor does when he informs relatives that the patient died. "There was nothing in the report requesting that you be re-assigned to Washington."

For a moment, Mullaney couldn't catch his thoughts as his mind fled from the painful present. Except his mind raced into an even more painful past—the look on his father's face when he told his father he was leaving the state police; standing beside his father's deathbed, realizing he would never receive forgiveness; the brokenhearted look on Abby's face when she told him she would not follow him to Israel. Now this . . . betrayed, abandoned once again. By a man he trusted. By a father he trusted. By a wife he trusted.

Mullaney knew he was still breathing, his heart still beating, but he didn't know how. He felt the cloak of death wrap around his heart and the enemy of hope steal his future. Time itself stood still.

What was wrong with him? What did he do . . . or fail to do? Was he just useless? Just a failure? Unworthy of trust or faithfulness? He thought Cleveland . . . that they were . . .

"Brian?"

Mullaney focused on the iPhone in his hand. Morningstar was staring into the lens with the urgency of a paramedic.

"Are you okay?"

Mullaney's brain sent a signal to his mouth to speak, but his spirit was so crushed his lips felt like tons of concrete and he couldn't force them apart. His body kept bending at the waist, searching for his stomach that had evacuated his lifeless carcass and crashed through the floor like a runaway elevator. *I trusted him. I was so sure. Now I've failed Abby again. What's the use? The result is always the same. What hope is there?*

"Brian!" Morningstar was trying to get his attention. He was saying something.

Mullaney tapped the red button at the bottom of the screen, and George Morningstar's image returned across the ocean to Washington, where he belonged. Where Mullaney belonged!

He pushed down the tab on the side of the phone that turned off the ringer and shoved the iPhone into his pants pocket. He got up from behind the desk, crossed the room, turned out the light, and locked the door. He walked the short distance to his bungalow and sat at the kitchen table, held his aching head in his hands. His breathing was labored, coming out of his lungs and through his nose like the chugs of a steam engine. *Why?* He didn't cry. But his huffing breaths were soon combined with pounding sobs, dry heaves of abandonment searing the lining of his throat, his face buried in his hands.

He was alone. And he was lost. And he was in agony.

What hope is there?

27

When Mullaney raised his head from the kitchen table, he could smell the burnt coffee and hear the TV—a soccer game from somewhere in the world—things he had turned on hours ago and forgotten about. His back hurt and his mouth felt like, and probably smelled like, the inside of a bowling shoe.

It was a long time ago, the last time he fell asleep at the kitchen table. Probably in his former life, when he was a Virginia State cop. He didn't want to remember why then, and he certainly didn't want to remember why now. The wound was still too tender.

Still in a fog, Mullaney looked around in the kitchen, checked the time. For a moment, he debated whether to make the effort to walk to the bedroom or stay there and go back to sleep. Not for the first time, Mullaney was grateful he no longer drank alcohol. Last night . . . now . . . would have been ugly. More ugly.

When he got off the phone with Morningstar it was after midnight . . . too late to disturb the ambassador. Now it was too early.

Mullaney, still fully dressed except for his suit jacket, pushed himself to his feet and stepped to the kitchen counter. He switched off the coffee machine, but there wasn't much he could do about the scorched glass pot except to take it off the burner to let it cool.

His bungalow on the grounds of the ambassador's residence was small, so it took only a few steps to enter the living area and turn off the TV. The silence felt like an oppressive weight on his heart. He turned the TV back on but turned the sound low. Then he sat on the sofa and looked for something to do.

What do you do at two in the morning when there's nothing to do? Go to bed? Stare at a wall?

Ten minutes later Mullaney was still staring at the wall, wondering why, knowing there would be no answer until he had a chance to talk to Cleveland. There had to be a why, a reason, something that made sense, that he could understand and digest. There had to be. Could he be that gullible, that foolish? Could he have missed something . . . caused something? Was there some offense? How had he failed?

Then guilt and shame invaded his thoughts. Two of his men had died today. Yesterday? They died trying to rid the world of this gang of Turkish killers. And now all he could think of was himself? His needs? His future?

Mullaney felt useless. Worthless. Helpless. And empty.

Exhaustion weighed on every muscle. He yawned, stretched out his arms, thought again about bed. His right hand brushed something on the side table.

Holy Bible.

Oh, no. You're not going to get me this time. There's no use when there's no answer. And there's no answer to this.

I will never put you into a conflict that I have not already equipped you to win.

Mullaney looked at the television. The sound was low, but he could swear the announcer was speaking Hebrew. Sounded like Hebrew.

But he knew what this voice was.

For decades, Mullaney had cultivated his relationship with God. It was prayer, yes. But more than prayer. Over the years, in quiet, still mornings, Mullaney had started writing in a journal. It helped him stay awake when his eyes were heavy, and it helped him focus on and record not only his prayers to God, but also God's responses to those prayers. He heard those responses not audibly, in his ears, but spiritually, in his heart and soul. There was a still, small voice that spoke to him. It was clear. And it communicated things that Mullaney knew did not come from his own mind. It was harder to put it any more plainly than that. And he certainly couldn't prove it to anyone if he tried. But Mullaney knew the voice—the still, small voice—that spoke to his spirit on so many mornings. He was speaking now. And Mullaney didn't want to hear it.

"Why are you talking to me," Mullaney said to the empty room, an angry edge to his voice and frustration clouding his already weary mind. "I don't want to hear what you have to say. If you were interested, you could have fixed Cleveland's report . . . made sure the transfer request was in there. If you can't do that . . . don't talk to me."

You need to change the way you think.

Now Mullaney was awake. He was itching for a fight. "Or what?"

What is the lie you are believing?

He looked again at the Bible on his right. No . . . not a time to read. It was a time to talk, a time to get down to business.

"What lie am I believing?"

He listened. Nothing.

"Okay," he said, his voice and his temper rising, "what—lie—am—I—believing?"

He listened. Then he heard his own thoughts. *Cleveland lied to me.*

Is that true?

It was a simple question. Mullaney stopped, took a breath, and considered. He didn't know whether Cleveland had lied to him or not. He hadn't gotten a chance to ask Cleveland. How would he know the truth until he asked? The air started leaking from his self-righteous anger.

"He promised to put the transfer request in his report," he said, his words morphing from pugnacious to prayerful, flowing from pain and not pride. Mullaney pushed himself forward on the sofa, put his elbows on his knees, and held his face in his hands. "But there was no request in the report. How will I ever get home in time?"

What's the other lie you're believing?

Now his thoughts started roaming through his mind, searching from compartment to compartment, looking . . .

"Other lie? What other lie?"

All the compartments his thoughts entered were empty.

"Please," Mullaney whispered, his words a reverent offering, "help me."

His thoughts entered the compartment that contained the memories of his home and his family. The girls were running into the house, laughing and teasing each other, still sweaty in their soccer uniforms. Sweaty and beautiful. Then Abby came in behind them, one arm wrapped around a paper grocery bag, a baguette poking out the top, the other clutching her keys and handbag, pushing closed the door.

Abby called out after them, "Homework!" and the word had the lilt of a Southern ballad. Then she turned and saw Brian. And a smile irradiated her face, her eyes dancing flames of delight, pure joy pouring out of her soul into his. "Brian . . . you're home!" She tossed the keys and the handbag on the kitchen island, placed the grocery bag beside them and came right up to Mullaney, pressing herself hard against his body. She placed her arms on his shoulders, her fingers in the hair at the nape of his neck. Her eyes, azure blue like the clear morning sky, looked up at his with a longing and a desire he felt in his gut.

"You're home."

Contentment, gratitude, safety.

"I'm so glad."

Abby pushed up on her toes, angled her head to the right, and kissed him with a fervor and passion that made Mullaney wish the girls weren't home. His breath caught in his chest. He was encased in her warmth.

What's the lie you're believing?

Entranced, enchanted, aching for the images in his mind, Mullaney strained to hold onto them—hold onto the warmth—as he was pulled back to his conscious world by the question he heard in his spirit.

A ragged tear ruptured his heart. The pain of the thought . . .

What's the lie you're believing?

"Abby doesn't love me." The words were ripped from his lips and invaded the room like the specter of death.

What's the truth?

Mullaney's breathing came from his depths. A leap of faith spread before him. Could he . . . would he?

"She's always loved me."

She chose you.

"She just wants me home. She wants to share her life with me, with our children."

And . . .

"And she's afraid."

Afraid of what?

As if all the lights came on in all the compartments of his mind at the same time, Mullaney saw and knew the truth.

"Afraid of the lie she's believing. That I don't love her, or our children . . . that I don't love them enough."

Enough for what?

"Enough to choose her."

Mullaney took a deep breath and washed his heart with the truth. The plain, simple truth that so often got lost in the hurried, the urgent, the critical.

He ran his hands through his hair and sat up straight. "Outside of my relationship with you, Lord," he said, his words a caress, "Abby is the most important person in my life. No one comes close. Nothing is more important to me than our marriage and our family."

And what's the truth?

It took only a split second for Mullaney to acknowledge the truth and accept the decision that the truth required. Suddenly, he felt clean . . . alive . . . energized . . . embraced.

"I'm going home." It was a statement of finality, of purpose, of character. "It doesn't matter what Cleveland did or didn't do, I'm going home. If I have to resign my position, forswear my oath, I'm going home. Nothing is more important."

Mullaney looked at the clock on the wall. Seven twenty at night in Virginia. Not too late. He pulled out his iPhone from his pants pocket and paused. He lifted his eyes and—as if he could see through the walls of his bungalow—stared up into the heavens. "Thank you."

"I will never leave you nor forsake you."

"Thank you." And he tapped the button for Abby.

Fairfax County, Virginia
July 21, 7:31 p.m.

Abigail Mullaney looked at the two file folders sitting on the table in the small kitchen, client files thick with reports, surveys, and polling data, and felt no compulsion or desire to touch them, let alone open them for review. She pushed aside the folders, put her coffee cup on the table, and sat down, resting her head in the palms of her hands. How did her life get so messed up?

Trim, athletic, and still stunning in her midforties, it was her intellect, her grasp of today's societal realities, her training and experience in molding public perception that had launched and sustained her successful career in the halls of corporate giants. It wasn't her father's influence or his money that bought her a place at the table. Abigail Mullaney was an A-list public relations wizard because of her own wisdom and cunning, not her father's.

So why was she here, sitting in this small kitchen in the guest house of her father's Virginia estate, just off the landscaped contours of a spectacular outdoor swimming complex? Her home on the other side of Fairfax County was empty. Her daughters were upstairs, probably fixated on social media. Her husband was half a world away in Israel, a country that seemed to be teetering between unexpected peace and violent chaos. Her marriage was hemorrhaging, spinning out of control in a downward spiral, and she felt powerless to make it stop.

She looked at the clock. Just past seven thirty. She was hungry, angry, lonely, and tired. And she was scared. Below the thousand-dollar tailored suits and the glamorous veneer of her striking beauty, she was petrified of the possibility that lurked in her future.

Why was Brian so stubborn? Why was she so stubborn? Why couldn't they get out of their own way and find a path that would take them back—or move them forward—into the settled, peaceful, blessed life that had once been theirs? Didn't he know how much she loved him? Didn't he know how much she needed him? *God, what's happening to us?*

Unbidden, a disturbing thought invaded her mind. Yes, Brian had been putting himself and his career . . . his honor . . . first. But what was she putting first? Hadn't her desires been just as diverted as his? Hadn't the glamour, the influence, the power that encircled her father, the astoundingly wealthy Richard Rutherford, enticed her back into the heady realm of the rich and famous—and influential—who ruled in Washington's society?

They had drifted apart because each of them was pulling their relationship in a self-serving direction. It was not just Brian. She was as much . . .

Her iPhone was on the table next to her now-cold coffee, its ringer turned off, its screen face down. Her eyes were closed, her spirit seeking God for an answer, when her phone rattled a few inches across the top of the table.

Let it go?

It rattled again.

Angered by the interruption, she flipped the phone over onto its back.

Brian? FaceTiming again? Suddenly, terror seized her heart. *Is he . . . ?* She grabbed the phone, hit the Accept button, and his face materialized on the screen.

"Brian? Are you okay?"

"Sweetheart . . . I love you. And I'm coming home." His face had that earnest set to it she had seen before, when he had made up his mind about something, but his voice was breathless, the words tumbling over his lips like a spring stream over boulders.

"Brian?"

"Abby . . . this has been one of the worst days of my life and now one of the best," he rattled on. "And I just wanted you to know, I love you and I'm coming home."

Abigail looked at his face on the phone in her hand, her mind trying to compute the words pouring out of her husband. An answer to prayer? So soon? "I . . . I don't understand," she fumbled. "What do you mean? What's happened?"

She listened to Brian work his way through his day. While her eyes never left his, her right hand cradled the phone in front of her, her left hand cupped under her chin, rested alongside her cheek, holding up her shaking head. He told her about the disturbing conversation between Webster and Cleveland, about the raid on the livery depot in the old city of Tel Aviv and the good men who had died there—his men. And he told her of his conversation with Morningstar, his plea for help in probing Webster's past, and the numb devastation he felt . . . betrayal . . . when Morningstar told him there was no request for his transfer in Cleveland's report.

"I was desolate," and she could see the anguish on his face. "I felt like giving up . . . like everyone had given up on me. Yeah, self-pity. But I was lost. And then God asked me, '*What is the lie that you're believing?*'"

Abby knew of Brian's journals, the growing number that filled a bookshelf in his office. He often read the journal entries to her, the ones that strongly impacted him or the ones that spoke of their life together. She knew the voice he was listening to. And she trusted that voice herself.

"And I realized all of the lies that I was accepting as true," said Brian. "And I need to ask your forgiveness."

A tear slid down her cheek, down the side of her left hand. Others started to form.

"I'm sorry, Ab . . . I've believed a lie that you don't love me—not enough to let me fulfill my duty. And that lie made me blind to the truth. That you love me so much you just want to spend your life with me, with our children. I'm sorry I've been so selfish, so self-centered all these years. Can you forgive me?"

There were words, but they were caught in her throat, blocked by the sobs that bubbled up from her lungs and escaped in gasps between her lips. She heard her husband's heart, and it was breaking hers—breaking hers free with gladness and thanksgiving. "I . . . I . . ."

"And, Abby," said Brian, the words coming out of him like an onrushing train, "God also told me that you've been suffering from fear . . . fear that I don't love you enough, love our marriage, our family enough, to put you first in my life. Well, I want you to know this. On this earth, you are number one, Abby. There is no one, nothing, more important to me than you. If I were to lose you, I would lose my life. I'm going to resign my appointment . . . I'm coming home."

Thank you, Jesus!

Then conviction struck Abigail in her spirit.

Her thoughts were in a tumble dryer of conflicting emotions, thrashing about in a discordant jumble. Abigail had been waiting so long to hear these words from her husband. But something wasn't sitting right. She pushed herself back from the table and tried to sort out her contradictory feelings, wiping the tears from her eyes. Yes . . . Yes! . . . she wanted him home. But, what about . . .

"Brian . . ." She paused, hoping to get the words right. "You've given me a precious gift tonight, one I will nourish and cherish the rest of my life. Thank you. I hear your heart, and I love it. And I long for you to be here with me and with our children. My body, my spirit aches for you."

"I—"

"Wait," Abby interrupted. "Brian, I'm sitting here in my joy, and my mind is grieving for you."

"What?"

Now the tears began again. But this time they were not tears of thanksgiving. They were tears of empathy and remorse.

"Who died today?"

Her husband recoiled from the question, a sharp intake of breath came through the phone, as if her words had stabbed Mullaney in the chest.

"Ed Mitchell. Bobby Collier." Mullaney spoke the names like the tolling of a bell at a funeral service. "Ed Mitchell has three kids. Meyer lost two of his men. One was his right hand . . . had been with him for fifteen years."

"I'm so sorry, Brian. They were good men."

"The best."

"Who killed them?"

She waited. She could see that he was collecting himself, trying hard to fit himself back into the role of DSS regional security officer.

"The same gang of thugs," Mullaney said woodenly, "who came after Atticus in Istanbul, who attacked us on the road to Jerusalem. The same gang who abducted Cleveland's daughter, who blew up the Hurva Synagogue."

"And they're still out there? They're still a threat?"

Abigail Rutherford hadn't been married to Brian Mullaney for nearly two decades without learning something about the man, the father of her children. She understood the conflict he was right now facing and the forces rending him between one responsibility and another.

"What are the two things you've always told me?" Abby asked. "'I will never shirk my duty, and I will never betray a confidence.' Right?"

His silence confirmed her intuition.

Abby leaned into the phone, getting closer to his image. "Brian, I hear your heart, and I love you for it. But the man I love would die a slow, agonizing death if he walked away without avenging the death of his friends by finding their killers and ripping them from the face of the earth. The man I love would wither away if he turned his back on Ambassador Cleveland and his daughter while their lives were still in danger. These men are terrorists . . . murderers of innocents. You need to catch them, Brian. You need to bring justice down on their heads. Hear me, my darling. Don't love me too much. Don't love me and lose yourself. Lose yourself and there wouldn't be anything left for me to love when you do get home."

"Abby, I . . ."

"And before you believe anything about Ambassador Cleveland," she said, her protective genes pumping full bore, "go and ask him face-to-face about his report. If what I've been told is true, Ambassador Cleveland is a man of character and integrity, honorable and trustworthy. He's not a manipulator or a deceiver. So if he told you he would request your transfer back to DC, I think you should believe his words until they are proven false. I feel it in my spirit, Brian . . . something else has happened here. You . . . you may have an enemy you're unaware of."

Mullaney's burst of laughter, clipped short, surprised Abby. That was another thing she didn't expect.

"Oh, yeah. I think Cleveland and I have the same enemy," he said. "Not entirely sure why, but I'm pretty sure I know who."

"Webster?"

"Noah Webster's certainly no friend," he said. "With George's help, I intend to learn more about my opponent."

A thread of dread wove its way through her thoughts. "Be careful. Webster's out for Webster. I think he squashes his enemies and takes no captives. But listen." She shook Webster out of her head and set her spirit on the miracle God had orchestrated this night, focusing her eyes on her husband, "Thank you for all this. Thank you for loving me, loving our girls, loving our life together. But Brian, go finish your job there. Please . . . be careful with yourself. Stay safe. But go get these guys, make sure the ambassador's safe, and then come home. I miss you now, more than ever. But we'll all be waiting for you, when the time is right. And you'll know when that time is. And I'll be here when it's over—no!"

Abby swatted a stray tear from her cheek. No more tears! "No, Brian. Not here. Home. I'll be waiting at home . . . our home. And I'll keep the lights on, and the bed warm, until you get back."

—◦◦◦◦—

She didn't know how long she had been sitting at the table in silence, staring at her phone, holding the mug that still contained cold coffee. Her prayers had flowed like a torrent once her wonderful conversation with Brian ended. Now she simply felt drained. But alive. Alive with hope, with possibilities, with gratitude.

Now, dear God, please keep him safe. Keep him safe, and bring him home.

Abigail Rutherford Mullaney took a sip of her coffee. It didn't matter at all that it was cold.

28

US Embassy, Tel Aviv
July 22, 8:45 a.m.

The urgency . . . no, the panic . . . Mullaney felt a few hours earlier had dissipated like fog at sunrise. Abby had heard his heart during his phone call home and was relieved by his determination . . . blessed that he promised to be home . . . no matter what. Now he just had to figure out how to get home, the best way, the right way, to fulfill his responsibilities here and get back to his family as soon as possible. Was there a way that he didn't have to outright resign from the State Department? A way that didn't feel like he was abandoning his responsibility? A way that didn't depend on Richard Rutherford?

He hadn't gotten much sleep, but he felt fresher than he did sleeping on the kitchen table at two in the morning. And he had an appointment to meet with Cleveland first thing this morning, as soon as the ambassador arrived at the embassy. Cleveland was hosting seven members of the Knesset's leadership for breakfast. Ostensibly, it was a chance for Cleveland to introduce himself. Practically, Mullaney knew, it was an opportunity for Cleveland to begin tracking the possible fate of the Ishmael Covenant, if it ever got to a ratification vote in the Knesset.

Mullaney had his phone in his hand to call Meyer Levinson when the console on his desk lit up.

———※———

The man who exited the elevator, escorted by the marine sergeant, was an enigma. Clearly elderly, but not frail. Thin, but not weak. Dressed in the black garb of a Jewish rabbi, but he looked like Barry Fitzgerald in a yarmulke—long nose and high forehead, arched eyebrows over cautious but inquisitive eyes. He had a large, wide-brimmed black hat in one fist and a pipe that looked like the end of a ram's horn clenched in the other.

When the call had come from the guard desk that there was a Rabbi Herzog wanting to see him, Brian Mullaney held onto a momentary glimmer of hope, hope that propelled him out of his office to wait by the elevator. But the man walking out of the elevator was not the Herzog he was hoping to see.

With a shake of his head, the man tapped himself on the chest with his pipe. "I also wish I was my son," he said, his voice shrouded in the lonely grief of a surviving father, his words released slowly, as if each one had been specifically selected for that moment and held a life of its own. "I am Mordechai Herzog, and I would most certainly exchange the dregs of my life for the hope of his. But that power I do not have."

About a head shorter than Mullaney, slightly stooped in the shoulders, he carefully measured the DSS agent from under the brow of his eyes.

"Rabbi Herzog," Mullaney said, extending his hand. "I'm sorry for your loss. How . . ."

Herzog took Mullaney's hand and locked it in a grip like a gnarled tree trunk. Mullaney felt as if the man were x-raying his character, searching for flaws, while he crushed Mullaney's fingers. "Well," said Mullaney, pulling his hand free and shaking out the pain, "I can see one family resemblance already."

"Hmmm . . . something my father taught me," said Rabbi Herzog, a faint smile touching the corners of his mouth. "You can often tell a great deal about the contents of a man's heart by the firmness of his grip. I can see why Israel trusted you."

"Well thank you, sir," said Mullaney. "Here, let's go to my office."

———⊰✧⊱———

Ankara
July 22, 8:50 a.m.

"An elderly rabbi just entered the US embassy," said the voice of the commander of the Disciples.

"And why is that important?"

"Because the winged ones were with him."

The Turk opened his eyes. *Perhaps there is an opportunity.*

"How many Disciples are there?"

"Two—one front, one back."

"Send two more. Then wait for my call."

29

"I appreciate your condolences, Agent Mullaney, and your kind words about my son. In Jewish tradition, he was buried yesterday." Rabbi Mordechai Herzog had his hat in his lap and the ram's horn pipe in his left hand. He kept looking at the pipe like a long-lost friend.

"I'm afraid you can't smoke that in here," Mullaney offered. "The entire building is smoke-free."

"How's a man supposed to think?" Herzog shook his head. "Too many rules these days. Imagine," he smiled, "a rabbi saying there are too many rules." He pushed the pipe into the pocket of his suit coat.

"How can I help you, Rabbi?"

"Me, you can't. But you I can help." Rabbi Herzog leaned forward. "When he left the ambassador's residence two days ago, my son sought my counsel about the surprising gift you brought him. You," he said, waving his hat at Mullaney, "I think you may have need of that same counsel. But warn you, I must. I am in strange waters here. I do not know the best way to proceed."

The rabbi was fidgeting in his chair, shaking his head. He looked at the hat in his left hand. He pushed it onto his head and spied at Mullaney from under its wide brim. "Agent Mullaney, do you believe in angels?"

Stunned, Mullaney sat back in his chair, his mind tripping to the incident on the loading dock in the Holon District. But Herzog swept on without waiting for an answer.

"No? I thought not. I also doubted . . . until yesterday."

Herzog reached into the inside of his jacket and withdrew an envelope. He held it up in front of Mullaney. The outside of the envelope was soiled and stained in spots.

"There is good and there is evil, Agent Mullaney. From the days of Adam's sons, good and evil have both walked this earth, always in conflict. At times, good appears to prevail. At other times, the darkness of evil seems to cover the world. But one thing is certain," said Herzog. "If evil is advancing, goodness is advancing as well. If evil powers are at work to destroy us, powers of good are also at work to protect us."

———◦◦◦———

US Ambassador's Residence, Tel Aviv
July 22, 8:53 a.m.

Cleveland had just escorted his guests to the front door of the residence, his breakfast with the members of the Israeli Knesset both enlightening and frustrating, when the iPhone in his jacket pocket began to hum and vibrate. The parade of black limousines was pulling away as he looked at the screen. "Blocked."

Curious, Cleveland pressed the green button to answer the call.

"If your patience hasn't been worn too thin by your breakfast guests, perhaps you would have some time for an old friend?"

The voice was distinct and unmistakable. But why would David Meir be here in Tel Aviv? Israel appeared to be coming apart at the seams, in the midst of armed insurrection and political crisis.

"Because I need your unfettered counsel," answered the prime minister of Israel, before the question was even asked. "I need your help. And I'm right around the corner."

"I've got all the time you need, David. I'll be waiting on the front steps."

———◦◦◦———

They kept the conversation formal and appropriate until they arrived inside Cleveland's office and the door was securely closed. Only then did Cleveland step close to Meir, grasp his right hand in a firm handshake, his left hand on Meir's right bicep in an expression of bonded friendship. "Good to see you, David. I'm sorry I didn't get to your office the other day. We ran into a detour."

"Yes, I heard. I'm happy you escaped without any serious injuries, and overjoyed Levinson's Shin Bet team could help find and rescue your daughter. How is Palmyra?"

"The physical damage was limited—some scalp wounds when they chopped off her hair. She's a tough, capable woman," said Cleveland, "but she's been traumatized and frightened beyond our comprehension, so I'm concerned for her mental and emotional well-being. Physically, she's a rock."

"Like her father," said Meir. "You've had quite a challenging few days since you arrived."

"And this one is just beginning," said Cleveland, pointing to the weathered leather grouping in the corner of the room. "I think I may be getting too old for all this excitement."

They sat facing each other, Meir on the brown leather sofa, Cleveland in the leather armchair opposite. "Coffee?" he asked.

"No, thank you. I'm already fueled up for the morning," said Meir. "One question, though. Are there listening devices in your office?"

Understanding the question, Cleveland got out of the chair, crossed to behind his desk, opened a drawer on the right and flipped a switch. He returned and settled himself into the chair. "Now you can feel free to speak. There will be no record of what's said here today."

"Thank you, Atticus." The prime minister settled back into the sofa, crossed his legs at the ankle. "It's not the reason I'm here, but is there anything you can share with me from your breakfast with the Knesset leadership?"

Cleveland did a quick rewind, assuring himself that there was no request to keep the elements of the conversations confidential.

"Honest?"

"Always."

"You've lost the confidence of a good number," said Cleveland. "But you know that. What I heard today, though, is that you've lost their trust as well. Some of your closest allies feel blindsided. Not that you kept the negotiations on the covenant a secret, but that its impact is so sweeping, such a monumental change in the course and fortunes of your nation . . . they feel betrayed that you didn't consult at least some of them before you signed the covenant, representing all of Israel. And frankly, there are so many parts to this treaty that there is something for almost all of them to oppose. You've got a tough road ahead of you, David. If. . ."

"If?"

Cleveland liked David Meir. He was a good man, admirable, honest, trustworthy. He had sacrificed much of his life to serve his country. And now, in what could have—should have—been his moment of greatest triumph . . .

"If you survive," he said. "If your government survives. There was open talk of a no-confidence vote."

"When?"

"Soon . . . perhaps this week . . . perhaps next week. But soon."

David Meir took it all in without flinch or grimace. Clearly he knew and understood what he was facing. "And you, Atticus, what do you think of this covenant?"

"Me or my government?"

"Your government I know. President Boylan has already contacted me personally. He wants to see the covenant ratified. He was very firm in stating his belief that an independent Palestinian state is critical for peace in the Middle East. And I was just as firm in stating my belief that an Iranian regime free of all international sanctions will simply have more money to spend on perfecting a nuclear weapon and an effective delivery system intended to destroy Israel and hold the rest of the region as hostage. Stalemate. But you, Atticus . . . I come here today for your counsel. You have a different perspective than mine. I trust you, and I respect your perspective. Tell me . . . what do you see?"

Cleveland knew it was time for truth.

"Confidentially, and speaking for myself, personally, I believe both of our countries are pursuing paths that will lead to disaster—ultimately to a Middle Eastern conflict that will spew devastation and destruction across the region."

30

Herzog held the envelope in front of his face, shaking it for emphasis. "This is the translation of the Vilna Gaon's second prophecy. It was given by my son to his aide, Chaim Yavod, just prior to the explosion of the Hurva Synagogue."

His eyes transfixed on the envelope, Mullaney flashed back to the man who had emerged from the ruins of the Hurva, who had been chased through the streets of Jerusalem for the box that he was carrying.

"How did you—"

"Angels, Agent Mullaney. Or I must be more accurate. One angel," said Herzog.

He lowered his hand and rested the stained envelope in his lap.

"I was sitting with my son's body, mourning his death, when an angel appeared to me. He showed me where this message was . . . the inside coat pocket of Chaim Yavod's body, which was in the same room." Herzog paused, turning the envelope over in his hand. "Perhaps you think me a fool or deluded? Lost touch with reality?"

Mullaney had a few memories of his own from the last two days. His mind flashed back to the moment on Malan Street when a powerful hand grabbed the back of his jacket and threw him behind a dumpster as bullets flashed past his body. "You would be surprised at what I've come to consider as reality. I don't doubt you for a moment."

"Good . . . then perhaps doubt me you won't when I tell you that the angel—Bayard he was named—sent me to you with a purpose. Not only this message to deliver, but also to bestow upon you the anointing of the guardian."

Like a slap in the face, a tsunami of fear swept over Mullaney, swamping and threatening his foundations. It was one thing to be engaged in the fight. He was okay with that. Went with the territory. It was what he was trained for—protect those who needed protection with all the skills and experience at his disposal. But always on the periphery. Part of, but never the center of attention. A guardian, yes. But this was something completely different.

The little man with the round face and inquisitive eyes had opened the door to a place where Mullaney had stashed all his fears. Was he good enough to be *the* guardian? Did he deserve to be given this anointing? Was he worthy? Was he able?

"You've got to be kidding. I can't do that," he said. "Not just because—"

Herzog held up his hand as a stop sign. "I know. You are reluctant not because my son perished carrying the anointing. It is not physical fear that attacks your confidence. You are reluctant because you doubt your worth. Is that not true? Why you? I know, believe me, I know. Because that same fear I felt, the same sense of unworthiness—even when a giant angel put his hands on my head, his huge wings unfurled, and spoke the Aaronic Blessing over me."

The rabbi leaned forward, his voice betraying the depth of his concern. "You have come face-to-face with evil these past few days. Not just bad men out to do evil. But evil itself. The same evil that killed my son and so many others. But you have also felt the touch of angels, I think.

"Angels, though created on a lower level than mankind, are immortal, their bodies don't suffer from pain and sickness. They are smarter, faster, stronger. They are not infinite . . . only God is infinite. And he makes all the rules, so he can wipe out angels—all angels—anytime he desires. And they don't have God's nature. They are not omniscient nor omnipresent. They are finite, supernatural beings.

"To us," said Herzog, "angels look like superheroes. And in many ways they are. But there are good superheroes and there are evil superheroes. I certainly don't understand it all. But I can tell you that super evil has been unleashed to try and thwart the purpose of the Gaon's prophecies. I believe we have yet to understand the ultimate purpose of his messages. But I also believe that super evil has sought to destroy the prophecies since they were first written over two hundred years ago, and super evil has persisted in its attempts to destroy the prophecies—and the men who have been anointed as guardians of those prophecies—right up until the present. So I am not surprised to find good superheroes . . . angels . . . working on our behalf.

"But Agent Mullaney, why . . . why now? Why this prophecy, this box of death, this supposed peace with the Arabs and the unleashing of this evil, all at the same time? About that have you wondered?"

This time Mullaney didn't hesitate. If he was going to get an answer in, it had to be quick. "Only in my sleep, and there's been precious little of that," he said. "The last few days, I haven't had much time to think about why things are happening. Too many people have died, and the ones responsible for those deaths are still out there, waiting, ready to try again." Mullaney could feel the level of his agitation rising. He got out of his chair, turned, and looked out the window. The day's heat was beginning to penetrate the glass. "I'm just trying to keep those people around me alive," he said, his comments as much for himself as for Herzog. He turned back toward the rabbi. "Which is another reason why I don't think I can take on this guardian role that you and your angel want to put on my shoulders. Wherever that box goes, the crazies go, too."

Rubbing his chin with his left hand, Herzog opened the palm of his right hand toward Mullaney. The envelope was still between his fingers. "So . . . you care not to know this message?"

US Ambassador's Residence, Tel Aviv
July 22, 9:10 a.m.

"Bluntly spoken," said Meir. "Why are you so confident that your president's policies or this covenant between Israel and its Arab neighbors will lead to disaster?"

"Persia must be stopped," said Cleveland, "on that we both agree. Removing the economic sanctions that have crippled the Iranian mullahs is ludicrous. The Iranians have not lived up to the terms of a single treaty in nearly three thousand years. Betrayal is a way of life for the Persians . . . it's how they do business. If you don't approach them understanding betrayal . . . knowing it will be part of the equation . . . you approach them as a fool."

Cleveland took a breath. Gathered his thoughts.

"Iran may be impoverished," he acknowledged, "but still its influence increases throughout the Middle East. It's infiltrated the region through relationship and Shia doctrine—Hezbollah in Lebanon, the Houthis in Yemen, the Badr Brigades in Iraq, and lately getting their talons into Bassad in Syria. Iran has become such a threat, King Abdullah has called in an IOU from the Pakistanis, asking for the nuclear weapons that have been waiting in storage . . . but you probably already knew that, yes?"

Meir nodded in agreement. "Yes, we are aware of Abdullah's gambit for nuclear weapons . . . perhaps the most destabilizing thing that could happen in our region at the moment." He continued to nod. "But spend no time worrying about Saudi nukes. That issue has been dealt with."

Wheels and gears spun in Cleveland's mind. "How?"

"Destroyed—melted actually—while still in their crates in the Gwadar Port."

Cleveland was not surprised. Israel's military and its leaders were vigilant, determined, and fearless. "Shayetet 13 is very effective."

A Cheshire cat smile spread across Meir's face—a smile that said, I know something you don't.

"What?" asked Cleveland.

"It wasn't us," Meir said matter-of-factly. "Somebody got there first. Our guys were on a submarine, just off the coast of Pakistan near Gwadar. They were getting ready to launch their mission when they saw the crates were destroyed and the ship that was supposed to carry the weapons to the Saudis had been sunk. We were ready to do the job, but we can't take the credit."

"Then who?"

"Don't know," said Meir. "We're still trying to figure that one out. It wasn't Delta Force?"

"Not us," said Cleveland. "At least, not to the best of my knowledge, and I believe Townsend would have briefed me before it happened. Who else is there? The Russians?"

"Don't know," Meir said again. "But they were well trained and well equipped. This was a very sophisticated job. Somebody else was very serious about not allowing the Saudis to get their hands on some nukes. But make no mistake, the nuclear button will determine the future of the Middle East: who has it; who doesn't; who's willing to use it. But you said you think Israel is also on a path to destruction. Why is that?"

Now it was Cleveland's turn to look like a Cheshire cat. His smile was knowing, informed, but sad.

"You know as well as I do, David," said Cleveland. "You are well read. Your faith is important to you, plays a crucial part in your life. What does your Torah say . . . about the Amalekites . . . about the location of the temple . . . about dividing the land? Where will you place your faith today, David? In the words of God or in the words of man?"

31

Mullaney looked at the envelope, curious about its contents but fearful of its implications. And now it appeared he could be entangled even more. But he was still on duty no matter how determined he was to get home. He still had to protect the ambassador and his daughter, the lives of all the diplomatic personnel under his care—and he still had to track down the rest of this Turkish cabal that threatened all of their lives.

Not only did Mullaney want to know what was in that message, he needed to know. There was clearly some connection between the Gaon's prophecies and the attacks against those who were guarding those prophecies. And Mullaney wanted to know what that connection was. Perhaps it would help them track down the killers. Perhaps . . .

"I do need to know what's in that message, Rabbi. But that doesn't mean I'm ready or willing to become its guardian. All this prophecy stuff has nothing to do with my duty or the critical importance of finding the killers of your son, of my men, or scores of others. I'll take whatever help I can get to bring them to justice. But I'm not willing to take on the responsibility of guarding the message itself."

"Yes . . . yes, I understand," said Rabbi Herzog. "Looking at this from your perspective, from my perspective, from the perspective of the world we occupy every day, you are being asked to take on a daunting responsibility, one that is difficult to accept in the normal course of events. But do you recall what the Gaon's first message said?"

Mullaney nodded his head and quickly remembered the wound that creased his skull from front to back. "It said when the Russians invade Crimea it would trigger the coming of Messiah."

"Almost," said Herzog, who settled back into his chair. "The Vilna Gaon was the wisest and most renowned Talmudic scholar of his age—perhaps any age. Earlier this year, the Gaon's great-great-grandson, who preceded my son as head of the rabbinate, revealed a prophetic message the Gaon received and wrote down in 1794. It reads:

When you hear that the Russians have captured the city of Crimea, you should know that the Times of Messiah have started, that his steps are being heard. And when you hear that the Russians have reached the city of Constantinople, you should put on your Shabbat clothes and not take them off, because it means that Messiah is about to come at any minute.

"Only months earlier, the Russians had invaded and annexed Crimea into the Soviet Union," said Herzog. "The Jews are awaiting the arrival of our Messiah. Christians are awaiting the second coming of the man, Yeshua, who we believe was the Messiah. But according to both Jewish and Gentile scriptures, this first, or next, coming of Messiah will be a signal that what is known as the end of days is upon us."

"Hold on." Mullaney was perplexed. Did he just hear correctly? "Just a moment, Rabbi. Can you say that again? I thought you said . . ."

"That I believe Yeshua of Nazareth was the awaited Messiah? Son of the living God come to earth to redeem men from their sins, resurrected from the dead, ascended back into heaven to sit at the right hand of God until the day of his Second Coming? I am a rabbi. A Levite. A defender of Torah and the Law, yes?" The furrow in Herzog's brow wrestled for supremacy with the twinkle in his eye.

Mullaney felt like his discernment was being tested. "Yes," Mullaney said, "but . . ."

"Listen, my friend," said Herzog, "the members of the Rabbinate Council had many contentious debates in private about this man Jesus. Primarily could this man, Yeshua, be found in the prophecies of the Tanakh . . . did he fulfill prophecy? Some say there are over four hundred prophecies or foretelling of the Messiah in the Jewish Law and the Prophets, others say it's only sixty. The actual number matters little.

"There was a mathematics professor who gave his six hundred students a math probability problem—what is the probability that one person could fulfill eight specific prophecies. The students calculated the odds against one person fulfilling all eight prophecies as one in ten to the twenty-first power. That's a ten with twenty-one zeroes after it.

"The professor gave his students an illustration: one in ten to the twenty-first power is like covering the entire world in silver dollars one hundred twenty feet deep. Mark an 'X' on one of the dollars, randomly bury it, and ask a blindfolded person to travel the world and select the marked dollar.

"When you purposefully study scriptures," Herzog continued, "it is clear that Jesus of Nazareth fulfilled *all* prophecies about Messiah—whether sixty or 360. In the natural, an impossibility, but also a truth that demands a response."

US Ambassador's Residence, Tel Aviv
July 22, 9:24 a.m.

Meir had been at ease, folded back into the soft corner of the leather sofa. But now he came to attention, his body pushed upright, his feet on the floor, his eyes riveted onto Cleveland.

"Six and a half million Jews live in Israel," Meir said, his voice echoing the sternness of a dictatorial schoolmaster. "More than half of them would declare themselves *secular* Jews . . . Jews by culture, but not by faith. Jews of no faith. I am sworn to protect the sovereignty and safety of all six and a half million, no matter what they believe and no matter what I believe. It's a simple, pragmatic equation. Before Ishmael, our enemies surrounded us and outnumbered us. Three times the Arabs have tried to crush Israel, to drive all of us into the sea. Now, after Ishmael, Israel is not only surrounded by a treaty of peace, but now our former enemies have sworn to be our defenders. And we all stand in opposition to the emergence of a Persian Empire of violence and subjugation. Since this coup in Iraq, I've had two telephone calls from King Abdullah urging me to do all in my power to have the covenant and its mutual-defense pact ratified by the Knesset. Perhaps he's discovered what happened to his anticipated delivery.

"But where is my choice?" snapped Meir. "What options do I have? Tell my people, 'I'm sorry, I won't accept this opportunity to save the lives of your children because it may offend some rabbis or be inconsistent with words written three or four thousand years ago?' Be serious, Atticus. If you were in my place . . . if you were me . . . you would do the same thing I'm doing. My people deserve this. My conscience demands it." He slammed a fist into his knee. "I have no choice!"

A desolate silence swallowed Meir's declaration. Cleveland felt emotionally wrought by Meir's argument. He understood the pragmatic realities. But he had and still lived his life in accordance with biblical principles. Blessings and curses. It was each man's choice. Believe the Word of God and live by it or risk suffering the consequences. So far, pragmatic politics had failed to trump biblical truth in Cleveland's life. He'd made mistakes. Oh so many. Some devastating. But never had he stepped out in direct opposition to the Word of God.

Would he? What if his president demanded it? Could he? Perhaps it was time to retire.

He spoke softly into the silence. "I can't stop Boylan. Neither can the secretary, although he's still trying. The Iran deal will go through."

"Then America is no friend of Israel."

"No," corrected Cleveland. "Then the president is no friend of Israel. America, that vast majority of Americans who move the country, stand firm with Israel. Millions of us pray for Israel, for the peace of Jerusalem, every day." He paused to pick his words.

"But I cannot stand and give voice to—speak in support of—a covenant that dares God's wrath." Cleveland leaned in from his chair. "David, divide the land of Israel, and you will be called into the valley of judgment. Is that what you want for your people? Will that save the lives of your children or put them more at risk?"

As if his face was chiseled into the ubiquitous Jerusalem stone that glistened in the light of so many Israeli mornings, the prime minister's face was implacable. "I have no choice, Atticus. It's futile to debate."

Cleveland let out a deep sigh. Oh, his friend. Such a big mistake. If . . .

"You're right, this is a futile debate," Cleveland agreed. "You will never get the covenant ratified. Too many are in opposition. Which is why I fear for you and your government. You, I trust. Who knows what leaders—what policy— may come next."

Meir's face remained impassive, unmoved. "The government will not fail. I have already secured the votes we need to ratify the covenant."

Cleveland was floored. "Labor? You are really going to get into bed with Labor? Talk about betrayal. David, Labor will spit you out at their first opportunity."

Meir closed his eyes, his shoulders narrowly rocking back and forth as if he were standing with the rabbis in prayer at the Wailing Wall. "But we will have peace. And we will have a temple. And my people . . . all of my people . . . will have a homeland they can count on." Meir opened his eyes. "Small price, Atticus. Small price."

32

Herzog was nodding his head in time like a metronome, a broad smile revealing teeth as white as the ivory keys on a piano. "Yes, Agent Mullaney. When an angel from the throne room of God prays for your soul and breathes into you a new Spirit that reveals the truth—well, that man has a choice to make. Believe the truth or flee from God.

"Bayard breathed into me a truth I have ignored all of my life. Our Messiah came upon this earth, and the leaders of the chosen people of God, like me, ignored him. All of the Torah predictions of the coming Messiah were fulfilled in a carpenter from a desert town of no repute. This Jesus . . . he is the way and the truth and the life. I know this in my soul without a doubt, and I have believed in my heart and confessed with my mouth that Jesus Christ is Lord. So, a rabbi? Yes. A Levite? Yes. But a disciple of Yeshua? Yes. Like Saul of Tarsus, a man confronted by the truth of Jesus, I am here to serve the living God . . . as strange as that still sounds to these ancient ears."

Rabbi Herzog turned to his right, then back to Mullaney. "Would you be so kind to indulge an old man and come sit here by my side?" he said, patting the arm of the chair next to his.

Mullaney got up and came around his desk. He took hold of the chair's back and pulled it around so that it was alongside, but slightly in front of the rabbi's seat. "The better to see you."

"Ah, yes . . . the face is the herald of the heart," said Herzog. "Thank you. We have much to discuss and time is running on us." He placed the stained envelope on top of his knee, close to Mullaney. Mullaney remembered the faces of the dead who had touched the box or the message without the protection of the anointing. He edged to the far side of the chair.

"I believe, no matter who you are, where you are, or what you declare as your belief system, there is good reason to consider that we are currently at the crossroads of scriptural prophecy," said Herzog. "If correct I am—and the truth of end times is broadcast to us every day on our televisions—then critical it is for all of us to understand what those scriptural prophecies mean for us today.

"And confident I am," said Herzog, placing his hand on the envelope, "that the heavenly messages the Gaon received are closely related to, or play a part in, the fulfillment of some of those scriptural prophecies. We are in a time, Agent Mullaney, that cannot be understood apart from God's Holy Word, in the Torah . . . and also in the books of the Christian Bible. And this second prophecy is intimately entwined with both the Torah and the Bible."

Herzog took the envelope in his right hand and lifted the flap with his left. He withdrew a piece of white paper and opened it.

"This is not the parchment upon which the Gaon wrote his prophecies," said Herzog. "I believe the original remained with the Rabbinate Council at the Hurva. This is a copy of the translation. By rabbinical tradition and practice, I expect this translation is complete in every way, including the addition of two lines of symbols at the bottom of the message—symbols I'm unfamiliar with and which I believe the council was unable to decipher. Forgive me," he said, bringing the piece of paper slightly closer to his chest, "If you don't mind, I'll just read it?"

"That's fine," agreed Mullaney. "I've learned to take no chances where the Gaon's messages are concerned."

"Excellent. What I will read to you was translated and decoded by my son and the Rabbinate Council. It reads:

> "When the times of the Gentiles is complete, when the sons of Amalek are invited to the king's banquet, beware of the Anadolian—he walks on water to offer peace, but carries judgment in his hands. His name is Man of Violence."

Mullaney waited. The rabbi stared back.

"That's it? There's nothing about Messiah in there." Mullaney was incredulous. Up until that point, he thought he had it pretty well figured out. The second prophecy would be similar to the first—watch out, Messiah's still coming! But this was all different. And Herzog sat there with a pleasant smile on his face as if they were talking about their favorite restaurant. "It doesn't make any sense to me," he said, "but by the look on your face I know you're going to tell me what it means."

"Many things . . . many things, Agent Mullaney. But on one thing you are mistaken," said Herzog. "This second prophesy does speak of Messiah. And even though it is 220 years old, it also speaks of this very day. What do you know of the sons of Amalek?"

"Not much more than what the ambassador told me, that Moses told Joshua he was to wipe out the tribe of Amalek from the face of the earth."

"Yes, well let's start there," said Herzog. "It's easier to explain." Herzog took the paper, folded it, and placed it back inside the stained envelope. He tucked the envelope into his inside jacket pocket then turned his attention on Mullaney once again.

"Amalek was a man, a descendant of Ishmael and Esau, and from him a desert tribe grew. They were nomadic but lived primarily on the western side of the Sinai Peninsula . . . what is now Saudi Arabia. When Moses led the people of Israel out of Egypt, their route took them through the land of Amalek, as they traveled toward Mount Sinai. The warriors of Amalek attacked the Israelites. First they attacked the end of the column—some say there were over a million Israelites in that exodus—where the old and the infirmed labored along.

"The next day, in the Valley of Rephidim, there was a huge battle between Israel and Amalek. Perhaps you recall the story. This is when Moses stood on a hilltop with his staff raised, and Aaron and Hur helped to keep his arms raised. Israel routed the Amalekite army. Tens of thousands were killed. But following the battle, Moses spoke a strong warning to Joshua. He said Joshua was to, 'blot out the memory of Amalek from under heaven.' God wanted Joshua to annihilate Amalek. Moses told Joshua, 'The Lord says, do not forget.'

"In many ways," said Herzog, "Israel and Amalek have been at war ever since. The people of Amalek are the desert dwellers, the nomads of the Sinai and the Middle East. The 'sons of Amalek' are the Arab nations, Agent Mullaney. And with the Ishmael Covenant, we have just invited the sons of Amalek to the table. In the ancient Near East—and even today in Levantine society—to invite someone to eat in your home was a sign of peace . . . a sign of a covenant of peace between those at the table. After the signing of the Ishmael Covenant, our prime minister hosted a luncheon for those who joined him in signing the covenant, the kings and princes of Amalek."

Rabbi Herzog gathered himself in his chair. "The same day Israel signed the Ishmael Covenant with its Arab neighbors, my son and the council deciphered a 220-year-old prophecy, which foretells of this very day when Israel has now invited the sons of Amalek to its table. Prophecy fulfilled, no?"

———⊰∘∘⊱———

Mullaney felt his head swelling . . . there was so much more. He looked past Herzog and caught a glimpse of the clock on the wall. What was keeping Cleveland?

"Excuse me a minute." He pushed a button on his phone console and called Jeffrey Archer, Cleveland's secretary.

"Jeffrey, it's Mullaney. Any idea what time the ambassador is expected at the embassy?"

"He's on his way . . . finally," Archer responded. "I'll let you know when he arrives."

"Okay . . . thanks. But Jeffrey, it's very important that I speak to the ambassador first thing, as soon as he gets in his office."

"I understand. I'll do the best I can. But his schedule today is already a shambles."

———⊰∘∘⊱———

Mullaney was conflicted. Here this elder Rabbi Herzog was taking the time to explain the Gaon's second prophecy and what it meant in light of very present events, but his time was running out. He had to see Cleveland as soon as he arrived at the embassy. He had to discover the truth about his transfer request and fast. But . . . what to do . . .

"Rabbi, I'm pretty sure we've only scratched the surface of this message and its meaning, which is very important for our government and the ambassador to understand. But I'm sorry, I don't have much more time this morning. I'm scheduled to meet with the ambassador as soon as he arrives at the embassy today. So is there any way we can wrap this up . . . or perhaps continue it later?"

"Oy . . . forgive me, Agent Mullaney," said Herzog, nodding his yarmulke-topped head. "Too much of your time am I taking. But there is so much revealed in this message . . . so much that is important.

"I don't know what conclusions you have come to about the events of the last few days," said Herzog, "but is it not curious that this second prophecy would be revealed the same day as Israel agreed to this Ishmael Covenant, a foolish document written by foolish men . . . an offer of peace that actually could be a portent of judgment?"

Mullaney stole a look at the clock, then flipped open his calendar. "Well, Rabbi, those are all important things I know . . ."

Mullaney's phone console lit up. "He's just walking in the door," said Jeffrey Archer's voice. "I suggest you hustle to be first in line."

Up, moving toward the door, Herzog came back into Mullaney's consciousness. "I'm sorry, rabbi." He stopped by the chair. "But I've got to speak to the ambassador immediately. Perhaps we can continue our conversation later? What are your plans?"

Herzog blinked, like a man coming out of a trance. "Plans? I have no plans," he said. "I . . . we . . . my plan was to speak to you, share the prophecy, pass along the anointing. I must help you understand about the times of the Gentiles and what that means for us today. And what does it mean about the Anadolian . . . or the Man of Violence? Or the day of judgment? And what about those other symbols on the Gaon's document that the Rabbinate were not able to decipher? What about them?"

Mullaney's mind and his heart were already out the door. "You're right and I want to know as much as I can about all that's in the prophecy. So why don't you just stay put for a few minutes while I speak to Ambassador Cleveland. When I get back, we can figure out what to do next. Okay?"

"But . . ." Rabbi Herzog's mouth gaped open, his eyes were wide, his hand lifted in objection to Mullaney's exit, ". . . the anointing!"

He gave Herzog a pat on the shoulder and was out the door.

⸻⸻✦⸻⸻

Ruth Hughes fell into step alongside Mullaney as he was heading toward Cleveland's office, "I need you," said Hughes, the US embassy's political officer. "We need to get moving right away."

"What?" Hughes's demand broke through the mental logjam caused by Mullaney's "need-to-know" from Cleveland about his transfer request and his mind-boggling discussion with the elder Rabbi Herzog. He stopped in his tracks and looked at Hughes as if she was speaking Martian. "Why? What's happening?"

Ruth Hughes was about half the size of Mullaney, but her presence belied her stature. A veteran of Middle East power politics after two decades as corporate counsel for Aramco, Hughes had spent the past two decades serving State Department outposts throughout the region.

"But first we need to talk to the ambassador." And just as quickly as she appeared, Hughes was gone, her high heels clacking down the corridor toward Cleveland's office.

Ambassador Cleveland was on the phone as Jeffrey Archer opened the door and ushered them both into his office. Cleveland held up one hand, palm out, as he listened on his phone.

Mullaney inclined his head to the right and whispered to Hughes. "What's this all about?"

But Hughes, still a striking woman in her seventh decade, with high cheekbones and eyes of glacial blue, was moving toward Cleveland, who stood behind his desk as he hung up the phone.

"Okay, Ruth, why the urgency?" asked Cleveland.

No one sat.

"We may have a problem in Amman," said Hughes. "I just got a call from Riley Whitaker. He needs me in Amman right away . . . says there is somebody there we need to talk to—like yesterday."

"Someone?" asked Mullaney.

"Okay, more than someone," said Hughes, looking at Mullaney out of the corner of her eye. "During my time at Aramco, I built close ties to most of the royal families in the Gulf states. The emir of Qatar wants to talk, and he wants to talk today, and—no disrespect to Whitaker—the emir said he would prefer not to share this information with an assistant agricultural attaché. The emir and his son were in Amman for the announcement of the Ishmael Covenant and will be there for only a few more hours until their entourage leaves Amman to head home. The offer is to talk now, to talk in person. And the emir says it's urgent."

"To talk about what?" asked Cleveland.

"There are a lot of people on edge about this covenant announcement," said Hughes. "People who were not consulted . . . people who are suddenly nervous because the world as they knew it just took a big 180 on them. People like me who think this so-called peace announcement will do nothing to bring peace to this region but only more turmoil. You told me to keep my ears open. Fear loosens a lot of tongues." She leaned on Cleveland's desk. "But from the urgency I just heard on the phone, this is about more than the covenant. If you ask my opinion, this is a lead we can't pass up."

"All right," said Cleveland, "go and see what the emir has to say. But why do you need Mullaney?"

Ruth Hughes was a pert five foot four, feminine but far from soft. She not only excelled at assessing—and taking advantage of—the shifting politics of the Middle East, but she also built lasting relationships and enjoyed the trust of both princes and peasants.

"I need more than Mullaney. We should bring Mr. Hernandez with us as well and have a team of DSS agents on the ground when we arrive in Amman."

"That's a lot of muscle," said Mullaney.

"Rule number one," said Hughes, leaning her arms against the back of one of the chairs in front of Cleveland's desk. "Never walk into a knife fight without a knife. Look, I'm certain the emir and his son will be accompanied by a couple of skilled, experienced security pros—not just guards, but people who are trusted counselors. I walk in on my own, I'm at a disadvantage right out of the gate. With Brian and Tommy behind me, we start on an equal negotiating plane.

"Second, I'll feel a whole lot safer with these two watching my back. There are countless individuals and organizations who will stop at nothing . . . nothing . . . to prevent the covenant from becoming a reality, who cannot coexist with a workable, livable peace and mutual defense pact between Israel and its Arab neighbors, or who are deathly opposed to an independent Palestinian state. And then there's that Turkish mafia who's proving to be deadly and determined."

Hughes pushed herself up from the back of the chair. "Third, I've known the emir for a long time, but we haven't spoken personally for more than ten years. A lot can change in ten years. While I'm eyeball-to-eyeball with him, I would covet the presence of these two as insightful and experienced observers who will help me sift the truth by analyzing what they see and hear."

All solid points. Mullaney couldn't deny the logic. But he had a point to make too.

"Mr. Ambassador, I need to speak to you, privately," said Mullaney, trying to keep any pleading from his voice. "It's very important."

As if he was rousing himself from a nap, Cleveland gave his head a slight shake and turned to Mullaney. "I'm sorry, Brian. I know you've been waiting all morning, and I apologize for being so tied up today. As soon as we're done here, okay?"

Then he turned his attention back to Ruth Hughes.

"When will you be back?"

"Five hours, max," said Hughes. "There's an unmarked Aramco helicopter getting fueled right now in a far corner of Ben Gurion airport."

"Normally, I wouldn't allow my top two security officials out of the country at the same time," said Cleveland.

Another valid point.

"Understood," said Hughes. "But we may not have another shot. The emir is a filthy-rich Arab ruler focused on self-interest and self-preservation, as are all the royal Arab families. But he's also a man I learned to trust as a voice of reason. He's on the board of OPEC and has sources that are precious to us."

"Okay," said Cleveland. "I'm not going anywhere today. If I'm not safe in the embassy . . ."

"Good. Thank you, sir," said Hughes as she turned on her heel to leave. "We'll leave from the garage in two minutes."

"Whoa," said Mullaney, reaching out to Hughes's retreating form. "How about fifteen minutes. I've got . . ."

Hughes was moving fast, already halfway out the door. "Okay . . . ten minutes. But don't dawdle."

Baghdad
July 22, 10:00 a.m.

The reception room used by the Iraqi government for formal occasions was just down the hall from the prime minister's office in the Baghdad Convention Center. This morning it had been hastily transformed into a television studio. The room was empty except for three men who sat behind a table covered in blue velvet, each one face-to-face with a myriad assortment of microphones. Each of the men felt smugly confident—but each for a different reason.

In the middle sat Samir Al-Qahtani, the self-proclaimed prime minister of Iraq after yesterday's coup. His combat fatigues were clean, neatly pressed, creases sharp. He looked like a man in charge. With his Badr Brigades militia keeping the streets of Baghdad quiet, he was.

To his right was Arslan Eroglu, prime minister of Turkey. He looked like he just stepped out of a GQ photo shoot—hand-tailored, navy blue, Italian silk suit; brilliant white shirt; and an elegant, lime-green power tie. Eroglu had, only minutes earlier, been whisked from the airport to the Convention Center in a black SUV with smoked-out windows.

On Al-Qahtani's left was the commander of the Peshmerga militia and the president of the Iraqi's Kurdish region. Three hours ago, he had laughed at the invitation. The governments of Turkey and Iraq had each tried to assassinate him several times in the past. He was not going to surrender his life so easily. But so many assurances had come from so many different sources that he finally had to consider that the offer he received was genuine. It was worth the gamble. So he got on the helicopter and now he sat at a table with his two greatest adversaries and they were about to make history—make the impossible happen—an independent Kurdistan. He was still wearing dirty fatigues, but he looked like a man who had just won the lottery.

The big double doors on the far end of the reception room opened, and a torrent of journalists flooded into the room, surrounding the table, taking photos, setting up video cameras, asking hundreds of questions that none of the three men at the table acknowledged.

When the onrush of swarming bodies slowed to a trickle, Al-Qahtani held up his hand. The room hushed, silent except for the click of camera shutters.

"Thank you for coming," said Al-Qahtani. "This is a historic day."

He introduced Prime Minister Eroglu.

"I speak for President Emet Kashani and all of the people of the Republic of Turkey when I welcome Commander Al-Qahtani to his new position as prime minister of Iraq," said Eroglu. "The Republic of Turkey recognizes the new government of Iraq as a rightful extension of the majority of citizens in Iraq."

Eroglu turned to his left and firmly grasped Al-Qahtani's hand. "Finally the majority population of Iraq has a government in power that reflects its interests and is committed to its safety and well-being."

Recognition. Al-Qahtani was not only grateful for the recognition of his government by Turkey, but he was also grateful for the clear message Eroglu's words sent to the Shia majority of Iraq. They were once again in power. "Thank you, Mr. Prime Minister."

Al-Qahtani turned to face the cameras. "As the leader of the new government of Iraq, I have invited Prime Minister Eroglu here to right an ancient wrong. Today, the governments of Turkey and Iraq will sign a binding proclamation. There are more than thirty million people of Kurdish descent living in Turkey, Iraq, and northern Syria. They are the largest people group in the world without their own sovereign nation. Today that will change. In this Contract for Cooperation, not only will Iraq and Turkey contribute thousands of kilometers of land for the creation of a new, independent Kurdish state, but Turkey has also agreed to open its dams and restore the normal flow of critical fresh water for both the Tigris and Euphrates rivers.

"Today, not only is a new nation born," said Al-Qahtani, "but a new partnership has been forged between two neighboring Muslim nations who can now turn their combined strength against common foes and common problems. History has been written today, and history has been changed."

33

Ankara
July 22, 10:37 a.m.

Even immortal ones needed time to stop and think. To analyze and understand the past. To project and anticipate the future.

Reclining on a divan in a dimly lit room inside his place of residence on Alitas Street, the Turk's eyes were closed, but his mind was weighing how to achieve his ultimate goal. Had the rabbis at the Hurva Synagogue deciphered the Vilna Gaon's second prophecy? Did they understand what it meant? And the box. Did the box have a power of its own? Could he use that power, absorb it into his own? Become greater . . . more powerful than . . . ? An interesting thought. But without the box and the message, so much was out of his hands, beyond his control. He needed to gain—

Like the sudden ferocity of a violent earthquake, terror engulfed the Turk. An overwhelming stench of putrid decay surrounded him as if he had fallen into a garbage pit on the equator. His eyes flew open. Staring back at him were the venomous yellow eyes of the One, his terrible and diaphanous red visage swirling like the core of a hurricane and erupting like explosions on the surface of the sun.

The Turk tried to speak . . . he tried to rise . . . but something gripped his throat and pressed his neck and his head back into the divan. No man touched the Turk. But this was no man.

"You think I can't reach you when I desire?" asked the malevolent face, its words like sharpened daggers, piercing what remained of the Turk's confidence. "I am not confined to that tomb in your basement. You are mistaken if you believe I come when you call. I choose to meet you in the dark. It suits my purpose. But don't think I can't find you."

The clenched fingers on the Turk's throat felt like a tightening vice grip, crushing his larynx and cutting off his oxygen. The Turk's arrogance was squeezed from his heart as the breath was cut off from his lungs.

"And don't be foolish enough to think I can't replace you."

The eyes of the One, a tumult of gray storm over the yellow pupils, reached deep inside the Turk, searching. "Do I need another?"

Panic seized the Turk. He had never before been in such jeopardy. What would happen to him if . . .

"My Disciples are being slaughtered, and you do nothing." The words were like a blunt instrument, wielded like a weapon of torture. "The Americans are still alive and the message is now in their possession. What"—the bony fingers squeezed once more—"have you accomplished?

"Do—I—need—another?" the voice thundered.

I cannot die. I cannot die. Panicked thoughts overwhelmed the Turk. *But if I am snuffed out, then what happens . . .*

The clamping fingers slowly relaxed, allowing the Turk a breath, but they were not removed. His attempts at an answer were stillborn, strangled in his throat.

"You have failed to control Eroglu. He thinks you bring him only suggestions, and he plans his own schemes. *He does not fear you!* His pride and ambition have poisoned him beyond your control. He can no longer be trusted to fulfill our requirements. He covets the nuclear weapons to give him earthly power, to overthrow Kashani and blackmail the West, but he does not have the courage to take the final step we have planned. He contrives for the creation of Kurdistan and the annexing of Assyria as a resurrection of the Ottoman Empire, with him as ruler. He is not a true Disciple. He must be replaced."

The Turk had been too lenient with Eroglu. He saw the man's weakness. Thought he could exploit it. But it was human weakness. And human weakness was unpredictable. He had waited too long. He had . . .

"Listen to me," demanded the One, his taloned fingers twitching spasmodically, "not to yourself. Do not lose your focus. There is still much to do, and time is our enemy. The weapons are not in your control. The treaty, with our opening, has not been accepted or ratified. What must happen for us to accomplish our goal?"

The fingers on his throat loosened. But the eyes of terror held him in place. The Turk searched for his voice.

"Destroy the message; betray the Persians; deceive the Jew; defeat prophecy."

"Yessssssss," the voice hissed, and venom dripped from every sibilant syllable. "And how much of the goal have you accomplished?"

He felt the bony fingers resting once again against his throat. Just a reminder. "Nothing."

It pained the Turk to admit how little he had achieved of their primary objective—defeat prophecy! There was one undeniable way to prevent the last-days prophecies of the Nazarene's book. And the Jewish book had shown them the way. Ezekiel, a madman, wrote that when this messianic imposter would return, his feet would land on the Mount of Olives, across the Kidron Valley from Jerusalem.

Two strategies were already well underway, either of which would make it impossible for him to return. At the Turk's insistence, Eroglu inserted a clause in the proposed water-for-gas treaty that would allow a Turkish company to build a shopping mall on the Mount of Olives and a causeway to where the new temple would be built—similar to the Mamilla Mall just outside the Jaffa Gate. The Turkish company would make sure to level that cursed mountain of rock before the mall was constructed.

In addition, there was Incirlik. Matoush was in place, ready to move on the NATO base and its supply of American B61 nuclear weapons. Once in their hands, they were prepared to unleash one of the stolen warheads, dialed down to its lowest explosive yield, creating a strategic weapon of limited destructive range, but one that would still obliterate the Mount of Olives and make it uninhabitable for decades.

But as of yet, the Turk had accomplished none of these things. Now he feared. Would he be replaced?

"Yessssssss, you have accomplished nothing," snarled the One. "The Lithuanian's message was unlocked in the Hurva, but you did not know that, did you?" His hand disengaged from the Turk's throat and his eyes turned to the right. "And now more troubling news arrives."

A second cadaverous hand was raised toward the door of the room, which the Turk had closed and locked. The One snapped his fingers and the door flew open. On the far side stood Assan, a gnarly fist raised to knock against the door. His eyes were wide in shock, and his mouth agape but wordless. One of the Disciples, who quickly prostrated himself across the doorway, was at his side.

Rippling fury assaulted the atoms of the air. "Why," roared the One, his voice an earthquake shaking the walls, "do you disturb us?"

US Embassy, Tel Aviv
July 22, 10:41 a.m.

Mullaney was about to speak to Cleveland when the floor shifted under his feet and the walls of the office appeared to warp. In a heartbeat it was over. Another one?

"Did you feel that?" he asked.

"Tremor," Cleveland nodded. "Something shook the earth."

They looked at each other, waiting. Nothing happened. Mullaney's time was running. He needed to ask his question.

Ankara
July 22, 10:41 a.m.

"Aaaahhhh," groaned Assan, who dropped to his knees and bowed his cowl-covered head to the floor.

"Speak!"

"Oh, Exalted One." Assan's mumbled words, spoken into the cold stones of the floor, barely resonated to the Turk's ears. "This Disciple brings a report. A rabbi sits in that demon American's office in Jerusalem, the winged ones by his side for protection. It is believed the rabbi has the deciphered prophecy in his possession."

Fueled by his humiliation under the grasp of the One and his repeated failures to destroy this message and its cursed box, focused fury erupted in the Turk . . . fury he was about to hurl across the room to bludgeon both messengers . . . when a flaming, yellow-orange beam scorched through the air toward the door. The beam sizzled the right side of the Turk's face. But it struck the prostrate Disciple on the top of his head and consumed his body, inch by inch, until it vaporized his feet and the shoes he wore.

The Turk looked up, to his right. The One's right arm was outstretched toward the door, the shimmering, flaming laser spewed forth from his skeletal hand. The One snapped his fingers closed, snuffing out the searing light. He slowly turned his eyes back onto the Turk. The fingers of his left hand moved, like a snake slithering across the Turk's throat. But it was the eyes, rimmed in red, pulsing with menace, that held the Turk transfixed.

"You think you have power," said the One, his voice a demeaning rebuke.

"Fail me again, and you will feel the full weight of my power upon your head, like that worm of a messenger." The One leaned in closer to the Turk, his breath the moldering decay of centuries. "So the message and the box are united once again. Having them both in one place may be to our advantage. And it may be your reprieve." The yellow eyes with the swirling gray storms of mayhem both petrified and entranced the Turk. He wished for their power. And he wished to be free of their control.

"You may have been mistaken from the beginning," slithered the voice. "You have pursued the message, the words of the Lithuanian, for generations. We have painfully learned of the power that is protecting that message. But it now appears that the box may have a power of its own. Now we know the message was removed from the box at the Hurva and deciphered by the council. They intended to reveal its contents and deliver it to the American ambassador. We knew the box was delivered to the American embassy and secured in its vault. What we didn't know, until now, is whether the message was extinguished during the explosions that destroyed the Jew's place of worship. But it exists. Outside of the box. So was it the box itself that brought death to the escaping rabbi?"

The Turk considered the possibility. The box of power?

He felt a cold squeeze on his throat. And words that assaulted him like a roiling, rushing avalanche.

"You must destroy the message—or destroy those who have the message—before it becomes known. There is nothing more important. Only then can we deceive the Jew into signing the treaty. And his thirst for water will unknowingly eliminate any possibility for the coming of his Messiah. But you cannot rely on Eroglu to write that treaty. Our goal must be fulfilled in that agreement . . . buried deep in the meaningless language . . . or on the firestorm that will annihilate the mountain. Do you understand what I require?"

His throat was raw and his mind was reeling from the One's verbal pounding. The Turk was unsure of his voice, but he squeezed out a response.

"Yes, Master."

"Tell me!"

"Destroy the message; betray the Persians; deceive the Jew; defeat prophecy," the Turk said, like a litany of prayer.

"Yesssssssss. And one additional task. Secure the box. And bring it to me."

An objection rose in the Turk's mind.

"Hear my words!" thundered the voice. "The box has power. I want that power in my hands. Remember this," the voice warned. "Not all immortal beings dwell on this earth. Some have already been sentenced to the lake of fire. A judgment we can both avoid . . . unless you fail."

The bony fingers wrapped around his neck like an enraged python, and the fiery face came so close the Turk could feel his skin sizzle. "So do not fail! Or you will join those others in their eternal suffering. Am I clear?"

The Turk was gasping for breath, flailing on the divan, terrifying visions of flames invading his thoughts when the fingers released his throat and all that remained of the One was the overpowering stench of putrid decay.

34

"Okay, Brian. I know the clock is ticking. What can I do for you?"

Mullaney was suddenly torn between duty and dread. *Duty first.*

"Quickly . . . the Rabbi Herzog we met at the residence? His father is here, also a rabbi, Mordechai Herzog. And he brought with him the deciphered second prophecy. Here . . . I wrote it down. It appears to speak directly to the Ishmael Covenant. That it's not a good idea. And it mentions a Man of Violence."

"How did he . . . ?"

Mullaney quickly shook his head. "Long story, too long for right now. But, sir," and now his stomach started doing flips, and part of Mullaney didn't want to hear Cleveland's answer, but he sucked it up and forged ahead, "what I really need to know is why you didn't include my request for transfer in your situation report."

Cleveland looked like he'd been struck with a plank. His head went back, his eyelids fluttered, and a surprised frown spread across his face. "What? What do you mean?"

Now Mullaney was confused. Maybe . . .

"Don't ask me how, sir—I'd have to betray a confidence—but I know someone who has read your report carefully. There was no ambassadorial request and no mention of me getting transferred back to Washington in your situational report."

A rainbow of emotions traversed Cleveland's face, from surprise to fury and back again. The ambassador took a step toward Mullaney, reached out both arms, and rested his hands on Mullaney's shoulders.

Mullaney's mobile phone chimed the arrival of a text message.

"That's Ruth," said Cleveland. "I'm sure she's ready to leave. But Brian, let me tell you this as clearly and emphatically as I can. The situation report that left my computer included the request for your transfer. I'll show it to you when you get back."

Cleveland looked deeply into Mullaney's eyes. "I'm sorry, son. You must have felt betrayed." Cleveland's voice caught a bit in his throat. "I didn't forsake you, Brian, or lie to you. I would never do that." Cleveland's big hands pressed into Mullaney's shoulders. "Now you've got to go. We'll figure this out when you get back. And figure out what to do about the message too."

A switch flipped on in Mullaney's memory. "Sir . . . Rabbi Herzog is still in my office. Can you ask someone to let him know I was called away? Ask him if he can come back tomorrow?"

Ankara
July 22, 10:55 a.m.

"Where are you?"

"At a coffee shop across the street from the American embassy. The rabbi remains, but the agent—

"I know. I have new orders for you. Find a place where you can speak without being overheard. Then call me back."

The phone on the stone table rattled to life. The Turk touched the screen. "Yes?"

"How can I serve you, All Powerful?"

"The scourge of our Disciples, this meddler Mullaney, is leaving Israel," relayed the Turk. "He is traveling to Amman in Jordan with the chief of Cleveland's security detail and another high-ranking embassy official. They travel in a helicopter owned by the Saudi's oil company."

"Then they may no longer be under the protection of the winged ones," said the commander.

"How many of our Disciples are in Amman?"

"Twenty," said the leader. "Well armed, well trained."

"Good. Summon them all. Have someone at the Marka Airport when the helicopter lands and follow them. Get yourself to Amman as quickly as possible. This is our opportunity. You will find them and kill them . . . all. Today. Do not fail me in this."

"You can rely on me," said the commander of the Disciples. "It will be done."

35

The Turk was dressed in his most ornate clothes, traditional garments worn during the height of the Ottoman Empire: a blood-red jubba, the thick outer shirt with sleeves that flared at the elbows to voluminous openings around the hands, the edges of this one stitched with pure gold; blousy, black pants, the salvar; golden slippers were invisible under the salvar; around his shoulders a flowing, black, cape-like coat with a cowl hood hanging from his neck, all of its edges and seams stitched in gold.

He stood in the middle of an underground room below the rear of the house on Alitas Street. The walls of the room were also blood red, strange symbols engraved with gilt on the four walls—some were small, violent looking swirls, others grotesques, unnatural animals, others huge astrological symbols. The room was armored and secured like a vault. In front of the Turk was a flat, stone table about six feet long, three feet wide, and three feet high. A runnel around the perimeter of the table emptied into a small hole at one corner.

Assan, his aide, was pressed into a dim corner, farthest from the Turk.

"Come."

The Turk watched for any hesitation. Now is when he most needed Assan. There could be no doubt today.

Assan quickly floated to his side. "Yes, Master?"

"The time has come for us to have another visit with our friend the prime minister," said the Turk. "As we planned, he is not feeling well today. It appears he caught an illness in Baghdad, and he is resting at home. Is the van prepared?"

"Yes, Master," Assan whispered. "The bodyboard will be covered. The two Disciples will be in the front, sealed off from the rear of the van. They will come in with the bodyboard only when summoned."

"Very well. And the prime minister's body guards?"

"They will fall into a deep sleep as they did last time. They will wake only at your direction."

"You are certain?"

"Yes, Master. We are prepared."

Assan refused to look up, but the Turk sharpened his focus on the top of Assan's bald, heavily veined head. He withdrew his skeletal right hand from the left sleeve of his jubba and held it outstretched, below Assan's downcast face. "You will see," he whispered, his words like a contagion, poisoning each molecule as they passed through the air. "Within the hour, my power will expand to greater heights than you have ever experienced. Hate, envy, greed, pride, ruthlessness . . . all the powers of darkness will flow into me and explode into a force that will perform miracles. Do not," he hissed, "doubt me."

The Turk could see the shivers rippling along Assan's spine. Good to keep him terrified.

"There can be no error," hissed the Turk. "The body must come back here immediately and be prepared on this table. You must be certain."

"Yes, Master, just as you say. I will not fail you."

"Bring up the van."

Amman, Jordan
July 22, 12:56 p.m.

"Who are those two?"

Brian Mullaney looked out the porthole window of the August Wetland AW135 luxury jet helicopter as it settled on its wheels and the rotors stopped spinning at the Amman Marka International Airport, the civil airport near the Amman city center. The unmarked Saudi Aramco helicopter had landed in a far corner of the airport on the flank of a private hanger. Two DSS agents leaned against the fenders of a gleaming black Lincoln Navigator waiting on the tarmac.

"Jasper Johnson and Ollie Trotman," said Mullaney. "I've worked with both of them before . . . top-notch agents."

"Well, they didn't have to bring the Sherman tank." Hughes got out of her seat and headed for the helicopter's door. "It's going to be pretty tough to remain inconspicuous in that power-mobile."

There were no sidewalks in Jabal Al Weibdeh, the old city section of Amman, and the streets were narrow and steep. Like Rome, modern Amman was a city built on seven hills. Jabal Al Weibdeh, sprawling across the top of one of those hills, was one of the oldest parts of a city that had been habituated for millennia, since the days of the biblical Ammonites.

Like an Olympic skier traversing a giant slalom course, Ollie Trotman guided the huge Lincoln Navigator through the labyrinthine streets of Jabal Al Weibdeh toward their destination, a small café west of the Amman Citadel and the Temple of Hercules. Across the street from the circular park in the middle of what was oddly named Paris Square, Café Kepi would have been right at home on the Place François in Paris, the quiet little circle just west of the Grand Palais and the Avenue Franklin Roosevelt in the Eighth Arrondissement.

Modern and quirky, a favorite of students who haunt the smoke-filled lower level, Café Kepi overlooked the small park that got its name from the deep green, cast-iron water fountain in its center, cast by the same artisans who created the sixty-seven large Wallace Fountains scattered throughout Paris. Commissioned by Sir Richard Wallace in 1872 to bring clean drinking water to poor Parisians following the destruction of the Franco-Prussian War and the Commune that followed, Wallace Fountains are now found and cherished around the world. Mullaney's favorite occupied a shaded lane in the Paris flower market—an oasis of peace and beauty one block from the throngs of tourists crowded around Notre Dame de Paris on Île de la Cité.

Riley Whitaker was waiting by the back door of the Café Kepi when the Navigator came to a stop in the narrow alley. Wearing a wide-brimmed Indiana Jones hat and sunglasses, weathered jeans, and scuffed boots, he looked like anything but a career diplomat. "They're waiting for you upstairs," he said after introductions. "Officially, I'm not here. And I'm not going to be part of the conversation upstairs. So Mrs. Hughes, unless you have another assignment for me, I'll be heading back to the airport and the chopper that's waiting to take me back to Qatar."

"Thank you, Riley," said Hughes, grasping his hand in hers. "You've been a great help to us. I'll make sure the right people in Washington know about this. I hope it won't be long before you get the sand out of your shoes."

"Thank you, ma'am. I grew up in the desert, so it doesn't bother me. But it sure would be nice to get back home for a while. Good luck upstairs."

36

When they entered the otherwise vacant upper room of the restaurant, he and Hernandez flanking the door to the quieter, nonsmoking second floor of Café Kepi, Mullaney could look past the shoulder of Ruth Hughes, out the window, toward the Paris Circle, and see the four caryatids—castings of robed women representing kindness, simplicity, charity, and sobriety—who supported the fountain's dome. And he could dream of the sweet afternoons he shared with Abby in the Paris flower market—afternoons long gone and far away. The dream vaporized quickly when they were approached by a young Omar Sharif look-alike in an expensive suit. "Thank you for coming so swiftly, Mrs. Hughes," said Prince Ibrahim. "My father wishes to extend his appreciation personally." The prince stood aside and motioned with his left hand to a small table in the middle of the room.

The emir stood as they stepped in his direction. But Mullaney was caught off guard. Instead of the stereotypical Arab chieftain in burnoose and caftan robe, the emir of Qatar was a man who looked more like the CEO of a wildly profitable tech giant than a king of the desert. The emir was well past middle-age but far from old, as tall as Mullaney and just as fit, wearing a perfectly cut black suit and a dazzling white shirt, open at the collar.

Just behind him, slightly in shadow, stood three men—two had the size and radiated the confident power of highly skilled security professionals; the third, smaller and thinner in stature, wore a scowl of displeasure.

Ruth Hughes stepped close and accepted the emir's outstretched hand. "Your majesty," said Hughes, bowing head and shoulders. When she came erect again, a broad smile lit up and warmed her face. "What a pleasure it is to see you once more."

Taking both of Hughes's hands, the emir embraced Hughes with his eyes, like long-separated siblings who had come home. "Ruth . . . it is good to see you again. Thank you for coming so far, so quickly.

The emir looked up at Mullaney, who had remained near the door. Hughes turned in his direction, not letting go of the hands that held hers. "Your majesty, may I introduce Brian Mullaney, regional security officer for the Diplomatic Security Service, now serving in Israel. Brian, may I introduce you to His Royal Highness, Sheikh Khalifa bin Hamad Al Thani, emir of Qatar, my friend."

For a moment, their conversation at the small table in the middle of the room was warm and animated, clearly a conversation between two people who at one time must have enjoyed a deep, personal relationship. One of these days he would ask. But the personal conversation didn't last. Almost immediately, Hughes motioned Mullaney to come closer. "Brian, please join us. The emir wants you to hear this also."

Hernandez remained positioned just inside the door as Mullaney stepped forward, put his hand on the back of a chair, and inclined his head. "Your Highness." Taking a seat, he was unprepared for the sheikh's bluntness as he addressed them both. His voice was flat, his words matter-of-fact, without trace of accusation. But they stung.

"You—America—you don't know who is your enemy. You don't know the catastrophe that is coming. And you have no time," said the sheikh, looking back and forth between Mullaney and Hughes.

"Yet," said Hughes, without missing a beat, "you called us here."

"Ruth, the geopolitical reality of today's Middle East is all about nuclear weapons," said the sheikh. He leaned into the table. "In spite of the so-called Ishmael Covenant, that reality hasn't changed. The Israelis have nuclear weapons. The Iranians will soon have nuclear weapons, no matter what your president hopes. And tomorrow, or the next day, the Saudis will have nuclear weapons."

"Tomorrow?" asked Mullaney, his mind automatically shifting to threat assessment. "We were told that King Abdullah called for delivery of the nuclear weapons Pakistan built for Saudi Arabia. Are you saying those weapons will be delivered tomorrow?"

The emir of Qatar turned his shoulders and his concentration toward Mullaney. "The Saudis' weapons were packed in crates, Mr. Mullaney, sitting on a dock in southern Pakistan, waiting for shipment," said the sheikh. "Last night, someone destroyed those weapons—melted them—and sank the ship that was waiting to transport them.

"Do you think one setback will deter Abdullah? He's probably placing another order as we speak. King Abdullah understands the realities and the risks he faces. But," said the emir, "my son and I agree that delivery of nuclear weapons to the Saudis will put to risk every life in the region."

There was nothing on the small table around which they sat. With his right index finger, the emir traced figure eights on the table top, his eyes carefully following every curve.

"King Abdullah is a fool and a madman." His finger stopped and he looked up at Hughes. "I wish he were the only one."

He took a deep breath and looked out the window, into the Paris Circle below. "You know your history, Ruth. Who is Ishmael?"

Hughes didn't hesitate. "Ishmael was the first son of Abram . . . Abraham . . . though not of Sarah. Tossed from the proverbial tent, along with his mother, Hagar, when Isaac was growing in Sarah's arms. Father of the bedouin, the wanderer, the desert people we today call Arabs. Enemy of Isaac, the father of the Jews, and ever since the enemy of all his offspring. So not only is Ishmael disinherited, he's banished as well, into the desert with his mother—presumably to die."

"Yes, this is true," said the emir. "Until Sunday, when the so-called Ishmael Covenant was signed, that story was only history. Sunday, Ishmael reentered that tent. The first Ishmael was the root, the source of the division that has fractured this land and destroyed its peace for nearly three thousand years."

For a moment, silence filled the room. The voices from the café below could be faintly heard, coming up through the floor.

"You don't believe the Ishmael Covenant will bring peace." From Hughes, it was a statement.

Before the emir could respond, a voice came from behind Mullaney.

"Father, may I speak?"

The emir looked up, over Mullaney's shoulder. "Of course."

"King Abdullah convinced my father and the other rulers of the Arab people that the enemy of our enemy is our friend. The Jews would never launch a war of annihilation against the Arab peoples. But the Persians would . . .

have already tried . . . almost succeeded. Peace with Israel would buy the Arab people a chance for survival. We all drank the Kool-Aid."

"But this week," interjected the emir, "my greatest fears have been confirmed. King Abdullah is not a man of character. He is not a man to trust."

"He's a madman, he endangers us all," snapped the prince. "He will bring devastation on us all. Abdullah serves only Abdullah. In addition to recruiting Arab leaders for his Ishmael Covenant, in the privacy of his inner circle Abdullah has also boasted of his Ishmael Curse. He intends to lead a resurrected Islamic Empire, stretching from India to Spain. To do that, he will need to use his nukes . . . to obliterate the Persians, yes, but to also annihilate the Jews. Well, cursed be his family and . . ."

The emir continued to look above Mullaney's shoulder. Although his face was benign, a weary smile barely reaching the corner of his lips, his eyes were delivering a message that the prince clearly received.

"Thank you, my son." The emir returned his gaze to his guests.

"The people of the desert, my people, are very patient," said the emir. "It's ingrained in our DNA. You have to be patient looking for water in an ever-changing sea of sand. It takes forever to travel from place to place at the slow gait of a camel. It takes patience to wait for destiny.

"Many in the West," he said, "postulate the greatest conflict in the Arab world is the split in Islam—the Sunni-Shia enmity that has endured for over fourteen hundred years. But there is a much older, much more basic conflict in the Middle East—the hatred and distrust between Arab and Persian. Your world tends to look at us all as nomads in robes and burnooses. That is true for northern Africa and the southern Gulf States. But it has never been true of the northern Gulf states. Iran and Iraq are Persian countries, not Arab. They are the seat of the original Persian Empire. The Persians have been the avowed enemy of the Arab for millennia, and each still wants to rule the Persian Gulf and be the heart of Islam."

The emir of Qatar sat back in his chair, put his fists on his hips, and skewered both Hughes and Mullaney with prophetic dread. "I can confidently tell you two things—no three—that should rob you of your sleep. One, King Abdullah will never embrace peace with Israel, no matter what he says with his lips. Two, a resurrected, nuclear-armed Persian Empire and an ascendant, nuclear-armed Arab Empire will never peacefully coexist along the Persian Gulf.

"But the third and greatest problem you face is that you do not know your enemy," he said.

There was a flatness to the emir's voice, as if he was stating a simple, universally accepted truth.

"If the Persians and the Saudis were your only problems, the world would still be a treacherously dangerous place. But we have learned that you have a much more pressing and immediate danger. The other great empire to rule this part of the world was the Ottoman Turks. There are some in Turkey today who plot for the return of the Ottoman rule over the Middle East.

"We are told there exists a scheme to steal some of the nuclear weapons from the Incirlik Air Base in Turkey. We do not know who is behind this scheme. But we have reliable information that someone in the government of your NATO ally is plotting to throw the region into more chaos.

"There are many in the Muslim world," said the emir, "who believe it is inevitable that, someday, the Israelis will use their nuclear weapons. Particularly if the Iranians combine a weapon with a delivery system that will reach Israel. Now it is possible both the Saudis and the Turks will also have these nuclear weapons, which leaves the rest of us, the rest of the Middle East, at a dangerous disadvantage. Ancient hate will not tolerate subservience. There will be war. And a war of thermonuclear weapons is a war none of us in the Gulf are likely to survive."

37

Mullaney's mind raced through the implications of the emir's warning. If the Qatari ruler was correct, then the US foreign policy in the Middle East was a shambles, built on a series of expectations and assumptions as solid as a screen door in a downpour. In the post-Arab Spring Middle East, the US envisioned its foreign policy as a three-legged stool built upon alliances with three of the most formidable and influential nations in the region: Israel, Saudi Arabia, and Turkey—Israel as a common-hearted democracy, Saudi Arabia as a coalition of convenience, and Turkey as a NATO member nation and home of the strategically critical Incirlik Air Base.

But this report was more than the political gamesmanship and posturing that were so often dictated by circumstantial forces that impacted American alliances with sovereign Muslim nations. America faced a crisis if—as now seemed likely—the Saudis were going rogue with their own quest for nuclear weapons. But Turkey? Would the Turkish government really sanction and support an attack on the armed forces of a fellow NATO ally—the American troops who maintained and guarded the nuclear weapons in Turkey? Could Kashani's fundamentalist-leaning rhetoric lead to an attack on American troops . . . an attempt to hijack American nuclear weapons?

"I'm sorry, your highness," said Mullaney, shaking his head, "but the idea that the government in Turkey would attempt to steal US nuclear weapons from a NATO facility on its own soil would be one of the most stupid moves in the history of the world. They would never get away with it."

The sheikh cast a glance at Hughes, but turned his full attention toward Mullaney. "Forgive me, Agent Mullaney, I mean no disrespect," he said. "But you do not understand the urgency of the threat you are facing. I have seen evidence that it was Turkish raiders who destroyed the Saudi's nuclear weapons on the Pakistani docks last night. These raiders were well disciplined and highly trained, but they were not Turkish military. They were a secret paramilitary group with ties to the Turkish government. I wouldn't be surprised to find President Kashani or someone in his government behind the raid. The Turks—the Ottomans—it's their unknown intentions I fear, and the ones you should fear also.

"You are not thinking with the mindset of a Muslim fundamentalist, Agent Mullaney. Whoever is behind this plot is not concerned with any possible repercussions. Their driving purpose is to do whatever is necessary, whatever is possible to hasten the arrival of the Mahdi, the final and greatest caliph of Islam. In the Koran, the Mahdi will bring revolution to the earth and establish a new world order based on Sharia law. The Mahdi will reign for seven years over all the earth, a time of justice, righteousness, and virtue where Islam will be victorious over all religions."

The emir leaned closer to Mullaney. "You see, Agent Mullaney, while all three of the world's great religions anticipate the coming of a future savior—whether Messiah or Mahdi—only the followers of Islam believe that the actions they take in this world, at this time, can accelerate the inauguration of those last days. Your enemies are people who believe that attacking the NATO base and stealing the American nuclear weapons will, ultimately, hasten the coming of the Mahdi and will annihilate all prophecy and possibility for the coming of a Judeo-Christian Messiah. Their goal is not to live peacefully and coexist in this world. Their goal is to overthrow this world. Any action that takes them closer to that goal is acceptable.

"It's not only the murderous barbarians of ISIS who believe they can pave the path for the Mahdi," said the sheikh. "Cut to the core and you will find the same goal at the heart of every Islamic jihadist who sees as his mission to bring terror and chaos into this world. Some researchers claim one percent of Muslims are at risk of becoming radicals. That's sixteen million people. How many of those one percent will engage in violent, jihadist terrorism? No one knows. But what we do know is that there is an army out there dedicated to the destruction of the West and the rise of an Islamic caliphate that will rule the world under Sharia law."

Sheikh Khalifa bin Hamad Al Thani took a deep breath. He sat back in his chair, away from the table and morphed into a regal monarch. "My family and I are part of the one and a half billion Muslims—the ninety-nine percent—who want to see our children grow up and enjoy a better life than we did, who want to spoil our grandchildren and attend their weddings. Who want to live beside you, Agent Mullaney, and share our lives with yours in peace and honor. We want you to know that we stand with you against this common enemy. An enemy that threatens the lives of my children and your children."

"Which is why you are here, why you called us here today?" asked Mullaney.

An eclipse of spirit enshrouded the sheikh's presence. He shook his head. "Not entirely." He turned to Ruth Hughes. "Ruth, most of this I could have told you over a secure phone line, you know that."

"I've been waiting," said Hughes. "Because this is why you asked Brian to join us at the table, correct?"

"Always insightful, Ruth," said the emir. He looked back and forth between the two Americans. "I came to warn you—both of you. There is someone in your State Department who is assisting those same people in the Turkish government who are plotting to steal the nuclear weapons from Incirlik."

A few years ago . . . a few days ago . . . Mullaney would have jumped to the defense of the people in his agency. Now doubt came like pollution, corrupting his confidence, and anger welled up in his heart like a tsunami. The swelling storm must have shown on his face.

The emir placed a hand on Mullaney's arm. "I want to be clear . . . I am not saying that someone in the State Department is complicit in an attempt to attack a NATO base and steal nuclear weapons. What we know, without a doubt, is that a relationship exists. I can't tell you how, but we have firsthand information from within the highest echelons of the Turkish government. There are ongoing, direct, and secret communications between someone in or connected to your State Department and individuals in the Turkish government. Not unusual. But we are also absolutely confident that those same Turkish officials are the ones actively communicating about an attempt to steal nuclear weapons from Incirlik."

The emir turned to Hughes. "That, Ruth, is why I urgently requested your presence. I wanted to speak to you personally, face-to-face, so there would be no doubt in you when you reported this conversation to your secretary of state." Sheikh Al Thani shook his head. "You cannot trust your superiors in Washington. Sadly I do not have a name to give you. So I just don't know who you can trust. There are—"

Like a hurled javelin, the small, thin man with the permanent scowl pierced their space, the two chiseled security men trailing closely in his wake, one with his arm protectively around the prince's shoulders. Taking the sheikh's arm at the elbow, he was lifting the emir out of his chair as his words hung in the air. "A thousand pardons, your Highness, but it is no longer safe. We must leave. Now." The two security guards closed around the sheikh and his son, front and back, as the small man hustled them both to the door. He cast one glance over his shoulder. "Leave. They are coming."

38

Ankara
July 22, 2:09 p.m.

The door opened soundlessly.

Heavy curtains closed against the sun, Prime Minister Arslan Eroglu's bedroom was bathed in a dense twilight, shadow upon shadow. Eroglu lay on the bed under a light sheet. In spite of the air-conditioning, Eroglu was perspiring heavily.

Like a mist drifting across a swamp, the Turk appeared to float across the room and hovered at the side of Eroglu's bed. His specter-like aide, Assan, was a ripple of shadow in his wake.

The Turk removed his hands from the sleeves of his jubba, reached up, grasped the cowl of his cape and pushed it back upon his shoulders. His voice came from the pit of darkness. "Arslan."

Far from wakefulness, Eroglu's body stirred, pulling the sheet more tightly to his chin.

"Arslan!"

Eroglu's eyes flashed open, terrified, his mind still only half awake. His shoulders shook, and he raised himself on one elbow in defiance.

"What are you doing here?" His voice sounded like sandpaper on soft wood, raspy and tearing at his throat.

"Arslan, you recently said you don't need me," the Turk whispered. "That is only partly true."

The Turk reached out the long, voluminous right sleeve of his jubba. A sepulchral hand of bone with only an onionskin-like covering of cracked and discolored flesh emerged from the folds of his sleeve. For the first time in ages, the Turk touched another living being, clamping his hand upon Eroglu's left shoulder.

"You may believe you have no need of me," said the Turk as he leaned closer to the bed, squeezing Eroglu's shoulder more violently, "but I most certainly have need of you."

From the black pit of his soul, the Turk summoned the essence of an ancient malevolence. Conjured up during hours in the red room, he unleashed a demon of darkness—the spirit of Soul Stealer—and set it to work on Arslan Eroglu.

A powerful current of hydroelectric proportions began pulsing down along the Turk's arm, through his hand, and into Eroglu. The Turk's right arm looked as if a distant thunderstorm had erupted under his skin—flashes of eye-searing light bolted along his veins, and his arm convulsed like claps of thunder against the side of a house—the violent storm coursing through his fingers and into Eroglu.

"Stop!" cried Eroglu. "What are you do—"

Eroglu's body started a rhythmic thrashing on his bed, each lightning bolt down the Turk's arm whipping Eroglu into more severe contortions.

"Stop!" he screamed, his words erupting from his mouth in violent fits. "What . . . are . . . aaaaaaggggghhhhh . . . please . . . stop!"

The Turk began repeating a mantra to the beat of the pulses invading Eroglu's body, Assan joining the cadence in a language few mortal men had ever heard. A whimpering cry weakly escaped from Eroglu's lips as drool rolled down over his chin.

The chanting increased in rhythm and fervor, and the Turk's hand throbbed on Eroglu's shoulder like a jackhammer on a rock.

Issuing a desperate wail, Eroglu's eyes burst open like eggs dropped from a roof.

Within a heartbeat, as Eroglu's eyes morphed in the rapidly darkening room, Assan stepped up behind the Turk.

The irises of Eroglu's eyes turned black, and the pupils began to glow with a dull yellow pulse. Swirling vortexes of gray thrashed across the surface of his pupils like storms on the surface of the sun.

Assan rested his arm across the back of the Turk's shoulders. He reached around the Turk and, pulling on the sleeve of his jubba, removed his limp hand from Eroglu's shoulder. Assan lowered the Turk's motionless body to the floor. Then he stood and fixed his gaze on the shell that was once Arslan Eroglu.

"Are you there, Master?"

The body that once held the life spirit of Arslan Eroglu looked up, and Assan quickly averted his eyes from the chaos that was erupting in the swirling gray-and-yellow phantom eyes that stared back from within Eroglu's skull.

"Yes, Assan, I am here," said the Turk's voice, echoing from deep within Eroglu's husk. "There is work to do. Take care with my body . . . I will call for it when I need it."

39

All of Brian Mullaney's training and experience snapped into place and into action in the span of a breath. "Move." He had Ruth Hughes up and out of her chair and moving toward Tommy Hernandez, who still guarded the door.

"We're going out the back. Check the stairs."

Hernandez pulled his 9-millimeter fully automatic Glock from his belt holster in the small of his back. Holding it in his right hand, he tucked it inside his suit jacket as he started down the stairs of the Café Kepi.

Mullaney directed his voice into the microphone tacked to the lapel of his suit coat, the one that looked like the State Department pin. "Jasper, bring the car around to the back of the building, fast. We may have a problem."

"They?" asked Hughes as she quick-stepped to the door. "Who could they be?"

"Don't know . . . don't care," said Mullaney. He put out his left arm as they reached the door, moving Hughes behind him and out of the opening. "And we're not going to find out."

His attention turned to the door and the stairs beyond. "Clear?"

"Clear!" came Hernandez's voice from the bottom of the stairs.

He turned to look at Hughes. There was no fear on her face. "My job is to get you back to the embassy alive and well. For now, you just follow me, okay?"

"Right behind you, Brian . . . right behind you."

DSS Agent Jasper Johnson was riding shotgun as Agent Ollie Trotman trolled the streets of Jabal Al Weibdeh, waiting for the call that Mullaney was ready to head home. Trotman never allowed the Navigator to remain in one place for longer than a few minutes, limiting the opportunity for anyone to ID the embassy's vehicle in a particular location.

"Roger that." Johnson kept his eyes straight ahead, scanning the flow of human and vehicle traffic that carpeted the road in front of them, and anxiety hitched a ride "We'll do the best we can, Brian. But these streets are a mess." He glanced to his left. "Mullaney's waiting at the back door."

"Tell him we're about ten minutes away," said Trotman. "It's going to take us some time to get through this crowd."

———※———

Mullaney stood in the doorway and took a slow sweep of the alley behind the Café Kepi. He wasn't looking for anything in particular. He was looking for anything out of the ordinary . . . anything that goaded his mind or trip-started his anxiety. He scanned the shadows behind stacked, empty crates. He peered into every window, especially those closed and covered. He ran his eyes along the parapets of the buildings on the far side of the alley, calculating shooting angles, and studied the shadows of the near-side roofs, emblazoned on the opposite buildings, looking for any movement.

He waited . . . two breaths, three breaths, four. Nothing. Mullaney turned away from the door, leaving it open so Trotman would know where to stop.

"Tommy, block that entrance from the restaurant. Don't want anybody stumbling back here." He guided Hughes to a crate away from the door. "I want you to stay here until the car pulls up." His shoulders took a half turn toward the open door before Mullaney turned back to Hughes.

"Ruth?"

"Yes?"

"Do you trust him?"

"Yes, absolutely."

The enormity of the report he just heard was attacking Mullaney's attention. "Then who do we trust?"

Hughes looked up at him from the corner of her eye. "Each other. Let's leave it there until we get back and talk to the ambassador."

"Still stuck . . . ten minutes out," came into Mullaney's earpiece.

———※———

Gocuk, Turkey
July 22, 2:28 p.m.

His fingers covered in the drippings of baba ghanoush and grilled lamb chunks, Turkish National Police Colonel Fabir Matoush hastily dropped the overfilled pita bread onto the paper plate on his desk. His other phone, the one supplied by his cousin, prime minister Arslan Eroglu, rattled incessantly from the left pocket of his uniform trousers. The paper napkins were already soggy and tattered. Matoush looked frantically left and right. No help. So he took his hands, shoved his fingers in his mouth, sucked loudly . . . looked at his sharply creased uniform pants . . . and reached down to rub his fingers back and forth through the new carpeting on his office floor.

Then he shoved his still sticky fingers into his pocket and pulled out the demanding mobile. It was Arslan. The time had come?

"Hello?"

"Good afternoon, Fabir," said Eroglu, his voice full of energy and power. "Is your family well?"

"Yes, Mr. Prime Minister . . . eh, Arslan. We are well."

"And are we prepared?"

It had been two days with no word, no communication. Matoush had been pleading with Allah . . . *let him forget me; let this madness pass* . . . that this moment would not appear. He felt like he had sold his soul to the devil.

Twice he tried to start the sentence, but the words would not come.

"Fabir? Are we prepared?" An edge had creeped into his cousin's voice.

He breathed. "Yes, Arslan, we are prepared. The men are ready. All of the crates have been delivered."

"Excellent," Eroglu purred. "Begin distributing the weapons tonight. You will unleash the weapons at dawn tomorrow."

Panic leapt into Matoush's throat. "Oh . . . no . . . that is not possible," he stammered.

"And why not? I have paid you well—for obedience."

Matoush scrambled to collect his thoughts. *Must be firm!* "For two reasons, Arslan, either of which alone would warrant this delay. First, the Incirlik base is vast and sprawling, and the bunkers containing the nuclear weapons and the crews who maintain them are scattered across the base. It would be foolish to risk this mission by trying to get all of our weapons placed in one night. We would look too suspicious. And second, there is a windstorm blowing through the region as we speak. The storm is not expected to dissipate until Thursday. Releasing the chemical weapons into a windstorm would not only be madness—there would be no controlling where they spread—it would also jeopardize our chances for success. The bomb crews and the guards would be unaffected if the wind was blowing the wrong way. We have waited this long, Arslan . . . prudence would be best."

Matoush held the slippery phone to his ear and waited for his fate.

"Very well, my cousin. I bow to your superior understanding."

Matoush cringed. Was it the words that were polluting his ear or the remnants of his sloppy lunch?

"Begin the distribution tonight. Proceed as you deem wise."

His heart stopped thudding. Matoush had some relief.

"But . . . at dawn on Thursday, wind or no wind, complete or not complete, you will rain death on the Americans at Incirlik, and you will bring me my nuclear weapons. Is that clear?"

"Yes, I—"

"It would be a tragedy for you if some illness suddenly came upon your family, would it not?"

Matoush was stunned, the images flooding his brain terrifying. "You would—"

"No, I would not. Unless I must," said Eroglu. "Complete the mission, Fabir. So both you and your children remain safe. Goodbye, my cousin."

40

Mullaney kept his eyes moving from Tommy Hernandez's back and the heavy curtains that separated this rear storage room from the front of the restaurant to the open back door. Without a sound, a huge body in a western suit appeared, blocking the back door. Mullaney's internal threat meter leapt into the danger zone, his finger starting to press against the trigger of his Glock—until . . . "Hello, Brian. I didn't expect to find you back in the storage room."

"Sultan?" said Mullaney.

"Forgive the intrusion, Agent Mullaney, but I fear for your safety and the safety of Mrs. Hughes."

"What are you doing . . . how did you know we were here?"

Sultan Abbaddi, commander of the Royal Guard Brigade, closed the door behind him. Abbaddi was a bank vault in a nice suit. A head taller than even Mullaney, Abbaddi's shoulders were half again as wide, his body half again as thick. The Brigade were personal bodyguards of Jordanian King Hussein II and as commander, Abbaddi had often accompanied the king in his meetings with the US ambassador and his security detail during Mullaney's tour of duty in Jordan. Mullaney had good reason to trust Abbaddi.

"Good fortune and good work, I believe," said Abbaddi. "All of our security forces have been working overtime to keep an eye on, and ensure the safety of, a number of high-profile visitors to our country," said Abbaddi. "You may have heard something about this little announcement that was made Sunday, yes? Sheikh Al Thani is one of the royals our teams have kept under twenty-four-hour watch since they set foot on our soil.

"Well, our men also continually monitor the activities of several cells who operate in our country, unsavory fellows with evil intent . . . Al Qaeda, the Islamic State, some freelancers. We started rounding them up a week ago in advance of Sunday's ceremony. About an hour ago we were tipped off about a new group. We thought they might be a threat to the king, so the military raided their home base. They were gone. But we found photos . . . photos of Mrs. Hughes and you. Imagine our surprise when our watchers followed the emir of Qatar to this café and then, not long after, you two show up. Why you are here, how they know—I'm not sure. But we believe you are their target. Today."

"How many?" asked Mullaney.

"At least twelve, well armed," said Abbaddi. He nodded his head toward the alley. "I have two men with me. Where is your car? We need to get you someplace that is more secure."

"Stuck in traffic . . . trying to get here," said Mullaney. He pointed toward the door. "These alleys are a dead zone—too tight and no cover. We've got to move."

Mullaney spoke into his lapel mic. "Jasper . . . where are you?"

"We're coming up to the end of the alley that leads to the rear of the joint, but that's as close as we're going to get," said Johnson. "You may need to come to us."

"All right, Jasper, we may have trouble. Can't be sure, but it's possible the Turks have tracked us down. We've just been alerted by three officers from the Royal Guard Brigade. They believe Mrs. Hughes is the target."

Johnson kept his eyes straight ahead, scanning the relentless traffic that blocked the road in front of the Navigator. "Roger that. Ollie, our team is waiting. And we may run into some unwelcome guests."

"Tell him we're still about five minutes away," said Trotman.

"The streets are clogged. It will take them a few minutes to reach the pickup point," said Mullaney, "which is down at the bottom of Jareer Street."

"Very good. Down is better than up," said Abbaddi. He turned to Ruth Hughes. "With your permission, Mrs. Hughes, my men and I will escort you to your vehicle."

"Thank you. Much appreciated."

Abbaddi moved to the back door, but stopped as he gripped the handle. He looked over his shoulder at Mullaney. "My men and I will lead. Allow us to get to each corner, wait for the signal that it's clear. Then move quickly to where we are. Once we found you, we put in a call to the police for assistance. We should be fine."

Mullaney didn't believe Abbaddi's attempt at reassurance. The big man's next move confirmed Mullaney's instincts. Abbaddi put out his large arm and moved both Mullaney and Hughes behind his formidable body and away from the door.

"Mr. Hernandez," said Abbaddi, assuming command, "would you be willing to act as rear guard?"

"Story of my life," mumbled Hernandez, who was spying through a gap in the curtains leading to the rest of the first floor. "Just one more rear to guard."

With the care of a cat burglar, Abbaddi cracked open the back door of the café but stepped to the side. "Rasheed?"

"Clear, Commander."

"Let's move." Abbaddi was out the door.

He cast a glance to his left, down the alley. Sultan Abbaddi was walking slowly, his shoulder grazing the walls on the right of the alley. One of his men was on the left, about to reach the first of several narrow intersections. The third was stationary, about twenty yards left of the open door, his back against the left wall of the alley, his eyes sweeping from one end of the alley to the other.

"We're coming up to the alley." Johnson's voice was flat and precise coming through Mullaney's earpiece. "Ollie will stay with the car. Let Abbaddi know I'm coming to you."

Mullaney saw the officer at the junction peer around the corner then lift his right arm in a holding motion. Mullaney's eyes remained on the alley, but he could feel Hughes's presence just off his left shoulder.

"Is it safe to move?" Hughes asked.

Her words were nearly drowned out by a throaty, reverberating rumble that rose up in anger to Mullaney's right. He barely had time to turn his head in that direction as two motorcycles thundered down the alley, hurtling in the direction of the café. And a volcano of violence erupted in the alley.

———————————

Jasper Johnson had one leg out of the Navigator when he saw the flash and the telltale wake of an RPG round.

"Incoming!" Johnson shouted. "Bail out, Ollie!"

———————————

Mullaney needed only an instant to register what was happening outside. Each motorcycle carried two bodies, a driver and a rider. The riders were shooting automatic weapons down the alley and closing fast on the back door of the café. Return fire was coming from Abbaddi and his men to the left. And a number of shooters opened up from the rooftops above.

With a move defined by decades of training, Mullaney rotated quickly to his left, placing his body between Hughes and the door, kicked the door closed with his left heel and spoke urgently into his lapel mic. "Code Red."

Nearly lifting Hughes bodily off the floor, Mullaney turned her away from the door and pushed her toward the cover behind a stack of wooden crates. He took one step when twin explosions shook Café Kepi to its foundation. The door to the alley was blown across the room, hit Tommy Hernandez square in the chest, and drove him through the curtains and into the next room.

Hughes buckled under the dual impact of Mullaney's urgency and the heaving floor of the café. She fell beside the crates with Mullaney landing atop her back. But the DSS agent threw himself off Hughes and scrambled to one knee, facing the door, his 9-millimeter Glock held firmly in both hands.

———————————

"Missed!" Ollie Trotman's voice came through Mullaney's earpiece, followed by a series of gunshots and a loud crash.

"Rooftop to the left," shouted Johnson. The sound of Johnson's weapon on rapid-fire nearly drowned out his words. "We can't get to you, Brian."

———————————

But Mullaney had no time to think about what was happening out in the alley. He put two rounds into the right temple of the first man through the blown door and then four rapid shots—two toward the shape of a man who stopped abruptly in the shattered portal as his comrade went down in a lump and two through the remnants of the door jamb. Which of the four hit their mark, Mullaney couldn't say and didn't care. The result was all that mattered . . . another body lying where the door had once stood.

———— ◦◦◦◦ ————

A three-foot-high stone wall on Jareer Street provided Jasper Johnson all the cover he needed. He could see Trotman on the far side of the Navigator, now using the SUV as protection. "Ollie," Johnson yelled over the sounds of the gunfire, "let's clear the roofs."

With his Glock held in both hands, Johnson popped up from behind the wall and emptied a clip at the muzzle flashes coming from the rooftops on the far side of the alley. That gave Trotman the split second he needed to reach into the back seat of the Navigator and pull out the Heckler & Koch MP5 9-millimeter submachine gun with extra clips duct-taped to its stock.

Trotman inched toward the front of the vehicle, laid the barrel of the MP5 on the hood at the base of the front windshield, and burned through three clips, laying down a withering fire against the parapets along the rooflines of the alley.

The muzzle flashes stopped.

41

"Stay here and stay down," Mullaney said to Hughes, who was on her side behind the crates. Gunfire reports ricocheted off the alley's walls, amplifying the number of shots. It sounded like several pitched battles occurring just outside the café's doors.

Mullaney inched to the side of the crates, the door ahead of him to the left. "Tommy?"

There was no answer. Mullaney risked a quick glance to his right. The heavy curtains had fallen back into place after the explosion. He couldn't see past them. He took a breath. Crouched down, he frog-walked to the side of the blasted doorjamb. He peeked right, up the alley, just to be sure. But it was empty. All the shooting was coming from the left of the door, down the alley toward where Abbaddi and his men had been standing.

These next steps would be tricky. Mullaney needed to step over the two bodies that lay on the floor of the clogged doorway, avoiding the spreading pools of red-black blood, and make it to the far side so he could look down the alley. Two steps. Maybe three. And all of that time he would be exposed, unprotected, as he passed by the open door. Out of the corner of his left eye, Mullaney tried to see the roofline of the building on the far side of the alley. Nothing.

Getting up out of his crouch, Mullaney bent over at the waist, centered his weight on the balls of his feet, and stepped over the first body, squaring his shoulders to the open door upon which he trained his pistol. Like a choreographed dance routine, his eyes never leaving the open door, Mullaney quickstepped, right then left, right then left, over the two bodies and threw himself against the wall on the far side of the door.

He couldn't help himself. Once more, Mullaney looked to the curtained doorway, hoping to see Hernandez pull his battered body into the room. But there was no movement, and he still couldn't see beyond the heavy curtains.

Put that aside. Focus.

"Get the launcher!"

Mullaney almost dropped his gun at the sound in his ear, an unexpected command from Jasper Johnson.

———————

Johnson slapped the last clip into his Glock and peeked over the wall. Trotman's relentless fusillade from the MP5 had shredded the stone along the parapets of the buildings on the far side of the alley. The firing from the roof had stopped. Johnson wanted to be sure. He held his Glock trained on the roof.

"Get the launcher," he yelled toward Trotman.

It took less than sixty seconds for Trotman to pull the weapon from the back of the Navigator. It was a standard Colt M4 carbine modified at the factory with the addition of a 40-millimeter grenade launcher. Lightweight and mobile, the Colt M203 grenade launcher was a deadly foe.

Johnson, his eyes on the rooflines, didn't see it. But he heard the launch, then a second. He didn't see the explosion either, wisely tucking in tight behind the wall for protection. A shower of pulverized stone fell upon his back. Then he was on his feet, running into the alley. "On our way, Brian."

———————

Mullaney flinched for a moment at Johnson's voice in his ear, but forced his focus out the door and down the alley.

One motorcycle was flat on its side in the middle of the alley, not far from the door. Probably the two dead men lying on the floor behind him. His eyes searched for Abbaddi and the Jordanians, trying to quickly discern friend and foe amidst the gunpowder smoke that filled the alley. But gunfire was pouring out from both sides of the alley.

Abbaddi was on the right, against the wall . . . one of his men was just left of the door . . . the other on the left at the first intersection.

Down the alley, on the right-hand side, a man in a suit lay motionless in the gutter. To the right, men were shooting from behind a stone wall. Return fire was coming from Mullaney's left. He couldn't see from whom, or where they were sheltered. But he knew his enemy was on the right, the far side of the alley. He cast a glance at the building opposite the door. Two of the windows were shot out, blood stained the window frame of the lower one.

Explosions, two, one right after the other, erupted from down the alley. *On our way, Brian.*

Sirens were closing in from the distance. Somebody on the far side of the alley ran out of a door to the side of the wall, firing across the alley as he ran. He didn't see Mullaney. Two taps on the trigger of his Glock and another body fell to the stone.

As if a curtain had fallen on the last act of a play, silence abruptly filled the alley. All the firing stopped. Mullaney could hear footsteps running up from the bottom of the alley and the anguished calls from one Jordanian to another. He glanced across the room, where Hughes was crouched at the edge of the wooden crates. But his head quickly snapped left and looked to the curtained doorway. Without losing his focus on the door to the alley or changing the aim of his Glock, Mullaney edged toward the back of the room, the last place he had seen Tommy Hernandez. He got to the curtained doorway.

Mullaney's hand was on the fold where the curtains opened when Jasper Johnson reached the door to the alley. "Brian . . . we're clear," he heard from behind him. But Mullaney's full attention was in front of him.

Tommy Hernandez was sitting halfway erect against the far wall, his shoulders propped up against the wall, the rest of his body stretched out on the floor. The back door to the building, now shattered in four pieces, lay on top of or beside him. A look of surprise filled Hernandez's face. His mouth was open as if he was about to speak. And a foot-long, jagged splinter of doorjamb was thrust through his left eye like a lance into a target.

Mullaney felt a hand on his right shoulder.

"Brian."

It was Jasper Johnson.

"Abbaddi's been shot. He's in bad shape."

And Tommy watched with unseeing eyes, an open mouth waiting for his forever silenced voice.

Mullaney grasped the curtain in his fist to keep his wobbly knees from buckling under his weight. "Oh, God . . ."

42

The lifeless body of the Turk lay stretched out on the stone table amid the brooding menace of the red room on Alitas Street. His form appeared shrunken within his clothes, as if the shriveled flesh alone hung onto the spindly frame of bone.

Assan was pressed into a darkened corner of the room, leaning heavily against the wall, his eyes on the cadaver of the Turk but his consciousness ever aware of the being sitting to his left. Assan's body still convulsed in spasms of pain, the breath squeezed from his lungs with every tremor, hours after the Turk's transformation. He had once before witnessed the Turk assimilate another human's body. While a miracle he could not explain, Assan could see and feel the effects of that assimilation firsthand.

He saw sweeping waves of supernatural power surge into the being on his left—the earthly shell of Arslan Eroglu which was now the host, the dwelling place, of the malevolent spirit of the Turk. But the process of assimilation not only ravaged the Turk's physical body, but also ravaged Assan's physical body as well. He had no explanation, only the ever-present agony that coursed through flesh and muscle. Clearly, this was the currency required by assimilation: a significant physical reduction in response to paranormal expansion.

Assan knew the Turk's spirit, now living inside Eroglu's husk, had ingested massive quantities of supernatural power. Assan was less certain whether his physical body, or that of the Turk, would survive the transformation. And this was only the beginning . . .

"We have suffered another defeat."

The voice, which sounded as if it were rising from the depths of the ocean, was Eroglu's but the eyes were those of the Turk. Assan could still not stare at those eyes.

Eroglu's body sat rigidly straight in a massive stone chair, opposite the stone table. Chiseled into the chair's surface were many of the same feverish characters and symbols that adorned the walls of the isolated red room. At the top of the chair's back, above Eroglu's head, was the carved symbol of a coiled serpent.

Eroglu's fingers were entwined within the lion's claws carved into the stone at the end of each arm of the chair, his grip tightening.

"Our commander lies dead, gunned down in the alleys of Amman, another victim of the American," the Turk growled. The being in Eroglu's body had the power to alter the sound of its voice, sounding either like himself, or mimicking Eroglu's speech. Now his voice—the Turk's voice—was rising in volume and passion. "This man, Mullaney, must be stopped! He was once a threat, but now he is a looming disaster. Each day he moves closer to a truth that could destroy all our plans."

Eroglu's head turned toward Assan but it was the Turk's eyes that pierced his averted countenance as he pounded his gnarly fist against the stone arm of the chair. "Find the commander's son! Time is against us and we must move quickly before the box of power eludes us again."

Truman Building, Washington, DC
July 22, 9:52 a.m.

It was unlike Noah Webster. He was late getting to the Truman building. Normally one of the first on hand at six thirty in the morning, it was nearly ten a.m. as he walked down the main corridor of the Truman building's seventh floor toward his office. Still he hadn't gotten much sleep. It seemed like he had just left the building, which he had less than six hours before.

He was feeling groggy—not at all like himself. Which is probably why at first all the furtive glances in his direction had failed to register, why at first he failed to notice the whispered conversations that ceased as he walked past. Just as he began to catalog the unusual behavior, Arthur Ravel, the assistant secretary of state and no ally of Webster's, stopped in front of him and offered a handshake.

"I'm so very sorry, Noah," said Ravel. "It was a shock to all of us. He—" Ravel stopped midsentence, clearly halted by Webster's lack of response.

"You don't know, do you?" Ravel took a step closer, not letting go of Webster's hand. "Senator Markham's body was found in his apartment this morning. He must have passed away during the night. I was told it looked like a heart attack."

Noah Webster recorded the words clearly enough, yet his mind was having a hard time processing the information. Markham? Dead? Then one statement captured his consciousness.

"Heart attack? The senator had a number of health issues," Webster said, still trying to sort through an unexpected reality, "but his heart was as strong as an ox. That's the one thing all the doctors agreed on."

Arthur Ravel released Webster's hand. "I'm sure they'll figure it out," he said, as he started to disengage. "Just wanted to tell you how sorry I am."

Washington, DC
July 22, 10:18 a.m.

"The terms for acquiring your services remain the same?"

Webster had made a hasty exit from the Truman building and was walking along the path skirting Constitution Pond, adjacent to the long, Lincoln Memorial Reflecting Pool on the Washington Mall, a few blocks from the State Department but much more secure. A cheap, throw-away mobile phone was pressed against his ear.

"Generally yes," said the voice on the other end of the call. "Depending upon the assignment."

The man—known to Webster only as the man in the Panama hat—and his organization were topflight professionals. Specialists in black ops, who operated well under the radar of international law enforcement, they surfaced and offered their services only at the recommendation of a current client. Webster was not a first-time customer.

"I want Abigail Mullaney, Richard Rutherford's daughter, followed consistently. And I want her to know she's being followed. And I want her to know her daughters are being followed."

"Tricky . . . but we can do it. Our assets will be in place tomorrow. Your fee will be the same as last time. You know how to wire the funds. Is there anything else?"

Anything else? An understatement.

"I wish I knew," Webster admitted. "There are multiple hands in play right now."

"Yes. Things are heating up."

"And there's Markham's death," said Webster.

"Yes, a warning signal, that," said the man's voice. "Somebody is starting to play hardball. Hits awfully close to home for you, eh? Is it Rutherford?"

"I don't know. But I need to know. Put on a full-scale surveillance of Rutherford—monitor all communications, shadow his every move."

"That will be expensive," said the man in the Panama hat.

"But necessary," said Webster. "I want his money. But it may come to a point . . ."

"Yes . . . safety. I know," said the voice. "We will be ready when you call."

Ankara
July 22, 5:24 p.m.

"Your father served us well, as did his father before him," said the Turk. They had tracked down the commander's son in Istanbul, and it was the Turk's voice that spoke through the mobile phone connection to the new leader of the Disciples. "Now it is up to you to serve us well."

"I am prepared to perform any assignment, Exalted One."

"Good . . . because it would be unfortunate if your family lost all that your father earned for them." There was no subtlety in the Turk's message. His words were intended to strike the new commander like brass knuckles in a velvet glove. "I understand they enjoy living in that villa on the Mediterranean, and your younger brothers have enrolled in very prestigious—and expensive—universities."

There was no hesitation on the other end of the conversation. "All of our family has sworn to you our allegiance. We are in your service, regardless of your favor. But . . . we are all grateful for the favor you have bestowed on us. How may I do your bidding?"

The Turk held a vision of the new commander in his mind. He had the same body as his father's—a taut, coiled weapon capable of extraordinary endurance and rapid, focused violence—only the son was thirty years younger and stronger. Equally proven, equally dependable. But unlike his father, the new commander—a livid, pink scar crossing along his hairline, down into a notch cut from the top of his right ear—passionately enjoyed the pleasure of inflicting pain. He was perfect.

"There is a flight leaving Ataturk Airport for Tel Aviv at six fifteen. Be on it, and alert the Disciples in Israel of your arrival. Call me when you arrive in Israel, and I will give you further instructions."

"It will be done," said the new commander.

"Good . . . for tonight you will have the opportunity to exert your revenge on the man who murdered your father."

❦

Amman
July 22, 5:30 p.m.

Ruth Hughes stood under the overhang of a metal roof. Mullaney, at her side, was leaning heavily against the wall of a deserted hanger in a distant corner of the Amman Marka International Airport. Across the tarmac, obscured from the view of the rest of the airport, four men were hoisting a heavy plastic body bag into the cargo hold of the waiting Aramco jet helicopter.

Hughes glanced to her left, away from the heart-rending tableau at the side of the helicopter, and tried to gauge the damage that was ripping away at Brian Mullaney. His face was hard, set, as if it had been sculpted, gray like aged marble. The life had fled from his eyes. Hughes stifled the sob in her chest that ached for escape and searched for words.

Her voice, when it emerged, was as somber as the setting. "It's a good thing Abbaddi's team intervened for us or we would probably still be negotiating with the Jordanian police."

"Abbaddi's team will slap a lid on this, so there won't even be a whisper in the newspapers," said Mullaney. His words were clear but had little life. "Not with all these Arab emissaries in town and with the ink still wet on the covenant signing."

Mullaney's eyes remained fixed on the helicopter. "Is he still in surgery?"

"I don't know," she said. "The hospital wouldn't release any information."

Mullaney shook his head. "Sultan's probably the toughest guy I've ever met. If anybody can survive those wounds, he's the one."

Jasper Johnson and Ollie Trotman backed away from the August Wetland AW135 as the pilot closed the cargo hatch. Hughes noticed that Mullaney flinched as the door was closed.

"Brian . . ."

Mullaney forced his head to turn aside, feeling like the flesh was being ripped from his eyeballs as they peeled away from the helicopter and its ravaged cargo. Tommy!

Ruth Hughes stood to his right, a mobile phone held in her upraised left hand.

"It's the ambassador."

The distance between them was only a few feet, but it seemingly took an eternity for Mullaney's arm to reach toward the phone and bring it to his ear.

"Yes, sir?"

"Brian, I've been praying for you since I first got the news." Cleveland's voice felt like an arm around his shoulders. "I'm so sorry, Brian. Tommy was such a good man . . . a fine friend."

Was. The word rumbled and echoed in the empty cavern inside Mullaney that was once the cherished home of Tommy Hernandez.

"Prayer," said Cleveland, "is the only thing I can offer you beyond mere words that sound so empty and futile. My prayers and a heart that breaks with yours. I'm so sorry."

It was hours before dusk, but still Mullaney felt a chill shiver along his spine. "Thank you, sir." His words hung like lead weights at the end of a fishing line. "I appreciate your thoughts and your prayers." The rotors of the helicopter began a slow turn, stirring Mullaney from the depths. "How can I help you, sir?"

The pause told Mullaney that Cleveland was carefully choosing his words.

"Under normal circumstances you could help me most, and help yourself most, by taking a few days off," said the ambassador. "But these are not normal circumstances. I don't think any of us are going to get much rest for the next few days."

Next. What would Mullaney do next?

"I believe we have two primary tasks needing immediate attention," said Cleveland. "The three of us will need to get on a line with Secretary Townsend."

"Gang of Four?"

"Yes." Mullaney heard hesitation in Cleveland's voice. "But I think you need to do something else first."

"Sir?"

"Rabbi Herzog is still at the embassy . . . waiting for you. I spoke to him after you left. He told me some of what he'd been sharing with you. He's a tough old bird. He said you told him to wait for you and he's going to wait as long as necessary because he's got . . . it's about the box and the prophecy, Brian. He said you are the only one he can share this with and that it's critical to share the information with you as soon as possible. So I commandeered the staff break room and put him in there until you got back. Sorry . . . never expected . . ."

The silence dragged on. Cleveland stepped into it. "Ruth can escort Tommy's body back to the residence. I think you need to go to the embassy first. Something is going on, Brian. I can feel it."

43

For five minutes—at least he thought it was only five minutes—Mullaney's head was back, eyes closed, as the driver navigated the streets of Tel Aviv on the way to the embassy. He was so tired, he struggled mightily to resist the sleep that beckoned. Pushing his head forward, he went back to scrolling through his phone, checking emails that had piled up in the last ten hours, quickly scanning over fifty text messages . . . until he saw the one from Morningstar.

"12:08 p.m.: blk frd 150 prst o"

That would have been 5:08 in the morning in Washington . . . well before dawn. Morningstar had been busy. Probably hadn't gotten much sleep himself. But what did it mean?

He scrolled further back through the earlier texts.

"11:32 a.m.: No time. Meeting someone who says they can help . . . could be the breakthrough we've been looking for. Talk to you later."

Mullaney thought for a moment. The first message came in while he, Hughes, and Tommy were in the helicopter on their way to Jordan.

Thirty minutes between communications. Nothing in the last eight hours?

Mullaney's sleep-deprived mind was suddenly alert and focused. He went back to the last text.

Black Ford 150. A good-sized pickup truck. But "prst"? Pursuit? Morningstar was being chased! At five in the morning.

Mullaney's mind turned quickly, beginning to catalogue possible scenarios, when the driver was waved through the vigilant and ever-present security and pulled into the embassy's underground parking lot.

US Ambassador's Residence, Tel Aviv
July 22, 7:57 p.m.

The marines, four across, were at attention on a lower step, white-gloved four-square salutes touching the polished brims of their hats. Two others, hoisting

American flags, flanked Ambassador Cleveland and his daughter, Palmyra Parker, on the top step as the black SUV carrying Ruth Hughes and the body of Tommy Hernandez pulled up at the front entrance of the ambassador's residence in the Herzliya Pituach neighborhood, just north of seaside Tel Aviv.

When the car stopped, no one moved except the marines.

It was as if the body of the president of the United States was in the back of the SUV. For the depth of grief Cleveland felt, the car could have been carrying the body of one of his sons.

The four marines snapped their salutes, their right hands slapping to their sides. In perfect unison of movement, the four marines proceeded solemnly down the steps. Coming around to the back of the SUV, they split, two on each side, flanking the rear hatch door. The hatch opened electronically, gliding up.

Hernandez's body had been transferred from the body bag to a casket at the airport, a crisp, new American flag draped over the casket. As if in slow motion, the two closest marines edged the casket out, hand over hand, as it passed on to the next marine. Once it cleared the car, they stopped all movement and stood like marble statues. Then with the grace of a ballet, they raised the casket to their shoulders and, with slow, mechanical steps, almost glided up the steps and into the residence, followed by the flag-carrying marines.

Ruth Hughes stepped out of the SUV and joined Cleveland and his daughter on the top step.

"How's Brian?" asked the ambassador as they followed the procession into the residence.

"Numb, I think," said Hughes. "Feel that way myself."

Cleveland stopped in the middle of the entry hall and faced Hughes straight on, a grimace crossing his face. "Forgive me, Ruth. I am being insensitive. That was a terrifying experience you've just lived through. How are you doing?"

Hughes put her hand on Cleveland's arm. "Thank you, sir. I don't think I've ever been that frightened in my entire life." Parker moved to Hughes's side. "And I've never seen so many acts of selfless heroism."

Like an aging prophet pondering a word from heaven, Cleveland nodded, rocking both head and shoulders. He slipped a hand inside the arm of both Hughes and his daughter and guided them along the hall in the wake of the marines. "We are blessed to have men like these. Lord, please keep them safe."

Mullaney bounded up the stairs two at a time, ignored the staff break room, and barreled into his office. He ripped the phone receiver off the console with his left hand and punched in Morningstar's number with his right.

The ringing continued. No answer. No response at all.

Mullaney grabbed his mobile phone and pulled up the text messages. He responded to Morningstar's last message: "Back to office. Cryptic message has me freaked. Where R U?"

He stared at the iPhone in his hand as if Morningstar would respond immediately, "At the library." But all of Mullaney's instincts told him his friend was in massive trouble. And he was half a world away.

Half a world . . . the light went on.

Mullaney tapped the green phone icon, hit Contacts, and tapped on Doak. Two rings and his brother answered.

"What's happening, Brian? Are you safe?"

"Out here is fine," said Mullaney, reciting the long-held code that father and brothers used when they were members of the Virginia State Police. "Be careful out there" were the final words they spoke to each other before going on duty. If any of them received a call from another that didn't sit right, standard operating procedure was to ask, "Are you safe?" And the answer they wanted to hear was, "Out here is fine." Any other response spelled trouble.

"Good . . . what's going on?" asked Doak Mullaney, often-decorated captain in the Virginia State Police.

"I think I've got a problem that needs your help."

"Shoot."

"All I can tell you at the moment is that we have a major crisis at State, and George Morningstar and I have been working on something sensitive. I don't know if there's a connection between the two, but I got these two texts from Morningstar before dawn your time."

Mullaney read the two text messages, spelling out the second message so Doak would get the obvious implication that Morningstar was in a hurry on the second text.

Without hesitation, Doak asked "Why was Morningstar being chased by a

Black Ford 150? You don't know, of course, which is why you called me. What kind of vehicle does Morningstar drive?"

Mullaney breathed deeply for the first time in minutes. "An old, beat-up Toyota 4Runner, rusted blue, couple of dents. Don't know what year."

"Okay," said Doak. "I'll find him. Call you back at this number?"

"Use my mobile . . . I don't know how much longer I'm going to be here."

"Okay. I'll call as soon as I have something. And Brian?"

"Yeah?"

"Try to breathe once in a while," said Doak. "And be careful out there."

"Be careful out there. And thanks, Doak."

———⋙●◉●⋘———

Ankara
July 22, 8:03 p.m.

The new commander called the Turk as soon as he cleared customs at Ben Gurion Airport. "The Disciples are already gathering," he said.

"Good. When you arrive at the rendezvous, divide the Disciples into two groups. Have one group on standby three hundred meters south of the American embassy and the second group three hundred meters north of the ambassador's residence. Ensure they are ready to move."

"Yes, Exalted One. May I ask what is our mission, so I will know how best to prepare my fighters?"

The Turk considered his new commander. His family had been faithful leaders of the Disciples for generations. Devoted. Reliable. This new leader would need to know what to expect.

"Our mission, as it has been for centuries," said the Turk, venom dripping from his words, "is preventing the prophecies of the Lithuanian from being revealed and destroying or capturing the box of power. But we now have a second purpose—revenge for all our Disciples who have been killed pursuing that mission—including your father."

He heard the quick intake of breath from the other end of the call. "Thank you, Exalted One. There is much to repay."

"One hour from now," said the Turk, "there will be two simultaneous earthquakes—one at the embassy and one at the residence. The earthquakes will inflict considerable damage, but they will not totally consume the buildings. They will defy the laws of nature . . . each earthquake will convulse only the ground upon which the embassy and the residence reside. The earthquakes will occur precisely at nine Tel Aviv time. Instruct your teams to remain three hundred meters away, so they will not be threatened by the initial, violent tremors. But I want the Disciples advancing on the buildings while the ground is still moving."

"Yes, Exalted One," said the leader. "Our men are well trained . . . and fearless."

"Today, they will need to be fearless," said the Turk. "Listen to me carefully. Our hope depends on your effectiveness."

"Yes, Exalted One."

"The box of power is being held in a secure vault in the basement of the American embassy building," the Turk explained. "The earthquake will breach the defenses of the embassy and rip apart its walls. Your Disciples will gain access to the basement. You will find a way to enter the vault and secure the box of power.

"You will have formidable opposition," warned the Turk. "Expect strong, armed resistance from the embassy security, but they are not your greatest threat. The winged ones are entrusted with maintaining the safety of the box of power. The earthquake at the embassy and your piercing of its defenses will trigger a response from the winged ones, and they will rush to its aid. The forces of darkness will attack them in the realms of the air, but you will engage them in the realms of the earth. Be prepared."

"It will be done, Exalted One."

"I want you, personally, to lead the attack on the embassy. And if the American agent should interfere, I want you, personally, to cut out his heart and bring it back to me as a prize."

"I will relish the honor, Exalted One. We will be prepared . . . and we will not fail."

"Commander . . . both the Americans and the winged ones will fight like gladiators to keep the box out of your hands. But if you gain access to it, do not touch the metal box! For you, it is certain death. Carry it only in the wooden box that protects it."

"Yes, Ex—"

"Your second objective is to pay back blood for blood, exact our revenge for all the Disciples who have fallen," interrupted the Turk. "While the winged ones are engaged at the embassy, we will also rain death upon the residence. Our man inside has informed me that Ambassador Cleveland, his daughter, and this meddling woman, Hughes, are all expected to remain in the residence. They will die tonight—either by the effects of the earthquake or by your hand. While the earth is moving, have your men breach the perimeter of the residence. In the confusion, your men will hunt down the ambassador and his daughter. If possible, slit their throats so they will survive long enough to watch their blood spill from their bodies.

"I want the blood of the Americans staining the streets of Tel Aviv just as the blood of the Disciples stained the alleys of Amman. You will kill the ambassador, kill his daughter, and any other American who gets in the way. I want them dead . . . tonight. Do you understand?"

"Yes, Exalted One. It will be done."

"Do not fail!" The Turk's words were more of a threat than a statement. "Or do not return."

44

Ankara
July 22, 8:10 p.m.

He had dismissed Assan from the red room. He wanted no distractions now.

Eroglu's body sat stiffly in the stone chair while the Turk's mind settled and focused itself. There was time before the Disciples were in position. Time to test the level of his newly assimilated powers. The Turk closed his eyes and concentrated on the image of Mullaney's face that one of the Disciples had captured on his camera. It was like compelling his life force through a keyhole in the space-time continuum. And even with his expanded power, successfully invading another being's consciousness required extraordinary concentration and was not always accomplished. He willed his presence into proximity with his adversary, into the space around Mullaney's body, and then began probing for access to Mullaney's mind.

The Turk could feel the weight of Mullaney's weariness, the emotional desert of his spirit. *Ah, yes . . . his best friend is now a lifeless hulk. Good. Suffer.*

***

US Embassy, Tel Aviv
July 22, 8:12 p.m.

Back in his embassy office, the building nearly silent at this time of night, Brian Mullaney was physically and emotionally exhausted. There was an emptiness inside that rivaled the black void that engulfed him upon the death of his father. He didn't have a chance to say goodbye to either Tommy or his father, who spent his last months in an Alzheimer's coma. Just as he never heard his father say, *I forgive you*, after Mullaney left the Virginia State Police.

Mullaney tried to clear the fog clouding his mind and focus on the elder Rabbi Herzog.

The rabbi was waving his huge, unlit pipe in Mullaney's direction. "Do you understand this time of the Gentiles? It is a concept that appears throughout holy scripture, both the Hebrew Torah and the Christian Bible. The prophet Yeshua of Nazareth spoke of the climactic season of humankind. Luke, the physician, recorded that Jesus told his disciples that a time was coming of great calamity, when the temple would be destroyed, a time of earthquakes and wars, of false prophets, famines, and signs from heaven. And then Jerusalem will be surrounded by great armies—a time of desolation, punishment, and wrath against the Jewish people.

"The translation authorized by the English King James says, 'And they shall fall by the edge of the sword, and shall be led away captive into all nations: and Jerusalem shall be trodden down of the Gentiles, until the times of the Gentiles be fulfilled.'

"The Jewish Torah also refers to this time. The prophet Daniel wrote of the holy place being trampled underfoot until 'When the power of the holy people has been finally broken, all these things will be completed.' The prophet Isaiah also wrote, 'but now our enemies have trampled down your sanctuary.' And the rabbi Saul of Tarsus, who saw Jesus, wrote to the persecuted Christians in Rome, 'I do not want you to be ignorant of this mystery, brothers . . . Israel has experienced a hardening in part until the full number of the Gentiles has come in.'

"Forgive me for the scripture lesson . . . the mind of a rabbi, eh? But the important point is this—if you believe scripture is an accurate and true recording of the words of God to his people, there is ample reference to these last days, to the trampling of Jerusalem, and to a time of the Gentiles that comes to an end."

"But the Gaon would have known that," Mullaney objected, his patience stretched to its breaking point. "He would have had access to both the Jewish and Christian scriptures. Him writing something about the time of the Gentiles is not unique. It's not a revelation."

"Yes, you are right," said Herzog, "but why is it here? What is the Gaon trying to tell us?"

With a leaden shrug of his shoulders, Mullaney surrendered to his exhaustion. "I don't know, Rabbi, and, to tell you the truth, right now I don't care so much. My body just wants to get some sleep, and my mind needs to stop thinking. No disrespect intended, but can you get to the point . . . soon?"

Rabbi Herzog thrust his head forward once, as if it was on the snap end of a whip, a physical exclamation point. Then he placed his hat, turned upside down, on the floor and, between words, began chewing on the stem of his pipe.

"In the year AD 70, Titus, son of the Roman emperor Vespasian, brought an army to Judea to subdue the rebellious Jewish people. The Roman army slaughtered Jews throughout the country, killed over one million Jews in Jerusalem alone. They completely demolished not only the temple, but the entire city of Jerusalem. The historian Josephus tells us Jerusalem was 'razed so completely as to look like a spot which had never been inhabited.' Then Vespasian ordered Titus to sell the entire land of Judea and sell it only to Gentiles. Thus, the time of the Gentiles began.

"Some," said Herzog, "think the time of the Gentiles came to an end in 1968 when Israel once again took full control of all of Jerusalem in the war against our Arab neighbors. Some see this reference to a time of the Gentiles as a spiritual reference, as the time when many of the Jewish faith will be converted to faith in Jesus as the Messiah. Personally, I'm more focused on what will happen, rather than why it will happen. From a spiritual perspective, there is a time coming that will end the present human age. It is believing, I am, that this time is upon us.

"So," said Herzog, "what does this new prophecy of the Gaon's mean? The sons of Amalek have now been invited into the tent by the recently signed Ishmael Covenant. It appears as if the times of the Gentiles has been fulfilled. And now this covenant proposes to divide the land of Israel to create a Palestinian state, which scripture tells us will bring judgment on all those involved. What is left that the Gaon wrote of over two hundred years ago? The warning about the *Anadolian*. That he walks on water to offer peace, but carries judgment in his hands. His name is Man of Violence."

Mullaney could tell Herzog was waiting for some evidence of understanding, but his mind seemed to be full of conflicting thoughts, a thicket of confusion.

"Anadolia, or Anatolia, is an ancient name for an area of land north of Israel, what was once called Asia Minor. It's the Asian landmass of Turkey, Agent Mullaney. Ankara is right in the middle of Anadolia. These words of the Gaon prophesy that a Turk, a man of violence, will come to Israel and offer peace for water. But what he truly carries is judgment. A Turk, Agent Mullaney, whose name is Man of Violence. Logically, no sense it makes, but in my spirit's depth, I believe your enemy, the murderer of your friend, is this Man of Violence. And still you don't believe you have been enlisted into this battle against evil? Still you refuse to take up the mantle of guardian?"

45

US Embassy, Tel Aviv
July 22, 8:19 p.m.

Herzog's head was down, either deep in thought or prayer. Mullaney waited. This was Herzog's story. Slowly, like the rising of the moon, the rabbi turned his attention back to Mullaney.

"Part of this new, proposed Ishmael Covenant grants to Israel the freedom to build a temple of worship adjacent to the current platform called the Temple Mount," said Herzog. "It would, in effect, be the third temple of God, following Solomon's Temple and Herod's Temple.

"But the temple proposed in this new covenant would be one of man's making, not one of God's direction. There's a problem with man deciding on his own what God wants—whether it's to build a place for God to live on Mount Zion or for each of us to decide what should or should not be part of our lives.

"Many years after Vespasian sold off all of Judea, the Roman emperor Julian, who was determined to stop the spread of this new sect—Jews who believed in Jesus—decided not only to restore Jews to Judea, but also to rebuild Jerusalem and the temple.

"Nine historians of that age attest to the same story. As Julian's workers set about building the temple, great explosions erupted and massive balls of fire burst forth from the foundation, burning the workers and making it impossible to access the site."

Herzog inched forward in his seat, drawing closer to Mullaney. There was an urgency in both his face and in his words.

"God has a plan for man, Agent Mullaney. And when man tries to interfere with or impede God's plans, the results are often disastrous for those involved. God also has a plan for you, Agent Mullaney. Why are you here now, in this place? Why have you been enlisted into the defense of this box and the message—or messages—it carries?"

Ankara
July 22, 8:19 p.m.

In the red room, the golden designs on the walls were pulsing with life, glowing in a macabre and random frenzy, casting cavernous shadows across the face of Arslan Eroglu's body, now occupied and manipulated by the Turk. The conjoined being's eyes closed, the body twitched and jerked as if speeding along a winding road. A smile of evil intent bared its teeth.

And a sulfurous vapor hung heavily over the stone chair and the table opposite.

The Turk projected his will across the nine hundred kilometers between Ankara and Tel Aviv, across the island of Crete, over the Mediterranean Sea, and into the US embassy on Hayarkon Street. In his desiccated right hand he clutched the photo of Mullaney as his mind sought to hold focus on the face and attempted to pierce Mullaney's thoughts.

How can you trust a god who would allow so many to be slaughtered . . . who would allow your best friend to be killed while doing his duty?

Are you so foolish as to put your faith in these mythical winged creatures and the absurd fantasy that any man can influence the supernatural realm?

Who is taking care of you? Who is helping you deal with your problems, your grief?

US Embassy, Tel Aviv
July 22, 8:20 p.m.

A thought floated through Mullaney's mind. How could he be so irresponsible as to get involved in this madness that was none of his business? He knew why he was in Israel at that moment. And it had more to do with the plots of vindictive men in Washington than the legacy of a Lithuanian scholar. "I haven't enlisted in anything. I've got a job to do—to protect the lives of those in my care and to hunt down this gang of Turkish murderers before they can kill again. I don't need and I don't want responsibility for guarding this message and its box."

The aged rabbi closed his eyes and wearily shook his head. Herzog's lips moved, but no words emerged from his mouth. When he lifted his head, Herzog had the look of a messenger with dreadful news. "Listen, my friend," he said slowly. "You don't understand. I've been sent here to you with a purpose, a mission, and that is to transfer the responsibility of guardian to you. You are being summoned. This calling is beyond your job. It is your destiny, your purpose. You were intended to be here at this time, Agent Mullaney. From before the dawn of time, you were called to this purpose. Do I understand it? Not at all. Do I believe it? With all my heart and soul. Perhaps a prayer you have prayed at some point? A prayer for God to use you in whatever way he desires? Who knows where such a prayer will take you . . . or into what responsibilities. Or into what danger.

"All I know," said Herzog, "is that the angel Bayard breathed into me the breath of life—eternal life. He breathed into me truth. And then he told me to come to you and pass on this mantle of guardian. God is calling you into his service, Agent Mullaney. But only you can answer that call. Or only you can reject it."

46

Mullaney sat up straighter in his chair. "And that's another question that's been bugging me. About these angels. If they are so powerful why don't they just zap the guys who are after us and put an end to it? If this Bayard can show up and tell you that the Gaon's deciphered prophecy was tucked inside the jacket of Chaim Yavod's body, why don't they show up when we need them?" The anger and frustration he'd stuffed into a dark corner for the last few hours began to fight their way to the surface of his emotions.

Herzog's head was nodding. "Yes . . . I suppose that would be convenient," he said. "Tell me, Agent Mullaney, were you ever physically injured as a youngster . . . fall and break a bone?"

"Sure. I was playing football. Ran into a fence. Broke my arm pretty bad."

"Why didn't the angels stop you from running into the fence? Why don't the angels stop an airplane from hitting a mountain? Why—"

"Why doesn't this angel of yours," snapped Mullaney, "step in and stop the killing? Where was he when Tommy was—"

It was the aroma that first distracted Mullaney. He smelled Christmas: cinnamon, cloves, brown sugar. And then a similar, stronger fragrance, like— Yes!—in church. The censers that priests shook around the altar during midnight mass on Christmas Eve. Wafting clouds of burning incense, ancient spices that—

There was a movement behind Herzog. Mullaney knew he was fatigued, devastated in so many ways. His mind a muddle. And now his eyes were failing him. The air behind Herzog appeared to quiver, as if an invisible tremor had displaced the very atoms of the atmosphere. And out of that shuddering space appeared a form that—impossible—a form that grew in size and materialized into . . .

His head crooked to the side, Rabbi Herzog was looking at Mullaney as if he had sprouted a second head. "He's here, isn't he." Herzog turned and looked over his shoulder. "Bayard is here."

———≈∘∘∘≈———

Ankara
July 22, 8:25 p.m.

A convulsion wracked the body of Arslan Eroglu and brought fire to the yellow eyes of bedlam.

The Turk's tenuous connection with Mullaney shuddered with a disturbance that hurtled across the kilometers. An enemy presence interfered with the projection of his thoughts. The Turk's consciousness wrestled frantically for control as he concentrated more fervently on the photo in his right hand.

———≈∘∘∘≈———

US Embassy, Tel Aviv
July 22, 8:25 p.m.

As the dancing atoms of the air settled, the form of a man materialized. The top of his head was above the frame of the closed door—about seven feet—and the feathered arcs behind his shoulders scraped against the ceiling. His muscled arms hung at his sides, one hand on the hilt of a massive sword in a silver scabbard, hanging from what looked like a belt of spun gold. A breastplate of silver covered his chest, the central piece of this warrior's armor. Thick, brown curls fell upon his shoulders. The hint of a smile dusted the peacefully benevolent face that belied the muscles, armor, and weapon. But his eyes . . . his eyes revealed the anguish of his heart.

"I am Bayard," said the winged warrior, his voice a balm for open wounds. "And we come with deep regret," he turned toward Herzog, "and with the same mourning we brought to Rabbi Herzog on the death of his son."

The angel—*the angel!*—turned his gaze once more on Mullaney. "I am aggrieved we could not save the life of your friend. He was a man of God and good conscience. Today, he is receiving from the Son of Man the rewards of his salvation."

With only a slight movement, Bayard stood at the side of Mullaney's desk. "Fear not, Agent Mullaney." A gently powerful hand rested upon Mullaney's shoulder—a touch he had felt twice before. Like dawn through a cloud-littered sky, light rose in Mullaney's spirit. "Join with the host of heaven and rejoice for your friend." A smile brushed the corners of his lips. "He rejoices for you." And a tear joined Mullaney's smile.

"Why—"

"You called," said Bayard. "You needed help. And you were asking the questions of humanity that only deity can answer. That is why I am here. To help you."

A lengthy string of urgent questions flooded Mullaney's mind as Bayard moved to the side, facing both Mullaney and Herzog at the same time.

"I can't answer all of your questions," Bayard said before Mullaney could speak. "What I can tell you is some of what you already know. Angels are real. But the purpose of angels is not for them to insert themselves into earthly lives on a regular basis. Nor is it our purpose to answer every prayer for help. Our purpose is to worship God and fulfill his purposes. Let me explain."

An angel in his office? In the embassy? Mullaney had to suspend his ideas of reality to remain in the room, in the moment.

Ankara
July 22, 8:26 p.m.

A brilliant, dazzling pulse of light—the brightness of a thousand lasers—collided with the Turk's consciousness, momentarily blinding both his natural and his supernatural sight and shattering his concentration. Around him, the red room continued in its macabre swirling dance. But within Eroglu's body—within the Turk's spirit—a lance of light had skewered his intent. And the darkness fled from the embassy in Tel Aviv.

US Embassy, Tel Aviv
July 22, 8:28 p.m.

Bayard set the point of his scabbard on the floor and, resting upon its hilt, lowered himself to one knee so he would be at eye level with both Mullaney and Herzog. "You are both men of the holy book. You are confident that these Scriptures—both Jewish and Gentile—are the inspired words from the throne room of heaven, the words of God for man." He turned his head, first to Herzog and then back to Mullaney. "Thank you for your faith.

"The scriptures speak often of my brethren. The letter to Jewish believers, known today as Hebrews, begins by making a clear distinction between the

Son of Man and we who are his ambassadors. It is written, 'Are not all angels ministering spirits sent to serve those who will inherit salvation?' So one of our purposes is to render service on behalf of those who were, are, and will be rescued from sin and death by the atoning sacrifice of Yeshua. But that is not all.

"In one of his most beautiful songs, the great worshiper, King David, wrote:

> The Lord has established his throne in heaven,
>   and his kingdom rules over all.
>
> Praise the Lord, you his angels,
>   you mighty ones who do his bidding,
>   who obey his word.
> Praise the Lord, all his heavenly hosts,
>   you his servants who do his will.
> Praise the Lord, all his works
>   everywhere in his dominion.

"We of the heavenly host are servants of the Lord God . . . I AM is his name," said Bayard. "As David sang, we do the bidding of him whose kingdom rules over all. Yes, we are mighty ones. But most importantly, we obey his word. Do you understand?"

Mullaney knew he was lost, but even the rabbi shook his head.

Bayard lifted his right hand and laid it upon his breastplate. "Angels know our assignments only when we hear a word that is spoken from the throne room of the Almighty Creator of heaven and earth. When the Lord of Lords declares a matter, we hear it, and we know that is our assignment. We can follow no other commands except those which flow from God. Man often asks why. But neither angels nor man can know why or understand fully God's thoughts. Our purpose is to obey his words.

"But there is a second understanding here. What King David was singing in his own language is that God's mighty ones also obey the voice of his word. The voice of God's word means that, sometimes, God speaks to men in that still, small voice they hear in their spirit.

"We of the brethren," Bayard continued, "cannot hear those words that come from the Holy Spirit of God directly to men's hearts. Those words actually need to be declared, spoken, by men. Often, you call that prayer. Only then can we determine and discern whether the words, the prayers, are from man alone, or whether they emanate from the throne room of God. When your prayers speak what the great Father is speaking, assignments are released into the atmosphere of the angelic realm."

Bayard shifted slightly to his left, bringing his full attention to bear upon Mullaney. A tingle of apprehension fluttered in Mullaney's breast but was instantly brought under the calming influence of supernatural peace. Unbidden, these words arose in his mind. *"And the peace of God which transcends all understanding will guard your hearts and your minds in Christ Jesus."*

Ankara
July 22, 8:31 p.m.

He could feel the slippage in the fragile grip of his mind on Mullaney's thoughts. Like his enemies, the Turk was not omniscient, omnipresent, nor omnipotent. He had power. More power than he had ever possessed. Yet even his power had limitations. He reached across space for Mullaney's mind and desperately hurled thoughts that might recapture his attention.

You allowed your best friend to be killed. You abandoned your wife and your children. So many have died. All those around you are in danger. You have failed . . . again.

An image pulsed across the distance in the span of a heartbeat. The Turk seized the image and reveled in it.

You will never be like your father!

47

With an enormous, armed angel kneeling only two feet from his side, apparently calling him into some cosmic, supernatural conflict between good and evil, Mullaney still felt a peace that was beyond his understanding and wiped away all his fears.

"Son of God," Bayard spoke the words into Mullaney's heart, "when you stood at the deathbed of your father, you breathed into his ears—over and over in those last hours—about the love of God, the gift of Jesus's atonement, and the simple offering of repentance that purchases entrance into eternal life with our Father. At that time, you spoke these words: 'Lord, if you will bring my father into eternal life with you, I will do whatever you ask of me.'

"That prayer, Brian, was neither a request nor a promise." Bayard rested his bulging forearm, covered with silver armor up to his elbow, on the edge of Mullaney's desk. "It was a prayer for salvation and deliverance for one whom you loved dearly. But it was also a prayer of surrender and submission, a prayer that echoed the words of the Father from the throne room and dispatched an angel to your father's side . . . an angel who, at that moment, served him who was inheriting salvation. Yes, good son, you will see your father again."

The fullness that was blossoming in Mullaney's chest moved into his throat and spilled over onto his tongue, which licked his quivering lips as his lungs tried to catch a breath. Mullaney tried to hold his chin firm, but it refused, shaking as the tears began rolling down his cheeks. He bit down on his lower lip to hold back the sobs of celebration.

Bayard moved his right hand to cover the tightly clasped hands of Mullaney. "Since that day, Brian, in response to your prayer, the almighty God of heaven has guided your steps and led you into his ultimate plan for your life, to be the last of the Gaon's spiritual sons, the final guardian. You have free will, so at times your will interfered with God's purpose of the moment, but never with God's eternal purpose for you. Circumstances may change your mind, but they can never change your destiny. Your eternal purpose—part of it—is here today. The Gaon's anointing, passed down through generations, now rests on you, Brian. Your life has been shaped, your heart and spirit prepared, to be the guardian, the last in the line of the Gaon's appointed heirs. To be God's warrior here on the earth. To do what only you can do."

With the solemnity of a soldier, Bayard stood to his feet and squared his shoulders. "The realms of darkness are in opposition to the plans of God. The evil one conspires to thwart God's work and destroy God's stated plan. This battle raged in the heavenlies before this earth was born. It rages today, both in this earthly realm and in the realms of the sky.

"In order to guard and protect the prophecies of the Gaon, I have contended with the man with the yellow eyes and his ruler for over two centuries. They are not the first, nor the last, that our enemy has dispatched to destroy the work of God. Those assaults will continue until the Son of Man comes in glory. But today, it is you and I, Brian, who are called to stand against evil.

"We are entering the final battle against those sworn to destroy the words which the Gaon received in the throne room of God. Rabbi Herzog is neither equipped, nor empowered, to engage that enemy. Nor is it my assignment. Neither Rabbi Herzog's son, Ambassador Cleveland, or Cleveland's daughter were prepared or called to this moment. While each has fulfilled an assignment that brings us to this moment, only you can decide whether or not you will accept your assignment."

———◦◦◦◦———

Ankara
July 22, 8:37 p.m.

No . . . he could not fail again! He must stop this. He must . . .

The Turk rallied all of the demons at his disposal and intended to unleash them to their demonic purpose, to destroy the intentions of their enemy and his minions.

But a force opposed him . . . a force he had battled all too often. A force as relentless as his own, but a force that would not move. Light rose up in that force, a light that darkness could not overcome. A light before which his demons of darkness must flee or be consumed. A light that drove the Turk back into the black canyons of his evil intent.

What was he going to do? He had sworn an oath as a federal law enforcement officer to protect the lives of the ambassador and his daughter—along with several hundred State Department employees—and American citizens throughout the Middle East. A ruthless gang of murderers, still at large, were responsible for the death of three Diplomatic Security Service agents, including his best friend. There appeared to be a traitor in the State Department who was in collusion with a foreign government—a government he'd been warned was about to attack a NATO base in order to steal American nuclear weapons. His wife and daughters were back in Washington, waiting to know when, not if, he was coming home. And now this angel was asking him to take responsibility for protecting a two-hundred-year-old prophecy and the lethal box that protected it.

This was crazy. How could he . . .

Brian Mullaney's mobile phone rattled to life in his jacket pocket. Grateful for the interruption, hoping to get his thoughts in order, Mullaney pulled out the phone. It was Doak.

He tapped the green icon. "Hi. What have you found?"

The pause told Mullaney almost everything he needed to know. This was not good news.

"I'm sorry, Brian," said his brother. "Morningstar's car went off a bridge on Yates Ford Road, out by the Bull Run Marina. He didn't survive. Two sets of skid marks."

"The black Ford?"

"Probably," said Doak. "Looks like Morningstar's vehicle was hit from behind. He was pushed off the bridge."

"Witnesses?"

"Too early. Not even dawn yet. Very little traffic at that time. Fortunate that a couple of fishermen spotted the vehicle . . . Sorry, Brian . . . it was underwater. What's going on?"

What's going on? Mullaney was asking himself the same question.

So many different pieces. Were they all random? Were some connected? All of them?

There had to be some kind of connection. He was sure of it. He just didn't know what that connection was.

But of one thing he was sure. *It's getting pretty dangerous to be my friend.*

First Tommy. Now Morningstar.

Brian Mullaney was feeling alone.

And angry. And determined.

Mullaney took a deep breath. "Tommy Hernandez was killed today."

"Awwwwwww . . ." The guttural growl that came out of Doak Mullaney sounded like a tribal call to battle. Brian could hear the fist pound on the desk through the phone connection.

"Look, Doak, stay all over Morningstar's death, will you? I don't know why, or how, but my gut tells me Morningstar's death is somehow connected to what's happening over here. There's a lot of evil on the move."

48

US Embassy, Tel Aviv
July 22, 8:45 p.m.

The door was locked. Most of the staff were long gone from the embassy, but even at this late hour, Mullaney didn't want to risk being interrupted. How could he have explained what was occurring at that moment in his office?

Mullaney stood in the middle of the room, Bayard at his right, Rabbi Herzog facing him straight on. His decision, at the end, had been a simple one. What was the right thing to do? What was the right thing for a man of faith, a man of character and integrity . . . what was the right thing to do in the face of evil? In response to a call for help?

Brian Mullaney knew it was the same choice his father would have made . . . *the same choice I'm sure he did make so many times during his life.* Danger was there. Standing up for what was right could cost him his life. It was not a price he wanted to pay. But if that was the price of character, dignity, and duty, it was a calculation he had made long ago and lived by for decades. The same calculation made by those in the other armed services who put their lives in harm's way every day they wore the uniform. Mullaney no longer wore the uniform of the Virginia State Police, as his father once did, as his brother still did. But he wore a badge of service, a badge of honor, a badge of sworn duty.

He would always oppose evil and the agents of evil. There was really no other choice. He had chosen for his life a course of character and service. He wasn't about to change that course now.

Rabbi Herzog lifted both hands and laid his right hand on top of Mullaney's head. His left hand, holding the stained envelope containing the Gaon's deciphered prophecy, rested along the side of Mullaney's face. He closed his eyes.

"The Lord bless you and keep you," recited Herzog. "The Lord make his face . . ."

Ankara
July 22, 8:46 p.m.

There was a subtle change in the cosmic force emanating from the embassy building in Tel Aviv. The Turk could not see into the room. He could not see into the hearts of those who were in the room. But he could sense, in his spirit, what was taking place. The mantle of guardian was being passed. In an escalating eruption of frenzied fury, he crushed the photo in the fist of his right hand. Now Mullaney was an even greater threat. But—

"Not yet!" spat the Turk, as Eroglu's body became as taut as a bowstring. "You fool!" His voice, a rising crescendo of shrieks, filled the room. "Do you think you have won? No! Not victory! You have only postponed your ultimate defeat. This earth is ours. And now I will declare my dominion over it."

Accustomed to working in the dark, the Turk's conscious mind navigated under the earth, looking for points of stress. He had found two in each location. He needed one more to create a triangular field from which he could control the movement of the ground.

Yes . . . there. That was the third at the embassy. Now he concentrated his search below the residence.

———

US Embassy, Tel Aviv
July 22, 8:46 p.m.

"The Lord turn his face toward you and give you peace."

As his senses registered some subtle alterations in his consciousness, Mullaney realized his eyes were closed. He opened them to find Rabbi Herzog holding the envelope in front of him. "Believe, I do, that this is now yours."

Mullaney looked at the stained envelope, thought about the death masks of Chaim Yavod and Haisha Golden, the cleaning lady in the ambassador's residence, who both had a fatal encounter with this message and the box that guarded it, and hesitated as his mind tried to override his emotions.

"The power is in the box." The voice of Bayard came from his right. Mullaney turned his head in that direction and looked up. The angel's benign gaze was fixed upon him. Mullaney felt . . . what . . . a stronger, deeper connection to this angelic being? "You may take the message. You may hold the parchment with the Gaon's original prophecy written on it. You may even touch the box, hold it in your hands, without being in danger of triggering its defenses. You are now the guardian. But I believe you sense something else, don't you?"

He tried to put words to what he was sensing. He suddenly felt as if he were operating on two different planes—two similar but not identical realities. And it was difficult to connect one to the other.

"You have entered deeper into the spiritual realm, Agent Mullaney," said Bayard.

"I can see more clearly." Mullaney was stunned. He didn't fully comprehend what he was experiencing, but it was as if a switch had been flipped and his world increased in light. "I mean I understand more. It's like a fog has lifted. And you. I feel more connected to you. The way I felt connected to the other troopers in Virginia. The way I feel connected to the other agents of DSS. Like now we're more comrades in arms, you know?"

Bayard was nodding his large head. "It's part of your destiny, your calling as the final guardian. You are being equipped, being given the tools you will need to complete your assignment. And one of those tools is a clarity of thought, a clarity of understanding. You will need that clarity of understanding. Please, open the paper in the envelope."

Mullaney realized that Rabbi Herzog was still standing there with the envelope in his hand—and a sheepish look on his face. "Yes," he said as he extended his arm, "I do believe this now to you belongs."

———————

Ankara
July 22, 8:53 p.m.

The Turk's concentration wavered as heat suddenly built up in his bony, gnarled right hand. His yellow eyes flew open, a seething sea of wrath, as the photo of Mullaney burst into flames between his clenched fingers. "Aaaaaaagggggghhhhhh!"

Bolts of pain scorched the Turk's right arm as he threw the flaming photo to the floor.

"NO . . . you cannot have it!" he screamed at the pulsing red walls. He forced his concentration back into Mullaney's office. All he could discern was that the mantle . . . the message . . . had been passed into his enemy's hands.

Eroglu's body jumped to its feet, its arms outstretched, its fingers extended and straining toward the south, every fiber in the body futilely scrabbling to seize control of the message that changed hands nine hundred kilometers away. "You cannot!" His wail rose in anguish and frustration and its passion shook the very gates of hell. "You"—his fingers grated the air, trying to pierce the distance—"you will never defeat—"

A surge of blinding light struck Eroglu's body in the chest, its power driving the body back into the stone chair, rending the Turk's desperate attempts at intervention, smothering his cries.

49

Mullaney's fingertips held the mottled piece of paper at its corners. He knew that some of the stains on the paper were blood. He didn't know what caused some of the other stains. Of those, he steered clear.

But the translation was clear enough. He looked at the words again and read them out loud:

> When the times of the Gentiles is complete, when the sons of Amalek are invited to the king's banquet, beware of the Anadolian—he walks on water to offer peace, but carries judgment in his hands. His name is Man of Violence.

"Look below the message," said Bayard.

Two lines of symbols were drawn along the bottom of the paper. They didn't look like anything Mullaney had ever seen before. He looked up at Bayard. "What are they? What do they mean?"

A smile that warmed Mullaney's spirit spread over the angelic face. "I'm afraid it's not that easy," said Bayard. "I don't know what they mean. Angels are not omniscient. Only God knows everything. But I can tell you two things. Deciphering these symbols is a critical part of your mission. And—"

"Wait," interrupted Mullaney. "What is my mission?"

The smile spread across Bayard's face once more. "I'm afraid it's not that easy."

Mullaney shook his head. "Of course not. So what's the second thing?"

Bayard pointed to the symbols on the paper. "In order to decipher those symbols, first you need to understand the box."

"There's kabbalah on the box," said Rabbi Herzog. "Is that what we need to understand?"

Bayard shook his head. "It will take more than kabbalah to understand the box. But all I can tell you is that your assignment will be determined by the meaning of the symbols on that paper. And understanding the box is the key to unraveling those symbols. The box is the key. That's why your enemy has been—"

Ankara
July 22, 9:02 p.m.

Eroglu's body pummeled back into the stone chair, his head fell against the serpent figure carved into its top. Inside Eroglu's husk, his eyes closed, the Turk fought to control his rapid breathing and recapture his concentration. With each slowing breath he repeated his vow. "You will not defeat me."

A malevolent grimace twisting his face, the Turk whispered the beginnings of an incantation that was as old as the earth itself. An incantation of dominion and an incantation of destruction.

His mind focused on the ground upon which the US embassy was built and upon the ground along the edge of the Mediterranean where the US ambassador's residence was located. His mind probed the ground, burrowed its way deep under the crust of the earth, and found the junction of tectonic plates, fault lines of structural instability.

By force of will, the Turk began to move those plates. His eyes closed, the Turk pushed his mind against the tectonic fissures under the earth of Tel Aviv. Then he turned his inward vision upward, through the stone and the soil and the sandy loam, up into the foundations of the US embassy and the US ambassador's residence. He forced his mind against the plates and then thrust them upward, an eruption of earthly force hurtling into the concrete upon which the buildings rested.

The earth moved.

ACKNOWLEDGMENTS

On each of my novels I've had the privilege to autograph, I've added the inscription "Ps. 116:12." It references this verse from the Psalms: "What shall I return to the LORD for all his goodness to me?"

There is no way to adequately thank God for all the blessings he has poured into my life—our family, our home, our health. And the stories.

None of the stories I've written have come from me. Honestly, I am only an instrument, a pen in God's hands. If you could see what these stories were at the beginning (usually only one idea) and how they emerged and developed over time, you would understand that all my novels have been birthed, sustained, and completed only because God's hand was on the writing and the writer.

I can't adequately express all that Andrea—my wife of forty years—has meant to my writing career. Her patience, encouragement, and good sense have sustained me through days and nights when the work became a burden and the way forward a mystery. Her sweet smile always lifted my spirit. And I loved the days we celebrated. Thank you, my sweetheart, for never giving up.

Thank you to our daughter, Meghan, for her wisdom, discernment, and clear thinking, and the brainstorming sessions that so often saved my sanity. To my sister, Pat, for being a faithful first reader. And to Pastor Nick Uva of Harvest Time Church in Greenwich, Connecticut, who first introduced me to the Vilna Gaon and helped me explore end-times prophecies. This book, and series, would be much shallower if it weren't for Pastor Nick's knowledge, wisdom, and support.

Some of the ideas about angels and their assignments came from listening to online sermons of Pastor Bill Johnson of Bethel Church in Redding, California.

Every author thanks his editor (if he's smart!). But I must offer special thanks to Janyre Tromp of Kregel Publications. The thoughtful exercise of her experience and her words of encouragement rescued this book, and this series, more times than I would like to admit. Thank you, Janyre . . . I wouldn't have made it this far without you.

To the rest of the team at Kregel Publications in Grand Rapids, including managing editor Steve Barclift, editors Becky Fish and Joel Armstrong, and marketing manager Katherine Chappell, thank you for making me look good.

And I'm deeply grateful to my agent, Steve Laube, who has helped me mature as a writer and always shared a deft word of wisdom when it was desperately needed.

And, once again, a special acknowledgment to Tina Heugh. Tina won a drawing—to use your name as a character in my next book—when I spoke at the Friends of the Bonita Springs Library luncheon in Florida. Tina asked me to use her mother's name, Ruth Hughes. The character of Ruth Hughes in the series is a strong woman of integrity, with a stellar business résumé. I was blessed when Tina later sent me this information about her mother that I did not know while I was writing: "My mom was a librarian for fifty-seven years, the last twenty as the first paid librarian at the Bonita Springs Public Library, where she ordered over eighty thousand books. Before that, she was head librarian for the University of Michigan Detroit branch. During World War II, she worked for Chrysler Engineering and is on the World War II commemorative wall in Washington, DC. She was civically active in Detroit as well as working. She became the president of the League of Women Voters after serving as membership chairperson. She also served on the boards of numerous committees. She was honored as one of Detroit's Top Ten Working Women. She is in Who's Who of Women of the Midwest and Who's Who of American Women. She was nominated to be president of the American Civil Liberties Union of the five counties of the Detroit area but had to decline because my parents were retiring to Florida."

Thank you, Tina!

AUTHOR'S NOTES

You've made it to the end of the second book in the Empires of Armageddon series, *Persian Betrayal*. But before we get into one of my favorite parts of the books—the author's notes that catalog a lot of the real people, real places, and real events I've injected into this fictional story—I want to offer you a reward for getting this far.

Here are two free opportunities available only to readers of the Empires of Armageddon series:

- How would you like to know more about the Vilna Gaon? I've written an exclusive fictional short story called "The Gaon's Revenge," loosely based upon the Gaon's known history, available only to readers of this series.
- In addition, I'll send you a monthly email post that will expand upon, with greater detail, one of the topics in these author's notes.

If you're hungry to know more about the Vilna Gaon, or more about the elements of reality woven into the plot of *Persian Betrayal*, just send me an email at terrbrennan@gmail.com, and I'll respond right away with these two special free offers.

Thanks,
Terry

———◦◦◦———

While *Persian Betrayal* is a work of fiction, several plot elements are based on fact.

Many historians cast doubt on the biblical story of the exodus—led by Moses, the escape of two million Jews from Egypt and their forty-year journey through the desert. While there is no definitive archaeological evidence of this massive migration of people, there are indications that the exodus story is more than myth. Many of the Levites in the exodus story had Egyptian names: Moses, Phinehas, Hophni, and Hur are all Egyptian names. The dimensions of the tent of meeting (tabernacle) and its surrounding courtyards specified in the

Bible are the exact same dimensions as that of the battle tent of Pharaoh Rameses II, for which we have archaeological evidence. The Merneptah Stele, dated circa 1219 BCE, is the earliest extrabiblical record of a people group called Israel. Set up by Pharaoh Merneptah to commemorate his military victories, the stone specifically mentions a people named Israel. In 2017 archaeologists discovered ruins in the Jordan Valley site of Khirbet el-Mastarah, adjacent to the Jordan River, which they believe are remnants of ruins from a nomadic people who they believe to be the Hebrews coming from Egypt.

One of the critical components of the exodus story is the Battle of Rephidim. After crossing the Red Sea's Strait of Tiran and marching south along a trade route, the Hebrew escapees passed through the Alush Gorge, where they turned north. Their advance was resisted by an army of the Amalekites. The elements of the Battle of Rephidim in the prologue are biblically accurate.

———◦◦◦◦———

The history of the Hurva Synagogue in Jerusalem is accurate as related in this series. Construction of the main Ashkenazi synagogue, now known as the Hurva, commenced in 1701. The Jewish builders fell into debt to Muslim moneylenders and, in the midst of a dispute over repayment, Muslims burned down the building in 1721. After two smaller synagogues were erected on the edges of the original ruins, disciples of the Vilna Gaon were granted permission for construction of the second Hurva, which began in 1855. That building was destroyed in retaliation in 1948, blown up by the defeated Jordanian Arab Legion after withdrawal of Israeli forces from Jerusalem following the 1948 war for independence. Israel regained control of Jerusalem from Jordan following the 1967 war, but decades of internal disputes and indecision delayed reconstruction of the Hurva. The third construction of the building was begun in 2000, and the nineteenth-century-style building was dedicated on March 15, 2010. The Vilna Gaon prophesied that when the Hurva synagogue was completed for the third time, construction of the third temple would begin. Construction of the third temple of God *has not* yet begun, but many believe completion of the third temple will be an imminent harbinger of the last days.

———◦◦◦◦———

The story of the Vilna Gaon—Rabbi Elijah ben Shlomo Zalman (1720–1797)—is accurate in all its historical elements. He was the foremost Talmudic scholar of his age and a renowned genius on both sacred and secular learning. The story of the Gaon's prophecy about Russia and Crimea, revealed by his great-great-grandson in 2014, is true and led many to believe that the coming of the Jewish Messiah was near at hand. The Gaon did attempt three trips to Jerusalem from his native Lithuania; the last one, only a few years before his death, ended prematurely in Konigsberg, Prussia. The story of the Gaon's *second* prophecy is a result of the author's imagination.

<hr />

The deeply held enmity and distrust between the Persian Shiite hierarchy of Iraq and the Sunni Arab Saudi royal family has raged for centuries. In 1979 when the Arab shah of Iran was overthrown, Ayatollah Khomeini actually declared that Sunni believers were not truly Muslims and demanded the overthrow of the Al-Saud family. That conflict continues today with Iran funding and supplying the rebel forces attempting to usurp Yemen, on Saudi Arabia's southern border, while Iran moves inexorably forward in its alliance with its fellow Shia believers in Iraq.

The potential for a nuclear confrontation along the Persian Gulf remains high. Iran continues its development of nuclear power—many believe for the purpose of creating nuclear weapons. And high-ranking US intelligence officials believe Saudi Arabia did in fact finance much of Pakistan's nuclear weapons program, pouring millions of dollars into its development. The intelligence community also believes there exists an agreement for Pakistan to provide nuclear weapons to Saudi Arabia when called for.

<hr />

For more than forty years, since 1979, the United States and other countries have frozen Iranian assets in their banks, in retaliation for when fifty-two Americans were taken hostage and held in Tehran for 444 days. Twenty to thirty billion dollars have been frozen in banks worldwide, including approximately two billion dollars in US banks. By 2014, two billion dollars would earn about one hundred million dollars per year in interest.

The question of accrued interest on those frozen funds, and how much interest is owed to Iran, continues to be a bone of contention. When four hundred million dollars was returned to Iran by the Obama Administration in January 2016—money the Iranians paid prior to 1979 for US military aircraft that were never delivered—the United States also sent Iran a payment of *1.3 billion dollars in accrued interest.* The money to pay that accrued interest came from the US Department of the Treasury's Judgment Fund, which pays judgments, or compromise settlements of lawsuits, against the government. In 2016, two US senators wrote in *Time* magazine:

> The Judgment Fund is a little-known account used to pay certain court judgments and settlements against the federal government. Each year, billions of dollars are disbursed from it, yet the fund does not fall under the annual appropriations process. Because of this, the Treasury Department has no binding reporting requirements, and these funds are paid out with scant scrutiny. The executive branch decides what, if any, information is made available to the public.
>
> Essentially, the Judgment Fund is an unlimited supply of money provided to the federal government to cover its own liability.

The descriptions of the last-days theology of the world's three great religions—Judaism, Christianity, and Islam—are accurate. All three religions trace their roots back to Abraham and claim to be part (though different parts) of the Abrahamic covenant that God established with mankind. And each religion waits for a climactic time in history, birthed in peace, when the long-awaited One (either the Messiah, Jesus's second coming, or the Mahdi) will be revealed. While the Jewish Messiah will usher in an eternal time of peace for a world united into one confederation, both Christian and Islamic end times anticipate an ultimate and definitive armed conflict, followed by a "final judgment" of the good and the evil.

The Diplomatic Security Service is the federal law enforcement and security division of the US State Department. DSS agents are unique in that they are members of the US Foreign Service, charged with protecting diplomats and embassy personnel who are overseas, but they are also armed law enforcement officers who have the authority to investigate crime and arrest individuals both on domestic soil and in collaboration with international law enforcement overseas. With nearly twenty-five hundred agents here and abroad, DSS is the most widely represented law enforcement agency in the world. DSS also provides security for foreign dignitaries in the United States, for the annual United Nations General Assembly in New York City, and during the Olympics. Descriptions of the State Department's Ops Center in the Truman Building are accurate to the best of the author's resources.

———

In the summer of 2014, the Islamic terrorist army called ISIS controlled more than thirty-four thousand square miles in Syria and Iraq, from the Mediterranean coast to south of Baghdad. The major Iraqi cities of Mosul, Fallujah, and Tikrit were overrun, including key oil refineries and military bases. The Iraqi army was in retreat and disarray. The world expected another offensive thrust from ISIS that could imperil the capital of Baghdad itself. And in late July of 2014, ISIS executioners began beheading captives and broadcasting the ghastly videos. It appeared the entire Middle East was at risk of being ravaged by ISIS.

———

Descriptions of the US embassy and the US ambassador's residence in Tel Aviv are accurate to 2014, before the US embassy was officially moved to Jerusalem in 2018. The US ambassador to Israel did host an enormous annual Fourth of July party, where over two thousand guests sprawled over the grounds of the residence and feasted on iconic American delights from McDonald's, Ben & Jerry's, and Domino's.

———

Over the course of nearly twenty-five-hundred years, the fertile crescent of the Middle East—from modern Turkey into the Tigris and Euphrates valleys in Iraq, down the Jordan Valley of Palestine, and across the top of Egypt and the Nile Delta—was but a portion of three vast, evolving, and at times competing empires: the Persian, the Muslim Arab, and the Ottoman empires. One of the fundamental beliefs of Islam is, in fact, that once an Islamic group or nation rules any portion of the earth, it rules that portion forever. Even though the Persians gradually converted to the Islamic faith only in the mid-seventh century, following the Muslim Arab invasion of Persia, if those empires were resurrected today, each would claim the same slice of the earth.

Opened in 1955, the Incirlik Air Base, located seven miles east of Adana, Turkey, includes NATO's largest nuclear weapons storage facility.

With one ten-thousand-foot runway and fifty-seven hardened aircraft shelters, Incirlik is the most strategically important base in NATO's Southern Region. At one time, the base had over five thousand NATO personnel stationed on its three thousand acres, in addition to two thousand family members. Adana, with a population of over one million, is the fourth largest city in Turkey.

NATO has operated a nuclear sharing program since the mid-1950s. Since 2009, NATO has stationed US nuclear weapons in Germany, the Netherlands, Italy, Belgium, and Turkey. While the United States and NATO maintain a "neither confirm nor deny" posture toward the numbers of its nuclear distribution, the Hoover Institute reported that the United States currently deploys somewhere between 150 and 240 air-delivered nuclear weapons (B61 gravity bombs). It is estimated that twenty-five percent of those weapons are stationed at the Incirlik Air Base in eastern Turkey, with most sources placing fifty B61 nuclear bombs at Incirlik. The B61 is a variable-yield nuclear weapon with an explosive yield of 0.3 to 340 kilotons. The "Little Boy" atomic bomb that destroyed Hiroshima in 1945 had a yield of 15 kilotons.

Other Notes: The mission and makeup of the US military's Joint Special Operations Command (JSOC) is factually portrayed. It is a quick-strike, highly trained force, its elements the best of Delta Force, SEAL Team Six, Army Rangers, and the Air Force's Special Tactics Squadron.

The possibility of "water wars" in the Middle East remains strong. Since 1975, Turkey's dams have cut water flow to Iraq by eighty percent and to Syria by forty percent. Work on a pipeline between Turkey and Israel was suspended

in 2010 after an Israeli raid on six civilian ships trying to run the Gaza blockade resulted in the deaths of nine Turkish nationals.

The Kurdish people, native to the mountainous regions of eastern Turkey,
northern Syria, and northwest Iraq, are the largest people group in the world
without their own nation.

———

Other than the basic facts and associated research listed above, the rest of *Persian Betrayal* is the result of the author's imagination. Any "errors of fact" are a
result of that imagination.

OTTOMAN DOMINION

Empires of Armageddon #3

TERRY BRENNAN

PROLOGUE

Thin and straight like a Popsicle stick in a good suit, Noah Webster stood behind the sofa, a sentry on duty. His eyes never fell to Senator Markham, seated in front of him and in earnest conversation with the chair of the Senate Foreign Relations Committee. No, Webster's eyes relentlessly swept the spacious but crowded room, looking for allies or victims. That was the breadth of his world . . . allies or victims. Not enemies. Senator Markham's enemies were inevitably victims . . . victims of Markham's power and influence. And Webster's ruthless wielding of that power.

Across the room, standing behind one of the columns that flanked the entryway, Joseph Atticus Cleveland took the measure of Webster and recognized a merciless man unwavering in his quest for even greater power. Cleveland broke his gaze away, pivoted through the arched entry, and headed in the direction he hoped would take him to the kitchen and that incredible aroma of mango and sizzling garlic that was causing convulsions in his stomach.

"Cleveland, isn't it?"

Turning toward the voice, Cleveland saw Noah Webster emerge from an overfilled dining room as the crowd parted like the Red Sea. His hand was held out, a handshake offering, expecting a response.

"Noah Webster . . . Senator Markham's chief of staff."

Trapped . . . make the best of it.

"Joseph Cleveland. It's a pleasure, sir. And I believe most of Washington knows who you are, Mr. Webster. It's kind of you to introduce yourself. But my stomach is demanding I follow this magnificent aroma."

Webster moved closer, his strong hand still wrapped around Cleveland's fingers. The slippery sweetness of gardenia banished the mango and garlic back to the kitchen and nearly overwhelmed Cleveland's outer veneer of composure. Inwardly, every warning siren was wailing.

Great-grandson of a former slave, Cleveland was four years into his career with the State Department and well into the lengthy and demanding process of applying for assignment to the US Foreign Service, with aspirations to one day earn a senior consular post overseas. Perhaps Ambassador Cleveland?

"Thank you, Mr. Cleveland. The aroma is captivating, but my duty is to remain by the senator's side should he need me," said Webster, who glanced left, then right, before skewering Cleveland with a look of menacing power. "Joseph, are you aware that Senator Markham is about to open his investigation of Major Lee's unlawful activities in the Defense Intelligence Agency?"

Noah Webster was thirty-one years old, the zen master of Washington politics, notorious within the Beltway. A striking black man—half Caribbean, half African American and self-consciously short—Webster was a formidable and forbidding force in the halls of DC political power.

Cleveland's knees felt like the warm mud along the French Broad River that flowed through his homeland in the finger of western North Carolina—they were soft and sinking fast. The sting of acid reflux overwhelmed his hunger. *Steady . . . remain steady. No fear. Please, show no fear.*

"No, sir," said Cleveland, his voice calm and his grip firm. "I wasn't aware of that."

"Yes . . . could be a nasty business." Webster's eyes narrowed, focused like laser-guided weapons. "You worked as liaison between State and the DIA, did you not? In Lee's office?"

"For a short time." Cleveland's voice was steady, but his heart was racing.

For nine months in 1985, Cleveland was on loan to the Defense Intelligence Agency, the organization that provides boots-on-the-ground espionage across the wide spectrum of US military operations. Routinely, twenty-five percent of the president's morning intelligence briefing came from DIA sources. Cleveland was assigned to a project run by Air Force Major Anderson Lee. His task was boring . . . insulting, almost. He was nothing more than an over-qualified, highly paid messenger. Until November 26, when subpoenas were served. Lee and his boss, General Isaiah Zimmer, faced the possibility of indictments on illegally diverting Pentagon funding and obstruction of justice. Cleveland had been kept in the dark by Major Lee and was innocent of any wrongdoing. But scandal is a fickle mistress, often condemning the innocent and the guilty with the same brazen impunity.

Without releasing his grip, Webster moved closer and lowered his voice. "The senator knows you are innocent of any complicity in this crime, Joseph. But so often there is collateral damage and others on the committee may not see, as clearly as we do, the distinction between being simply a messenger boy and a conspirator. I'm trying to convince the senator that you don't even need to be called as a witness. We wouldn't want to jeopardize your pending appointment to the Foreign Service, now would we?"

So there it was. The bait and the trap. Clearly Webster knew exactly what Cleveland's responsibilities were and who he reported to at the DIA. True to his Washington legend, Webster was offering Cleveland a deal—a way out of possible trouble. But what did Webster want in return?

Cleveland tilted his head to the right, a question entering his eyes and his voice. "Is there some way I may be of assistance?"

Webster smiled, and Cleveland feared his knees would lose all control. If a smile could threaten annihilation, Webster's smile was nuclear.

"Oh yes. You will be of assistance to me, Joseph." Webster's smile grew wider. "Or you will join Major Lee in a federal prison."

Webster finally released Cleveland's hand. He half turned back into the dining room, but looked over his shoulder. "Enjoy your dinner, Joseph." And with a nod of his head, Webster vanished into the crowd.

Cleveland placed his right fist in front of his lips, wrapped his left arm over his stomach, and hurried off in search of a restroom. It was bad form to vomit in the midst of a reception for movers and shakers, for allies and enemies.

1

Brian Mullaney's world lurched sideways. The floors and walls of the fortress-like US embassy in Tel Aviv undulated like a drunken jellyfish. What looked, felt, and sounded like an earthquake had Mullaney's internal threat monitors off the charts. Again.

In the last seventy-two hours, Brian Mullaney's world had raced like an avalanche from the rational to the inexplicable. And through each of those hours, a rising tide of violence had haunted Mullaney's every move—a pervading and relentless carnage that had claimed six American lives, including that of his best friend.

Now to his right, an eight-foot-tall armed angel hovered above the convulsing floor, and to his left, a terrified, bearded rabbi sat flat on the seat of his pants. But after what Mullaney had experienced the last few days, nothing came as a shock.

The angel, Bayard, pulled an immense, gleaming silver sword from the scabbard at his waist. The sword was suffused with light and thrummed like a chorus of heavenly voices; a stiletto sharpness honed its edge.

His wings flexing behind his heavily muscled frame, Bayard was prepared to go to war.

"We must hurry," he said, looking toward where the door to Mullaney's office had once stood. "Our enemies are here. They are pursuing the box of power."

It felt as if every molecule in the building had a mind of its own and each was heading off in different directions. Mullaney's office was twisted like a wet rag being wrung out . . . the corners of the room appeared to be melting . . . and the wall opposite was ripped apart.

Regional security officer for the Diplomatic Security Service, responsible for the security of all United States diplomatic personnel in the Middle East, Mullaney's six-two frame was still lean and muscled at forty-four. A nineteen-year veteran of the DSS, he instinctively placed a hand over his earbud and turned slightly to the mic in his lapel to give orders to his DSS agents and the marines guarding the embassy. "Lock down the building . . . mobilize all security . . . double the guard at each entry point and do a floor-by-floor, face-to-face accounting of all staff. Stay alert!"

Mullaney stumbled around his desk and grabbed the elderly rabbi, Mordechai Herzog, by the arm. "C'mon . . . you're getting under the desk."

"I don't know if these old bones can squeeze in there," said Herzog, the former chief rabbi of Israel's Rabbinate Council, his eyes darting back and forth, watching the moving walls.

Mullaney pulled Herzog to his feet and emphatically moved him toward the desk.

From across the room, the armor-clad angel called through the groans of a building in torment. "Guardian . . . follow me when you can!" The air seemed to be shifting back and forth as much as the walls as Bayard's form evolved from solid to amorphous to vapor. And he was gone.

Guardian. That was a new title Mullaney needed to absorb. Passed down through generations of rabbis for over two hundred years, the guardian's responsibility was to protect and defend both the prophecy of the Vilna Gaon and the lethal box of power that contained it. Only minutes earlier, Rabbi Herzog had spoken the Aaronic blessing over Mullaney, transferring the mantle of guardian to the DSS agent.

Mullaney hadn't fully grasped why *he* was ordained as the final guardian—Bayard had called him the last in the line of the Gaon's appointed heirs. But after Bayard's warning, he fully suspected that this earthquake was being used by the gang of Turkish terrorists who had relentlessly pursued the box from Istanbul, where it was brought out of hiding only seven days ago. Only the guardian, under the power of the anointing, could touch the box of power without incurring a horrible and instantaneous death. But Mullaney had no doubt that those same murderous thugs were now invading the embassy in order to raid the vault where the Gaon's bronze box was currently secured.

Rabbi Mordechai Herzog was sprawled on the floor under Mullaney's desk, desperately clinging to its legs, as the building continued to convulse in chaotic jolts.

"Follow him?" Mullaney squeezed out of his chest. "How can I follow him?"

Another violent eruption throttled the embassy and a cascade of concrete crashed into the middle of the floor, missing Herzog and Mullaney by inches.

He looked at Herzog, who was sitting on the floor under the desk, his frail legs pulled up underneath his body. "Stay here. You're safe."

"Where am I going? I can't get up."

"I'll send help."

<hr />

US Ambassador's Residence, Tel Aviv
July 22, 9:02 p.m.

Palmyra Parker felt as if her shoes were moving across the floor while she was standing still.

Daughter of Joseph Atticus Cleveland, US ambassador to Israel, and his de facto chief of staff, Parker was in the security office in the north wing of the ambassador's seaside residence in the Herzliya Pitch neighborhood of Tel Aviv, going over the street maps with DSS Agent Pat McKeon and the ambassador's driver. In the wake of Tommy Hernandez's death, McKeon was the interim head of the ambassador's personal security detail. In any one week, seldom did the ambassador's vehicles take the same route to the embassy. Cleveland was planning to leave for the embassy early in the morning, so Parker was helping to sketch out a new route. She felt a tingling in her feet.

"Did you feel that?" asked the driver.

Parker had her mouth open to respond when the wall behind the driver appeared to morph into an *S* shape. Her knees buckled.

One hand grabbed the side of the desk and the other hand went for her phone, but . . . everything stopped.

The intercom buzzed. "Did you feel that?" came the voice.

McKeon hit the intercom button that connected her to every phone and every mobile earbud in the residence. "Tremors," she said. "Find the ambassador and let me know where he is." McKeon paused for moment. "Let's take it to code yellow. If there aren't any more shakes in the next half hour, we'll dial it down again."

She released the intercom button and turned toward Parker.

"We used to get these all the time when I was stationed in New Zealand,"

McKeon said. Turning back to the map, she said, "I can't remember the last time Israel had—"

As if she were on the string end of a mad puppeteer, Parker felt like all the joints in her body were out of her control. Everything was moving, but independently and haphazardly.

Instinctively, Parker reached for the stability of the desk. But her hand grasped only air. The desk was tilting to the left and sliding across the floor. Parker turned to the driver . . . as a piece of concrete fell from the ceiling and sliced away half of his head.

"My father!" screamed Parker. She would have been running for the door. Except she couldn't get one foot in front of the other to run. And because the door to the office had disappeared.

Ankara, Turkey
July 22, 9:02 p.m.

In the red room of the house on Alitas Street, downhill from the Citadel in the old city of Ankara, cryptic golden designs on the crimson-painted walls were pulsing with life, glowing brightly in a macabre and random frenzy. The stabbing strobes of light cast cavernous shadows across the face of Arslan Eroglu's body, now occupied and manipulated by the Turk, relentless enemy and pursuer of the Gaon's box, malevolent leader of the Disciples, and servant of evil incarnate—the One. Its eyes closed, the body twitched and jerked as if speeding along a winding road.

The Turk willed his otherworldly power roughly nine hundred kilometers beneath the Mediterranean Sea, once more to erupt along fissures, through the bedrock and dirt, colliding with the foundations of both the US embassy and the ambassador's residence in Tel Aviv, thirteen kilometers apart. They were the only buildings in Tel Aviv under assault by the Turk's power to move the earth.

A massive wave of energy hit the two buildings simultaneously. And the Turk felt the collision.

The face contorted in pain, the body violently thrown back into the stone chair, Arslan Eroglu's vocal cords emitted a desperate, keening wail that sounded as if it had risen from the gates of Hades.

"You . . . will . . . die." The voice of the Turk emerged from Eroglu's throat, ripped and raw. But a smile of evil intent bared its teeth.

And a sulfurous vapor hung heavily over the stone table of sacrifice on the far side of the room.

<hr />

US Embassy, Tel Aviv
July 22, 9:04 p.m.

Two jagged fissures tore the rear wall of the US embassy building on Herbert Samuel Street. The new commander of the Disciples stood behind a seawall, the vivid blue water of the Mediterranean only a dark swath of black. The sweeping crescent beach was dimly washed by ambient light, but the commander ignored the beauty behind him. His focus lay on the fortified and heavily protected building across the street. His other teams at the ambassador's residence were well-trained, fervent believers. They had their assignment—swift, merciless slaughter. The commander's target was the embassy and the Gaon's bronze box, held in the embassy's vault.

Surrounded on this side by anti-tank barriers that blocked the only entrance to the rear parking garage, the US embassy to Israel was big, square, solid, and ugly. Situated in the middle of an eclectic downtown neighborhood with a mixture of hotels and restaurants, along with small, local shops topped with apartments on their upper floors, the sidewalks around the embassy building were studded with concrete-filled bollards—four-foot-high steel cylinders embedded into the sidewalks—linked together by a steel beam. The ground floor of the massive building was solid, windowless stone. But now ravaged by the ongoing earthquake, the defenses at the back of the embassy were rent by two huge gashes running vertical to the ground, one to the north, near the corner of the building, another to the south, near the ramp to the underground garage.

Along Herbert Samuel Street, men in civilian clothes, ID lanyards slapping against their chests, raced to the jagged fractures in the embassy's walls. Locally hired security professionals, most of them former members of the Israeli armed forces, they formed the majority of the embassy's security force.

The commander, a young man with a livid pink scar rising from his right ear along his hairline to the front of his forehead, glanced at the floor plan of the building in his hand. Elevated into his new role by the Turk only hours earlier, he was taking the place of his father—killed in a gun battle with Mullaney and his allies in Amman. Not only was the new commander determined to fulfill the orders of the Turk and secure the lethal box of power, he was also determined that Agent Mullaney would lose his life in its defense.

With a wave of his hand, as another jolt quaked the ground under his feet, the six Disciples to his left began working their way to the gash at the northwestern corner of the building. "Keep them occupied."

Then the commander, a finely honed weapon capable of extraordinary violence, turned his piercing black eyes on the growing fissure near the parking entrance. "Follow me," he said, and a dozen black-clad Disciples rose from their hiding places.